SIGNIFICANT

SHANEN RICCI

Copyright © 2022 Shanen Ricci

All rights reserved. Without limiting the rights under copyright reserved above, no part of this publication may be reproduced, stored in or introduced into retrieval system, or transmitted, in any form, or by any means (electronic, mechanical, photocopying, recording, or otherwise) without the prior written permission of both the copyright owner and the above publisher of this book.

This is a work of fiction. Names, characters, places, brands, media, and incidents are either the products of the author's imagination or are used fictitiously. The author acknowledges the trademarked status and trademark owners of various products referenced in this work of fiction, which have been used without permission. The publication/use of these trademarks is not authorized, associated with, or sponsored by the trademark owners.

Formatting by Stacey Blake
Cover design by Shanen Ricci
Editing by Traci Finlay
Proofreading by My Brother's Editor

"He's more myself than I am. Whatever our souls are made of, his and mine are the same."
—Emily Brontë, Wuthering Heights.

PLAYLIST

"Birthday"—Anne-Marie (Don Diablo Remix)

"Play With Fire"—Sam Tinnesz

"Who I am"—The Score

"Man or a Monster"—Sam Tinnesz

"Broken"—Isak Danielson

"Champion"—Bishop Briggs

"Oxygen"—Winona Oak & Robin Schulz

"Ocean Eyes"—Billie Eilish

"Inside My Love"—Delilah

"Heal"—Tom Odell

SIGNIFICANT

PART I
HELL-BENT

Significant *adjective*
/sɪgˈnɪfəkənt/
Synonyms: Meaningful. Rare. Special.
1. Important enough to have an effect and be noteworthy.
2. Having a special and secret meaning.
3. Something everlasting and undeniable.
4. Aaron LeBeau.

CHAPTER 1

Crashing into you

Flags wave proudly in the sky. Engines scream as they race down the track. The crowd cheers with thunderous roars.

Everyone is here for something.

Monte Carlo is known for its expensive luxury and its expensive guests. It exudes money. The elite gather in the VIP paddock, the oversized yacht, to sip pricey champagne by the pools and build their connections. They take photographs next to the Formula 1 drivers, exchanging selfies among celebrities and paying deference to the royalty. The only race they are in for isn't the one happening on the track, but the one of social climbing.

Some of them are indeed here for the love of the race. To watch the racers driving passionately, passing in front of you in a flash. Feeling your body vibrating, the adrenaline rush passing through each of your cells. The fans are jumping, cheering the drivers with their home flags. They traveled from across the world to attend the Formula 1 Grand Prix.

Not in my case.

I'm not here for the race, nor the social gathering, even if I did travel from New York for the event. Nina Braham, my cold, demanding, and authoritative boss sent me as *bait* to accomplish the impossible. *Succeed or get fired* are my only options.

There is no way to prepare for the unattainable. You just have to go blindly for it. *Celebrity Magazine* would say nothing is impossible if you're dressed up for the part. I'm more of a Rapunzel type. Since my college graduation, two years ago, I write my column from my tower—otherwise known as my one-bedroom cozy apartment. I don't do glamorous. My life could be summarized by an absent father, an unsatisfied mother, and a talent to close my heart off.

I'm a loner, an introvert who's living risk-free, painting on canvases who will never see the light of day. If it was up to me, I'd have been a starving artist—but some dreams get crushed. After being rejected by many art schools, I went for the second-best thing: journalism. And now, I can't afford to fail in that too.

But today is different. It's a new start. A blank canvas. If I live up to the unrealistic expectations of Nina, and prove myself, I'll secure my job and my income. I'm blending into this land of milk and money, dressed up in a tight marine-blue cocktail dress, revealing my long legs and thin yet athletic body. The right amount of makeup, slight and unnoticeable, a touch of mascara to liven my hazel eyes. My honey-blond hair sways with the wind, in harmony with the wild agitation of the crowd.

I have two certainties. One, I need that interview. Two, I have no idea how to get it. Truth is, I'm probably not the right person for this Augean task. I've never worked hard to get an interview before. People were willing and happy to talk about themselves. They confide in me easily, considering me like the typical *sweet* girl next door. Which is actually why she chose me as bait. It's a test and being 'not good enough' is something I can't allow myself to be today.

I jump out of my seat when the men next to me scream with excitement. I stand up and lean toward the ramp to watch the action. The Formula 1 number 7 is taking the lap at full speed, executing dangerous maneuvers to take the lead. He sets the crowd on fire by capturing all the attention. Driving brutally, fearlessly, bending the track to his will. That man is the main reason everybody is here today. He is everyone's obsession, to the point where you either hate him deeply or worship him.

He is like an angry god, going by the driver nickname *Wolf*.

Wolf is known for his provocative racing. Reckless and indomitable, he could be the definition of sin with a killer instinct. At twenty-five, he has acquired years of victory—*and years of conquests*. I have a theory that women should avoid certain men at all costs: the bad boy, the unavailable bachelor, the alpha male... and by some dark miracle, Wolf fits all of them.

1. A feral racer with dangerous driving skills. *Bad boy.*
2. Handsome. Emotionally unavailable. Bazillionaire. *Unavailable bachelor.*
3. Powerful. Mysterious. Dark. *The alpha.*

Wolf makes his own rules and plays his own game. He hasn't done any interviews; his past is erased, completely inaccessible. He has graced hundreds of headlines but remains a mystery. He possesses such a heated temper on the track, and yet I've heard that a glance from him will freeze your soul and make you submit to him. I've never met him, and frankly, I can't understand how one man could have such an impact on anyone. Distant, unreachable, this man looks damaged, if you ask me. *But aren't we all?*

I awaken from my thoughts as the crowd gasps for air, the track falling silent when Wolf tries a dangerous maneuver, as he is already racing at full speed. He is in a skirmish at the chicane with Louis Harmil, known as Golden Boy. He sets a blistering pace, his racing forceful, intense. There are no overtaking opportunities on the track, and yet Wolf doesn't reduce the pace. My heart skips a beat, while I'm magnetized by how fearless this man is. He takes a sharp turn, having total confidence in his car when he begins to lose control.

Tire squealing.

Air hissing.

Metal crashing.

Wolf slams brutally into the barriers. He is forced to retire from the race. Everyone starts to panic. I'm in shock; nobody can get out of a crash like that without an injury. But as inhuman as Wolf seems to be, he gets out of his cockpit, assuring he is fine to the crowd. Wolf smashes his helmet furiously on the ground and strides toward his pit in anger. His team approaches him, but he leaves without a word, disappearing through his paddock.

The media start to demand answers, eager to solve Wolf's enigma until a point they're forgetting the race that's happening around them. Wolf, the man who had all the talent to become a legend, but ends up being pictured as a villain in a world full of heroes. So it's true. His sponsors complained about his lack of humanity. He refused to have a publicist, doing the strict minimum at his duty of crowd-pleasing. He was unreachable, an undefeated king, until he made that one mistake on the track. A mistake that could put his reign in jeopardy. The French racer just lost the Grand Prix in his hometown. And as for me, I need to figure out how I'm going to be able to find the reason I came tonight.

The after-race party is at Rubis Lounge.

VIP guest lists. Models and movie stars. Sports celebrities. Musicians and literal royalty. It's exclusive, glamorous, magical, and deep pockets are required. Individual passes cost more than a thousand euros. I've spent a significant amount of money and used my boss' connections to be able to get in here. This is my last chance…

At the open lounge, acrobats are performing aerial silk dances. The club is packed, people dancing, gyrating their bodies. As for me, I remain still, stuck in the middle of the party, thinking I haven't been to a place like this since college. Right now, I feel like a guest in one of *The Great Gatsby* parties. Fireworks, huge bottles of champagne, confetti—it's another level of grandiose. And like all the great parties, there are troublemakers.

My stomach turns instantly at the sight of the ghost of my past. He hasn't changed—a pink sweater over his shoulders, a pale blue Lacoste shirt, his Ivy League haircut, and the same irritating judgmental look as he sips his cocktail. Stephan. The man who broke me on every level, leaving me with scars I cannot forget.

Stephan's gaze meets mine, a wicked smile on his face. My legs petrify. As he approaches me, I don't hear the music anymore, just the sound of my palpitating heart. He shouldn't be here, and I'm not prepared for unwanted surprises.

"Elle. What are you doing here?" he sheers with his snobbish tone.

I clear my throat, thinking this has got to be a sick joke. "I'm working. What is a lawyer doing at a Formula 1 party?" I can't let all the time I've taken to rebuild myself and the confidence I've gained to fall apart. I cannot let him reach me. *You're a new woman now, Elle.*

"Networking." He leans toward me, his repulsing breath paralyzing me. "I'll see you around"—his eyes travel the length of my body, before smiling viciously—"my sweet." My blood freezes hearing the pet name of my past. My sweet. *Don't cry, my sweet.*

I turn around, gasping for air, trembling as I head toward the bar to find a seat where he won't be able to see me. I call out to the bartender. I need something strong to escape my nightmare and his words resonating through my mind.

Minutes pass, alcohol flows through my system, and I notice everyone having the time of their lives. Couples are kissing, beautiful people are flirting, friends are laughing. And me? I might as well send my resignation. I'm trying too hard to erase the sweet and weak Elle, but I'm not sure if broken Elle would be better company. At least, this one doesn't feel.

I was sent to be bait, but I've attracted the wrong fish.

A fish I need to forget.

"Something strong," a man with a delicious, husky voice orders while taking a seat next to me as if he has heard my thoughts.

He captures my attention. His brows are knitted together while his gaze stops in my direction. I can't look away. I'm, for an unknown reason, spellbound. His piercing stare is from a deep ocean blue, contrasting with his obsidian hair. A rebellious strand is on his forehead as a slow lethal smile stretches on his lips. He is unreadable, tenebrous, and screams of every nuance of darkness and conflict as if he's holding the gates of Hell inside of him.

I notice his sculpted body underneath his light blue tuxedo. He has the features of a Greek god. A troubled Greek god, surrounded by a magnetic and powerful stygian aura. A perfect masculine jawline with chiseled cheekbones, full watering lips, and a straight-edged nose. He empties his glass in one go before turning his body to face me.

"He is not worth it." He scans me with intensity, tilting his head, before licking his upper lip seductively like a predator eager to taste his prey.

I arch my eyebrow. "Excuse me?"

"That sorry excuse for a man you're thinking of," he states in a raspy voice, sure of himself.

"There are no men on my mind." I sip my drink, trying to look away from his magnetic gaze. I shouldn't have said that. I just gave him the green light to approach me, but after all, it was what I wanted.

His eyes, darkened by desire, travel the length of my body. My pulse hitches, my lips feeling suddenly dry as I close my thighs tightly, resisting his overpowering charm. I'm not used to being seen, unraveled like that. I didn't come here for a flirt, I came here to save my job—to get that interview. But then again, I'm incapable of deciding if the timing is perfectly wrong or perfectly right.

"Good." He leans closer to me, his masculine scent intoxicating my senses. "Otherwise, I would have offered to fuck him out of you."

I gasp at his direct comment. He isn't ashamed. He is enjoying this, even. A ghost of a smile spreads on his face, analyzing my reaction. He is a mix of ice and heat, of forbidden and need. A daredevil with the beauty of an angel. I was the bait, supposed to trap the unreachable one. But instead, he's trapped me.

He is the hunter.

I'm the prey.

Wolf.

CHAPTER 2

Obsession

I just crashed into the man who radiates dominance. The man who is himself the epitome of danger. Dangerously dark. Dangerously attractive. *Wolf.*

Wolf, whose real name is Aaron LeBeau.

The man I've desperately wanted to meet all day.

The man I'm here for.

"You crashed your car earlier. It seems that you have your own problems to solve."

"Ouch." He bites his lower lip, the corner of his mouth quirking up in an amused smile. I just piqued his interest. Something tells me he isn't used to people facing off against him. He is used to being a dominant, to having it his way.

"I suppose I deserved that one," he admits. "You're right. I completely wrecked my race. But apparently misery loves company."

"Apparently." *And tonight, misery found Wolf and me.* "Some things are better left… forgotten."

"I couldn't agree more," he states. "I'm looking forward to getting to know you tonight, Miss—" He draws in a long breath, waiting for my introduction.

"Elle. Monteiro."

His piercing stare claims my body, not hiding the fact he's undressing me in his head. In a second, he has the power to make me feel naked, plunging into my soul.

The words of Nina crawl back into my head. *"Get him to talk. He's just a man."* But Aaron isn't just a man. The media portray him as a predator. He makes women his conquests for the night, they're devoted to him while he doesn't give anything back. *"Find his weakness, try to get the interview by any means,"* she ordered. Others have tried, he remained without empathy, scaring them away, which gave him the headline of the *heartless racer*. Many magazines have contacted him, and yet he has refused them all, not caring for bad press. No, you can't trick a man like Wolf.

The only thing you can hope to have from him is his attention. And he gave it to me. But I fear what I'd have to do to keep it. Wolf has some sort of power emanating from him. A darkness I wanna lose myself in, and that terrifies me. That unwanted attraction is playing to my disadvantage.

He could be some kind of Greek god, but I'm a mortal.

And gods used mortals. Not the other way around.

"Elle." The way my name rolls off his tongue, so sweet and soft, makes me feel sultry. "Shall we make this night better for both of us?" He gets out of his seat before leaning toward me, his elbow on the bar.

"You're used to getting what you want, aren't you?" I tilt my head, my heart pounding, realizing I'm playing in the big leagues now.

He closes the distance between us and I get up abruptly from my seat, overwhelmed by his impressive six-foot-three height. Even standing, my five-foot-seven looks small and vulnerable. Our chests almost connect, the electricity between our bodies sparking. His Adam's apple popping up. He is all man. All power.

"Always," he whispers.

I swallow, ignoring my desire to drown in my misery, ignoring an attraction I shouldn't indulge. "Well, I certainly can't give you what you want."

"You're wrong. You can give me exactly what I want," he says as an affirmation. A certitude he'll claim what he is looking for.

"I believe the contrary, Mr. LeBeau." *But you, you could be the answer to all of my problems.* I pull away from him, taking a step back. I'm experiencing a duality, two parts of me fighting. Fear and desire. Saving my job or escaping my past.

A satisfying, wolfish smirk appears on his face. "Interesting."

"What?"

"You. You are interesting."

Resisting him makes the hunt even more enjoyable for him. He will test my limits, my boundaries, my ability to resist my own lust. The game has just begun. And neither of us is willing to lose.

"Probably because I don't have any romantic interest toward you." I've never been the type of woman to reply back, to look for confrontation. I'm a good girl. The one who plays by the rules, the polite and docile one, but it seems like Wolf brings out a new part of me.

"Liar." He sips his drink before his azure-blue gaze pierces me again. "You want to fuck me as much as I want to fuck you."

I mumble an incomprehensible comeback. I'm not aroused by his words—no, it's worse than that; his direct sincerity creates an obsession in me to find out. It's like he has bewitched me, placing new cravings in me. Cravings I can't allow to exist.

"I'm here on business. I'm a writer for Celebrity Magazine." He lifts an eyebrow. "My boss sent me here to write an article about you. I've been meaning to interview you all day."

His expression changes radically. The playful look in his eyes is gone, his jaw clenched.

He turns his back to me and asks the bartender for another drink, a brutal silence rising around us. I knew it. My only choice was to go directly to get what I want from him—before he takes what he wants from me. After all, an interview is supposed to be a manipulation, a calculated risk between a certain degree of sexual tension and knowing your boundaries. And clearly, my boss—and I—overestimated me by thinking I could be the bait. I thought I had healed. I thought I could get back to the person I once was. I was wrong.

Aaron isn't stupid enough to share his life just by the sight of a potential lay. The man could lay every woman in this room. But he suddenly turns back, his burning gaze on me. "What about you? Would you like to get to know me?"

"Yes. It would help my article to have your cooperation." I struggle to speak, knowing he isn't referring to this level of intimacy. He caresses his lower lip with his finger, destabilizing me. He knows he is in a situation of power, and the only thing I'm left with is begging. "My future is on the line with this article."

He beholds me with a rare intensity, his eyes roaming over each of my curves, inspecting me closely. "I'm not here to dig dirt about your past. It's only to glorify your bachelor status for a women's magazine," I keep justifying myself. But yet, nothing. He remains cold as ice, merciless, a lone wolf who doesn't care about anyone. I'm lowering myself at his feet for his own amusement. He won't help me. *This is stupid.*

"I can't do this," I grumble to myself.

I grab my bag harshly, fully deciding to call it what it is—my downfall, a night of humiliation. I just want to leave. I can't keep holding on to false hope. I'm rushing away from the bar when something stops me.

His hand clutches my wrist, his breath near my nape. He slides his fingers into the center of my palm, making my heart hammer across my chest. I turn to face him, the tantalizing feel of his touch proving an electric attraction linking us.

"Maybe I can help you." Aaron takes one step closer, I take a step back and hit the wall behind me. His hands trapping me against the wall, he leans toward me, wetting his lips. No escape. "I usually hate gossip. I'm very… private."

"Why do you want to help me, then?" Legs weakening. Breath quickening. Lips begging. He is too close, too sure of himself, too dangerous.

"I'm following my gut." He clears his throat. "Would you like to dance?"

I'm wide-eyed with confusion. Dance? What does dancing have to do with this? This man is an enigma.

"Miss Monteiro, you don't get to know someone by asking questions. You get to know someone by sharing moments," he adds.

"And Mr. LeBeau, I bet the moments you're used to sharing with women are the ones without clothes involved. And I'm not that type of columnist."

"I actually prefer the hunt. I'm a competitor, after all." A self-confident smirk slides onto his face. He is overly aware of the impact his words have on me. "And I'm not asking the columnist in you to dance with me, but the woman." He finishes his drink in one go. "I believe neither of us wants to talk about our jobs tonight."

"Be careful not to crash again, Wolf. I doubt your alpha male ego could cope with it," I tease him.

But my amusement stops when I spot Stephan's gaze on me across the dance floor. His vile eyes daring me to be the weak woman he knew. But tonight, I'll make the right choice and will not redo the mistakes of my past. My attention turns back to Aaron who's awaiting my next move. I conclude this is the worst timing for Wolf and me to have met. My need to escape forces me to play with fire, without caring about the consequences, while he's looking for prey to hunt. This could only end up in breaking each other's rules. An exchange of privacy—that none of us would have planned.

He slides his palm to my lower back, a gesture not pushy and yet teasing enough to send guilty goose bumps over my whole body. "When I want something, I always get it. And I intend to prove it to you. Shall we?"

I should hate his arrogance. I've never met someone who sends so many red flags, who represents everything I despise. A controlling alpha. An endless player. The type of man who believes he's royalty, the world bowing at his feet. But for an unknown reason, I feel the need to get closer.

Heart against head. That's how obsession triumphs over reason.

I know I'm going to regret this choice. I'm no match for him. I let him lead me to the center of the dance floor where everyone is dancing as if the world ends tomorrow. Their eyes are stuck on Wolf, observing him from afar without daring to approach him. They are all an appeal to sex and sensuality, but me—I'm not like them. I don't dirty dance, I don't jump in the air recklessly, I don't party. I'm always in control. *And he seems to be, too.*

He clutches my waist and connects our bodies to the pulsing tempo of the music. His fingers travel from my spine to my waist, his eyes boring into mine. He is playing a game, a game of control, a game of lust—and I'm giving him the answer he demands. Moving my hips. Tangling my fingers into my hair. Touching my neck.

I'm not *sweet*. Not anymore.

He spins me around, my back now facing his torso. I twirl my hips on him, my eyelids closing, my head rotating slowly backward. I'm losing control, unleashing something I thought I lost in myself. I feel alive. His hands take control of my hips, commanding my movements to his pace.

His breath on my neck, his woody musky scent invading my senses, heating up my body. I let the intoxication of him, of the alcohol, lead me to an unknown territory.

But I won't submit so easily to him. I push him to his own limits, my hands fondling my waist, the edges of my breasts, then through my hair. He reels me around for our longing eyes to connect, the azure-blue of his gaze now a dark black like a tormented ocean, betraying his growing desire.

A game of power, that's what we are playing.

"I'm trying to be a gentleman. But I promise you, if I lose control, I won't be able to be one any longer," he threatens me.

He brushes my cheek with his fingers before cupping my nape with his hand. We're disconnected from what's happening around us. The crowd is jumping. Confetti is exploding. Smoke is rising. And me, I'm consumed by a burning heat, a need for proximity. His face so close to mine is tormenting my ability to resist him. I want to feel again.

"Unless you want me to lose control," he mutters under his breath.

He waits for my signal to break the few inches separating us. My lips urge to taste his. I open my mouth, panting, ready to push my boundaries. Just a step. My past collides with my present. *I'm not sweet.* I need to be someone else. Someone free just for one night. Tonight, I'll get to know who Wolf is.

His predator charm lures me in, his sweet lips so close to mine they could almost touch. "Tell me to stop or I won't."

Fuck it. "Aaron. Take me away."

He captures my hand and leads me in the direction of the elevators. We find our way toward all the people dancing, kissing, making decisions they'll probably regret the morning after. Once inside, we don't say a word to each other. When the doors close, the only sound is the one of our panting breaths, of our animal connection, of the inevitable that is about to happen.

I swallow, excitement melting with anticipation, owning me. His gaze meets mine, trying to read my needs, my desire for him. But the problem is not what I desire, it's the reason why I desire him. I shouldn't want him. But he is what I need. Aaron LeBeau is no Prince Charming, no white knight—he is something else entirely. Something powerful.

"You wanted to know me, Elle? You are about to," his raspy tone promises, while all I can think of is only one thing. *Kiss me.*

Without warning, as if he could read my mind, his lips crash onto mine, a wave of pleasure intoxicating me. Aaron LeBeau's kisses are everything I've expected them to be. Passionate. Demanding. Urgent. I melt under the fierce heat of his drugging kiss. I'm at his mercy as he pushes his tongue in my mouth, possessing me. His lips move over my jaw, my chin, before nibbling on my neck.

He lifts me up, my thighs bracing on his hips when we arrive on his floor. I'm caught in a crossfire, a crossfire that is Aaron LeBeau. He kisses me with a greedy hunger surpassing everything I'd expect while we enter his suite. I don't pay attention to what is around us, all my attention is focused on him. He creates in me the need to sin, the need to taste darkness. He is demanding more, making me oblige to him, taking control of me, until the point when my primal craving possesses me.

I can't deny the carnal passion between us, and yet, it is more than just a desire of lust. It is a desire to escape. Two lost souls using each other.

We crash on his bed, the satin sheets caressing my back, as his herculean body covers mine. I'm falling down the rabbit hole, losing myself into his Adonis features. I bite my lower lip, losing my senses, welcoming all the new inebriated sensations. I don't drink. I don't have one-night stands. I don't do reckless. I giggle, a heat burning inside of me, alcohol probably intoxicating my veins. He furrows his eyebrows, analyzing my face with deep intensity, like he's battling something. I urge his body closer to mine, my back arching, yearning for his touch, opening my mouth to taste his lips once more. Wolf has me where he wants, at his mercy, but he doesn't act.

"You're not yourself, *ma belle.*"

Wolf backs off, leaving me alone in his king-size bed.

"I didn't take you for a quitter," I mumble, struggling to keep my eyelids open, pouting like a child whose favorite candy has been taken away from her.

The bastard laughs. *Beautiful and arrogant bastard.*

CHAPTER 3

Just the beginning

I feel the rays of the sun warming my face. I throw a pillow on top of my head, the daylight hurting my eyes. I stretch myself, my head hurting, feeling like a truck drove over my whole body. I shouldn't have drunk that much last night. *Last night?* Crap.

Wide awake, I open my eyes and look around me. Definitely not my bedroom. Everything is so bright, so luxurious, so big. From the massive windows with silk beige curtains to the three-person canapé with fresh roses, this place looks like we jumped back in time to the old Grecian era. I glance at my dress on the floor, my heels a few inches apart, and start to put everything together.

Wolf and I did share a heated kiss last night. I can't believe I lowered myself to his arrogance. But nothing more happened, right? I scan what I am wearing. Positive point, I'm dressed. My blue lace panties are here, and I'm wearing a white fancy silk shirt, smelling just like him. Something addictive and sensual, like an erotic scent of rosewood with sandalwood and amber, a powerful and refined fragrance. Which brings me to the negative point, why am I wearing Aaron's perfectly shaped shirt?

"*Ma belle.*"

I struggle to swallow, beheld by the view in front of me. I just arrived in a mythological setting. Aaron LeBeau is facing me, with only a small white towel to cover his perfectly proportioned herculean body. He is the epitome of sex. Water drops are sliding down throughout his muscular chest to his well-defined abs. His strong arms are contracting as he winds his fingers through his wet hair. I notice the tattoo of the face of a wolf howling on the left side of his chest, behind it a skull with the number 7 on it.

The dark inking of the drawing expresses a profound murky pain and anger, which leads me to believe it isn't random. I'd define myself as an artist—even if I haven't finished any artwork in months and never gathered my courage to expose my art to the world. But one thing I learned is that art always has a meaning, a story on an unconscious level. This tattoo is proof that Wolf has a secret—*and a heart.*

I bring the sheets closer to my breasts when I feel Aaron scrutinizing me. I'm ashamed of my actions yesterday. The way I allowed myself to fall so low, and yet I feel empowered by the way his regard betrays his yearning for me. I shouldn't. I was supposed to use him for my article, and instead, I'm in his sheets. It looks like a win for LeBeau. He's devilishly wrong, and I'm broken enough to know a man's interest doesn't last. I need to snap out of it. My heart starts racing, my insecurities resurfacing at the thought that Wolf might have seen me naked, and I probably embarrassed myself enough for my ego to cope with it.

"Aaron. What am I wearing?" I knit my eyebrows together, mad to have been so reckless. I always take care of myself, and wearing Aaron's shirt is proof of my failure to do so last night.

"You're wearing a shirt." He sits on the corner of the bed, a ghost of a smile stretching his lips. I inhale deeply. I'm not in the mood to play his game. It might be amusing for him, but I will not burn myself willingly.

"Tell me what happened last night," I command.

"Breakfast first." He tries to get up from the bed, but I tackle him.

I'd played Wolf's game last night. I fell under his spell, but I have too much pride to let him win this round as well. Even while the bastard enjoys the view of me sitting on his lap, my messy long hair brushing against his cheek, my hands trembling to steady myself. "I need to know! We didn't sleep together, right? Why am I wearing your shirt?"

"Someone is feeling bossy this morning." He yanks me to him, shifting my body in one move while clutching my waist, so he can position himself on top of me. I look small compared to his muscular body dominating me. "But I prefer to be the one on top," he adds.

I'm breathing harder, the sudden proximity making my breasts connect with his strong torso. There is something about him that magnetizes me, a power he exercises on me—a power I shall never give him again. I look away, incapable of meeting his predator's eyes. I need to deny this alchemy, even if every nerve in my body is reacting to him, begging to be electrified with him. I've sworn off men, especially the ones who send so many red flags.

"I'm pleased to notice your attraction for me wasn't because you were drunk."

I shove him away, lifting myself out of bed. "I wasn't myself; I'm not attracted to you. I'm not one of your easy girls!" I storm around the room, looking for my clothes. "And, trust me, you aren't my style." My eyes narrow. I want to burn him the same way I felt burned by how I lower myself to his man-whore charm.

"And yet, you responded to each of my touches with twice the intensity I gave you. Sounds like you're lying to yourself." He gets out of bed and walks in my direction.

No, I'm not going there. "I don't like men like you. You know, the type of men toying with women," I shout while looking for my damn phone. "You think you got it all figured out, Wolf? Well, let me tell you, scoring a woman who got drunk isn't very impressive. It's desperate! You and your alpha male ego are desperate."

By snapping at him, I realize I'm not angry at him, but at myself. I was the weak one, the one who lost control, the one who couldn't resist my primal needs. I let Stephan get to me, I wasn't strong enough, and I probably ruined my chance at getting that interview. Old fears rush back. I have too many emotions inside of me and I'm exploding. Maybe I'm angry at men after all.

Aaron's jaw clenches as darkness flickers in his eyes, my words sticking in his craw. I rush toward the bathroom, but he chased after me. He blocks the entrance, caging me with his muscular arms.

"I don't fuck women who don't want me. And I don't abuse women. It's always consensual." I start feeling the embarrassment rushing through my cheeks, but he is not done with me yet. "Last night, you fell asleep.

I changed you so you'd be comfortable and gave you my bed to sleep in while I took the fucking sofa." He leans toward me, and my back hits the wall under the pressure of his angry eyes. "So no, I didn't fuck you, nor take advantage of you. I'm not a pig, in spite of what you think of me. I'm not. That. Desperate. Elle." He articulates each of his words like daggers into my heart.

"I'm sorry." I look down, not daring to meet his eyes, knowing I was way out of line. "It's just, I freaked out when I saw I was wearing your shirt and couldn't remember the rest of the night. I didn't want you to…" I huff, my fingers rubbing nervously together. The words of my mother are haunting me—*Never show your insecurities to a man, or he'll give you more reasons to doubt yourself.* I manage a fake smile. I'm not vulnerable.

"I've been a gentleman, Elle." And weirdly, by reading into the powerful intensity of his stare, I believe he's telling the truth. But he's a man. *And men are liars.*

"Did I embarrass myself yesterday?" He snorts at my question, pulling himself next to me on the wall. And I couldn't be more convinced that some questions are better left unanswered.

"Well, I bet you were looking cute as a lobster mascot."

I throw my head into my palms. I told Aaron LeBeau my most embarrassing story, admitting I was crushing on a football player during my teenage years—and that he made fun of me while I was wearing a lobster outfit. Great.

"I needed the extra money," I growl.

"Oh, I would pay you a thousand dollars to cheer for me as a lobster," he chortles as I roll my eyes. I realize this is the first time I'm seeing Aaron LeBeau laughing. He's usually so intense and in control.

"I really can't figure you out, Elle." Our eyes connect briefly before I turn my face away, not trusting myself from plunging into the azure-blue of his eyes. "The night certainly went an unexpected way."

"You can't have it all, Aaron," I tease him.

But when he wets his full lips with his tongue, I instantly regret my comment. I remember my ex saying he used to like that I was so docile. Not anymore. At least not with Aaron. The hunter is back and wants to activate my horny—yet feisty—emotional state.

"I can. Don't confuse my respect for you last night with me

withdrawing from the race." He approaches me, and I gasp, knowing I'm the race. "I need you to be fully conscious the day I thrust my cock inside you, because trust me, it'll be something worth remembering, Elle." His confidence and bluntness should give me the ability to take a pit stop from whatever this is, and yet I can't help but lose myself into the abyss of his soul. His fingers travel the length of my arm, to my neck, to stop at my chin. "You know us, it will happen."

"It won't," I mumble, probably trying to convince myself more than him. "You had your chance." Even a man who likes a challenge as much as Wolf will not push to conquer me if he knows it's a dead end. And I need him to believe that for my self-preservation.

Our moment is interrupted when a man barges into Aaron's suite. "Aaron, we need to talk about what happened—" He stops at the sight of us—halfway undressed, a guilty expression on our faces.

I recognize that man. He's Mattias Longfoard, the CEO of Aaron's racing team. He's known to be an exigent man and a figure of respect and power in the Formula 1 industry. He might be sixty years old with long gray hair, but he is an Italian shark. Longfoard has led the Amorino F1 racing team to dominate the past ten seasons, six of which they finished first. Four of them won by Wolf.

"Fuck, Mattias. I—" Aaron curses, but Longfoard stops him by raising his hand, expressionless. He leaves his suite, shaking his head, and grumbles in a language I don't know.

Wolf storms after him in the hallway and closes the door behind. I feel like an outsider. An outsider who shouldn't be here. I gather my things quickly, looking for my blue dress and my leather jacket. I rush toward the bathroom to see my reflection in the mirror—god, I look like a mess. My mascara has dropped, forming black circles under my eyes; the alcohol has made my golden skin look pale, my hair messy. I dress quickly and check my phone, The Wicked Witch—aka my boss—has left me five messages asking about the article. And I don't have enough for it. I need more than an anecdote, I need to unravel who Wolf is. I tap to reply, but my phone battery dies.

Fuck. I leave my cell phone number on Aaron's bed with a thank-you note. I hope he'll get the memo to call me for the article. He's my last hope. I rush to the elevator, praying it will open quickly. I glance at Wolf arguing with Longfoard in the hallway. I'm such a coward to leave like this.

My heart is bouncing, my nerves are shaking. Please, hurry. I've been a supporting character my whole life, and then suddenly I'm cast to play the main character. The heroine. It's too much for me. A rush of inexplicable and contradictory feelings is traveling throughout my body. Fear and excitement, a guilty and liberating adrenaline storming into me. I enter the elevator and push the *zero* button.

I inhale, closing my eyes for a second, dazed by the crazy hours I just experienced. When I look up, I see Aaron standing in front of me like a vision. We stare at each other, losing ourselves in the moment, memorizing each other's features. I mouth to him I'm sorry, feeling ashamed at running away. I believe another man would have been mad or would have forced me to stay, complained about my actions, but he curls his lips into a dangerous smirk, as if he could read me.

"This is just the beginning, Miss Monteiro."

"Is that a threat, Mr. LeBeau?"

"No. It's a promise."

The elevator doors close.

My heart races.

… Breathe. I need to breathe.

CHAPTER 4

The right word

I readjust myself during the elevator ride, looking at my reflection in the mirrored glass. I tuck a strand of my hair behind my ear before caressing my neck with the tips of my fingers, remembering Aaron's touch on my skin. The carnal passion. The lust. The need. I put my black leather jacket on, to notice that it isn't mine, judging by the red bands on the side and the cut—it's Aaron's. For a moment I simper; this jacket represents him. Powerful. Daredevil. Rebellious. The opposite of me. His words haunt my mind… *It is just the beginning.* I'm certainly just a game for him. A race he has to win. A flag he has to take. Nothing more.

I stride into the lobby. I need to head back to my hotel as fast as possible. But my plans are compromised and the memory of my night with Aaron vanishes when I hear a voice I know way too well calling me out. I'm praying that I am wrong, but when I look back, *he* is here standing behind me. Stephan, faking a smile as he scans me from head to toe. His mother is shaming me, even if she's talking on the phone. She doesn't even bother to greet me from where she is. I feel like a virus from which she needs to keep a safe distance. Felicia Walton, or as I call her moray Eel, is the classical Upper East Side wife. She lives only for the 4G's: Gold, Gossips, Galas, and misoGynist values.

"Elle. Seeing you twice in less than twenty-four hours, how

interesting." Stephan lets out a dry laugh. "You're still wearing the same clothes as last night."

I tighten my fists, hiding my discomfort with a proud smile. "It's not any of your concern, Stephan." I close Aaron's jacket on my chest and peek at the side. I got this.

"Oh, my sweet…"

I swallow, and my pulse accelerates. *Don't call me that.* "I'm not your sweet," I articulate, but my lips are trembling. *It's been almost a year, Elle, don't let him get to you.*

His vampiric gaze meets mine. I want to run away, but my legs are glued to the floor. I know what he is going to say, what he is going to do. He's manipulative and vicious. I can't let all the work I've done to rebuild myself fall apart, all the confidence I've gained fall into ashes.

"I saw you dancing with Aaron LeBeau." A sardonic smile spreads on his face as he approaches me. "I can't believe you fucked him. Didn't take you for the kind to open your legs so easily." The whisper of his voice is like a blade. He takes a step closer to me. *No. Don't.* My breath sharpens, my heartbeat increases… *I don't want to feel like nothing.* Not again. I need to escape him.

My lips open, but I'm left with the incapacity to respond. He grips my wrist, seizing me hard, yanking me closer to him so I can smell his nauseating breath. "I should have known that sooner, treat you like a one-night stand like he did. That way I wouldn't have been bored to death in bed by you." I close my eyelids, thinking about all the therapy I had, his words bleeding me, making me feel worthless. Broken. Undesirable. "You know it was *your* fault, my sweet."

He pulls back, a dry smirk on his lips when Felicia, his dear mother, calls him out. He answers his mother, covered in charm, before she leaves. He has always been a manipulative snake—*no one would believe me.* After all, he's a brilliant lawyer from the elite social class, and I am a nobody.

"You're disgusting."

"My sweet, you can't fight me. I was the only one who cared for you." A lie. I take a step backward when he clutches my arm with a polite smile. "I'd let you suck my cock though, just like old times."

Stephan continues to speak, but I don't hear him or see him. Everything becomes blurry, and I feel my world falling apart. I feel the demons of my past haunting me again. I start to sink in my own nightmare, letting it consume me, not looking for an escape anymore. I feel weak. Destroyed. Broken. I lose hope until someone pulls me out of my nightmare.

I don't know what happened, but Stephan is now a few inches away from me, and a strong arm is protectively encircling my waist. I look up to see my escape. Aaron LeBeau. A white shirt contrasting with his tanned golden skin and dark jeans—the man exudes power no matter what he's wearing. Just his presence makes me forget my momentary pain. He's like a shield, and for the first time, it feels like Stephan can't reach me anymore.

"Ma belle. Are you okay?" Aaron tightens his grip on me, testing my reaction. I nod, managing a gracious smile even if I know my eyes are wet and my body is shaking. "You look good wearing my jacket." His face is cold as stone, but his comment appeases me. How can simply his presence calm me down and ease my fears?

He narrows his eyes at Stephan, taking a step closer to him, dominating him by his charisma and his height. The two men stare at each other. I've never seen Stephan so weak and impuissant. He can't compete against Wolf.

"Do you have a problem with my girlfriend?" I peer at Aaron, dazed by him calling me his girlfriend and by his authoritative tone. But he doesn't look at me and keeps tightening his gaze at Stephan. He is rescuing me. Again. And I don't mind. After all, nobody has ever stood up for me before.

"Girlfriend?" Stephan's face goes awry, like the thought of someone liking me shocks him to the bones. "No, no problem, man."

Wolf's gaze darkens in disbelief at Stephan's comment. I can't stay here anymore. I can't let Stephan manipulate him. "Aaron, let's go," I beg him, and he finally breaks eye contact with the ghost of my past, before twining his fingers with mine and pulling me away to the corner of the hallway.

"How can you let him talk to you that way?" Aaron's tone is imposing and enraged. He crosses his arms on his chest, clenching his jaw.

I want to reply that I'm emotionally broken, that Stephan damaged me and my capacity to feel alive, to believe in myself. That I'm weak and a mess. But instead, I snap at him, "Why did you say I was your girlfriend?" He uses flirting to change the conversation? Well, I use anger.

He lowers his eyebrows, clearly not expecting my answer. "Are you seriously asking me that?"

I'm about to leave. I can't support this—people telling me what to do, being everyone's puppet, having to explain myself. But Wolf captures my arm, stopping me from leaving. His touch is nothing like Stephan's. It's the opposite—warm, protective, addictive. It's a touch I'm not used to feeling. "I couldn't let him treat you that way," he adds.

Oh, no, it's until now, I realize he heard Stephan's words insulting me, reducing me to nothing. He saw how weak I was. He must take me for—

"You look beautiful," Aaron states as if he could sense my doubts rushing back.

Beautiful… One word can cause you suffering while another can make you feel alive again. One person can make you feel the worst about yourself when another awakens a new part of yourself you didn't believe existed until you met him. My lips curve into a smile, and I'm thankful that he doesn't push me to open up to him. Maybe that's because he understands me. Wolf certainly has demons of his own, just like me.

"Let's get out of here," he commands.

I nod and follow him toward the exit. We step outside the hotel, and I notice a red LaFerrari Aperta, a car that costs more than two million dollars, in front. I smile, not even surprised by his choice of car. We enter his fancy babe-magnet, and Aaron revs the engine with a powerful sound that makes my heart bounce. There is something magnetic about him. I still can't figure out what it is. I mean, I've never been turned on by a man racing his engine, but Aaron creates in me a new need, a new obsession. His tongue darts out of his mouth before licking his upper lip as he switches to the next song, *Who I am* from the Score, pulling his sunglasses on. The lyrics couldn't symbolize him more. And I wish someday, someone will not *try to change me.*

We make a quick stop at my hotel room so I can gather my things quickly and change before my flight back to New York. I agree to go with him to

God knows where—even though I don't trust myself with Wolf. I apply a slight touch of mascara and some gloss as an attempt to look pretty. I decide to wear my lucky white lace summer dress and my brown heels. It has a deep V-neck, so I choose to not wear any bra under it. I bite my lips nervously, is that too much? Will I look ridiculous revealing that kind of cleavage with my small breasts? *Screw it.* Screw my insecurities.

I head down to see Aaron waiting for me next to his sports car. When he sees me, he takes off his sunglasses, laying eyes on my whole body, observing every inch of it. I can't help but wonder what he is thinking. When I approach him, my confidence starts to vanish. *I look ridiculous.* I put my hair in front to hide my cleavage and pull my dress down. I try to mask my discomfort by squeezing my bag in front of my breasts. I'm used to being invisible, not in the spotlight. He opens the car door for me, and I rush to enter when—

"Wait," he says, stopping me from taking a seat.

His eyes drag over my body once again. What is he gonna say? Is there something wrong? But instead, he takes my bag and throws it on the seat. He brushes my hair softly with his hand and pushes it behind my back, exposing my cleavage. My eyes are begging him to stop contemplating me, to stop torturing my insecurities, to stop comparing me with—"You look gorgeous, Elle. Never hide yourself." I look into his eyes, questioning his sincerity. He isn't smiling; he is staring at me with a deep intensity. He meant that.

"Your jacket." I hand him his leather jacket, feeling the need to change the topic.

He hands me mine, and we take our places in his car. My heart is still aching from his compliment, knowing I shouldn't let it get to me. He raises up his engine, the brutal sound of the motor giving me goose bumps.

"I hope you are ready." This isn't a question, but an affirmation.

I raise my eyebrow. "Where are we going, Aaron?"

"That's for me to know, and for you to find out," he says seductively, a bad-boyish grin on his face.

I put my seatbelt on in defeat while he puts his sunglasses on and opens the car roof. In one maneuver, he drifts his car out of the parking lot with a powerful speed that makes my heart instantly jump. I grab a hold of the door in surprise. I feel something new, a thrill, a need for speed.

He notices my reaction and smiles in victory. "I hope you aren't afraid of speed."

"Of speed or of you?" I challenge him.

"Both," he chuckles. "Did you know that"—he bites his lower lip, his gaze holding mine—"a man drives like he fucks?"

On that sentence, he presses the accelerator and takes my breath away. I'm propelled into an adrenaline rush at a blistering speed.

His driving is… overpowering. Electrifying. Intoxicating.

Point taken.

CHAPTER 5

The agreement

We arrive at the viewpoint of Monaco. I'm speechless by the breathtaking sight; the fancy buildings seem so tiny, they look like Lego bricks. It feels like we are on top of the world. A world where it's only us. No one around. As I crawl closer to the edge of the cliff, I can feel my stomach turning into a knot. A few steps farther and I would step into the void. I look at the horizon to focus on the deep blue of the sea instead while positioning both of my hands on the stone to stabilize myself. Aaron is sitting on the edge of the rock, inviting me to take place next to him. It's not until I settle down—not so close to the edge—that I realize how high we are. I've always been afraid of heights, but something in me wants to defy my fear. Probably Aaron.

"I come here when I need to think," he says, lost in his thoughts. "Or when I need to yell. You can try, nobody will hear you." He remains stoic.

"I'm more of an introvert."

Aaron stands up on the edge of the rock. One more step and he would be falling into the void. He remains there, staring at the sea with sinister confidence. The confidence of a man who isn't afraid of death. A daredevil provoking fate. A silent wolf without a pack. I can't shake the idea that something is haunting him. He has this dark aura surrounding him that screams danger.

He turns to face me, offering me his hand to hold, his hair wild with the wind. I shake my head, grabbing harder at the rock behind me. I'm already paralyzed by sitting on the vertex of a cliff; I can't possibly stand, not even being a few feet away from the edge.

He ambles toward me, leaving the verge, and squats facing me to offer his hand again. This man doesn't understand the meaning of fear. I accept it in spite of myself, wanting to prove to him that I'm stronger than I appear. I stand on the rock at a safe distance, but my heart starts to bounce hard. I tighten my grip, probably hurting him, as he poses his other hand behind my lower back, his gaze scrutinizing me. I focus on the view. It looks so different when you're standing; it's empowering, powerful. I simper, feeling proud of myself for this accomplishment. I would have never imagined I could stand so high, even though a minute later I'm back on safe land. Maybe I'm stronger than I think.

We head back to the grass, the adrenaline still in my blood. For the first time in my life, I feel alive. I lean closer to the white myrtle tree as I notice Aaron lost in his thoughts. His eyebrows frown like he's trying to make an important decision.

"Aaron, what happened with Longfoard—"

He overlaps my question with his. "Tell me something about you, Elle."

I chuckle at the bluntness of his question. "What would you like to know?"

"Anything."

"Fine. I'm twenty-three, and I don't have any siblings. It has just been my mother and me." My face closes at the thought of my mother. She and I have always had a complicated relationship and pleasing her came at a high price.

"What about you? Any siblings?" I change the subject, not letting my gloomy thoughts get to me. I already know Aaron's father is André LeBeau, a multibillionaire and chairman of LeBeau's luxury hotel chains.

"I have a brother."

I open my mouth in surprise. But then again, I did my research on him two days before flying to Monaco. That's the reminder, we only know what Wolf is showing willingly to the world. "How old is your brother? Are you close to each other?"

"Trust me, you don't want to dig into my past."

"Why?"

"Because Elle, I'm not a good man," he replies in a rugged tone. And yet, his darkness is appealing to me. I feel the need to elucidate the Wolf enigma.

His penetrating stare hits me with the same intensity it did last night. He spreads the blossoming tree branches away from his face, our bodies almost pressing together. I grip the trunk of the tree behind me, ignoring the shimmering arousal by the sudden proximity. Wolf's breath is soft but shuddering, like a predator savoring the conquest yet to come. He tucks a strand of my hair behind my ear. And this could feel like a movie scene—if we weren't both emotionally unavailable.

"What kind of man do you like, Elle?" His tongue flicks out.

"I like a gentleman. I'm more the type of girl to go for the Prince Charming than the…" My voice is trembling like a whisper, my lips in a haze to taste sin one more time. I scan him from head to toe. "…than the hunter."

He cracks a dazzling smile. "Fairy tales are nice, but… I don't think you want a gentleman in bed." He stares at my begging lips. "And you, you are not destined for boring."

That's when I understand what we have in common. We both hide our feelings, our demons, by using an escape. Him, he fights his demons by indulging his desires, the need for flesh, the need to be in control—of himself, and of someone else. Aaron LeBeau isn't a womanizer, but a broken man trying to fulfill an empty void. And I am a distraction. His need to escape. The one he can't have. Yesterday, he couldn't claim the flag that was his to take, so he takes something else. Me.

I pull away from him, knowing where this discussion will go. He leans against the tree, clearly amused by my reaction. I walk around him, distracting his mind as well as I can. "How did you get into Formula 1?"

"Probably like everyone. I've started as a karting driver when I was a teen and made my way through Formula 1 a few years later, but you probably know all that, that's basic internet knowledge."

I snort. "Then, do you like racing?"

He pauses. "It's a part of who I am. Something I was born with."

"And yet, you're not like the other racers out there." His gaze locks on mine, startled by my comment. "I mean, being in the spotlight is part of your job. The other racers care for their fans, they are friendly and let the public adore them. But you, you are—" *Heartless. Fury. Enigmatic.* "—different." I've seen how the crowd watched over him, stuck between angst and deep admiration. Why does this man create such deep and contradictory emotions in everyone?

"I don't like to put on a show more than I have to with the press conferences. Actions speak louder than words." And on that, I couldn't agree more with Wolf. Celebrities often leak information about themselves to gossip papers or post on their social media out of the fear of becoming irrelevant. As a columnist, I learned more about a person by their environment and daily actions, than by their press release.

He takes a step toward me and I'm sensing he'll take control of the conversation. "What about you, Elle? Every time I'm trying to unravel who you are, you're backing off."

"Sometimes, it's better to withdraw from the race." Especially after crashing into Aaron's game last night.

"Oh, *ma belle*, you aren't withdrawing. You're just too afraid to go full speed." A ghost of a smile spreads on his face. And, just like that, I believe that's the first real discussion we exchanged.

"You asked me what happened with Longfoard earlier?" I remain silent, waiting for him to continue. "Well, at the end of the season, I'm out of my contract." He peers over me, his eyes sparkling as if he is having a revelation.

"I know." It's not a secret Aaron's two-year contract ends this year, but he shouldn't have a problem renewing it, being one of the youngest and most titled racing drivers of his generation despite his reputation.

"If you had billions, would you invest your money in someone like me?"

I frown my eyebrows in confusion. "I don't see why not." I won't praise his ego, but he is hell-bent, I can't possibly imagine someone able to refuse him.

"Well, I'm a risk. A risk that some sponsorships won't allow. They can't tame me, and a feral driver is a dangerous one. I can make them win big, or lose big. The way I race and my lifestyle don't please them." He studies my expression. "But I need to make them trust me, to show them some… humanity and engagement. If I give the media something about me, they'll leave me alone. I want to race in peace without worrying about not getting a contract due to how the media paint me. That's why I believe we could conclude a mutual agreement."

"An agreement?" My eyes open wildly in surprise.

"Yes. I'll do your interview if you come to the Canadian Grand Prix with me. By accompanying me, they'll believe I'm settling down. In my world, happiness doesn't sell. Once they see I've let someone in, they'll get off my back."

I open my jaw in shock as I chuckle, thinking it's probably a joke. But when I see the glazed and fixed look on his face, I know he meant it. "You can't be serious. I'm sure you have plenty of women who would like to keep you company and play the groupie."

"They don't care about who I am, they care about what I represent." I hold on my breath at his statement. For a second, he sounded like he was almost… lonely? "You see, in order to care for someone, you need to get to know the person. And no one knows me. Plus, I'm not one to trust people."

"But you trust me?"

"I don't, but I believe it could be a mutual salvation, on every level." He approaches me closely as I stare at him with bewilderment. "On a professional level, I save your job, you save mine." He bites his lower lip seductively. "On a personal level, I can give you a good time." He licks it slowly like a predator siccing his prey. "The best, even. Last night was a promise."

Last night. Our heated exchanges. The chemistry radiating between us. Wolf is a danger, corrupting each of my cells under his power. I pull away from him, my breath getting heavier, not believing how my life took an unexpected turn.

"You need me as much as I need you, Elle," he adds.

"You're wrong, I don't need you." A lie. Without his help, I'd never have what I need—*but I don't want to need him.*

"You do. You need someone who will awaken you, someone reckless. I know you have a fire inside of you—especially since I had a preview last night—but you are afraid. Afraid to live." He takes a step closer. "Afraid to have pleasure." A step closer. "Afraid to be imperfect. Afraid to exist as yourself." His last words hit me. All my life, I've tried to reach perfection, to please everyone by being someone I wasn't, until I forgot who I was to begin with. A woman with a dream, with a desire to escape her cage to fly free. "Plus, you need me for your article."

Using each other.

That's all it has been since the moment we've met. We both needed an escape until we trapped ourselves into a mess. "You don't know me."

"I do know that last night you were feeling pretty free and alive, and that's clearly not in your habits." His gaze burns me, and I know he's probably right. The twenty-four hours spent with Aaron have been the most liberating ones. But that's not the question.

"I can't, Aaron." I swallow. "Why are you even interested in me?"

"I've made it clear, I want you." His lips curl into a confident smile. "And I know it's not one-sided." He contemplates each of my features like he is trying to understand me, to read me. "I take every 'intimate relationship' as an agreement between two parts. I have rules. This doesn't have to be any different."

"And let me guess, those rules benefit you and not your one-night stands?" I cock my eyebrow, I'm not as sweet and naive as he thinks I am. I know about his after-races conquests, about women who don't last twenty-four hours of his interest.

"I'm always honest. Both parts know what to expect. Sex. Pleasure. Orgasms." He accentuates every word. How come a man can be so cold, distant, and at the same time so sinful, undressing me every minute? How come he can act like a gentleman while being dirty? How come he represents the opposite of what I want, but I'm for some unknown reason magnetically attracted to him? He is a mystery.

"I'm not interested in sex. I'm not one of your fangirls who obeys you kindly. You can't control me."

"And you, Elle, you can't control yourself all the time. Or you'll end up waiting for a dream that doesn't exist."

"You're wrong," I mutter.

His fingers tease my bare skin, tracing my spine and electrifying my nerves, as his other hand attuned our bodies together. His intense gaze meets mine, analyzing my reaction to his touch, giving me a chance to back off, but I remain receptive.

"Am I?" He skims his hand up my waist, the edge of my breast, like a poison running through my veins.

"Yes." I ache, losing control of my own body.

"What if I prove the contrary?" He rubs his lips close to mine, his husky voice bewitching me. God, I can't want him.

"You—"

He collides his lips into mine without a warning, and I give in. Let him consume me. My skin flushes hot. I'm melting under the fierce heat of our drugging kiss. He awakens every nerve of my body. Taking more. Claiming more. Burning me more. And I'm relishing every moment of it. I open my mouth eagerly to let him take the lead. I'm overpowered by all of Aaron, afraid he'll be my addiction.

Our tongues dance together. His hands clench my waist, passionately creasing the material of my dress. I abandon my control to the man I barely know, the man who creates an empyrean pleasure in me. Scorching my senses. Crushing me. My fingers intertwine in his hair, our kiss almost violent to the point where I could make him bleed. To the point where I don't need oxygen to breathe.

The wrong man who brings to life all the right things.

A damaged god breaking the mortal.

A story that promises only tragedy.

"So, Elle, do you want to be mine?" He stops our kiss but maintains the proximity between us.

Mine. I'll never be someone's property again. I could succumb to Wolf, but he'll never have more from me. I could never go out with someone for casual pleasure. I could never accept the rules, the expiration date written on my face. Being his flavor of the month to allow him to ditch me after I'm of no use. He'll never have my heart, my broken heart, that has been shattered into microscopic pieces.

It's unassailable.

But he could still own my pride. And that I won't allow.

Rules. Agreement. Game.

It's not like I have a choice. I need his help to show that I'm valuable. Securing my job while dazzling Nina with the article no one has been able to obtain. I fought my whole life to be where I am today—for my independence. And hopefully someday, my freedom. After all, I have nothing to lose. What's left of me is a deep, consuming hunger.

A need for revenge.

How weak I've become, how Stephan destroyed me. I felt ashamed for so long, I can't be seen anymore as the sweet, docile girl who couldn't stand up for herself. The one who wasn't perfect enough. I'm tired of hearing the demons of my past. Maybe Aaron is my only choice, my only possibility for a brighter future. My escape.

He sets the game.

I set the rules.

A mutual salvation. Nothing more.

"Yes, I accept," I mumble. He quirks his eyebrow in surprise. "But, I won't date you, and even less sleep with you. That's a non-negotiable rule." Again, I don't know if I'm trying to convince myself or him. *Probably both.*

"One date. Give me one date to change your mind." He remains unflappable as if he were expecting my answer.

I mean, who wouldn't want to date him? To have the illusion you can change a man like Aaron. That you'll be the one to be different. Significant. I'm not naive enough to believe that. I know I'm a challenge, the one who resisted him. Nothing more.

I'll use him to save me. Not destroy me.

And for the wrong reasons, I reply, "Fine. One date."

It's just a date. It doesn't engage me in anything.

And yet, I was supposed to interview Wolf but ended up playing his game. Trapping myself into a deal to gain my freedom.

"I have one rule as well," Wolf states. "I'll answer your questions, but my past is off-limits. I don't tolerate people seeking dirt and unfounded gossip."

"I'll write only the truth."

He smiles, probably appreciating my honesty. "Smart answer." He leans, whispering in my ear, "I have a feeling, Miss Monteiro, that we will both try to break each other's rule."

He heads toward his car, enjoying this, thinking that he will acquire one more victory to his shelf.

One thing is sure, none of us can afford to lose this race, because anything could happen.

We are standing in awkward silence in front of each other in the airport hallway. It's the last call for New York, and I keep looking nervously at my ticket. I crave more. But I need to think straight. It was just a weekend, a carnal need, nothing more. *You'll forget about him.*

It's not special.

It's unreal. Chimerical.

You'll save your job, and gain Nina's trust, it's all that matters. Not him.

"Well, goodbye Aaron." I gather my dazzling smile, the one I perfected after so many years to hide my emotions.

"Goodbye, Elle."

Our faces almost connecting, I anticipate the kiss that is yet to come, and my lips part willingly to have one last taste of sin, eager to break my own rule. But a wave of disappointment rushes through me when he aims for my cheek to kiss instead. I swallow my discontent.

A hint of a smile stretches on his lips, and I know it was part of his plan. "I'll contact you for our date."

Desire comes from frustration.

But Wolf hasn't tasted my bitterness. It might be his game, but I know all about frustration. And I surely will not give him what he hankers to claim.

I'll be his frustration.

I walk away from him to give my ticket to the flight attendant. Before disappearing through the boarding area, I look back one last time. When I see Wolf standing still, his charismatic aura circling him, a mix of spellbinding and conflicted, of darkness and triumph, I know he is an enigma I need to solve.

He was right.

Us, this is just the beginning.

CHAPTER 6

The frog, The Knight, The Prince

"Aaron freaking LeBeau!"

Tania screams, attracting the attention of all of our coworkers who are now glaring at us. I shush her as she comes down from her desk and twirls her chair closer to mine. I'm usually working from home as much as I can, but I needed to fill out Tania with my epic weekend with Wolf—and confront my boss. Judging by her malicious smile, her you're-so-naughty look, the interrogation had just begun. She pulls up her dark raven hair into a bun. Tania has a dazzling personality; she's always wearing warm fall clothes that complement her alluring amber skin. She has been my only friend here. I've always been admiring, almost envious, of her no filter personality and how confident she is about her body and desires.

"How come you didn't sleep with him?" She bites her pen, sinking into her seat.

"He only wants me for sex, Tania."

"Is that so bad?" She scrutinizes me, a proud smirk curving on her lips. "I mean, if there is one person casual sex is worth it with, that would be Aaron LeBeau." I roll my eyes. "Maybe casual sex is exactly what you need."

"I don't need it. I'd be insignificant for a man like Aaron, I'm just another trophy for him to claim," I snort, having my fair share of the male testosterone. They race after you to bolster their ego, and once they accomplish their mission, you're old news."

"Why did you accept his agreement, then? You're not the kind of woman to act impulsively, nor to open to a guy so easily."

"I guess it was revenge." I shrug, knowing revenge wasn't my only motive. Sure, I want revenge on what Stephan did to me. I won't allow myself to be weak or sweet again, and getting the article is the proof I've changed. But Aaron awoke something different in me, a sort of new exhilarating freedom. I frown my eyebrows, too proud to admit that to her. "I was attracted to him, but it doesn't mean anything."

"Well, that's the first time a man got your attention after—" She swallows and hesitates to continue, aware that Stephan is a sensitive topic for me. Even if Tania doesn't know the whole truth, she witnessed my degradation over the months and saw me losing my spark. "You closed yourself. You need to feel the heat, someone that will make you feel like the goddess that you are." I simper at her comment; she has her own unique way of giving advice. Playful, flirty, and yet she's overprotective of the people she loves.

"I'm serious, Elle. Think of sex as therapy. It doesn't have to last forever." I raise my eyebrow, so she searches for a more sensible metaphor. "Maybe he isn't your Prince Charming, but he might just be what you need in order to find your prince."

"You mean the frog before the prince?" I chuckle, having no idea where she's going with this.

"No, frogs are for assholes. I mean the hot knight. The one who offers the princess a good time before she marries the boring prince who has all the spotlight." She might be good at gossip, but definitely not at fairy tales.

"Knights aren't part of the fairy tales," I answer sarcastically.

She arches her eyebrow, pointing her finger at me. "You don't know that. Maybe the jealous prince deleted the knight from the book. Maybe it isn't the truth. Princes are old news. A sexy, rebellious knight… someone who fights for what they want, not a spoiled rich brat who lounges all day in silk pajamas, gathering dust while others build empires."

We start to giggle, forgetting we aren't the only ones in the bright office on the tenth floor. But then Tania's expression changes radically, her eyes wild, she spins her chair to the other side without a word. I feel a shadow behind my back, hands on her hips in an authoritative gesture, and I instantly recognize who it is.

"Elle. In my office."

I turn around to face my cold and soulless editor-in-chief, Nina. Black stilettos, tight black business dress, her silver-gray hair cut into a square on her shoulders—her looks scream of order and rigidity. At the office, no one dares to approach her. We could say Nina Braham lost her heart many years ago and sold her soul for power. She got remarried to the director of Black Publications, Albert Black, a seventy-year-old billionaire, while she's still in her prime forties. Weirdly, a couple of weeks later she was assigned as editor-in-chief, and became my boss. Nina's opinion is therefore the only thing that matters.

I swallow and follow her with heavy steps to her lifeless office. She has a breathtaking view of the whole city, while her black curtains are always closed. She doesn't let any light enter. She sits behind her desk, her legs closed in a position of power as she scans me from head to toe. I feel like a helpless bug. I take a deep breath, approaching the spider trap, repeating in my head the same word: *Confidence. Confidence. Confidence.* After all, I accomplished what she demanded—and what no one else could achieve.

"I don't see the article about Aaron LeBeau." Her gaze tightens in my direction, inspecting me.

"The interview is settled for the Canadian Grand Prix. He offered me an exclusivity."

"Almost impressive. Tell me, Elle, how did you get that interview?" Her lips curve into a dry smile. "I've sent two other writers, and yet, you're the only one who got an interview, if in fact what you say is true."

I breathe heavily, trying to calm my nerves. Of course, she didn't trust me with this. Nina always has a backup, and by the way she studies me over, I could guess she wasn't expecting that I would be the one succeeding.

"You sent me as bait, Nina. I just did my job."

She cackles, making my skin crawl. "Sure. I believe you got well acquainted." She raises her eyebrow, scanning me like I just piqued her interest. Vicious as she is, she's probably certain I slept with Wolf to secure myself an interview.

My nerves shaking, I feel the need to justify myself. "I've remained professional. Nothing happened. Aaron agrees to—"

"Aaron? You're on the first name bases, now?" I clear my throat, incapable to stand up for myself. After all, I did conclude a deal with the devil to get that interview. "Well, you're impressing me, Elle. Having you on our team wasn't a mistake after all."

A wicked smile stretches on her face. "That said, I'm expecting more than superficial curiosities from this article. Aaron LeBeau has secrets. I want you to hound him. I don't care what methods do you use. If you deliver this to me, consider your job secured. If not…" She draws in a long breath. "… don't bother coming back. You already deceived me once a year ago. This is your last chance." She waves her hand at me in a way of saying I'm dismissed.

Right. I nod, knowing a negotiation is off-limits with Nina. Monaco wasn't the last step toward freedom, it was only the first step. The first step into Nina's mind games. I stand from my chair and start to retire from her office.

"Oh, and Elle?" I turn to face her. "I'll be following whatever is going on between you and him, closely." *Of course, she will.* "I'll be away in Paris for the next couple of weeks."

I nod, hiding my feelings of deliverance at the thought of being weeks free, without Nina.

From 16 to 7. Interesting.

I've been searching for information about Aaron for the past hour on the web. It'll be adequate to say my past week has been used to fulfill this mission; getting to know the man who's occupying my thoughts. I've concluded LeBeau isn't a social media fan. He is one of the racing drivers with the most fans, having millions of followers, and yet he follows only a few people with the strict minimum of posts on his page. The only article that catches my eye in this pool of gossips around Aaron is, *From 16 to 7*. Wolf had changed his car number suddenly without giving an explanation two years ago.

His driving became even more aggressive, dangerous and unpredictable. He made some reckless mistakes and got into many skirmishes with the other drivers, which gave him his nickname, Wolf, and his reputation with countless of women. My gut was right, something happened to Wolf.

I search more on the web, trying to find information related to Wolf's family. He said he has a brother. But the results I find on the web are like nothing I imagined. *Aaron LeBeau absents from his brother's funeral.* I click on the link. Aaron's brother died two years ago. Nothing else is written. The LeBeau's family has been trying to keep the media away from the funeral and the reason of the death. But... why would Aaron miss his own brother's funeral? Could he be that cold-hearted? Why Wolf is so determined to be pictured as a villain?

I snap out of my thoughts when I receive a text message from the racing driver in question.

Aaron: I believe I owe you a date. See you tomorrow.

Tomorrow? I wasn't even aware he would be in New York by then. We've exchanged a couple of texts the past few days. He is being his usual flirty self, and I, playing hard to get. A game of cat and mouse. He'd sent me a friend request I've accepted only a couple of days later. Weirdly, I've become active on social media, only for one purpose, him seeing it. Even if I hate to admit it, I've been enjoying it and encouraging his hell-bent desire to claim me.

Our last conversation was about the picture he sent me from his oversize yacht in Monaco. I replied to him that I wished the water could freeze his ego, before he snapped with, "Ma belle, there's ego, and there's reality, and the reality is, I'm sailing my megayatch for the afternoon before boarding a private helicopter that'll take me into the city, where my 16,000 square foot penthouse awaits... ego no longer factors in when your reality exceed most people's dreams."

"You have a way with words, Wolf. I'm surprised it worked on so many women," was the only comeback I could think of.

"I'm more of a man of action. Plus, you know what my mouth can do. But maybe you need a reminder?" He did win this one. And that's the reason why I ignored him since then.

Me: What if I am unavailable?

Aaron: I know you're playing hard to get, ma belle. I'll be there at 7pm.

And here he is, Mr. Arrogant, in all his greatness. Aaron doesn't ask, he goes for it at full speed. I almost regret texting him my address a few days prior. I'm making it too easy for him.

Me: You're so full of yourself.

I chuckle at my answer, savoring our game, and how daring I am with him. But then, he left me on *read*. Something that never irritated me before—until now. I feel the urge to continue the discussion, but end up waiting impatiently for a text that doesn't come. Irritation grows on me by the second, questions haunt my mind. I'm overthinking. Impatient. Needy. And I hate that.

I head back to my cozy bedroom and throw my phone on the beige blankets of my bed. After taking a shower, I changed into my red grenade pajama, ready to call it a night. But when I see my screen lighting up, my heart bounces like a teenager receiving a reply from her crush. *I'm pathetic*.

Aaron: So, you never thought of me since Monaco?

I smile coyly, holding my pillow against my chest. Of course, I did, but that he'll never know. I check the time, it's eleven p.m. which means it must be five a.m. Aaron's time.

Me: I believe you should sleep.

Aaron: How could I sleep when I have you on my mind?

Me: How many drinks did you have?

Aaron: None. I'm not usually drinking during the racing season.

Aaron: See. Training.

And to my surprise, he attaches a picture with it. He is at the gym, already lifting weights. Shirtless. I need a moment to process the picture. He has the beauty and the strength of a Greek god working for his own Olympia. Water drops are dripping from his sculpted chest, his ripped muscles are contracting, his wolf tattoo howling on his chest. His body is an appeal to bend over his desire. His devilish smirk is his promise to claim what he's here for. He doesn't even hide it. The bastard knows his strengths, and he is using them to destabilize me.

He embodies all seven of the deadly sins.

Which makes me a sinner.

Aaron: Your turn.

I bite my lower lip, my heart pounding, fueled with the desire to let Wolf fantasize about me. I run toward my bathroom to readjust my hair and apply a slight touch of mascara and a bit of blush. I don't realize yet, how this is a bad idea. Aaron probably receives on a daily basis hundreds of pictures of models. And then there is me. But for a moment, I don't think about them. He asks, and I oblige. Weakly. Does that make it right? No. Does that make me significant? No. And yet, my gut seems to believe it's such a great idea.

I hop into my bed and start taking a few selfies. Obviously, none of them seem right. I don't want to send the wrong message. I'm not like *them*. I throw my phone next to me, not feeling good enough, obsessed with a need to awaken his lust. Finally, I decide to take it back and select a decent selfie. I'm smiling coyly, my head tilted to the side, and I'm probably trying too hard to appear cute. It's not provocative, not even near sexy, but it's simple. Me. I'm not sure if my girly bedroom—in the grayish and salmon pink tones with fluffy pillows and quotes on my wall—sends the right message either. But with him, I don't want to pretend. I close my eyes and… sent.

Me: Heading to bed.

Aaron: Damn. Beautiful. But if I was there, you wouldn't stay fully clothed any longer.

I giggle, returning to the innocent teenage years when I read his reply. I'm heading to a dangerous and fatal game, and yet for the first time in years, I feel awake.

Me: You know that won't happen. Goodnight, Aaron.

Aaron: Oh, Elle… You shouldn't begin something you can't finish.

Me: I believe I already did. You can't win every time.

I know I will regret sending this message. I'm teasing the player himself, burning myself willingly to the point where I won't be the master of my fate any longer. I've stuck myself into a circle. The more I refuse him, the more he hunts me and the more I'm feeling the need to succumb to his power over me. And the worst, I'll do it all again. Every fucking time.

Aaron: I'll make you pay for your teasing tomorrow. Goodnight, ma belle.

That was a promise.

And each promise of Wolf is a certitude.

CHAPTER 7

Love

Elle: 8 years old

Little birdie.

Daddy calls me that, and today I want to make him proud. Birds can fly in the sky, so I climb the old tree of our garden to sit on the branch. A step closer to the sky. I stare at the dirt on my dress and on my hands, my fingers colored by the pastels. Mommy is gonna be mad, she spends her time cleaning and cooking, she's never smiling.

A robin is singing. I recognize him from the pretty orange color of his pelage. I believe he's cheering me up, or welcoming the spring. My arm up, I incline my palm toward the sky for him to lay on it. I feel lonely—boys are stupid, and girls don't like me. Mommy told me it's because I'm pretty. I think it's because I'm weird. I'm always drawing, putting colors everywhere.

The bird flies away on the higher branch. *Crap.* I dare to look at the ground. Oh no, it's too high.

"Daddy," I cry out, fear paralyzing me. How am I gonna get down? I'm higher than Daddy's height, and he's a giant.

Dad is on the phone, discussing adult things that make him most of the time angry. I continue on calling him until he turns around and his brown eyes meet mine. "Daddy, I'm stuck. Please, help me."

He sighs, "I'll see you tonight, Selene." *Selene?* I've seen a beautiful blond lady once in Daddy's car with this name. Dad hangs up and walks in my direction before looking up. "What are you doing up there? Where is your mother?"

"Mom is at the supermarket." *You were supposed to take me to the park today, but you didn't.* "I wanted to be friends with the bird." My legs start to shake as I lean toward the huge branch, gripping it tighter when the wind begins to rise.

"For fuck's sake, Elle!" I don't like it when Daddy raises his voice, just like when I dislike when he's wearing his expensive business clothes. "Just jump, I'll catch you. I don't have time for this."

I nod my head sideways. "No, it's too high. Please, take me!"

"I'm not gonna climb out there, jump, Elle." Oh, no, I've annoyed, Daddy.

"Promise, you'll catch me?" *I'll never climb again. I promise.*

"Yes. Come on, hurry up!"

Both of my hands still on the branch, I pull my legs in the void, ignoring my fear. "Daddy, are you here?" If my hands stop clutching the tree branch, I'd fall. Would I die?

"Yes, Elle."

"Okay. I'm letting go." I close my eyes. It's fine.

Daddy will catch me.

Daddy is behind me.

Daddy loves me, he'll never let something happen to me.

"Shit," Daddy sighs while I let go of the tree branch.

The bird peering at me, I scream, watching the sky as I fall the same way I do like in one of my nightmares.

Humans don't fly.

Humans *fall*.

I hit the wet grass, falling on my side. It hurts, and my knee tingles of burning heat. I move my leg. Blood. But I don't cry yet, not until I see Daddy on the phone, ignoring me.

He didn't catch me.

He lied. *Again.*

Then, I cry, my heart hurting so much. When he finally notices me on the ground, he hangs up for the second time paying attention to me. *I trusted you, Dad…*

"Stop crying, Elle." *Why?* "You're not injured, this will serve you as a lesson."

I cry even louder, seeing Dad's face cold as stone. "You didn't catch me. You lied. I'm hurt," I sob, showing him my bleeding knee.

"In life, people don't catch you. Nobody will ever love a weak person."

"Dad…" He walks away from me, leaving me on the ground.

He steps on my favorite pastel pencil, breaking it apart, before throwing on the ground the drawing who was in his pocket. The one I've made for him.

Dad, come back.

Don't abandon me.

Love me.

I spot Dad's luggage in the hallway of our home, while the voices keep screaming. Dad is leaving without saying goodbye. *I don't understand.*

"Don't leave us, please," I hear Mom begging Dad. "You wouldn't abandon your daughter."

I hide behind the door halfway opened, taking a peek. Mom is trying to take his hand, but he pushes her away. Her eyes are wet and tears dark from the mascara that dropped on her cheeks.

"I've invested enough in that child. I'll send you money." He is walking away from Mom, before she blocks the way, tears in her eyes.

"I love you. Don't leave. I'll do everything you want, I'll be better, I promise," she pleads, crying.

"You have a month to leave the house. My lawyer will contact you."

She falls on her knees, her head bows down before taking Dad's hands, kissing them, wetting them with her tears. "Please, I know you love me. I need you."

He forces Mommy to meet his eyes with his thumb. "But, I don't."

No.

Dad walks in my direction as Mom lies on the floor, still crying. I want to help Mommy, but I don't. *I don't understand.* When Da—Father opens the door, I swallow my tears. He doesn't deserve this. *I wish I didn't love him.* His eyes lock on mine before he leaves without a word. I want to run after him, but I can't. My leg hurts from the fall, and I have an ugly bandage on it.

The door slams.

He's gone.

He abandoned me.

I look over at Mommy, she's in pain. I walk toward her as fast as I can to hug her.

I still have Mom.

"Mommy, are you okay?" She doesn't reply for a moment, as a tighten my hug.

Then, she takes me by my shoulders, obligating me to face her. Her dark hair is falling on her face, her eyes red, she doesn't look like Mommy anymore. "Never love a man, Elle. They'll just break you."

"But I loved—"

Slap.

Mom's hand hits my cheek and it hurts, but I remain brave. "Never say that word, ever again."

I nod, afraid to disappoint Mommy too. She pulls herself up, swallowing her tears. "There is no such thing as love. Men are bastards. Use them, manipulate them, because if you don't they'll destroy your pretty heart instead." She walks away as if her heart has left her chest, leaving me alone.

I lost Mommy too.

She's gone.

I glance at the window to peek at the bird, teasing me with his freedom. He abandoned me too, just like Dad did to us, stealing Mom's heart, and breaking her wings.

Go away.

I hate you.

Love and fairy tales were lies.

There are no such things as happily ever after. People leave. People abandon you.

I'll never fall again.

CHAPTER 8

Sexting is wrong

I'm late!

It's 6:58 p.m. and I'm facing an issue every woman faces in their lives. A closet full of clothes and nothing to wear. After staring at my outfit choices, I decide to go for simplicity. The last real date I had was with… never mind. I opt for my favorite jeans which grant my glutes justice, with my comfy suede heels and my black silk blouse.

But maybe it's too simple? Someone like Aaron might want to go to a place where I'd look underdressed and uncomfortable. And as for tonight, it's the opposite of what I want. The doorbell rings, pulling me out of my overthinking. I try to calm my nerves, but the contradictory feelings rush into me.

I open the door, and my heart races a thousand miles per hour when I see Wolf standing on my doorstep. Charismatic. Devilishly handsome. Magnetic. I feel butterflies in my stomach when I glance at his flirtatious grin. His elbow on the wall, his fingers playing with his obsidian hair, he screams of bad boy vibes with his leather jacket. I simper, realizing it's the same I borrowed from him when we met.

"*Ma belle?*"

I bite my lower lip at the sound of his husky voice. I bow my head to the side, and suddenly, resisting him feels like a bad idea. He's creating an urgent craving in me. I've never felt the need to have sex. I was fine without it, and truth is, I've never taken pleasure during intimacy. But seeing him makes me reconsider my need. *Maybe I should invest in a vibrator.* I mean, I wrote about it, but I've never tried it. Thinking about Aaron's hands caressing my skin, his kisses trailing down my neck, his voice bewitching me until I—

"*Ma belle.* You are staring." I snap out of my thoughts. *What an idiot!* My cheeks flush red when I realize how awkward I must have looked.

"You look flushed." He grins. "I bet your thoughts were quite… intense." His last word rolls off his tongue, he's enjoying this way too much.

I give him a friendly shoulder tap before letting him enter my place. I stand stiffly next to my couch, readjusting my blanket, tossing my unfinished paintings under my couch, hiding my romance novels behind the shelf of books about mythology, art, and psychology. He scans my whole place in silence. I feel so little—he's probably used to the sumptuousness, but I'm far from a billionaire. At least, everything I own is thanks to myself, and that's something I can be proud of. His gaze drops to the painting I have in the middle of the wall, he furrows his brow, tilting his head.

"What's this?"

"It's *Everlasting* from Romeo Di Angelo. Obviously, it's just a print." I smile coyly, remembering the history this painting has for me. It was my own escape. My hope.

Romeo Di Angelo was one of the most influential painters of the eighteenth century, his paintings have sold millions. *Everlasting* is the story of true love. The man, who is depicted as an angel, is in the sky, capturing into his arms his beloved. But demons are holding her feet as she's desperately crying in pain, her light pink dress halfway ripped and dirty, like he just saved her from Hell itself. As for him, a mask of fear is on his face as he battles demons of his own. They are trying to separate them, to break the man's wings for them to fall. This painting is a cry for help. The only light is around them. It's from deep sadness, and yet it has been my hope. The promise that true love will win it all.

That love could someday exist.

Little girls dreamed to be princesses—well, when I was a child, I dreamed to be that woman. The one who escapes her demons, the one whose love is so pure and strong it frees her. This painting has been my secret. Art was my escape. The only world where I can let my desires run free, without having to face the consequences. I wasn't allowed to believe or feel love. I've been raised to believe it's a lie, that it rhymes with abandon and destruction. My own obsession with love destroyed me, until a point, the word itself has no meaning for me anymore. It was bane vocabulary for my mother, and a weapon of destruction for Stephan.

Love is a willing submission to the other. Nothing else.

"Why do you love this painting so much?" He tries to read me, and I'm intrigued by his interest in it.

Because I wish she was wrong.

"It was my escape, sort of?" I shrug, not ready to explain my past to Aaron. "It made me believe in a brighter future. I feel emotions, and I—" I laugh shyly, knowing he wouldn't understand me. "It's stupid, right? It's just a painting, I know."

"It's not stupid, Elle. Not stupid at all." And for a moment, I allow myself to feel like I'm not alone.

We break our eye contact. Aaron clears his throat and I cross my arms on my chest. One more thing in common—we don't patronize ourselves with the talking and we neglect our emotions to perfection.

"Can you give me a tour?"

"It's pretty small…" He raises an eyebrow at me. "Fine," I capitulate.

A kitchen and a bathroom tour later, we arrive at my… bedroom. And for an unknown reason, my heart starts racing. Perhaps from the memory of our steamy texts haunting my mind. I lean across my desk, watching Aaron walk like an elegant tiger across the room. He observes with curiosity my whole place, a satisfying smile on his face just as if he had me all figured it out.

As he approaches me, I grip harder on the wood of my desk, unconfident with being a few inches from him. It's been weeks since we've seen each other, and yet he strikes me just like he did the first time. He hovers over me, placing both of his hands on the desk.

"So this is my bedroom." I lower my voice.

His gaze darkens vibrantly with arousal as he wets his lip with his tongue, unveiling me with just a look. Sexual tension. Magnetism. Craving. We are like opposite forces magnetically drawn to each other. His left thumb lifts my chin up in order to oblige me to meet his scorching stare.

"Remember when I told you... you shouldn't begin something you can't finish?"

My cheeks flush red at the thought of my reckless texting. One thing is sure, I can't let him have his way with me. I can't let him know he has control over my body. Wearing red undergarments tonight—undergarments he shall not see—wasn't the smartest decision.

"If you're hoping to take me on my desk without even being on a date, you're wrong," I say, defending myself.

"That wasn't my intention... for tonight." He angles his face closer to mine so our lips are dangerously close to colliding.

I swallow, ignoring my palpitating heart. "Don't get your hopes too high."

"What if I could prove to you that you want me as much as I want you? An honest game." His raspy voice is like a whisper, an invitation to sin.

He traces a deliciously light trail down the column of my neck with the tips of his fingers, his gaze locked on me as I nod, giving Wolf the green light. I'm determined to prove to myself that he can't affect me as much as he claims he could. But when he kisses my neck slowly, a wave of pleasureful goose bumps travels around my whole flesh. He isn't wasting his time. He knows what he wants, and he is here to claim it. To claim me. And I'm letting him intoxicate my senses. He kisses the lobe of my ear as I pull my head backward, closing my eyelids, facing my guilty pleasure. Igniting into him.

His fingers tease the neckline of my top as he watches me breathing heavily, my thighs squeezing themselves harder. He is playing a game of lust, and he won't stop until I beg for his kiss, his touch, and admit our attraction. He knows I'm resisting him, and he is enjoying it. His hand clutches my waist as he leans dangerously close, and my lips part, ready to submit, to steal his control by giving him what he needs.

"I'll not kiss you, Elle. Not now. Not until you admit you want me."

He backs off, his mission accomplished. Bastard. I immediately amble toward my bed to grab my bag. Wolf is creating within me such contradictory and intense feelings. I'll not admit I want him. I'll not give him the checkered flag to be another insignificant conquest. But yet, I want to get back to him.

I notice his piercing gaze on me and decide to bend over seductively to reach my bag. I can feel his eyes dragging over me with lust. But by arching my back in a 'sexy' way, my bra unclasps itself from under my top with a loud noise. That's just great. I was in such a rush that I hadn't clipped it well, and now I'm paying the price. I try to clip it back, but the rasp of his voice interrupts me.

"Let me do it."

I turn myself so my back is facing him, feeling like at this pace we will never leave for our date. *Not our date. His date.* I place my hair on the side of my shoulder while he unzips my top slowly. We are awfully close to each other, too close. He skims his hands on my skin delicately, creating shivers all over my body. He clasps my bra in one move, which is a reminder of all the practice he must have had with his conquests.

He moves his lips closer to my neck. "Red. Nice choice." I try to ignore his comment as he zips my top back up. I repeat my mantra. Undergarments he shall not see. Undergarments he shall not touch. Undergarments he shall not rip.

"You won't see more of that, I'm afraid."

"I wouldn't be so sure about that."

He kisses my nape, and we're back into our spiral. A game of power, a game of running back and forth from the other. His hands find my hips and pull me closer to him. His lips move over my earlobe before nibbling on my neck again. His erection on my back. I start losing control. He grips me harder. I'm flushed. I can't breathe. When I'm about to ask him to end my suffering, he reels me in to face him.

His hand possessively cups my jaw, angling my head up, while his calloused finger caresses my lower lip. "I was right. You want me." On that sentence, he pulls away from me and lets me hang there unsatisfied as he walks toward the door. *That controlling bastard!* "I told you I'll make you pay for your teasing." He flashes me a victorious smile as he leans on the door.

Nicely played, but the race is not over. I move closer to him and stare into his eyes, darting my tongue out of my mouth. "Aaron."

"Yes?"

I look down at his pants. "You are still hard." I wink at him before leaving my bedroom. "From where I stand, you are the one who wants me."

I believe I just won the pole position.

"Aaron! I can't believe it!" I exclaim, excitement rushing through my veins. We are standing in front of the fair. The Ferris wheel is spinning, big attractions are dazzling through the dark night. It's the perfect summer evening. I've never been here before. It was my dream teen date, but I never found the right man to bring me here. I wonder if Aaron could read my mind. Tonight, I didn't want to go to one of those fancy places, I wanted excitement. That's the thing with Wolf, he does the unexpected.

"Shall we?" he addresses me, watching me acting like a five-year-old child.

I nod and follow him toward the fair entrance. The atmosphere is magical. People are gathering around a variety of attractions. Happiness is the only emotion of the night. The festival music, the food treats, fireworks… and Aaron LeBeau—who laughs at me seeing me trotting around the attractions. Wolf laughs. That's unusual. He has more charisma, power, and money, than every man I ever met, and yet he is so simple.

Some people recognize Wolf, and he waves politely at them with a charming smile. He even agreed on a few pictures that the most courageous fans dared to ask, which confused me even more. Wolf isn't the type of man to cares, to be that open with people. Am I wrong about him?

"What?" He stares at me, probably noticing my bewilderment.

"You're just not how I imagined you'd be."

"What type of man do you think I am, then, Miss Monteiro?"

To be honest, I have no idea. But instead, I reply, "I'd say the arrogant alpha type."

"If that's what you're into." He smirks with confidence.

"I also believe there is more to you than you're letting us know."

He doesn't answer and we continue to walk toward the main attractions where it's getting more and more crowded. So much so that I grip Aaron's arm to not lose him among the people.

"I'm sorry… I didn't want to lose you," I mutter.

"Is that a way of saying you want to be closer to me? Because that can certainly happen."

"You have to stop flirting with me, Aaron." I can't let myself succumb to him, not at the price of being insignificant to a man like him.

"I will stop flirting with you when you stop denying our attraction." I swallow at his comment, knowing I'm throwing away a perfect date because of my issues. "You feel our chemistry as much as I do. There is nothing wrong with it."

But you, Aaron, you are wrong.

"This is just a game for you." I cross my arms over my chest as he stops walking to position himself in front of me, frowning his eyebrows.

"A game?"

"Yes. You want me because you can't have me."

He is the hunter and I'm the prey, it's not a healthy connection between us, it's a twisted role-play. The moment I am in his bed, he will stop paying attention to me. And I will have to suffer the consequences of being humiliated.

"I'm just a challenge. I can't have a good time and be…" My voice quivers as I finish my sentence. "I can't be… insignificant." *To you or to anyone… not anymore.*

"Who says you have to be insignificant?" His tone is serious, deep.

I narrow my eyes, determined to prove my point. "That agreement of yours. Women play by your rules, you fuck them, and when you're bored, you pretend they never existed… insignificant. You can't expect me to bend to your desire just because you are used to getting things your way."

"It is the only kind of intimacy I can offer, yes." He admits with sincerity. *Who would ever agree to that?* "I don't do the whole nice boyfriend thing. I'm not that type of man."

He's right, he's not. He's the type of man mothers warn their daughters about. The one who screams of every shade of bad, breaking the good girl innocence. The one you know you should stay away from, but has turned your own body against you. A sinner, a danger you cannot escape. Wolf trapped me from the start.

"I'm not insignificant," I repeat, looking at my feet, denying my unwanted attraction for him. "Once you get what you want from me, you'll lose interest."

I glare at him as he stares at me with an unreadable expression on his face. "So you think that I just want to fuck you once?"

"Pretty much," I reply, not breaking our eye contact.

A sly smile curves on his lips as he reduces the distance between us. He takes all his sweet time to answer, scanning me.

"Well, I guess I'll just have to fuck you and prove you wrong."

I shake my head in disbelief. I'm uncertain if I dislike his dirty talk or if it's actually turning me on. *Prove me wrong...* Perhaps because one night won't satisfy his needs, and never will it satisfy mine.

"*Ma belle*, if something's gonna happen between you and me—and it will—it's gonna happen more than once. Trust me." By the gravity of his tone, I feel it's a promise.

It isn't about a one-night stand. It is for a long, slow-burning ride. But a ride to where? Probably to Hell.

Using each other for our personal needs. Using our cravings to escape our darkness. Transforming our darkness to a source of pleasure. To forget.

We are caught in a spiral, without brakes or a possibility to stop the inevitable.

CHAPTER 9

A spark in the darkness

I can't believe I'm doing this.

My fists tighten, my pulse is accelerating, it's too high. I close my eyes. I got this. Aaron is sitting next to me, not noticing my anxiety as we are going higher and higher on the Ferris wheel. I should have told him I'm afraid of heights, but I wanted to prove that I am stronger than my fears. And now, my small drop of courage leads me to the verge of having a heart attack. Even children are on the Ferris wheel, I can't be that weak. I look down, my fists gripping the bar tighter.

"Are you okay?"

I nod and manage a fake, unconvincing smile. I can't show him I'm scared of a kiddy attraction. I need to change the subject. "Aren't you afraid of death when you race?" *Hey, Aaron, let's talk about death on a first date.* Not that I'm anxious to die on the Ferris wheel.

"No." He shrugs.

"Why?" How could he not? One bad maneuver. One mistake. One second. And he could die. He is putting his life in danger willingly.

"I have nothing to lose. It's even thrilling to defy death during each race." He stares at me, trying to read my reaction.

"What's so thrilling about it? And what if one day you lose against death?" I can't believe he isn't scared. Every person would be scared, but then again, he is Wolf.

"To be in control. It doesn't matter if I lose or if I win, what matters is that I forget." I meet his tenebrous gaze, wondering what happened to him. Why is he so—

"No!" I yell in horror as the Ferris wheel stops at the highest point. I'm stuck in my worst nightmare. I start to panic, moving my hands stressfully. My mouth vibrates with fear, my muscles shaking. I hear the sound of the creaking metal pieces, there must be a problem. Something is wrong. I close my eyes, hoping it's just a nightmare and that I will wake up soon.

"Look at me," Aaron orders with calmness and control.

I shake my head on my knees, incapable of opening my eyes. "I can't. I'm scared, I can't—" I try to deny the tears of fear sliding down my cheeks. This is humiliating. I wish Aaron could be gone, that he didn't have to witness my poor self paralyzed by fear. My whole body is trembling, I don't hear the music of the fair anymore, trapped in my own nightmare.

Aaron's hand reaches for mine, twining our fingers together. I tighten my grip on his hand, squeezing him, knowing that he probably regrets pursuing me. The strong wind hurling. Our cabin shaking. Metal cracking like death knocking at your door. No. No.

"Come closer to me." He is so serene, while I'm collapsing into my demons. He leads our hands closer to his body as an invitation.

Without thinking, I crash brutally on his torso. He offers me his chest to lie my head on, wrapping his arms around me. He caresses my back as I toughen my hold around his waist. He seems unbreakable—his body is strong, his expression cold as ice and yet his touch is comforting and caring. And I let myself go. I cry, letting my anxiety out, reviving a painful memory. I hold Aaron tightly, fearing he will abandon me. I don't want to be alone again.

My eight-year-old self is trapped in an endless nightmare of her past, in a memory she wishes to forget. The memory that started her downfall. A memory that left her with an incurable fear. *He said he would catch me.* I swallow my tears, my hands clutching Aaron's shirt at the memories haunting my mind. *He told me to jump.* Two meters. *Why didn't you catch me?* I jumped. I jumped, and he wasn't there to catch me. I fell. My nightmare. I need to forget this. I snap out of my thoughts when I feel Aaron's touch bringing me back to reality.

Silently, he caresses my hair softly with the tips of his fingers, his other arm squeezing me closer to him. With my body attuned to the proximity of his, I don't feel alone anymore. *He catches me. He is here.* And just like that, my past self feels protected, secured. For the first time in years, I actually feel like I'm not alone anymore. I forget the heights, I forget where I am, and our heartbeats connect in symbiosis.

"Take a long breath, hold it for three seconds, and exhale slowly. Count to ten," he commands while continuing to brush my hair. I do as he says, and I feel my heart calming itself. "Good. Now, try to remember a peaceful memory, or a place. Do not think about what could go wrong." I nod.

A few minutes later, I have enough courage to open my eyes and move my head up to face him. His gaze is dark, mysterious and… concerned. I lose myself in reading his tormented soul, and I understand something. He knew. He understood. The way he calmed me down in a couple of minutes, the way he wasn't judging me, mocking me. He had lived through something similar. A traumatic experience.

"You are safe." His voice is grave and powerful, for an instant it is just us. No game. No hiding. He erases the trace of my mascara on my cheeks with his finger gently. "Nothing will happen to you. I promise."

His fingers trail a path along my jaw as I open my mouth, my eyes still wet from my tears. I pull my face closer to him, begging him to kiss me. Our lips are a few inches from colliding together… but the force of the universe acts against us.

The Ferris wheel starts working again, pushing us closer to the ground, away from my fear. We immediately pull away from each other's embrace, pretending this moment never happened. It was a sign. He isn't meant to be my Prince Charming, we aren't meant to kiss. But he is meant to ease my soul, to take away my darkness—he is the troubled knight.

"Thank you, Aaron." My voice betrays my embarrassment for being so vulnerable. "And I'm sorry… I'm sorry for being a mess. I'm just… I panicked."

"You don't have to apologize. It was actually pretty brave of you to face your fear tonight." He's becoming himself again, his expression impenetrable.

I had a glimpse of Aaron's humanity. His touch felt so protective, gentle, while usually he is led by a demanding hunger, a controlling behavior, and a heated passion. Tonight, I'm discovering another side of Wolf.

"I really can't figure you out, Aaron."

I recover my emotions and we are back in the middle of the fair attractions, eating churros. We have conquered the arcade games, and he won a stuffed toy, ready to bring to life the "Ferris cliché date," as he called it, but what he hadn't anticipated was the little girl crying because she couldn't get her unicorn. He offered her the unicorn, and that gesture made me happier than any stuffed toys he could have won for me. I couldn't be more convinced that there is more to Aaron than he's letting us know. I'm sure of it. Which makes him even more dangerous and hard to resist.

The broken man rescuing less broken people.

We arrive at the claw crane machine. I notice a teddy bear key ring wearing a racing suit. *That would be perfect for Aaron.* I take Aaron's hand and lead him toward the arcade machine, a corny smile on my face.

"Nobody ever wins on the claw crane machine."

"I will." I raise my eyebrow, looking for my money, but Aaron already bought the tickets for the game. "I could have bought it myself."

"I never let a woman pay, and even less the woman I'm on a date with."

I roll my eyes at his comment, wondering where this new gallantry came from. "I don't mind."

"With me, I'll never let you pay. You can argue with me, but you know I'll have the last word." I pout, even if a part of me is melting in front of his assurance. All alpha. All man. All controlling.

Twenty minutes later, I end up insulting the machine, and Wolf has spent more than a hundred dollars on this game—for a random two-dollar key chain. He is fabulously rich, and here I am trying to win him a meaningless trifle. I must look pathetic to him.

"We should go… it's fine if—"

"No! Let me try one more time!" I'm mad at myself for not being able to do this. I slap the machine harder—I can beat the silly machine, for God's sake! And then, the claw grips the stuffed teddy bear, and I finally win. I did it. I pick up the key ring proudly and hold it up to Aaron.

"This is for you, Mr. Arrogant," I simper childishly at him. "But I want to pay you back, it was supposed to be a gift."

"No, you won't." A smug smile stretches on his face as he bows dramatically in front of me. "What counts is how devoted you were for the past twenty minutes to win this for me, Miss Monteiro."

"Oh, shut up!" I laugh at him, pushing him gently away.

"No, really. I don't usually receive gifts." His raspy voice hits me as he contemplates the ridiculous key ring in admiration. "Thank you, Elle."

I try to deny my blushing and the heat reaching my stomach. The man who has everything is impressed by my miserable attempt at doing something ridiculously small for him. *No, don't go there, Elle.*

We continue to walk around the carnival. I have never laughed this much. It really is the best date of my life, and yet so simple and natural.

"It's Aaron LeBeau!" A kid that's approximately twelve years old runs to Aaron before jumping into his arms. Wolf chuckles as he greets him and autographs the kid's hat. "I want to be a racing driver just like you! I watch all your races on TV! You are the best!" he exclaims joyfully.

"Thank you, buddy. You know you can become anything you want, right?"

The child waves his hat. "Henry! Look who I am with!" A child around the same age peers in our direction a few meters away; they look similar. Both with brown hair and blue eyes.

I chuckle at the scene, loving the innocence of children. But when I glance at Aaron, he isn't smiling anymore. His face is blank as he takes a deep breath, looking over Henry like he has seen a ghost. I pose my hand on his arm, and he immediately looks back at me, managing a quick smile.

"This is my brother! My dad likes him better. I'm always the one to get in trouble. But he is boring sometimes. He doesn't like racing," the kid explains with a shrug as his brother stops paying attention to us.

"Henry, huh? What's your name?" Aaron kneels in front of the kid.

"I'm Lucas!" He delivers a huge, proud smile to Wolf.

"Well, Lucas, you remind a lot of myself at your age." Lucas' eyes dazzle with joy at the comment of his idol. "I have a brother named Henry, too. We were always so different, and we used to fight all the time. But—" Aaron stops for a moment, and I'm speechless. It's the first time he is talking about his family. He flashes his casual grin. "—I'm sure he loves you. Don't be too hard on him, okay?" The kid nods. "You'll make a great racing driver, Lucas. I'm sure of it."

"I wish I could see you racing for real... but my dad..." Lucas sighs. "I asked him for my birthday to see you. But he is against it." I feel my heart shatter witnessing the sadness in Lucas' eyes.

"You know what? I'll have free seats reserved for you. Ask your dad to call this number. It's my agent." Aaron hands him his personal card before winking playfully.

My lips part in surprise. Wolf is the opposite of what I was expecting him to be on this date. Wolf has a heart. Wolf is caring. And Wolf is suddenly winning me over. Lucas jumps with happiness, hugging Aaron, making him lose his balance and fall on the ground. I feel emotions rushing me when I notice the kid's tears of euphoria and Aaron smile.

But then a man starts yelling, approaching us. "Lucas! Come back here!" Lucas immediately steps back and stands next to the old man in front of us. Aaron gets back on his feet next to me.

"I'm sorry if my kid was bothering you."

"On the contrary, sir. I just offered your son free seats for my next race. Here's my card and—"

The dad throws his card away. "No. This obsession needs to stop, Lucas. Why can't you be like your brother?" the dad yells at his son, who is trying to defend himself. "I don't want you to be a brainless racing driver!" How can he be so harsh? And in front of Aaron. This man has no respect.

Aaron's eyes narrow at the mad father. "You can't talk to your kid like that. You should respect his dream, not—"

"Don't tell me how to educate my son. Let's go, Lucas." The kid is about to leave with his father when I step in front of them. He can't disrespect Aaron that way.

"Did you know that Aaron LeBeau graduated with honors from college with a business degree? Training to be a racing driver is as hard as training to be an astronaut." All those hours searching for Aaron on the web are worth it. "Let me tell you what's brainless. Judging people without knowing. And while we are at it, a brainless racing driver wins more than the entire salary I'm sure you collected for the past thirty years." I don't know where my sudden confidence came from. The father murmurs something to himself and storms off with his son. Aaron offers a genuine smile to Lucas before he leaves.

"The kid. Lucas. He reminds me of myself. The younger me." Aaron seems lost in his thoughts, staring nowhere. "I thought I was helping him. But now, I realize I've made things worse."

"Worse? You couldn't know his father would act this way." Is he seriously blaming himself for being nice to a child?

He shakes his head, changing the subject swiftly. "How did you know about my studies?"

"Research, Mr. LeBeau." I grin victoriously at him.

"You are sending me mixed signals, Elle." His voice husky, he passes his fingers through his hair, turning his back at me.

"What do you mean?"

He faces me again, his eyes vibrant with conflict. "I'm a patient man, and I have been honest with you from the beginning. I want you." One step closer. "And I know you want me, too, otherwise we wouldn't be on a date. But yet, you keep resisting me… mixed signals." One step closer. "What do you want, Elle? No games. Honest truth." A few inches separate our bodies, our gazes fixed on each other. "I'll back off if you tell me you don't want me. The ball is in your court, Elle."

He waits for my move. My agreement. My sign. I feel my heart racing, being in the position to deny us. Our improbable attraction. This magnetism uniting us. Wolf's soul speaking to mine. He's a tornado of contradictory feelings. If passion was a human, it would be him. Destructive and pleasureful. And again, I let my body take control of my mind, ignoring the consequences.

"I want you." Three words, a cataclysm of feelings.

His hard body pressing against mine, he takes my jaw into his palms before his lips crash savagely on mine. I would have never thought a simple kiss could awaken each cell of my body, each of my senses. His kisses are demanding, urgent, powerful. It's not sweet or tender. He wants me and he is capturing my lips, possessing every inch of them.

His touch makes me feel a new form of lust and creates in me a galvanizing, greedy hunger. He weaves his tongue around mine, and I moan, forgetting we are in public. My body explodes with sensation, magnetically attracted to him, relishing each moment of it. Each of his ardent kisses are corrupting me, sending me into oblivion. It's terrifying and addictive. He takes a part of my soul with him, leaving me wanting more.

"Fuck. If we weren't in public, the things I'd do to you." Things, I couldn't wait to find out.

He breaks our embrace and leaves me breathless from our exchange, my whole body burning. "Are you ready for the next part of our date?" A roguish grin spreads on his face.

"This wasn't the whole date?"

"A part of it, yes. I'm leaving for the Canadian Grand Prix tonight. My jet is leaving in a couple of hours."

The Canadian Grand Prix? Wasn't I supposed to come with him? But it wouldn't make sense. It's only Tuesday, and—

"And, you're coming with me, *ma belle*…"

CHAPTER 10

The fallen god

Aaron LeBeau hates labels and has his own sayings.

Dating him means resisting him until giving in. For him, a relationship equals an agreement. The pleasure without the emotional connection. There is an expiration date before it even began. As for my presence at the Canadian Grand Prix, I'm only here on a mission to unravel Wolf's humanity, delivering my part of the agreement, even if we both know I came here willingly. But why? When I'm with him, I have an indescribable rush, I'm insatiably in need of adventures.

I still can't shake what happened tonight. A few hours ago, I was on a date with Aaron, beat my biggest fear, and then took his private jet—his luxurious, oversized, private jet. I had to maintain a safe distance from him during the few hours we flew. Everything is uncertain apart from one thing, freaking Wolf is corrupting my soul.

That freedom makes me remember the person I was before Stephan three years ago. Dancing with my friends, celebrating the end of the semester, feeling free, confident, a firecracker. Until Stephan arrived. He was everything right on paper, polite, charming, destined to be a brilliant lawyer—the epitome of perfection. *Love is not a feeling you could rely on. Don't wait for something that doesn't exist,* my mother used to say. And that's the reason I gave Stephan a chance. On our first date, he wined and dined me at one of the most bougie restaurants in New York, drawing me with his words, and his incredibly persuasive personality. He was thoughtful, not letting me drink as much as I wanted, and showed his desire of engagement asking me to be his girlfriend—I mean, he was already talking marriage. He filled the emptiness then gnawed me, paying attention to me, and offering me what every woman probably wanted. Even if I was convinced I wasn't this kind of girl. That's how I open my boundaries to a man I barely knew. Aaron is the opposite of Stephan, but what if he could break me the same way?

I snap back to reality, when I hear the laugh of a few drivers having a friendly conversation in the middle of the Canadian Grand Prix hotel. The teams begin to put the materials inside their paddocks. Reporters surround us, families and girlfriends are taking pictures together, and as for me, I'm acquainted only with Wolf.

"Aaron!" A man of approximately fifty years old walks toward us, a dazzling smile on his face. He's one of the few people dressed casually here. Jeans, a checked shirt, a beard of a few days, messy brown hair, and kindness in his gray eyes. *An outsider? Like me.*

The two men engaged in a friendly hug before Aaron turns to face me to introduce us. "Elle, this is Thomas, our team principal and my agent." *Maybe not an outsider.* "Thomas, this is Elle."

We greet each other politely with a coy smile. I can tell that Thomas is as uncomfortable as I am with introductions. "So, Elle, I heard a lot about you." *Really?* "I'm curious to know how you managed to make him changes his ways." He throws his arm around Aaron's shoulder. "I could use her tricks to make you listen to me."

"You aren't a woman, Thomas. You can't use her tricks." Aaron flashes his grin while Thomas rolls his eyes, and within a second my cheeks turn red. Wolf directs his attention to me. "If you'll excuse me. I need to see my teammate."

He leaves me with Thomas, and my gaze can't help but follow him, my thoughts uncontrollable. I watch Aaron talking with his teammate and a few other drivers, captivated by his magnetic charisma. Wolf occupies all the attention with just a gesture; he radiates of dominance. But not in a fake way. He is himself without caring what other people think.

"Aaron is a great man." Thomas smiles, noticing the way I'm staring at Aaron.

"Indeed, he is," I reply sheepishly.

"He has his own demons and he doesn't trust people easily, but... he has a lot to give." Thomas' voice is filled with kindness.

"How did you discover him?" I convince myself I should ask questions for the upcoming article, while in reality, I'm collecting a vivid interest in knowing everything about Wolf.

"I took him under my wing when he was just a teen. That kid borrowed a kart—without permission, before racing it on track. He claimed he was better than my other students." He chuckles, peering over at Aaron, pride in his face. "Well, he was right. He already had that fire in him. I mean, at nineteen he already placed P2 in a world championship."

"As he said, he always gets what he wants." I can't help but laugh. That he does. Otherwise, I wouldn't be here.

"I was starting to get worried about him. The life of a racing driver isn't easy, he needs stability." When Thomas looks at me full of benevolence, I feel like a teenager who just got her boyfriend's father's approval. "He's more of a loner type. His teammate always has his family to cheer him on, but him..." He sighs. "He believes he doesn't need anyone, I just think it's hard for someone like him to trust someone."

"It must be hard to develop real relationships when you're famous. Sometimes it's better to push people away, so you aren't disappointed in them," I say truthfully. I need to remember that Wolf and I are playing a game. A game that never involves feelings or emotional connection. I can only be insignificant once our *agreement* expires.

"But apparently he let you in, isn't it?" A playful smile slide on his face.

"*Ma belle*, we should head to our room." Aaron comes back to us, placing his hand on my lower back. His entrancing touch sends goose bumps on my arms.

"It was a pleasure to meet you, Thomas."

"You too, Elle. I'll see you soon." We smile at each other before Thomas' attention drifts to Aaron. "And no dirty business before the race, Aaron." *Oh, god!* I feel the blush on my cheeks as Thomas leaves us, laughing at my shocked face.

When we reach our bedroom, doubts start consuming me. We have a room on the top floor with an amazing view of the track. Our balcony is illuminated by the beautiful twilight. The atmosphere is fueled with romanticism—it's spacious, it could be honeymoon worthy. And more importantly, there is one king-size bed. Only one. I'm gonna share a week, alone, with Wolf. Can I trust him? Probably not. Yet, I believe he'll be a gentleman. I almost feel like his personal escort, maybe this agreement wasn't such a good idea. Only one way to find out.

"So… which side of the bed you want to take?" My voice etches, revealing the fact I haven't slept alongside a man in a long time.

"Whatever you want. I'll sleep on the sofa." *What?*

He throws his bag on the sofa which he transforms into a tiny bed. I'm studying him with confusion. Wolf wants to fuck me. Wolf invites me here. But sleeping in the same bed as me, that he can't do? I don't believe he did that out of gallantry—no, it's something else. He glances at me over his shoulder. "It's not personal, Elle. It's just, I always sleep alone."

I mumble a vague okay, my voice betraying my disappointment. What's wrong with me? As he goes to the bathroom, I place my suitcase on the bed and tie my hair into a messy bun. I search inside my bag for my beauty products, still wondering why he doesn't want to sleep next to me. Is it because he can't fall asleep next to someone? Is it because he doesn't want to get emotionally involved with someone? It's hard to tell.

I decide to take a shower once I notice Wolf is done. I carry my products, and our paths meets halfway, our gaze connecting intensely with each other. I look at the ground, ignoring him, not believing I'm really doing this.

It's a one-time thing.

Just a few days away from everything.

I enter the bathroom when I hear his phone ringing on the sink. "Aaron, your phone!" I grab it and open the door to give it back to him but catch a glimpse at the WhatsApp caller ID by mistake.

Monica.

She's beautiful. In her profile picture, she's smiling, showing her incredible teeth. Her deep blue eyes would bewitch any men, her wavy brown hair looking like a hair commercial. For an instant, I wonder—who is she to him? *Who cares.*

"Thank you, Elle." He takes his phone as I manage a smile and feel something…weird. Jealousy? Seriously? It's ridiculous.

I hear him cursing a few times on the phone but decide not to eavesdrop. During my shower, all my thoughts are occupied by Aaron. Mysterious and enigmatic Aaron. I change into my Bordeaux satin shorts and camisole and check my phone.

Aaron: Heading to the gym. Don't wait up.

Liar.

I might not be an expert about Formula 1, but I do know about sports. You are supposed to keep your energy before a competition, follow a training schedule—which doesn't include a gym session at night, abruptly. Great, Wolf asks me to come here just to screw another woman, probably gorgeous Monica. I refused him sex (for now, at least) and he isn't the type of man to wait for a woman forever. I storm into the bedroom, trying to not let my temper affect me. I take a book in order to relax and head toward the balcony to feel the fresh air on my face. Almost all the lights are off, except for one huge bay window on the right.

The gym.

I take a closer look at it and see Aaron running on the treadmill—alone. He is fast, focused, as if he is in a war against himself. Fuck. He wasn't lying. *Talk about trust issues.* I sit on the chair and switch my focus between the book and Aaron for god knows how long. I've never seen someone so hell-bent. He stops the treadmill and sits down on the floor looking exhausted, his hands resting on his forehead. He seems haunted, worn out, like he went over his own limits.

I check the time and notice it's been two hours since he's been gone and already past midnight. My instincts take control of me at that moment. I'm not thinking clearly, I'm directed by a powerful imaginary force. I take a deep breath and grab my waistcoat, leaving the room. When I open the door of the gym, I find Aaron by the window, his back facing me. It's too late to head back now.

"Aaron," I drop, unsure of why I'm really here. When he hears my voice, his piercing stare meets mine as he sips his bottle of water. "I'm sorry, I didn't mean to intrude… I just saw you from the balcony and I was wondering if you were okay."

"I don't need a babysitter," he replies darkly. His eyebrows frown, his eyes narrowing at me with a deep intensity. Message received. He wants me gone.

I notice how silly I look. We don't even know each other, and here I am storming into his personal space. I nod at him, understanding that this is a bad idea. I'm about to leave the gym when he grabs my hand, his touch sending an electrifying sensation throughout my body. For the first time when I read his eyes, I find a vulnerability I've never seen in him before. He—who is usually always in control, always so strong, fearless—now seems like a haunted child waking up from a nightmare, trapped in a feral man's body.

"I didn't mean to be rude. It's just, it's what I do." He clenches his jaw.

"What do you mean?"

He walks toward the huge bay window. "I train harder than everyone else to escape my thoughts. I need to be the best. If I let myself go, I'll get consumed by darkness." I meet him in front of the view, the moonlight lighting up half of his face. Half seraphic. Half broken.

"What are you talking about?"

"My past doesn't concern you." His eyes like blades pierce into mine.

"You must be lonely," I whisper, probably thinking about myself. He analyzes me in confusion like I'm an enigma he needs to solve. "Keeping everything to yourself. Sometimes it helps to talk to someone." I should know. I'm lonely, too.

"You don't want to know why I am this way. The reason I drive." *The reason he doesn't get close to anyone.* "I'm broken." His sharp and cold tone doesn't push me away. Instead, my heart feels for him, even if he guns his eyes as if I'm his enemy. "I don't need your pity, Elle," he adds with mistrust before storming away to pick up his bag.

"This is not pity, Aaron. It's called caring." A word he probably doesn't know the meaning of. I wonder what happened in the last two hours to make him change drastically in behavior. What scars is he hiding, to deny his emotions?

"You should care about your own problems." His words are meant to hit me.

"I don't know what happened to you, but it's not a reason to act like a selfish jerk. We all have our demons!" I howl at him, leaving the gym.

He walks behind me in silence. I might have acted out of impulse.

Did I really call him a jerk? I just made assumptions without knowing a thing about his life. He closes the bedroom door behind us. I feel the need to apologize—after all, he doesn't owe me anything—but he beats me to it.

"The seventh of the month is a bad day for me." *Seven...* just like the number of his car, and of his skull tattoo. "Goodnight, Elle."

Sometimes words have other meanings than their actual significations. Sometimes we have to read between the lines to find a new understanding. And, in this case, opening to me could mean he's sorry.

"Goodnight, Aaron."

I crawl into my bed, and when I'm about to turn off the lights, I hear his voice. "Thanks for caring."

I smile at him. I turn off the lights. There is hope.

He might be broken, damaged, crushed by a past he isn't ready to share with the world.

But, I'll discover who Wolf is, at the price of reawakening my own demons.

CHAPTER 11

Enliven me

Wolf is discussing race strategy with his team and prepping for the car testing of after tomorrow. In the meantime, I've gathered the most popular questions asked about him. I doubt it will please Nina, but if it pleases the readers, my job will be secured. Plus, Wolf is too controlling to deliver information spontaneously. I've set up the camera to record the interview and to give my article an interesting visual—we're all aware of his good looks.

Sitting on a chair, my legs on the balcony railing of our hotel room, I tuck my top up my belly to take in the rays of sun on my skin while waiting for Wolf. My sketchbook on my lap, I'm hesitant to give it a try. Art is like riding a bike, you can't forget how to do it. But it feels like an eternity I've made my hands dirty and played with colors. Honestly, it scares me, because you can't control your creativity. You can't hide from your subconscious. Art is honest. You can't lie with your feelings. You're expressing your secrets desires, your fears, your darkness, and your light—without knowing it in the first place.

But I don't have colors. I have only a charcoal pencil. *What much of damage can I make with a single pencil?* I decide to draw the track with a racing car, having a pretty good view of it. *See. Easy.* An idea hits me. I turn the page and lose track of time, feeling inspired for the first time in months. I draw a bird on the shoulder of a man in a racing suit, both walking away from the darkness—*talk about Wolf's obsession*. I blend the color with my fingers before highlighting the wing of what seems to be a parakeet, and I'm in the impossibility to deny I have a thing for birds. The last time I painted one, it was in watercolors. Big brushstrokes of black. Red coat of paint. Drips of sangria melted with water.

"That's beautiful."

I blench when I hear the voice behind me bringing me back to reality. Wolf. I quickly close the sketchbook, embarrassment rushing through my cheeks. "You weren't supposed to see that," I snap.

I've never shown my art to anyone willingly. (Apart from art schools, but they described my art as too simple without deep meaning.) When my mother found my paintings, she told me to focus on a real career, preferably one who allows me to meet important people—what she meant was men with a consequential wallet, high social status, and unmarried. Stephan told me to stop my irrational dream and made me understand my art was taking 'too much place', whatever that means.

"Well, I already had a glimpse. Can I see it more closely?" He reaches his hand toward me, not even sorry, convinced I'll hand him the key to my subconscious.

I clutch the book closer to my chest. "No, it's personal." His gaze wanders on my fingers and nails darkened by the charcoal. I immediately hide them behind my back, looking shamefaced. "I tend to get dirty when I draw or paint."

"I'm working with mechanics and cars, having your hands dirty is sexy in my world," he drops in a confidence impossible to resist.

I untie the knot of my top to cover my belly and lay a strand of my hair behind my ear. There is no one like Aaron to make you feel sexy in the worst possible moments. This is dangerous, I don't have for habits to expose my true self to someone.

He laughs. "You've got lead on your cheek."

Aaron steps toward me like a tiger, reducing the distance between us. He brushes the charcoal on my cheek with his thumb in a caring and soft gesture. I look up, meeting the blue ocean of his eyes focused on his task.

He pulls away, and I do what I do best—pretending Wolf's touch isn't getting to me. "Thank you."

"You can thank me by showing me what you've been drawing." His fingers trail a path along my arms, to my hands, until my sketchbook.

"It's far from finished. Plus, I'm doing this just for fun," I lie. But when Wolf doesn't move, I know he won't give up. Would it be so bad if he sees it? Yes. *He could see a piece of your soul.* No. Who cares what he thinks? *This way, he'll probably lose interest and you'll be able to kiss goodbye to that unwanted attraction.*

I hand him my sketchbook, before biting my nails while he inspects each of my drawings. Is he pretending to be captivated? As he keeps on turning pages, taking his time, my nervousness hits another level. "I told you, I'm not that good."

"I think it's amazing. You're talented, Elle," he answers instantly.

"Really?" My eyes open with bewilderment.

He hands me back my sketchbook. "Yes, really. You shouldn't be shy to show them to the world."

"It won't interest anyone."

"Well, it interests me. And I'm hard to please." A hint of a smile curves on his too appealing lips. "I had a question. Why did you become a columnist? Was it your dream?"

I think about his question, his interest leaving me confused. No one ever asked me what my dream was. Truth is, writing about gossips is far from what I expected it'd be, but it pays well, and pleased my mother at first. I've never liked to report dirt, but I did have an interest in human nature. I thought if I could understand the people around me, I could prevent myself from not being broken again. It obviously didn't work out.

"I guess I wanted to connect with people, learn to get to know them. I mean, sometimes you just want to forget yourself, and have a glimpse of someone's else life." *That's overshared, Elle. And pathetic.* "It's less risky, while you can live an adventure through words."

"You have to take risks in life, otherwise you're already dead. But you didn't answer me. Was it your dream?"

"An artist," I state. "My dream was to be an artist. But I know it's an unrealistic one." I wanted to create beauty out of nowhere. To enliven broken things—as I couldn't fix myself. To leave a trace. For my art—and I—to matter. But, art is sharing a part of yourself to the world, and that

I'm not ready to do. Not only it wasn't good enough, but dreams don't pay rent. Plus, inspiration can betray you at any moment.

"It's unrealistic because you believe it is. You're good, Elle."

I brush him off, uncomfortable to talk about my wants and needs. I made a decision and I'm sticking to it. "Anyway, that's in the past. I'm pretty happy with my life and job, just as it is." *Am I, really?*

"If you change your mind, I won't mind posing naked for you." His voice sounds too husky for his playful tone.

"I doubt your ego could fit on the canvas," I tease him.

"My ego isn't the only thing who will struggle to fit in, *ma belle*."

Oh. My. I decide to ignore that comment. "Well, you owe me an interview, Wolf, remember?" I point at the camera set in place.

"Fine, let's get this over with." He clenches his jaw, clearly not hiding his lack of enthusiasm.

Wolf takes a seat. I roll the camera before sitting in front of him, taking my notes with me. "Ok, so, I'm gonna ask you the most popular questions I got."

I clear my throat, taking my professional voice. "One, what's your pre-race routine?"

"I focus on the race to come, visualize the track and my win, while listening to music. It's important to build your focus before a race," he explains in his usual cold, detached tone, crossing his arms on his chest.

During the following questions, Wolf keeps his mask of the *Heartless racer* on, as if he fears to show an ounce of humanity that could be held up against him. "Your favorite quote?"

"I'll go with Rocky Balboa; 'It ain't about how hard you hit, it's about how hard you can get hit and keep moving forward.'"

"Great, next one is—" My notes drop on the ground and I curse. Aaron lets go of a smile despite himself before I give him a death glare. I get back into my seat, as Wolf covers his mouth with his hand, hiding his amusement. *Bastard.* "Next question. What's your type of woman?" It looks like a question I could have asked.

"Physically, I'd say naturally beautiful." Suddenly, his eyes behold mine and I feel myself melting in my chair. He smirks arrogantly. "And for the rest, a woman with a strong personality…" His gaze drops to my legs that I tighten together. "Athletic." He leans toward me. "Funny. Plus, I have a thing for…" *I'm in trouble.* "… Artists."

Ok. Time to move on. Am I really his type? *Move on, Elle.* "Well…" I almost choked when I read the next question, blushing hard. Too late to back off. "Your favorite sexual position?" My voice sounds huskier than what I've planned.

He laughs beautifully as if the camera between us is inexistent. "Why choose only one? Let's say, with the right woman, I can be into vanilla or into more… passionate exchanges." Let it to Aaron to not say the actual words while being a next level of dirty.

I cough, praying the next question wouldn't be a sexual one. "How do you see yourself in five years?"

"Having won five more championships." Of course. "Honestly, I like to live in the present, by doing my best each day. We don't know what the future is holding on."

"Favorite color?"

"Red victory."

I can't help but laugh, having more fun I ever had doing an interview. A few more questions later, Wolf and I are successfully done with it. "That was great, thank you." I turn off the camera, before importing the card directly to my computer.

Aaron stands up. I don't need to turn around to know he's right behind my back, feeling his magnetism and our connection sparkling all around the room. "You're making it really hard for me, Elle."

"Hard?" I play the innocent. He's so close to me, only a few inches separating us. He could easily crush me between his sculpted body and the desk in front of me.

"Yes." *God. That husky voice.* "I don't give interviews and here I am." I turn around to face him. He wets his full watering lips, while I play nervously with my fingers. "Plus, yesterday you stopped denying that attraction between us, maybe—"

"It doesn't mean I'll succumb to it," I justify myself. "Again."

"Oh, you will… again. After all, you're all mine this week."

A satisfying smile curves his lips as he steps away. How will I survive days being at Wolf's mercy?

CHAPTER 12

Pole position

I open my eyes slowly, perceiving only a blurry shadow in front of me. My sight becomes clearer and I see the most enchanting view ever. *Aaron?* This isn't a dream. I cover myself by bringing the silk blanket up to my nose so I can hide my goofy smile. The red color of his racing suit vibrates throughout all of my body. His lock of hair falling on his forehead lightened by the sun feels like a movie scene. His Greek god features are creating the need for my body to belong with him. Wolf in all of his splendor.

"Good morning, *ma belle*." I simper and greet him back, pulling the blanket lower under my arms. "I have a practice session this morning. Would you like to come watch it?"

"Yes, I'd love to come," I reply still half asleep, playing nervously with my hair. After all, it's only seven a.m.

"Perfect. I'll see you on the pit wall in half an hour." *Wait? What?* "Don't be late."

I throw off the blanket in one move and run to catch him before he leaves. "Aaron, wait!"

He is already outside the room calling to another driver in the hallway. His piercing stare meet mine, undressing me without shame. His attention travels to my lips, my breasts, my legs, while I'm giving him a *you can look but you can't touch* look.

"Did you know that your pajama is... transparent?"

What? I look down and notice my black panties is visible from beneath my silk shorts. The small tissue of my top offers him a perfect view of my pointing nipples and of the shape of my breasts. *Oh god!* I quickly cover my chest with my hands, my eyes throwing raging flames at him. His annoying self laughs and dares to push my buttons.

"Thanks for the preview. Very sexy." His tongue wets his lips, while his mouth curves into a lascivious smile. "Sexier than what I imagined. And I have a wild imagination, *ma belle*."

I don't know what irritates me more. His arrogance, the fact he undresses every inch of me without even trying to hide it, or, his brutal honesty.

I slam the door on him. *I hate him!*

Forty minutes later, I'm obviously late and walking on the track trying to spot Aaron's pit wall, with my old-fashioned white converse, my favorite slim jeans, and a white off-shoulder top. Racers are already here doing test practice with their respective teams. The screaming sounds of the engines rumbling around us.

"Watch where you're going!" a woman shouts after bumping into me while she was taking the perfect selfie from the perfect angle.

"I'm sorry, I didn't mean to—" *Why am I even excusing myself?*

"Tourists aren't allowed here," she replies apathetically before scanning me from head to toe. She's the living version of Barbie with her dirty blond hair, her marine-blue eyes, and her generous breasts. "Whatever." She rolls her eyes before getting back to her activities, ignoring me.

I finally spot Aaron and his team making adjustments to the car. When he notices me, he puts his helmet on the table next to him and ambles in my direction. *Danger.* I bow my head to the side and bite the inside of my lip, lost in my new fantasy. My new craving. My new need. I always thought the slow-motion walk was purely a cinematic thing, but now I know it's real.

Wolf is strutting toward me, like a sexy hero who just achieved the impossible, the firefighter who rescued innocent people, the soldier coming back from war. He passes his hand through his hair seductively and begins to open his racing suit while flashing me the type of grin that makes you flush. I want only one thing. His lips on mine. To make me the heroine of my imaginary movie. I'm yearning for his touch, for our bodies to connect. I've never been into racing drivers, nor fantasized about any man before. But now, I'm convinced of my undeniable attraction for him. He is taking the pole position of my thoughts, and I can't stop him.

"Let me introduce you to the team," he says casually while I swallow, trying to erase the mental image of him from my mind.

I greet every member of Aaron's racing team, from the engineers to the mechanics—and Thomas, who sends me a friendly smile. "Aaron is about to test the car. Do you want to watch the testing with us?"

"I don't know if I should. I mean, I don't want to intrude." My mantra used to be: hide from the spotlight, don't go into an unknown territory, and old habits die hard.

Aaron steps in while putting his gloves on. "Nonsense. I'd prefer to hear your voice on the headset than Thomas's."

Thomas rolls his eyes. "Well, I have your back on the track. Without me, you'd be a reckless driver without a proper strategy." I laugh as the two men joke around. Aaron is a completely different person with him, it's like he is free of whatever demons he's carrying on.

"That's true, but you get to boss me around and I know you love that."

Thomas chuckles despite him. "If only you would listen, that would be more effective."

Wolf jumps into his cockpit before putting his helmet on. "Where would be the fun in that?"

Aaron's Formula 1 racecar leaves the pit to do the installation lap to test functions, and I take a seat in front of the monitors inside his paddock with the other engineers. Thomas hands me a headset, connecting Aaron with him and his car crew.

"Why is Aaron's nickname, *Wolf*? I have my guess, but I believe there is a story behind it," I question Thomas.

"Because Aaron is a lone wolf. He is unpredictable and dangerous to others." He shakes his head while smirking at me. "His previous teammate called him Wolf because he was an individualist. During his first year in Formula 1, he was supposed to race behind him, but…" He laughs. "He couldn't follow the orders. He raced aggressively against him and stole his first place." *This sounds exactly like him.* I can't help but smile. "In the end, he became the lead driver of Amorino racing and stole the spotlight from the other driver. He didn't take it well."

"Who was the driver?"

"Louis Harmil. He is racing with our main competitor now." I open my mouth, that name is definitely familiar to me. Aaron got into a skirmish with Harmil in Monaco, and I read the two men have a lifelong rivalry.

I hear Aaron's voice in my headset. "We need to adjust the front wings. I'm not feeling it."

"Copy. Rise up the engine," Thomas commands, his eyes not leaving the screen, as Wolf presses his pedal, gaining speed.

A couple minutes later, the team starts working on the car adjustment. After that, Aaron is back on the track, racing his car faster during the straights. And for the first time in a long time, I feel like I belong here. I don't understand everything about racing, but I feel comfortable. I never felt that way around the parents and friends of my ex. Probably because I always tried too hard to be someone I wasn't.

"We need to maximize the power on the rear wheels. I don't want to be overtaken down the straights." Wolf struggles to speak while racing his car at a blistering pace.

"Copy. Box the lap," Thomas replies.

"Do Formula 1 drivers need to learn about mechanics?" I ask, genuinely uncertain.

"Yes and no. They need to know their cars and adjust themselves to it, but most of them don't go deep into the details. Aaron does. He's overworking himself more than most of the drivers out there. He helped the team buildup the perfect car. That kid knows a lot."

"A kid?" I can't help but smile. "That's not a word I would use to define, Aaron." *More of a twenty-five-year-old alpha.*

Thomas lets out a loud guffaw. "Yeah, for me, he's still the reckless teen I knew from back then."

My discussion with Thomas is interrupted when Wolf completes his last lap, before discussing with his engineers. I don't want to disturb them so I decide to walk around the pit lane and check my messages. All of them are from Tania, asking if I have decided to make Aaron my 'knight' in my fairy tale.

I start typing, looking up to meet Wolf's gaze but to my surprise, I spot him with the Barbie of earlier. She's talking with him—and not in a friendly way. She also brought her gorgeous friends to accompany her into her seduction quest. Great. I've met the evil queen trying to make of my 'knight' her own.

"Aaron, love! How have you been?" Just the sound of her perched voice talking to him and stroking his arm makes me cringe.

"Hi, Amber." *And the perched voice has a name… Amber.*

I clear my throat, watching the show from afar. Jealousy strikes me at full speed and unleashes all of my inner demons. She's clearly flirting with him, giving him the bedroom eyes, but he does nothing. He doesn't flirt back, but he doesn't push her away, either. I know I have no right to be jealous. I shouldn't be jealous. Someone like Aaron doesn't do relationships, and we have nothing going on. Just a lie. An agreement. But my body is burning from the inside. I've never been the jealous type, and I can't possibly understand why this is happening to me. Probably because they are gorgeous, an appeal to sex. This is the type of women he goes for. Not me.

Then Aaron's gaze meets mine and a confident smile spreads on his face. But I don't smile back, I'm too busy doubting myself, hating him for something he is allowed to do. *He can fuck whoever he wants, I don't care.* I'm just his possession for the week, that's it.

Barbie notices that his attention fires back on me and aces up her game. She pretends to laughs, practically giving herself to him in front of his whole crew. Amber is sending a message, claiming her territory, displaying her true colors. Aaron analyzes me, but I won't give him the satisfaction to show my jealousy, even if I'm struggling to hide it. We maintain an eye contact, until he drifts his eyes to Barbie, giving her exactly what she desires—his attention.

She's like a tarantula, spreading her venom, seeking her next meal. I have a dark storm of emotions within me filled with doubts. Am I burning myself willingly? My stomach turns instantly, a pain in my chest, seeing Aaron busy with the court of women surrounding him. Women who believe by being submissive to him, they'll be unforgettable. But we can only be insignificant to a man like Wolf. This is all a dream, a fantasy happening in my head. Nothing of this is real. Not our date. Not this Grand Prix. I'm just part of his game, and I surely don't want to race against all the women battling for the pole position to be in his bed.

"Hi, sexy. Are you looking for something?" a husky voice interrupts my thoughts behind me.

I turn around to see…

Louis Harmil. Aaron's number one competitor and a man-whore. He is known as the man who has it all. The perfect son, the perfect racing driver, and the perfect amount of money. Louis is chewing his gum, his sunglasses on, wearing his white racing suit. If Aaron is the alpha, Louis is the Golden Boy. He tangles his hand into his messy blond hair before pulling his sunglasses off, giving me a glimpse of his green piercing eyes. He is not very tall, probably five-foot-eight, but he has a certain charisma. He is less good looking than Aaron, but something tells me he has no problem getting women to fall at his feet.

"I'm just waiting for someone."

I search for Aaron's gaze but he is busy talking with his team—and still surrounded by the horde of tarantulas. The grinding sounds of the motors are exploding around us, making my heart race. The mechanics are working on the cars, the reporters are already here, and I… have no idea what I am doing here. I need to remind myself that Aaron is wrong for me. He has nothing to give. *Nothing but a heartbreak.* But why is my heart beating so fast? Why do I feel that miserable? *Why can't she stop flirting with him!*

"I see. You are with Aaron. He seems… busy," Louis replies, noticing the mask of jealousy growing on my face. *Yeah, right, busy.* I usually hide my emotions very well, but with Aaron, I feel so transparent. I feel like the wall I've built for years to protect myself is silently falling into aches. I feel vulnerable. "So, you're his new girl," Golden Boy adds, seeing I'm not paying attention to him—a thing he probably isn't used to.

"And you are Louis Harmil." My lips curve into an amused smile.

"So, you do know my name." He raises his eyebrow cockily and smirks in a way that makes me understand he is flirting with me. "You don't have to worry about her," he says, pointing at the Barbie tarantula near Aaron's garage. "Amber is a bit offensive, but she's not that bad."

"I'm not worried," I answer in a dry tone, my voice betraying my insecurities.

"Be careful." He puts his hand on my back while guiding me closer to his garage and away from the pit lane as a car in testing approaches us.

I quickly remove his hand from my lower back and glance at the ground in confusion, not knowing how to act with him. "I'm fine." I readjust my hair behind my ear.

"He shouldn't have left you alone in the pit." He stares at Aaron, who is busy with his team. Golden Boy's attention fires back at me as he passes his fingers through his blond hair. "At least, it's giving me the opportunity to get to know you." He darts his tongue out of his mouth seductively, a thing that usually turns me on when Wolf does it, but with him… nothing. Which proves that Wolf is my Achilles' heel.

"Louis. I'm flattered, but I have no interest in you."

He nods, trying to hide his disappointment with a seductive smile. "You can't blame a man for trying."

"I believe you aren't lacking women in your circle." I point out the obvious fact to him as I finally detached my focus from Aaron to peer at Louis, noticing he has a certain charm. He and Aaron could be similar somehow. Both of them are flirtatious, competitive, and used to getting what they want. But Louis is more welcoming than Aaron. He has less darkness and doesn't have the same aura. Aaron's screams of alpha vibes and power. Louis is more of a Hollywood celebrity type.

"We aren't. But I'm a commitment kind of guy, when I find the one." He smiles while looking at his team prepping his car.

"I doubt that." I snort.

He chuckles, not offended. "I can see what Aaron sees in you. You're direct." He winks at me in a playful way. I raise my eyebrow, waiting for a cheesy line, but instead, we both laugh. I end up enjoying his company more than I thought I would.

"Aaron and I used to be friends. I know him better than anyone else."

My jaw drops in surprise. "I can't picture you as friends." Probably because they both compete for the same spot.

"There are a lot of things you probably don't know about him." He snorts, speaking to himself. I start tensing. He is right. I know nothing about Aaron. He is a mystery. A mystery I made a deal with blindly. How many secrets does he have?

Louis notices my reaction. "I'm sorry, I guess he's secretive with everyone."

And here is the reminder of how I shouldn't get involved with Aaron, or else I'll end up being one more trophy he claimed. My thoughts are interrupted when I feel a strong arm capturing my waist from behind. I don't need to turn around, I know who it is. I recognize his woody scent. He is the man who makes my heart races. The man I used as an escape. The man who will be my downfall. Aaron LeBeau.

"Louis." Aaron's eyes narrow at Louis, a muscle twitching in his jaw. He is squeezing my waist harder, almost hurting me without realizing it.

"Aaron, we were just talking about you." Louis' lips curve into a polite smile, even though I can tell he is as tense as Aaron.

The two men are caught in a staring contest. A car testing on the track passes near us, leaving behind it the rough sounds of the engine amplifying this warfare. There is more than a competitive rivalry, there is a dark secret linking them. In spite of their apparent calm, it's evident that at any moment the situation can spiral out of control. A house team passes near us, people start hurrying around, but the two men keep on eying each other without blinking.

"Already trying to steal what's mine, Louis?" Aaron attacks, as I witness the possessiveness in his voice. *Mine? Like hell.*

"I would never. We all know that you are the one who is a ladies' man," Louis replies.

"At least it's always consensual on my side." And it's a victory by K.O. for Aaron in this first round.

Louis swallows, tensing a bit, before smiling widely at me. "Well, I better go. I have a Grand Prix to win." He passes in front of us and puts his hand on Aaron's shoulder, whispering something I couldn't understand. Aaron's jaw clenches immediately, whatever he heard getting on his nerves.

He pushes Louis' hand away and turns around to dominate him by his height. Their faces are a few inches from each other, their eyes narrowing like blades. I feel that round two is about to start.

"If it wasn't for the no fight policy, I'd knock the shit out of you." The alpha male threatens the Golden Boy, his fists tightening. I glance around to notice the other teams watching us.

"Aaron, stop," I snap, unsure if it is wise of me to step into their fight. Why does he hate him so much? He is acting way out of line.

Louis smirks and raises his eyebrow. "Listen to your girl." He puts his sunglasses on and leaves victoriously. "See you on the track... Wolfie."

I take a deep breath, feeling relieved that Louis left, and no damage was done. But as usual, I thought too fast.

Aaron's gaze slices straight to mine. "What were you doing talking to him?" He frowns and sighs before heading at a fast pace to his empty garage. I follow him, not understanding his whole proprietorial attitude.

"Do you know how he treats women?" He crosses his arms on his chest, leaning against the table behind him, his eyes darkening at me. He plays with his tongue inside of his mouth in order to hide the fact he is burning inside... *jealous*. He is jealous. *Like I was*.

At this moment, I want to tell him that I felt the same way when he was talking with his bimbos. I want to tell him that Louis doesn't interest me, but there is no place for honesty in this conversation. If I'm honest, if I show my jealousy, I lose. It's a game. A warfare of jealousy. A warfare where our demons are battling together, destroying ourselves as our souls melt under the bitterness of our thoughts. A warfare for power. Instead I reply, "What's your problem, Aaron?"

"My problem is that I can't stand him flirting with you," he says in his raspy, domineering voice. His Adam's apple bobs up—he acts like he's claiming what his. But I don't belong to him. I never will.

"Louis was actually very kind. Unlike you, he has some manners," I retort. I want to hurt him, to prove to him I'm not his propriety.

"Don't be stupid, he just wants to fuck you." He is trying to remain in control, but I can tell he won't be able to keep his control for long.

"And that's not what you want, maybe?" I raise my eyebrow in provocation, jealousy consuming me, the thought of Amber spitting her venom at him still haunting my mind. "Or maybe you want to fuck me first? That's all it is about, right?" I'm beginning to lose my temper and I couldn't be more thankful that nobody is around us. I snort and shake my head.

His eyes keep roaming my face without a word for a moment, before speaking with an authoritative and forceful tone. "I don't like to share, Elle." His mouth sets a grim line before he emphasizes, "No, scratch that. I. Do. Not. Share."

His threat resonates through my mind, my heart jumping, anticipating what will happen next. Aaron denies his emotions by indulging in the desire of the flesh. He can't dominate nor tame his feelings; therefore, he loses himself in a distraction. Me.

Within the next couple of seconds, I'm pinned against the wall. His eyes darken with intense craving as he pinches his eyebrows. But this time, it's not his lust for me that pushes him to get closer. It's his need to be in control. To make me bend to his will. To be his perfect distraction. He squeezes my waist, connecting our bodies, his scorching look burning me. He searches for my authorization, for my desire to have him. But my past jealousy transforms itself into a deep sadness. I will never let a man take control of me again. I can't play his game, because I will never win. I'm hurt and vulnerable.

"Then, you should find someone obedient. Like Amber," I articulate, looking at the ground. My mother used to tell me that showing my jealousy to a man is the assured way to get him to hurt me. *"If he knows your weakness, he will use it against you,"* she repeated constantly.

You can't change a man, but you can give him the whip to tame you.

"What if I want you." It isn't a question, but an affirmation. *He wants me.* But the real question should be, until when?

I swallow, forcing a smile to hide my weakness. "Not satisfied with your fan club, Mr. LeBeau?"

"I'm not a liar." He lifts my chin up, and I brave to meet his eyes. "Amber is the sister of my teammate. I fucked her many years ago, but it meant nothing. I've been honest with her from the start, it'd never happen again. She's irrelevant." I can't help but feel ashamed about my reaction. Not for judging him, but for being weak. Showing him my jealousy, that I'm not indifferent to him. And especially for giving him the opportunity to continue playing with me.

"I guess I'll have to prove to you where my mind is." His gaze is not leaving mine, tormenting my spirit and my ability to resist him. This animal magnetism is radiating from us at full force.

"How?" I ask.

"On you."

His lips crush mine, and I'm caught into the tornado of lust and inexplicable emotions that is Aaron LeBeau. His palm grabs my chin as his other hand clutches our bodies together. I'm melting under his touch, his tongue claiming mine. Seductively. Dangerously. Fiercely. His strong arms encircle me into his embrace as our kisses grow stronger, eager, deeper. Deeper into our darkness. Eager to escape. Stronger for me to be broken, to need him until the point of no return. A moan escapes from me as he bites my lower lip gently. I'm crashing at full speed every time I'm in his embrace, and I cannot stop.

"Your lips taste like heaven," he adds while my body is exploding of sensation under the fierce heat of our yearning.

He awakens my senses, creating a new craving. A craving for him. My sinful addiction. Leaving me wanting more. Begging for more. He pushes my boundaries and shakes my beliefs. Everything I wanted, I hoped for, my unanswered questions don't matter anymore. I'm directed by an animal impulse to satisfy my needs.

There is no rule of how to win warfare—*especially with Aaron LeBeau.* Just to embrace it. To give in.

We are stuck on a battlefield and there is no escape. Only certainty. Us, that thing linking us, it's real. We might end up in bloodshed, or take the road of a dangerous skirmish. But we might also save ourselves from our own demons.

That's the thing. In warfare, your enemy can become your ally at any moment. Maybe I don't have to race against him. But with him.

CHAPTER 13

The ashes of our past

"Your helmet." Aaron hands me the helmet that I accept shyly.

I still can't believe he booked the entire karting exclusively for us for the whole hour. Aaron has the afternoon free, tomorrow he'll test the car again before racing on Sunday. He is screaming of bad boy vibes with his leather jacket and ripped jeans. The memory of our heated kiss is still haunting my mind, his touch leaving me craving for more. He is intoxicating my soul. *I need to snap out of it.* One thought at the time. One obsession at the time. I need to show him I'm not the damsel in distress of our first date. My curse was to be invisible, but with him, I feel very much alive.

I start to feel anxious; I've never raced before and I certainly don't want to make a mess out of myself. I try to clip my helmet but struggle to tighten it.

"Let me do it." He approaches me as I bite my lip, meeting his eyes like a defenseless doe. His masculine hands touch my skin gently as he clips it in one movement. He readjusts my hair, pulling it out of my face. I need to break out of this moment or we won't do karting—*but do me*.

"This isn't a fair race, Mr. LeBeau. You are a racing driver." I lift my eyebrow before jumping into my kart, pretending I'm not at all anxious. I mean, it's not like he didn't explain to me the rules of karting, but instead of listening to him, I was fantasizing over his sweet, perfect lips.

He leans closer to my kart, his face dangerously close to mine. "Never admit defeat before being defeated." He winks before leaving to take place into his kart.

There is no way back. I step on the kart pedal and start racing. The outside track has three undulating corners, one tight hairpin, two colossal straights, it's perfect for fast speed and mastering the kart. I take the first laps at a slow pace, still insecure and not trusting myself with my driving skills. Something is holding me back, I can't seem to go faster. *Damn it, it's just a freaking kart.* Every time I begin to gain in speed, I panic and feel the urge to slow down, afraid to lose control. Aaron is patiently racing behind me; he doesn't want to rush me. He is giving me time to adapt, to tame my kart.

I hear the rasp of his voice from behind. "You need to trust yourself, Elle."

Trusting myself... that's the thing, I don't. How could I? My mother used to repeat constantly that I was her greatest failure. I couldn't be imperfect, I couldn't exist as myself. Just as with Stephan. The man who wanted to tame me. To make me his personal project. The man who said I wasn't capable of achieving anything on my own. The man who broke me, physically and mentally inking himself into my soul. I'm broken. I stopped living, fearful of being imperfect. Fearful of being hurt again. Fearful of discovering *they* were right.

"You should go ahead, Aaron, I'm too slow for you." I blink away the tears while looking at the track.

"We race together." *Together...* I turn my head to lose myself in his eyes behind his helmet. I find in it a new strength. A new hope. His words give me the confidence to push harder, to try harder. After all, life is like a race. You can be careful, but not live fully. You can crash and end up bruised. But mostly, you can awaken.

I take a deep breath, and my feet step on the pedal. Harder. Longer. I'm soon caught in a hellacious speed, losing control, freeing myself from my demons. I hear Aaron's voice from afar cheering me on, but I can't listen clearly. I'm in some sort of trance, where my new self is battling her older, insecure, and damaged self. Freedom. I had to wear a mask for so long that I ended up forgetting who I was beneath it, what I wanted and deserved. Sometimes, when you can't express your feelings because no language can possibly describe them, you need to find a new way to let them go.

So, I race.

I race my demons.

I race my soul.

"I race you, Aaron!" I yell at him, a huge smile on my face.

I've never felt so good, so free. Aaron stays behind me, holding himself back and letting me win. I can't help but smile, knowing he is doing this for me. "Race for real, LeBeau." I cock my eyebrow at him, my voice sprightly. "Or I might think less of you."

He laughs, gripping his steering wheel. "I was just trying to behave."

Aaron races his kart so fast that within the first seconds he distances himself from me. Damn him. I try to hold on to him as much as I can, but I need to assume my evident defeat. He already finished his lap and is on the departure line, waiting for me.

"Satisfied?" He takes off his helmet, smirking.

"Not quite," I respond in a flirty tone before passing in front of him, racing my car as fast as I can.

I let the speed consume my body. I'm pushing the kart toward the speed limit, exceeding 50mph, mastering it during the curves. I feel energized, I'm letting go of my insecurities, liberating myself. I'm caught in a war between the old me and the new me. The more I feel the speed, the more I disconnect myself from the world. It feels like a dream. I finally understand why Aaron is racing. In each race, he is freeing himself. In each race, he becomes something stronger than he is. I don't think about crashing, I don't think about failure anymore.

I escape.

I hear Aaron's voice behind me telling me to slow down, that I'm going too fast. But I can't. I don't want to. I don't want to head back, I don't want to feel. I'm caught in a world where my problems don't exist, where I am someone else. I need to get closer. Closer to the finish line, closer to my own limits. I race like my life depends on it. This is it, I'm here. I take the tight corner, not reducing my speed and—

No! I lose control of my kart. I slam on the brakes, but it's too late. I crash into the wall in front of me, and within the next seconds, I'm ejected from the kart. I fall on the ground, my helmet crashes on the hard tar, reducing the impact. *Shit.* My heart is beating, waiting for something wrong to happen. Seconds… minutes… I don't know how much time has passed. I open my eyes, looking at my bruised hands from my fall. I stay seated on the ground, trying to figure out if I have broken anything, calming my nerves. It's just a scratch. My top is ripped where my shoulder and clavicle hit the ground, but it's a shallow cut. I peer in front, Aaron is running toward me brutally throwing his helmet. He is speaking, but what he is saying? I frown my eyebrows, trying to collect my focus while pulling my helmet out, but I hear only my heart hammering in my chest. What was I doing? I could have hurt myself badly.

"Fuck, Elle, are you okay?" Wolf leans down next to me, touching my face with his calloused hands. He caresses my forehead, my cheeks, before brushing his fingers over my shoulder where I got hit.

I remain weirdly calm, still under the shock of what happened. I close my eyes, trying to breathe and ignore the mental image of my crash. How could he do that? Crashing and getting back on track? I'm terrified, of what could have happened. I'm fine—physically at least, mentally I feel so stupid to have been that reckless. Once my heartbeat slows down, I open my eyes again to meet Aaron's haunted and concerned eyes, like I just crushed the life out of him. He scrutinizes my body, his expression darkening into something new… sadness?

"Are you ok? I'm sorry, it's my fault, Elle." He shakes his head, unhinged by what happened.

"I'm fine, Aaron. It's just a superficial scratch, I didn't break anything." I manage a smile, but his expression remains darkly stoic.

"You have blood on your shoulder. You are not okay," he drops, cold and dry. "This is my fault. I'm making only bad decisions… I shouldn't have brought you here."

"It's not your—"

"You are hurt because of me, damn it! And it could have been a lot worse!" I've never seen him so angry, devastated. His eyes redden with anger, his eyebrows pinching together. This is not the same Aaron I know.

I reach for his hand, but he pushes it away, distancing himself from me with a mask of fear on his face. "No, I did this. This is my damn fault!" He stands up and puts his hands on his forehead while screaming curses.

"Aaron—" My voice is low and panicked.

"Don't speak! Don't say a freaking word!" His eyes bore into mine with hatred, like I'm a mistake. Someone he wants to get rid of. A ghost who's haunting him.

"Don't—" *Don't yell. Don't talk to me this way. It makes me feel worthless again.*

"I told you to not. Say. A. Freaking. Word." His tone is menacing and authoritative, he's becoming what everyone told Wolf was.

Tormented.

Angry.

Haunted.

Aaron vanished to become only fury.

"Stop!" I yell, feeling the demons of my past reaching me. He isn't the only one who is broken.

It feels like we're both falling to the underworld. He's the tormented sinner who's staring at me as if I'm one of the Furies punishing and cursing him. A tear slides down my face. He is scaring me. Not because he exposed a new part of him. The part he has been hiding for so long. The damaged part. The one of someone lost between a memory and the present, stuck in his own fear. But because he is pushing me away like a nobody, leaving me on the ground like he couldn't care less. I'm not his enemy, but I can't help him, I can't force him to open up to me.

"Don't cry, please." His voice softens, his vulnerability sparkling through his eyes. "Fuck, I'm such an asshole. What am I doing?" he mutters to himself.

He sits in front of me, reaching for my hand. "You are scaring me, Aaron," I reply. But when he drifts his gaze away from me, I know my words hurt him. I intertwine my fingers with his. "You are scaring me, because I can't figure out why you are destroying yourself. I don't know what happened to you."

He helps me stand up, our bodies folding together. He encircles his strong arms around my waist. "You're the one who scared the shit out of me when you fell. Seeing you like that…" He stops for a moment, lost in his demons. "You should hate me, and yet here you are, trying to understand why I was an ass with you."

"I told you, I'm fine. I'm not made of porcelain."

"Let me be the judge of that. I need to take care of you."

He starts to lead us toward the exit, when I stop facing him. "First, let me understand you."

"You don't want to go there." *But maybe I want to know your darkness.* The tips of his fingers brush my chin and erase the mark of my tear, our gaze lost in each other. "I'm destroying myself like you said, so no one else can. It's probably the worst kind of control but it's the only one I know." He takes a deep breath, his expression cryptic. "That's why I have nothing to give. Not to you—not to anyone."

My heart shatters hearing his bitter words. Words I can relate to. Only someone who knew only pain could speak this way. Love is probably an unknown emotion for Aaron, and I'm heading down a dangerous path. Connecting with the man whose darkness is speaking to mine.

He dips down and swoops me into his arms, bridal style. I wrap my arms around his neck, facing his duality. He has the stature of a Greek god and the regard of a troubled man. Alpha and vulnerable. He is the man who makes me feel significant for a second in his arms, while I know he'll never let anyone matter to him. Close and yet unreachable. Wolf could be similar to the angel of the painting *Everlasting*, someone who has the capacity to rescue you while fighting demons of his own.

"You are better than you think, Aaron."

He remains focused while carrying me. "I'm not. And if you are smart, you will stay away from me."

"Stay away? Is that what you want?"

"No. But you know I'll ruin you. I'll use you for my personal needs." He is distancing himself emotionally, not daring to meet my gaze. "It's what I do. I'm selfish, Elle. And I always have what I want."

Crashing makes me realize life is too short to be wasted on fear.

I always find a deep beauty in the most broken things.

And he won't be an exception.

CHAPTER 14

Healing ourselves

We drive to our hotel in silence. All the emotions experienced the past hours get to me, until a point I sink into sleep, letting the nightmares of my past awakened.

A memory I tried to forget poisoned my mind, and no matter how hard I try to wake up, I cannot.

"I love you…" Stephan whispers, squeezing my hand. Love, a magical word. A word no one has ever said to me. "But, if you don't change, you know it won't work, right my sweet? I love you, but you need to make efforts for us, right?" He cups my cheek, and I nod. *If Stephan doesn't share your beliefs, they are therefore wrong.*

But he loves me, that's all that matters, even if he has been criticizing a few of my actions. I couldn't understand why as it was a part of who I am; "you stayed home all day you could have cleaned", "painting is useless, you should focus on us", "why are you so shy and awkward?", "the way you think is stupid", "she's just a friend stop being insecure"… In those fights, I feel like the only one who has to change. God, I'm making so many mistakes… he is the one working late hours at the office, while I'm working as an underrated writer for a gossip magazine. He has a lot on his mind, so I try to avoid conflict. I hate that we fight about my incapacity of not being the woman he wants, no matter how hard I try to solve us. But he loves me. I'm certain that no man will treat me the way he does, I couldn't afford to lose him. After all, he is the only one there for me. My mother loves him. She's her ideal son-in-law and hopes that someday we get married.

"I love you, too, Stephan." Do I really love him? I don't think so. I wish, but I've been conditioned to never feel love. I feared all men would be like my father. My mother trained me to seduce without caring after she destroyed the remaining pieces of my soul. Love is a sign of ownership, but Stephan is different.

He glances at my Angelo Di Romeo. "That painting will have to go when we live together."

"You know I love this painting, Stephan." He already convinced me my paintings were a waste of time—or it'd be just for fun, not a real career.

"Oh, my sweet... you know it's childish. It's just a painting. Me, I'm real." He cups my cheeks before kissing me tenderly. "I'm exhausted, I have been working all day."

Stephan falls onto my couch, opening his arms to hug me. Hugs have become rarer with him, and just this simple gesture makes me the happiest. And I, too, have a surprise for him. Underneath my jogging pants and my sweater, I have on black lace lingerie. I want to feel the lust in his eyes. I sit next to him and throw my sweater over my head, biting my lower lip. He scans my bra with an unreadable expression.

"Do you like it? The vendor woman told me it was a hit," I say coyly, pretending I'm some kind of model.

He snorts. "For a woman with breasts, yeah," he says while looking at his phone. Every nerve and fiber tense inside me. I've never felt unconfident before about my body, but then again, the only man I've been with is Stephan. I lost my virginity to him, and yet, I thought I'd impress him more, naked.

"Don't look at me like that, my sweet. You know I'm joking, right?" I might know it, but his mean jokes about my body make me feel worthless. I'm probably overreacting, but I feel put down. He cups both of my breasts with his hands, pulling them out like a push-up bra or a boob job would do. "Hmm. Like that—perfect." He laughs, and I decide to put my sweater back on.

That's the thing with Stephan. Sometimes, he is perfect, giving me gifts and sweet attention—in public—but sometimes I feel the need to be someone else to be able to handle his criticism. Is that what relationships are?

"Come here." He opens his arms, and I simper. I pose my head into his chest as he caresses my hair. Love. I want to believe in it.

But then suddenly, he unzips his pants and pushes my head toward his cock. I pull back immediately. "You know I don't like giving head, Stephan… I'm not in the mood." Truth is, I thought sex would be better. People talked about it, but as for me, I found it… boring. We have sex often, but it's mostly because I know he'll be happy after.

"I don't understand. Other women like to do it, it's a normal thing. Come on, Elle." He strokes himself. Being with Stephan has made me realized I'm probably frigid. I want to overcome that—someday, with time. Giving head is a repulsive thing for me. It makes me feel owned.

"Can we have sex or cuddle instead?"

"Elle, I had a rough day today. I just want a release. Come on, just a minute, my sweet?" He holds my hand before putting it on his cock to stroke himself. "Elle, I love you and I never want to cheat on you, but at some point, you need to please me, or I'll end up making a mistake someday. And we don't want that, right?" He poses his hand behind my head, caressing my hair. "I'm doing everything for us. I'm pleasing you, I'm the one who's making all the efforts."

I swallow and nod as I approach with my mouth, ready to take him. He's your boyfriend, Elle, you can do this. Plus, I don't want to be alone.

He pushes inside my mouth without a warning, pulling my head brutally to his cock for me to take him whole, not caring that he's choking me.

And I suck and feel humiliated.

No.

"*Ma belle?*" The voice of Aaron brings me back to reality. I open my eyes, hoping the ghost of Stephan disappeared fully. "Are you okay?"

My breath has quickens, and I nod, noticing we're parked in front of the hotel. "Sorry, nightmare."

Stephan is gone.

You are not the same woman anymore.

He can't get to you.

"Can I do something?" I stare into his troubled eyes as he reaches for my hand. I find it easier to chase Stephan from my mind with Wolf by my side.

"No, it's all forgotten."

Aaron doesn't say anything, giving me the time to cool down, before he insists on carrying me to our room.

"Let me take care of your cuts."

Aaron lifts me onto the bathroom sink of our hotel room, not waiting for my reply. He fixes his gaze on the dried blood covering my shoulder and collarbone. I've never seen him so concerned, so murky. It seems we are both haunted by a memory, consumed by a past, I want to ease.

After a traumatic event, people adopt different approaches to it. They can ease their darkness by trying to survive any way that they can and learn to live with it. Or they can repress their memories, being the dominant to them—and to everyone. To feel that they are in control, while they aren't. They are their own slave, their kingdom being their prison. And I believe Aaron is one of them.

He applies pressure with a clean tissue near my collarbone, but my long sleeve shirt doesn't provide him full access. His touch is mechanical, focused, as if he has disconnected his heart from his brain.

"Aaron," I whisper, hoping to reach him. "Are you—"

He hands me one of his shirts. "Your sleeve. I need you to change."

"It's fine. I trust you." With my eyes fixed on his, I'm determined to take a leap. Giving him the proximity he needs while battling my demons. I can't let my ghosts get to me.

His hands slide down my top, his fingers caressing my skin as he lifts it over my head, revealing my black bra. My heartbeat accelerates at a dangerous pace, my breath cut, I've never let another man see me since Stephan. Aaron looks upon me with an expression I can't picture. Hatred? Desire? Pain? All of the above. I've been bruised, but he creates something new in me. Something wild.

"You should wear my shirt."

"Why? Am I repulsing you, Aaron?" I defy him, swallowing my last drop of courage. I won't let my past define me. I won't let another man tarnished my confidence.

He starts to clean my cut near my collarbone, his fingers caressing my skin sensually. They slide lower near the entrance of my breasts as I'm gripping the washbasin behind me to calm my nerves. Every one of his touches is erotic. Galvanizing. He isn't only healing my body, but the bruises of my past. Erasing Stephan's disgusting touch with a tender one.

He is giving me a new hope. A hope to rebuild myself. He slides the strap of my bra down before our eyes connect intensely.

"No, Elle. You are making it very hard for me to resist you." He inhales deeply, as if his control is escaping him.

He massages the healing cream tenderly below my collarbone, encroaching on my breasts. I bite my lower lip, my eyebrows frowning, welcoming the guilty pleasure that his touch creates in me. He bandages my shallow cut before positioning his body between my legs. Aaron caresses my thighs before squeezing them, a soft moan escapes me, heat streaking down into my belly.

"The way you are reacting to my touch, it's driving me insane," he growls in his raspy voice.

He wrinkles his brow, his mouth lowering dangerously close to mine, while my lips part, eager to taste him. His thumb brushes on my cheek, a dilemma visible in his scorching stare. It's as if he is hesitating between breaking me or freeing me. Between revealing his darkness or his light. Wolf hides his emotions by the desire of the flesh. As for me, I pretend to be perfect, seeking approvals—*To be loved.* Seen. Desired. Until him. This feral racing driver becomes my addiction. My escape.

Our lips, magnetically attracted, meet in a lustful kiss, finding our freedom. His hands seize my waist, pulling us closer, while my fingers wander into his stygian hair. Electricity sparking between us. Captured in the moment, I lose myself in the abyss of his soul, giving him what he relishes. *An escape.* I moan toward the fierce heat of our tongues dancing, colliding, melting. He is claiming and possessing my lips, and I doubt Wolf will stop here. He's a conqueror, he'll continue until my heart follows. Until he owns my whole self.

Our kiss slows down into something more sensual, taking our time to savor each other's lips slowly but deeply. We finally break the kiss to be able to catch our breath, and I find my opening to learn more of Wolf. "Aaron… the way you reacted at the track earlier," I mention. "What happened to you?" For an unknown reason, I feel the need to get closer to his darkness. The need to heal together.

"Forget it." He hands me his shirt, his whole attitude shifting a three hundred sixty degrees turn.

He heads toward the bathroom door before I stop him by grabbing his wrist. "I can't, Aaron. You asked me here. If something happen between us, I should know—"

"I've told you my past is off-limits. If you want a heart to heart conversation, you should find yourself a good *boyfriend*. I don't do small talk."

"I'm not your enemy, Aaron. Have you ever thought that perhaps I'm interested in learning to know you? It doesn't have to be clinical and robotic between us. We can be friends," I snap at him, crossing my arms on my chest. Yes. I just admitted that us, it will happen. Twice.

"So… you want to be friends with someone who will try to use you for his personal needs? Is that what you want, Elle? To be treated like a nobody?" He snorts, shaking his head.

I am incapable of speaking. He hits me with the somber truth. I'm heading with him into a road with the possibility to live my worst fear. Being used again. Being insignificant, with my consent, and with all my heart. And was I ready to do it? Probably. *What's wrong with me?*

"Maybe you are as screwed up as me after all," he adds before leaving.

An hour later, I take a seat on our balcony wearing his black shirt while watching the golden sunset warming my face. I text with Tania a bit to try to clear my mind of Wolf. A thing that I find impossible to do. This troubled racing driver is haunting my thoughts. The irony is, I've been obsessed with perfection. And now, I'm obsessed with a man who is far from perfect and yet seems perfect to me. I laugh, I'm ridiculous. It's been only a few weeks since I've met him, but I have the feeling that I'm getting emotionally involved to a point of no return.

Probably because with Aaron, I don't have medium emotions. I'm all or nothing. He is an extreme. He is the answer to my job, the answer to my pain, but yet he is a problem. A problem who just appeared next to me. I peek over at him, watching him staring at the sky. He exhales, leaning toward the railing and running his fingers through his hair, massaging his scalp. Mysterious Aaron. He creates in me a dark pulsation; I can't decide if he provokes the best or the worse in me.

He sips his drink in one go, and I could guess it isn't his first one tonight. "Thomas is gonna kill me, drinking so close to a race."

And for the first time, I decide to share my past, hoping that one day he'll share his with me. "You know why I am afraid of heights?"

His eyes slice straight to mine, sparkling with an aching torment. I draw in a long breath. "I was eight, and I was climbing in a tree. I didn't know how to get down. My father told me he would catch me. And, I believed him… I jumped to fall into his arms. I jumped, but he stepped aside, letting me hit the ground." I sigh, remembering this painful memory. "I fell down in the grass, broke my leg. He told me to stop crying. He didn't care. It was my fault. An eight-year-old girl's fault, that her father didn't love her enough to care. It was a lesson. That nobody will ever catch me. That nobody will ever…" *Love me.*

I smile, trying to hide the fact that saying this out loud hurts me more than I thought it would. "He left, and I never saw him again."

That day, I lost my mother too. She remarried for money right after and taught me to never open my heart. She has been broken and trained me to be perfect and heartless. I was her revenge against men, she shaped me to her desire. But by trying to protect me, she broke me. And she couldn't see it. I start to feel that my coward of a father was right. Men broke *us*. They try to make me bend to their will, abuse me, and serve themselves before leaving me. Used. Alone. Ashamed.

"I want everything, Aaron," I speak, disgusted. I want revenge. I'm tired of not being enough, of feeling powerless. My jaw tightens as I meet the dark angry part of myself. The one I've been trying to suppress for years. I've been hiding, pretending to be someone I'm not for so long that I lost sight of who I am.

I've been manipulated. Conditioned to obey. It feels like my life has never been mine to begin with.

"That I can understand." Our gazes connect, and I lose myself, admiring his cerulean eyes tainted with burning flames by the light of the sunset. "For what it's worth, I would have caught you," he adds.

You already did.

"You already have everything, Aaron. A brilliant career, every woman you want, money, good looks." The list is long. How could someone like him possibly understand me?

"Every woman except one, apparently?"

I smile at his comment, proud that he recognizes my weak attempts at resisting him. "You can't have everything without sacrifices. I pushed my limits to become someone. I was driven by the need to excel, to be invincible." His tone, profound and determined, betrays his fear. He never wanted to be insignificant. *Like me.*

"I have nothing else to lose." He frowns his eyebrows like he is trying to erase a painful memory. His fists tighten. Darkness flickers in his eyes.

"So, it means you lost someone."

"My brother," he drops before swallowing. His eyes widen in fear, like he didn't mean to say that out loud.

I reach for Aaron's hand to intertwine my fingers with his, but he pushes it away. He's unreachable, detaching himself from all emotional connections. That's why he doesn't sleep in the same bed as a woman, that's why he never stays with them for more than a night, that's why he races dangerously. *He loved his brother.* Love rhymes for him with pain and suffering. He associates a positive word with his torment. He is lonely. A lone wolf.

"I know what it is to—"

"You don't know anything." Flames of angst lick through him as rage throb in him like a heartbeat. "I don't need fucking saving."

"You are better than you think you are. I know it." The way he acted with the kid at the carnival, his concern for me, shows he cares more than he thinks. Someone as passionate as he is couldn't be heartless, the headlines were all wrong about him. The opposite of love isn't hatred—it's indifference. "I'll prove it to you."

"That's a risky bet you're taking, Elle."

I stare at his icy eyes. He stares into my warm hazel eyes. There are no words left. Only actions. We both know what we need. We knew from the start this moment would happen. A moment when our carnal desires can't be ignored. A moment to escape. To lose control.

"Aaron," I whisper, my voice weak.

"Elle," he drops, lustful and desperate.

My heartbeat quickens with one certainty—tonight, I won't be insignificant. I'll allow him to serve himself—but this time, on my call—to reach my freedom.

"Use me."

CHAPTER 15

An animal craving

Aaron is my own aphrodisiac, sending a bolt of glowing fireworks inside my whole body. I'm ruled by hungry greed, tasting Wolf's lips like an animal. He is a vortex of sins, blossoming each of my cravings. Crushing my control.

Aaron pins me hard against the wall of our bedroom, his muscular body pressed against mine, while he cuffs my wrists with his strong grip. I'm vibrating, humming with lust, not caring if he wants to possess me. I don't mind anymore. I just want to connect. To quiver under his touches freely.

A moan escapes me as he weaves his tongue around mine. He lifts me up, my thighs bracing on his hips as he curves my butt cheek with one hand and my nape with the other. His kisses on my neck send a wave of goose bumps across my whole body. I run my fingers down his back, craving more, feeling his erection pressing on my stomach. I know tonight, I'll answer every one of his desires. Each cell of my body eager to receive his touch. Head spinning. Heart beating. Me, simpering. He puts a spell on me.

"Elle." His domineering and sultry tone enlivens me. "If you continue to tease me, I won't be able to stop." His eyes, insatiable and drugged with lust, bore into mine. He's giving me one more chance to escape.

"Don't stop," I pant, my doe eyes begging him to kiss me. I've never felt this intense urge to be pleased. I'm inflamed with the need of him.

His fingertips travel down my neck sensually to the edge of my breast as I hold my breath, apprehensive of what he will do next. He slides them lower, reaching my belly. "I want to fuck you hard and passionate, Elle."

Wolf has everything from a predator. The physique of Adonis, the voice of an alpha, the touch of the Devil. I'm powerless. His brutal honesty arouses me. His wolfish grin tempts me. His lecherous gaze haunts me. Aaron isn't the type of man to ask. He takes what's willingly offered without looking back.

"I've been wanting to make you mine since the first time I saw you." He leans toward me, his delicious lips kissing the lobe of my ear while his hand begins to slide near the entrance of my panties. I feel my ability to keep my eyes open weakening, his tantalizing touch makes me helpless and bound to his desire. He is so erotic. Manly. In control. He exercises a mind-blowing torture on my soul. Every nerve in my body replies to him, asking him to touch me.

He plays with my panties, creating a slight friction between my center and the satin fabric. His fingers slide inside before tracing circles around my clit, pushing me where he wants me to be. When he notices my wetness, a ghost of a smile spreads on his face. He finally puts pressure on my clit as I start moving my hips instinctively to his touch, enslaved by my own body.

"You'll scream my name as you reach your orgasms, tonight. I want to make you bend to my desire all night," he whispers in his lascivious tone. "I want you to be *mine*." He dots my throat with his sinful kisses, heading down my collarbone before stroking one finger inside me. *Dear god!*

My hand immediately grips his shoulder as I moan louder than expected. My body is exploding when I meet the arousal in his eyes. He is teasing me. Commanding me. He pushes deeper when he notices I've adjusted to him. His left hand travels inside my top to cup my breast. I'm imploring him to continue, to erase the past memories I have of sexuality, and to finally accept my own pleasure. Not being ashamed anymore.

"I want…" These are the only words I manage to speak.

"What do you want, Elle exactly?" He enters a second finger inside my entrance, stroking me at a faster pace while putting pressure with his thumb on my clit. My nails dig down his shoulder as I feel myself panting in ecstasy. Bliss. He sends me to the edge, knowing the impact he has over my body, and he is enjoying it. I'm giving him the control he needs, he is giving me the pleasure I've never experienced. I feel my orgasm nearing. I'm gasping for air and I want only one thing. Him.

"You… I want you to fuck me, Aaron."

His lips capture mine again, wild and full of hunger. His fingers move inside me faster. Deeper. I feel my legs weaken. I'm hot. Wet. Caught in a tsunami, a hurricane of passionate feelings. I hold on to him as his hand grabs my hip possessively.

"Stop, or I'm gonna come." But he doesn't. Instead, he pumps his fingers harder, faster, kissing me with a fierce heat that burns my soul. I close my eyes, part my lips searching for air, and throw my head backward, offering him my throat to claim. I've gone to the seventh heaven and I'm not ready to head down.

"Not now," he commands as he marks my neck. His hand curves around my ass, squeezing it, clutching our bodies closer together. I can't hold it anymore, I'm so close. My aroused nipples are pointing hard at him, my head is spinning, my heart is leaving my chest. I moan. I can't, I'm gonna—

"Come." He pushes his fingers into me one more time, applying pressure on my clit, and I come.

My orgasm crashes around me without restraint. I collapse into him, feeling like he just took my soul with him. His hand cups my cheek, his arm encircles me, letting me catch my breath and my senses for a couple of seconds.

His skilled fingers lift my shirt over my head. I stand in front of him in my black lace underwear, hypnotized by the craving in his eyes. He is Aaron LeBeau, the man who's dated beautiful women, and I'm the woman whose ex told her the sex was bad with her. A woman who has been broken, and has lost confidence in herself. And suddenly, I feel shy, scared, ashamed. I want to cover myself, I want to know what he is thinking. I swallow hard, thinking about Stephan's voice telling me I was boring, comparing me to other women. Fucking me like I was a sex doll. Serving himself. Putting me down. And I've accepted everything because I've never known anything else. I've never thought I could be worth more.

Pleasuring him—*willingly or not*—because it was my duty. Stephan never looked at me. I was invisible. But at this moment, with Aaron, I don't feel invisible anymore.

He gets on one knee and slides down my panties, before kissing my wetness. I close my thighs taking a step back. Nobody went down on me before. Aaron doesn't insist, noticing my evident shyness. His gaze is not leaving mine; he is taking his time, observing me, controlling himself until the edge. He is testing his boundaries until he unleashes a storm of sin on us. I try to shut up the voice of my insecurities, the nightmares of my past. He stands up and unclips my bra before caressing with the tip of his fingers the naked flesh of my arms. He slides it on the floor, and I'm naked. Naked in front of a man fully dressed. Every nerve in my body is itching to feel his touch. I'm in a haze, experiencing a craving for him I never thought I'd have for anyone.

His eyes drag over me, taking in every inch of my naked body. Savoring me. I'm the flag he wants to take. The trophy he wants to claim. The woman he couldn't have—*until now. What am I doing?* He is reading my soul, and I'm scared. I'm scared he sees me for who I am. I'm scared he sees my past. My insecurities. With all the other men, I've played a game. Pretended to be perfect, but with him... I can't hide. I cover myself with my hand, the fear of him seeing me taking control of me.

"Don't." He grips my wrist and brings my body closer to his.

"I'm not—" I stop, daring to meet his eyes while searching for my words. But I can't tell him what happened with Stephan. I can't tell him how broken and insecure he made me. He won't understand. "—I'm used to being invisible."

"Not for me."

He lifts me up and brings me to his bed. But he doesn't come. My nakedness is completely exposed to him. Aaron's eyes are roaming at me as if I'm an offering. A gift he wants to unravel, a woman who he granted the status of goddess just by the power of his stare. He unbuttons his shirt, slowly, sensually, before throwing it off and offering me a perfect view of his herculean body. His muscular arms contracting, his ripped, well-defined abs facing me, he is... *perfect*. He begins to unbutton his jeans, and I try to calm my nerves. Fear and excitement rush into me.

"You don't have to hide yourself for me." He throws his jeans and boxers away, standing naked in front of me. A naked, broken god. My heart is pounding, everything about him screams alpha. From his powerful and charismatic aura, his sinful body, to his hard, well-endowed manhood. Stephan's control made me feels scared, abused, worthless. Aaron's makes me feel safe, desired… a Delilah or a Cleopatra.

"You are very beautiful, Elle." I feel my cheeks redden as he leans over me, positioning himself on top of me in the bed. I want him. I need to feel him. I need his touch. Not as an escape, but as a remedy. "By far, the sexiest woman I've met. And I'm gonna show you how you are making me fucking crazy." His arm encircles my waist before lifting me up, pushing me toward the head of the bed.

"I'm gonna fuck every inch of your body and own every part of you. You'll see how much I want you." He opens with his teeth a condom before pulling it on over his hard cock.

Our eyes connect, and for an instant, I hear only the sound of my pounding heart, caught in an everlasting moment. Waiting. Anticipating. I yank him to me, our lips meeting softly at first before a cataclysm of passion explodes between us. He handcuffs both of my hands over my head with his hand, obligating me to bend to his will. He disposes a trail of kisses along the length of my collarbone. I abandon myself to him, his control, his everything. He lowers his mouth, teasing on his descent before closing over my nipple, his tongue working across me. Kissing. Sucking. Claiming. His other hand squeezes my breast, tugging my nipple delicately between his thumb and forefinger. I part my lips, yearning for his touch, moaning as he keeps his attention on my chest. A heat of forbidden pleasure reaches my stomach when, with a flex of his hips, he slams into me.

"Aaron!" I arch my back in a scream of bliss.

"Fuck, Elle. You feel so good," he groans.

He pulses in and out, blurring the fine line between pleasure and pain as I adjust to his length. I close my eyes, moaning his name as he hits different parts of me, kissing the soft spot behind my ear. He lets go of my hands and my fingers rake his back, my legs encircling his hips. I clench my muscles around him, arching my back, pushing my chest up, to feel where our bodies join. Each time he goes deeper, harder into me, I realize how much I've been yearning for him. He takes my breath away, our connection ripples through every cell of my body.

His strong arms grab the headboard as his eyes darken with lust. It feels like he is afraid of breaking me, not trusting himself with his carnal need for me. He clutches the headboard harder, his muscles contracting, and for a moment I feel he could break it. I grab the sheets of the bed, my heartbeat accelerated, an intense heat irradiates in me, I feel my next orgasm approaching. The second orgasm of my entire life—in the same day.

"Aaron, I—" His lips crash on mine, his palms cupping my jaw as he hits the end of me and I yell out his name in a scream. He fills my neck with delicious kisses, giving me the time to catch my breath.

"I'd ruin you for another man, Elle." *He already has.* The question is, would I be able to ruin him for another woman?

Aaron lifts me up, so I sit on his lap. I'm urging for more. He caresses my hair, and I close my eyes abandoning myself to him, offering him my throat to claim, as his mouth pleases my nipple. He runs his skilled fingers through my clit, massaging it at the perfect pace. I tense and rock my hips to meet his measured drives. His hand slides under my butt cheek as I press my pelvis farther into his, my fingers lost in his hair, my arms pulling him closer to me. I'm panting harder, caught in some sort of liberating trance. Wolf knows the effect he has on me, he is pushing my limits, testing my boundaries. He wants to be the only man in my mind and to mark my body with his touch, claim it, possess it. I bite my lower lip, incapable of keeping my thoughts straight. Our paces connect. Our heartbeats synchronized. Our moans melt together.

He groans, "You are mine, Elle."

Mine. A thing I promised myself I'd never be to anyone. And yet, at this precise moment, I'm his. I wonder if he is this possessive with the women he has been with. Is it just a game? Is it because he wants to be in control? Or is it me? There is a deep connection uniting us, I feel it. I've never been wild, nor let my primal lust take control before.

He pulls away from me, and he positions himself behind my back. Wolf lifts my body up, so my back is touching his strong torso, reducing the distance between our bodies. His left hand cups my breast as his right hand immobilizes my waist close to him. He enters me, and we move in synchronization like a sensual dance, slow but deep. Intense.

"Say it, Elle." He kisses my nape, taking control of the pace as I feel myself exploding. I can't hold on anymore.

"Don't stop." I'm panting, not understanding why he needs me to admit those words. He doesn't do relationships, he doesn't do romance, feelings, engagement, but he wants possession. He has control over my body. I'm vulnerable, burning myself and yet, I know he is waiting for my word to unleash itself. To lose control. To explode.

"Elle." His husky voice betrays his arousal and capitulating is the only option.

"I am yours." *And I'm gonna regret it.*

"I never lose control but with you, it's hard to not—"

"Lose it," I order, driven by an animal impulse. He protests, but I order him one more time to lose it. I need all of him. No restraint. No control. Just us.

And so he does.

Our chemistry is exploding into something passionate, brutal, intensely liberating. He starts pounding me with ferocious thrusts as I yank my hips down to meet him. I grab the sheets in front of me, offering him a perfect view of my back, when he lets go of his hold on me. I'm magnetized by him. He burst me into flames. We crash into lust together, and there is no comeback. That night we lose control. He is like nothing I've experienced. Everything that would have been a turn-off for me, that made me feel insignificant, is with him something I crave.

He is my descent to Hell, and my flight to Heaven.

My world ignites.

He fuels my soul.

"Aaron. I can't hold on! I can't… I can't—" His hands grab my waist as he pumps into me with intensity. The bed shaking, our moans getting higher and more intense, I believe the rooms surrounding us could hear our exchanges. I love the feel of him, I'm not ashamed anymore. It feels so good, so right, while I know this is wrong. My hair in his fist, he pounds harder into me, losing our primal instinct into each other. I've never been so free, his thrusts may be brutal, but his touch is passionate, liberating. I'm pushing his limits as well as he is pushing mine. My legs start to shake when he rolls me over so we can face each other.

"Are you okay?" he asks, concerned. His eyebrows frown, his gaze stuck between desire and fear.

He seems afraid of breaking me by his loss of control, probably not trusting himself. I nod my head as an answer, unable to talk. His concern for me makes me believe he isn't used to this kind of chemistry, to such passionate exchanges. Maybe I'll be able to mark him as well as he marked me.

By allowing him to take control, he is losing it to me tonight.

He pushes in me again, staring into my eyes with deep intensity. He buries his head into my neck, his tempo increasing, my body tingling as I feel myself climax. He is taking me to the edge as I crumble beneath his touch. I'm bewitched. Dazzled. Ensnared to him.

"I want to watch you come," he groans, his hands capturing my waist, as I arch my back with pleasure. His eyes, full of lust, are not leaving mine. I bite my lower lip and feel the heat of blissful ecstasy, the sparks of hot flashes invading my body.

We come together. Breathless. He consumes me. Enthralls me. Enraptures me.

It doesn't matter how long I've known him, what matters is how our souls recognize and connect in symbiosis. It's inexplicable. Haunting. *Significant*.

He has the power to heal me or to break me. He is as destructive as he is magical.

An everlasting addiction.

CHAPTER 16

Cursed 7

Silence.

Neither of us speaks. Most people express themselves with words. Artists express themselves through their art. But us, it's chemical. Our bodies expressed themselves for us. We keep on staring at the ceiling, lying on the bed, lost in our thoughts. I've never felt so driven by someone. I can't see clearly when I'm next to him. He consumes me. Turns me into aches until I'm reborn. But when our physical contact breaks, he is distant. Something unapproachable. And I'm left feeling—

He jumps out of the bed without a word and heads toward the bathroom. I watch him walking away from me. Farther away. Distancing himself. He closes the bathroom door, and I hear the water of the bathroom sink running. He got what he wanted from me… now, this is over. I'm one more. My heart aches, my chest hurts, and I've sold my soul to Hell.

I'm feeling insignificant.

I quickly dress, putting on my silk top and my shorts before heading toward the balcony to take a breath of fresh air. I'm cold, but I don't care. I feel like I've been sunburned and now I'm paying the price for exposing myself to Aaron, without protecting my heart from him. I look over at the full moon, shining and smiling wickedly at me. Judging me. *Happy now? You got fucked by Aaron LeBeau.* I need to swallow my pride and to call it like it was: animal sex. Casual sex. Nothing more. I needed him, I can't regret my choice.

"Elle," I hear his husky voice call from behind me.

I take a deep breath, commanding myself to not let my emotions lead me. When I turn to look over him, he is already fully dressed, wearing something sporty that shows his muscular body underneath, and he looks gorgeous. Is it so bad that I want to do it all again? He is like a drug, and I'm an addict. But unfortunately, no anonymous meetings will help me solve my addiction. I thought succumbing to my desire would drive me away from him, but instead, it left me craving more. I'm the Red Riding Hood and I've fallen into the lonely Wolf's trap.

"You are going out?" I stare expressionless, pretending to be disinterested. We don't owe each other anything. He is not mine. He'll never be.

"You shouldn't stay on the balcony or you are gonna catch a cold," he replies, distant, like nothing has happened between us.

"I'm fine." Truth is, I'm freezing, but he doesn't need to know that.

"I'm heading to the bar downstairs. Do you want something?" I shake my head, no. I feel like he is forcing himself to have this conversation. He doesn't want to talk to me. He wants to leave.

I was his escape, and now I'm the one he needs to escape from.

"Goodnight, Elle. Don't wait up for me."

And just like that, he leaves.

Message received.

One step. One breath. One song. It's seven a.m., the sun begins to rise. I'm running somewhere near the track. I don't think Aaron saw me leaving, he was still asleep. The music rising from my headphones is bleeding into my ears as I'm trying to escape my thoughts. Mental flashbacks of our heated night are capturing my mind, haunting my body. Him… the way he touched me… our synchronized breathes… his raspy voice. His scent. The sweat of our bodies connecting. *Snap out of it!*

An hour or so later of running, I still can't erase the images of last night. My five senses remember everything. I run faster to erase the mark he left on my soul, but the more I'm pushing, the more I'm falling. So, I stop out of breath near the hotel, my hands on my knees and my head down, my eyes blinking.

"Problems?" I catch sight of Louis Harmil in front of me, sitting on the stairs with a cup of coffee. He looks like he hasn't slept all night, as if he has seen a ghost.

"What about you?" I retort and stand up, adjusting my ponytail.

"It's better to be prepared." He is lost in his thoughts, eying the ground. "Aaron will cringe if he knew you were talking to me."

"He doesn't own me." I raise my eyebrow, aware that I just hinted to Louis that something is wrong between Aaron and me. Not my smartest decision.

"Trouble in paradise?" He smirks, his emerald eyes meeting mine. Is he enjoying this? His mood changes radically. I really can't figure him out.

"No. Not at all," I lie.

"You know he won't change his ways for you, right?"

"That won't work on me, Louis. I know you don't have Aaron's best interest at heart." For an unknown reason, I start feeling anxious when Louis chuckles at me.

He puts his cup of coffee in the trash before standing in front of me, anger sparking in his eyes. "And neither does he with yours. You should probably wonder where he was last night… and with who."

He leaves, and I feel like I just received a dagger in my heart. The venom he spits consumes my cells, and I'm left with intense jealousy and pain. Is it possible that he already moved on? A couple of hours after he marked me. All of my insecurities come back. He used me in a way I thought he never would, breaking the confidence I've tried to regain. I need to know. I rush into the lobby, my heart racing, anxiety taking control of me. Once again, I wasn't good enough. Once again, I've misplaced my trust. Once again, I'm stuck in my old ways.

I'm almost at the elevator, rushing, my head spinning, not thinking straight, and ignoring everything around me when a hand grabs my wrist. I turn back and I see him. Aaron LeBeau in his red racing suit. He has circles under his eyes, messy hair, his gaze is impenetrable.

"Elle. I have been looking for you! Where were you? Your phone is off!" he shouts.

"I've been running," I reply in a dry tone, trying to keep control, to not be weak. I remember my mother's words. *If you cry once in front of a man because of him, you give him the certitude that you belong to him. The certitude that he will break you again. The certitude that he owns you.*

"You could have just told me." His possessive tone irritates me. I chuckle, clearly amused.

"Why do you care? I heard you were well occupied," I snap, my eyes narrowing at him. Truth is, he has always been honest with me. I've accepted the game—burn my rules, I'm the one at fault. He furrows his brow, trying to understand my change of behavior. I shake my head. "I don't care who you bang—or how many women you bang in one night—but I thought you wanted to take racing seriously."

"Aaron, I couldn't—" A beautiful woman walks toward us checking her phone. When she notices me, she gives me a bright smile. "Oh, you must be Elle. I'm Monica."

Monica... the woman who was calling Aaron a few nights ago. I stand speechless, viewing both of them. Monica is gorgeous. She's the definition of every man's dream. We are probably around the same age. She has shiny dark-brown wavy hair, a top model smile. She's dressed in a tight red dress that accentuates her generous breasts. Monica has curves in the right places, deep smoky eyes, she's definitely a predator. And me, I'm wearing my sweaty leggings and my sports bra that's great for comfort—not so great for valorizing my body. I can't help but feel jealous and uncomfortable. This is the type of woman he goes for.

"Monica is like family. I was with her last night," Aaron adds before looking straight into my gaze. "Talking. As friends. She knows about our agreement." My jaw drops. In a couple of seconds, hundreds of questions pop through my mind. Who is she? Why did he tell her? How close are they? But more importantly... did he ever sleep with her?

"And God knows he doesn't do friendships with women." She chuckles. I smile shyly, trying to hide my discomfort.

"I really need to head to the qualification race. We'll talk later, Elle?" Aaron asks while his fingers reach for my hand, his touch reviving in me what happened last night between us. Every time his ocean eyes meet mine or he touches me, I'm powerless. Magnetized. There is only one answer, to take a leap of faith—trust him.

"Elle and I can watch the race together. If that's okay with you?"

"Sure." This is my opportunity to get to know her.

"Great. I'll see you later, *ma belle*." He gives me his usual smirk, that immediately reassures me. In my experience, if a man has something to hide, he would never let his two secrets together. It's a risk. And Aaron might be a player, but he is a smart one.

He faces Monica and arches his eyebrow, a playful tone in his voice, "And Monica. Be nice. Don't tell embarrassing stories." He puts his sunglasses on and leaves the two of us alone.

"Well, I better change."

She laughs. "I'll come with you."

She keeps scrutinizing me on our way to the elevator. We exchange a few brief smiles but remain silent until we enter. "I'm sorry to show up out of the blue. But you don't have to worry about me. We are like family. He sees me as a sister."

By the tone of her voice, I feel that she's genuine. I'm relieved. But also scared… the thought of Aaron sleeping with someone else almost broke me, and I know it's a question of time before this happens. I'm not special. There is no us, or if there is it's the darkest parts of ourselves connecting. It will lead to our destruction, and I need to protect myself from crashing at full speed.

"If I'm being honest, I thought you and him were involved romantically before," I reply.

She snorts. "Never happened and never will. And it's been ten years we've known each other." She turns to face me. "Don't get me wrong, Aaron is a great guy and all, but he is not the one who has my heart."

"That's refreshing to hear." It's nice to talk with someone close to Aaron. Especially a woman who hasn't her claws in him. "For how long have you been with the one who has your heart?"

Her expression changes. Her eyes darken. She starts to play nervously with her fingers, turning her ring. An engagement ring. I immediately regret asking her this question.

"Hmm. I believe Aaron told you about Henry? His brother."

"He mentioned him, but he's very private." I fear what she's gonna tell me next, my heart already aching for her.

"You know, he never mentions him to anyone, so that's a lot coming from him. He must trust you, Elle." And yet, I know nothing about the enigmatic Wolf.

"Henry was your husband?" I understand at this moment the reason she is close to Aaron. They are linked by tragedy. He doesn't let anyone in, but she's the one who belonged to his brother. She's the other part of Henry. Monica isn't a threat; she is like Aaron. She has lost a part of herself. She's broken.

"We were engaged. We hadn't gotten the time to… get married. He was the love of my life." She manages a bright smile, but I notice the tears forming in her eyes. Aaron hides his brother's loss by the desire of the flesh. Monica probably hides her loss by smiling, dressing seductively and showing a perfect image of herself—just like I did for so many years. Hiding how imperfect you are by pretending to be perfect.

"Monica, I can't possibly know what you've gone through, I'm sorry. Nobody deserves that." I don't want to ask what happened to him, I believe it's a story for Aaron to tell me willingly.

"I'm still broken, but Aaron was here for me…" She sighs. "That's why I'm here. On the seventh, it was the day Henry died. So, I called Aaron to see if we could meet up during the Grand Prix, I didn't feel like being alone." That's why Aaron's reaction changed suddenly after the phone call, that same night he was haunted at the gym. The seventh, just like Wolf's car number. Everything made sense, except one. *Why did Wolf never come to his brother's funeral?*

"Oh, if you need time with Aaron, I can give you space."

"Aaron needs you, Elle." I open my mouth in surprise. *Needs me.* How could he? I want to tell her that he needed me, but not anymore. After all, I'm probably the one who needs him. She notices my expression and adds, "He cares more than he'll let you know. He just needs time."

"I know, he is a good man." I try to hide my blush.

"I really hope you won't give up on him. He might pretend that he is strong, but at heart, he is just like a child afraid to be abandoned again." *Abandoned?* I wonder what part of his past he is still holding on to.

"We aren't together, Monica," I deny.

"Oh, Elle, you still don't understand, do you?"

She raises her eyebrow, and the elevator door opens.

"Understand what?"

"All of this."

CHAPTER 17

Two negatives make a positive

In the first nine minutes of the qualification race, I let my thoughts wander, obsessed with Wolf racing. He is powerful. Charismatic. Fearless. I spent the next nine minutes getting to know Monica. I understand why she and Aaron are friends—she's funny, kind, and strong-minded. The qualification race ends with Aaron claiming the pole position for tomorrow's race. The commentators seem impressed by his comeback, the odds are in his favor for the championship.

A couple minutes later, Wolf is laughing with Thomas as his crew is taking care of his car. When the two men finally notice us, Thomas hugs Monica and me before leaving. Aaron beholds my gaze, and flashes a self-assured grin that makes my cheeks flush as red as his racing suit.

"*Ma belle.*" Two words. I only need two words to make my heart shiver.

We continue staring into each other's eyes, ignoring the agitation around us. I attract Wolf's attention on my lower lip, biting it. I can feel it, he is still craving me. He may be the hunter, but I'm a doe fully willing to be chased.

"Well, if anyone is looking for me, I'll be… somewhere else," Monica adds, glancing at the both of us with a wicked smile stretching on her face before leaving to talk with Thomas.

"Monica seems to like you. I have no idea how you won her over, if I'm being honest. She never liked a girl before." Aaron reduces the distance between us.

"I'm just being myself. She's great. And she is also… gorgeous." I tuck a strand of my hair behind my ear, looking at the floor.

"I guess she is." *Of course she is.* "But not as much as you."

I study him, looking for the truth. "You don't have to lie, Aaron. You already had me—we are past the lies of a first date."

His scorching stare hits me as he furrows his brow. "I don't lie, Elle."

A man has never looked at me the way Aaron is. He has the gift to express his raw desire for me with such intensity that I feel glorified. Reborn into the type of woman I want to be. He creates new confidence in me, making me feel beautiful.

"Plus, you know you are my style."

"And what's your style, Mr. LeBeau?"

He approaches me, his eyes traveling the length of my body. "I believe you've already asked this question, but …Great legs, delicious mouth, beautiful eyes and smoking hot body."

I push him away, laughing at the way he spoke those words. "Why do you have to make every word sound dirty?"

"It's a gift."

Thomas calls out to Aaron; they have to discuss the race strategy this afternoon. Monica comes back to us, giving me an I-know-you-like-him kind of look. She probably listened to our conversation.

"Elle and I are going to Luxure this afternoon," she addresses Aaron before switching her attention back to me. "You'll see, they have great clothes."

From the look she's giving me, I conclude I don't have much choice in the matter. I bet she's not a huge fan of my ripped jeans and my casual top. Aaron picks up his bag and opens his wallet while I'm joking with Monica about my fashion sense.

"My treat." Aaron hands me his credit card, a proud smirk on his face. I scan him, shocked. How am I supposed to react? Is he trying to buy me? That's what men with money usually do. I'm no trophy wife. I'm not that type of woman.

"No." I snap at him.

"I insist."

"I can't. You are already paying for everything here. I won't. I can pay for myself." I push his credit card away.

"Elle, I have more money than I need. I'm not expecting anything." He hands me back the credit card. "Plus, my net worth is five hundred million—"

"I don't care how much money you have. I won't take advantage of you," I shout.

"For God's sake, just accept it, Elle. I'm trying to do something nice!" His temper sparked with annoyance.

"No."

Anger pulse through his veins, before surging through him. "Fuck! Is it so bad that I want to *please* you?"

Please me? He swallows down his frustration. Even Wolf seems surprised by his reaction and his choice of words. He didn't want to admit that. He hands me his credit card again and now I take into my palm, before he gathers his stuff and starts leaving his garage without a word. He seems upset, like by refusing him I've hurt his feelings. He thinks I've rejected him. He cared. He cared, and I pushed him away. Did he really want to do this gesture just to please me? Without another motive?

"Aaron, wait!" He turns back to face me, his expression cold as ice. "Thank you… but I won't buy anything expensive."

"Don't think about money, please. It's my treat." He glances over at Monica whose eyes have widened, shocked by our exchanges. "For the both of you."

He leaves before I can reach for him. He is still upset. Does he regret what he said?

"Well, fuck! I didn't know you were that close." Monica gives me a sinful look.

"He is just being nice." I brush my fingers through my hair awkwardly. She snorts before raising her eyebrows theatrically while we exit the garage and head toward her car.

"We are an agreement, that's it," I remind myself, using the term of how Wolf describes whatever relationships he has with women.

"You know, Aaron doesn't do something he doesn't want to do."

"Unless he doesn't have a choice."

"Aaron is the best racing driver out there. Do you really believe he couldn't win Longfoard nor the media in his own way? You can't oblige a man like him to do something. He doesn't follow the rules. If he did it, it's because a part of him wanted to," she points out, sure of herself.

"This doesn't make sense. He's doing that to be in peace, that's it." I frown my eyebrows, not believing her theory.

"Sometimes your unconscious knows better about what you need and want. Maybe you were linked by destiny."

Linked by destiny? How could two screwed up people be linked together? Nothing good can come out of it. Science says two negatives make a positive. Two negative charged ions can heal together to create a positive outcome. But our chemistry is extreme. It's destructive and doomed from the start.

"Monica." We turn around to see Louis standing in front of us, his skin as white as death. He is staring at Monica like he has seen a ghost. He seems crushed. Cursed. I peek over at her to notice her eyes have reddened with hatred.

"Let's go, Elle," she shouts while opening the door of her car.

"Monica, can we talk, please?" Louis begs. His usual flirtatious grin is gone. He seems weak in front of her, torn between his emotions, like something crippled inside of him.

"Stay away from me, Louis!" They are caught in a staring war, in which Louis is losing to the blades Monica sends him.

"I'm sorry. I've never meant to—" Louis' eyes soften in a tormented way. Is that regret? Pain? He is always so sure of himself, but now he seems devastated. Agonizing in his body.

"You're sorry?" Monica laughs nervously. "Because of you, I lost everything! I trusted you, and you leaked naked pictures of me for fun into your dumbass drivers' group chat!" She shakes her head in anger. "You got what you wanted, you screwed me. Now leave me alone! You can rot in hell!" She slams the car door, and I open my mouth in shock.

"Mo—"

"Louis, leave her alone. I can't believe you did that. This is disgusting." My lips curve into an expression of disgust, understanding why Aaron warned me against him, saying he doesn't respect women. He is a creep. He went from Golden Boy to fuck boy, losing my respect.

I hop into her car, and Monica races her engine fast to distance herself as far away as she can from Louis. "I'm sorry you had to see that." Her eyes are locked on the road.

"For what it's worth, I know what it is to put your heart into the hands of the wrong person."

"Thank you for not judging me, Elle." I smile at her, letting her know that I'm here if she needs to talk. "I want you to know I'm not a whore. After Henry's death, I wasn't myself. Louis was our friend. I always knew he had a crush on me, and I wanted to heal, you know?" Just like I wanted to forget when I'd met Aaron.

She exhales, her hands grabbing the steering wheel harder. "So, I slept with him. How classy of me, right? And then we start getting very close. We used to send… steamy pictures to each other, when he was away… but it turns out, he used me. He leaked these compromising pictures of me in the group chat, probably to impress the other drivers." By the way she talks about Louis, I could guess she started to open up to him. To trust him. Being betrayed is the worst feeling.

"It's not your fault, Monica. I've been used in the past, too. You couldn't know he would do that. Were you able to make the pictures disappear?"

"Yes, they were gone the same day, but I was already too ashamed. I didn't want Aaron to know, to think I'd betray Henry like that. Of course, he did know, all the racers received the pictures. I thought he would hate me, but he didn't. He blocked the pictures, dealt with Louis, and defended my honor in front of the others. I'm very thankful to him, even though I still can't face any of them." This is why Aaron hates Louis. The rivalry between them. The reason jealousy hits him when Louis tries to get closer to me.

"He did what was right. And he cares for you, I don't believe he'd hate you. When you suffer, you aren't capable of making smart decisions. You just want to forget. To reinvent yourself." I don't know if at this moment I'm talking about me or her. But I learned something, Aaron cares. I was right.

"It's funny, Aaron used the same words as you. Something about forgetting." We arrive at the shopping center, and she takes a deep breath, finding her smile again. "Here we are. No talking about Louis, please."

"You should try this on," Monica encourages me with a smile, noticing my hesitation.

I stare at a black leather skirt and a leopard silk shirt. For some reason, this outfit is calling out to me. It's very sexy. Very not me. And yet very appealing. It's been a long time since I've dressed sexily. I've always dreamed to unleash the femme fatale within me—if she still exists. And somehow, I want to feel beautiful for myself and for a particular someone. I want to be bad, wild, and free.

"You know what? I think I will."

I take the outfit with me into the fitting room.

The leather skirt curves my waist tightly and gives justice to my shaped glutes. I've never been more thankful for my lifting sessions. My legs appear longer with the black stilettos. The silk shirt is showing the right amount of cleavage. And I feel… desirable. I let go of my ponytail and let my hair down wildly to my waist. The doe becomes a tiger, and I love it.

I leave the room and smile at Monica, who is seated on the ivory sofa in front of me while I'm imitating a model pose. She opens her jaw, amazed, her hand covering her lips. I'm done hiding. I'm done excusing myself. People stopped looking at me because I was too afraid to be… me. I've decided to find myself again.

"Wow. You are perfect. I can't imagine Aaron's face when he sees you wearing that. Damn, I knew you were beautiful, but this is another level." Monica's attention brings over the vendor woman who didn't greet us earlier—probably thinking we couldn't afford this place. After all, no price was put on the outfits. "Isn't she beautiful?" She arches her eyebrow at her, and I can't help but chuckle. I love Monica's feistiness and honest speaking—*just like Aaron.*

"She is, Madame. Unfortunately, this item is a new collection and—"

"That won't be a problem. My friend here is dating Aaron LeBeau. Money isn't an issue for us," Monica snaps at the vendor, who immediately gives us her fakest smile before leaving.

She gets up and ambles toward me, crossing her arms on her chest. "I hate those kinds of people. I grew up being poor, and people looked down on me when I was with Henry. I've never fit in. I won't let that happen to you."

I change, and we reach the checkout to pay for the outfits. My heart is beating, fearing the price.

"Three thousand." The rude woman smiles at us in a wicked way.

I stare over at Monica in a panic, my eyes wildly open. I can't. This is the price of three months of rent. I've never spent that amount on myself. She nods at me, encouraging me to use Wolf's card. I glance over it… this time, I don't want to use him. I'd been with Stephan for the comfort, the safety of a future. I've dreamed for a man to treat me like I'm special. I've always been a huge fan of the *Pretty Woman* scene, when Edward treats Vivian like a princess on a shopping day. But with Aaron, the fact he wanted to please me, I couldn't. It's exactly what I wanted, but accepting it would mean I accept more with him. More that he couldn't possibly give me. That it's real. That I could possibly fall for him. I hand her my card, swallowing hard, doubting it will pass.

"Elle. What are you doing?" Monica shouts.

"It's okay." *You are doing the right thing, Elle.* My mother always depended on men. On me. I won't be like her. *I'll just take the outfit back tomorrow.*

"Your name, please?" the rude woman asks.

"Elle Monteiro."

She taps on her computer. "Oh. Your payment has already been taken care of." She hands me the bag of clothes and my unused card. "Have a good day," she says in a robotic tone.

I look at Monica in surprise. Who paid for it? How is that possible?

"Don't look at me like that. I just told Aaron where we were going. He probably knew you wouldn't use his card. And let's face it, any shop would kill to have Aaron LeBeau's mysterious woman photographed with their clothes on." Monica grins, probably telling me less than she knows.

That arrogant driver doesn't give me a break. He takes all of my breath away. Occupies each of my thoughts. And now, he is racing his way to my heart.

Aaron: I'm at the track. Text me when you are here. Ps: I'm inviting you to eat tonight. And no. You. Can't. Refuse.

I smile childishly, reading the text Aaron sent me, wearing the outfit *he* bought today, my eyes made-up with smoky brown eye shadow and my lips with glossy lipstick. Gloss that probably won't stay long on my lips. I'm doing a hundred steps in front of the hotel. Dying of anxiety. Shaking with anticipation.

"I should go. Let me know how it goes." Monica hugs me before walking toward her car. We exchange numbers. In such a short amount of time spent together, I already know she'll become a close friend.

She turns to face me one more time. "You know, I don't have many girlfriends. You never judged me based on the way I dress, the way I look, or for what I've done. So thank you, Elle." I simper at her. "Aaron is very lucky," she adds before waving at me.

I take a deep breath as I walk toward the pits to find Wolf. I feel butterflies in my stomach, the wind leading me closer to him. My heart races. My breath quickens. The golden sunset is warming the track in an orange tone. The scenery feels magical. It's like this moment was meant to be. I'm feeling like a teenager going to prom with her crush.

Aaron is talking with a few drivers, dressed up in a marine-blue suit with a white dress shirt underneath. All the attention is on him. He is charismatic. Handsome. God-like. I repeat my mantra. *Confidence. Confidence. Confidence.* I spot Aaron's teammate catching sight of me as I'm walking toward them. His jaw drops and he pushes Aaron's shoulder with a head nod, telling him to look at me. When Wolf turns around, our eyes connect.

All the attention is suddenly turned on me. The golden light is warming our faces, our eyes tainted in a feline color, my hips moving like rumba music is accompanying us. All I see is him. The man who enlivens each of my body cells. The man who dazzles me. I smile at Aaron nervously as he bites his lip, his eyes stuck on mine. Sparkling with desire. Observing each of my moves. He swallows before giving me his brightest smile, and I chuckle.

This moment is everlasting. The world around us seems to stop. Aaron rushes toward me, our bodies ready to express themselves. We are like two magnetic elements drawn to each other. Awakening the silent volcano inside of us. And together, we generate a nuclear explosion.

Two negatives make a positive.

Like the atoms, we are hit with an electrical arc discharge. An electrifying touch that creates a force. The discharge slams into us at full force, hitting all of our cells, knocking our control out.

Creating… something else. *Something new.*

CHAPTER 18

Race me

He crushes his mouth against mine, hot and angry. Kissing me with an intense ardor that scorches my senses. It's real. Not for the game. Not to escape his darkness. This time, we don't use each other, we ease into each other. My entire being is relinquishing the last drop of control I had.

I bite his lower lip, driven by an animal impulse. An unbreakable impulse. A need for him. My hands grab his hair fiercely while he presses our bodies together. I hear the other drivers playing around, teasing us by whistling at us, but I don't care. His tongue enters my mouth, dancing in harmony with mine. We deepen the kiss until neither of us can breathe. Until the sun drops. Until the darkness rises.

"You'll be my downfall, Elle," he whispers, his hands cupping my cheeks. Every time his lips collide with mine, every time I abandon myself to him, I feel alive. He is my fuel. He revs up my soul. "I'm losing control so easily with you."

"And is it wrong?"

"I have no fucking idea." His arms encircle my body against his as I look up at him, feeling secure. Happy. "One thing is for sure, that outfit won't stay on you long."

"You don't like it?" I play with my eyelashes.

"Love it. Especially when I know what's underneath it." I cover my face with my hands, bringing my head to his chest. He is so bold. So direct. So Aaron. "You know you're gorgeous, *ma belle.*"

He takes my hand firmly, leading us toward his car. He opens the door for me, and I remember I still have his card. I take it out of my purse and hand it over to him. "Thank you. I want you to know I was about to pay for myself."

"I know. And I told you, when you are with me you will not." He leans toward me, and I find myself captured between him and his sports car. "Don't try to argue with me on this subject ever again, or I'll fuck you to heaven right here."

I cross my arms on my chest, pouting at him, trying to make a point. Which obviously doesn't work as his annoying, arrogant self laughs at me. "Cute."

I'll get you back, Wolf. You won't win the next round.

A short and fast ride later, we take an elevator to the top of an immense building. Floor ninety-six. When the doors open, I'm transported into another universe. The restaurant has a 360-window view of the whole city at night. In the middle of it, there are acrobats juggling fire, dancing with veils, the piano music hypnotizing my heart. The dome lets us see the bright stars. The dark tones of the place are illuminated only by the flames of the dancers and the candles on each table. It feels like a dream. A midnight reverie coming from another culture. A reverie full of possibilities. The server dressed in a fancy tuxedo leads us to our seat in a private area.

Aaron pulls up my seat. "This is the Minuit. There are only two places like this in the world. Here and in Morocco. The owner designed the restaurant for his wife. I met him a couple of years ago. Great man."

This is simply beautiful. Enchanting. Dazzling. Every minute with Aaron is an adventure. An endless dream. He orders for both of us, as I was still undecided on the menu. With our eyes firmly set on each other, we remain in silence, until time passes way too fast. Even after eating a couple of expensive dishes, I'm still starving—for him.

"I wanted to apologize for yesterday, Elle." I clear my throat, I never expected an apology from Aaron. "After we had sex. The way I left you," he adds, his eyes stuck on mine.

"You don't owe me anything, Aaron." I sip my wine, trying to hide my feelings. I can't let him know it hurts me more than I thought it would.

"I know. But I respect you." He leers over the flames, pinching his eyebrows as the color of the spotlight warms our faces in a flaming red light. "I don't usually lose control the way I did last night. I hope I wasn't too… passionate." His eyes are back on mine and have darkened.

That's when I understand. He freaked out. He lost control to me. A control he will never regain. A control he needs to have due to a scar he is hiding. He is afraid of something, but I can't tell what.

"Last night was perfect," I comment shyly as he searches for the truth in my eyes. Is he afraid to break me? Hurt me? My cheeks redden, he was the hottest sex of my life. I've never been so free, so animal with anyone.

"You haunt my mind, Elle." And he haunts everything of me. "I usually fuck and forget. I thought having you would satisfy my… appetite. But it's worse." He sighs, and I forget to breathe.

He leans closer to me, his stare vibrant with arousal. "I'm thinking about your naked body, the way you taste, it's driving me insane." The crowds applaud as the performance finishes, but our eyes are stuck on each other, ignoring everything around us. "I constantly. Want. To. Fuck. You," he emphasizes, articulating each word in a commanding and forceful tone.

I close my legs tighter, the pulse of my heart resonating through my whole body. I cannot continue down this road. I'm haunted by his touch. Breathless by his kisses. Possessed by him. I've never experienced such extreme emotions. Emotions that are destined to be beautiful and romantic, but with him, it's not safe. It's dangerous. Crepuscular. I'm the master of my soul—not him.

"We don't want the same things." It feels like I'm trying to convince myself. Freaking hormones. Freaking LeBeau. Is he even human?

"Probably. But we do have something in common."

"What?" I arch my eyebrow as the next performance begins. The romantic music has gotten darker, faster, the fire has risen higher.

"We are both obsessed with each other. And the way to end this obsession is to give in." His caliginous, darksome eyes are stuck on mine. I feel Hell has come to collect my soul. My punishment is to crave endlessly this tempestuous man I shouldn't. "To give in to our desire until this obsession stops."

Obsession. Addiction. I thought our connection was purely physical, carnal. But could it be more on a deeper level? Could we really stop this obsession as he calls it? This is unhealthy. Wrong. We can't give each other what we need. We are opposite. There is no future, no hope for us to heal together. And I'm afraid. I'm afraid my obsession will grow harder, deeper into my soul. I'm afraid to fall in love.

"I don't know, Aaron."

He swallows his drink. "This wasn't a question." He angles his head toward me, a feral smirk on his face. "I think we are stuck with each other. No matter if we want it or not," he adds, and I know he is right.

We can't deny our connection. We can't stay away. We can only take a leap and burn ourselves. Hoping to be significant. Hoping to heal and not unleash a nuclear bomb among us. Life is like a chess game. I'm the queen and he is the king. On the same team, we can be unbreakable. But against each other, we have no chance to survive. Destruction or redemption. That's a risky bet.

"You have an answer for everything, don't you?" I take the cherry he left from his dessert and put it in my mouth, fully decided to show him I can play, too.

I lick the cherry seductively, in and out, before sucking it slowly, my eyes provoking him. I break the top of it. And swallow. I lick my upper lip, bite my lower lip, unleashing my doe eyes. He stays silent, his eyes locked on me, as his tongue plays inside of his mouth. A thing he does when he is about to explode.

"Elle," his raspy voice states like a warning, and a rush of adrenaline travels the length of my body.

I bow my head to the side, and with my feet, I take off my heels from under the table. "Yes, Aaron?" I reply, playing the innocent.

I slide my feet up on top of his pants until reaching the area of his manhood. Luckily, the table is draped with a white sheet and no one can see what's underneath. He coughs, surprised by my action. I dart my tongue out of my mouth, licking my upper lip once more, my feet stroking him as I know he is growing hard beneath his pants. I caress my collarbone with the tips of my fingers, pushing my silk shirt delicately to the side to give him a preview of my lace underwear.

"Fuck, Elle. I'm hard now," he groans.

I smile wickedly before pulling myself off my chair, satisfied to have played the player himself. "I don't know what you are talking about, Mr. LeBeau."

"Oh, *ma belle*… I hope you are ready to get fucked, because I'm gonna make you pay for your teasing." I'm pushing Wolf's limits, giving him a red light, and he is about to push mine once the light switch off. "I'll come to find you as soon as I—you know."

I head toward the bathroom, still smiling, enjoying my first lap of victory. I glance over at him, almost sure he is watching me walking away. Which he is—his elbow on the table, his hand covering his mouth before smiling in spite of himself. He wants to race me. And I cannot wait to do it all again.

I readjust myself in front of the bathroom mirror, trying to cool down. What am I doing? I'm teasing him with things… things that I hate to do. Did I really stroke him with my feet? Licked a cherry the same way I… but it didn't make me feel ashamed. I felt overpowered.

I wait for him by the elevator, remembering a race isn't a sprint, but a marathon. I check my phone's messages, and suddenly I feel strong arms encircling my waist from behind. I know it's him. I recognize his touch. His scent. His aura. He squeezes my back against his strong torso before kissing the lobe of my ear.

"It's time to teach you a lesson." *Red. Red.*

Heart burning. Head spinning. Heat reaching.

The race is about to begin.

CHAPTER 19

Owning you

When the elevator doors open, he takes my hand and leads me inside. It's just the two of us in our long descent down to the garage. He doesn't wait until the doors close to pin me against the wall in a hasty movement. A satisfying smirk appears on his face when he notices the blush of excitement spreading on my cheeks. He cups my face with his palms, devouring my lips in a feverish and explosive kiss. In just a couple of seconds, his passion sends me into oblivion. I'm possessed by the greedy hunger of our kisses, forgetting everything around us. Danger. He is an addictive danger.

There is no warning against Aaron LeBeau.

You can't take precautions, you can't fight back.

"You are gorgeous, Elle." His words set me on fire. My desire for him is escalating. Inflaming me. Amplifying until it consumes me.

He lifts me up against the wall, my thighs bracing on his hips as his hands curve around my butt cheeks and I run my fingers down his back. I'm bewitched by the heat of his kisses, melting under his possessive touch. My shirt is unbuttoned. My skirt is lifting up. My collarbone is aching for his kiss. I can't slow down, and neither can he. We are racing together at full speed, until we are pushed off the track when the elevator doors open, and two older men scan us. Aaron pulls away, positioning himself in front of me, while I'm buttoning my top back up.

"Mr. LeBeau?" the older man asks, a confused look on his face. Aaron clears his throat, trying to act all professional. *Too late Aaron, we've been busted like horny teenagers.*

"Gentlemen." He smiles, giving them a polite head nod before swooping me into his arms, and I giggle, noticing the what-on-earth-happened expression on the faces of the two men.

We burst into laughter together as we enter his flashy sports car. He revs up the engine, and in one movement reverses the car at a fast pace, making my heart skip a beat. I hate his assertiveness. I hate that his playboy tricks are working so well on me.

"I thought you were supposed to help my reputation, not damage it, Miss Monteiro." He exits the garage, driving in a haste. I simper, knowing he wants to get to the hotel to take me on my bed as fast as possible.

"Maybe I'm as sinful as you." I bat my eyelashes as his eyes sparkle with appetite for me.

"Oh, yeah?" He drifts his car on a 180-degree turn. I hold on to his leg, the speed pushing me back to my seat. He enters a parking lot, leading us to the rooftop of a building. The way he drifts his car during the tight turns, the music inhaling my senses, I feel like I'm in a *Fast & Furious* movie. We are racing our way up, until he parks his car on the skyscraper, where it's just us. I admire the view of the stars shining in the sky, the city lights sparkling all around us, the pink lights of the parking lot, feeling like we arrive to another world.

Desire blossoms heavy in my belly when I meet Wolf's tenebrous gaze. I know what he has in mind. He has the gift to push my limits, to make me forget my fears, my insecurities. I yank him closer to me as his lips brush on mine slowly. His hands trace up my ribs to the edges of my breasts. He trails open-mouthed kisses down my neck, winding his fingers through my hair while I close my eyes, accepting the pleasure consuming me. Aaron's hand moves inside my panties, and his lips curve into the smile of a sinner when he realizes how wet I am. He slides my thong down before opening my legs wilder.

"Yesterday, I lost control. Tonight, you'll lose yours to me, Elle." I already lost it. Our lips meet sensually as he unbuttons my shirt before throwing it in the back seat. I moan when his skilled fingers set me on fire. "You'll come for me, yelling my name in that sweet voice of yours."

His stare is wild, his pupils darken as he tries to read my needs. He pushes one finger inside my entrance and a heat invades my body. He moves his finger inside me, slowly, at a measured place as I bite my lower lip to keep me from moaning his name. Truth is, I've never had sex elsewhere than a bed. I doubt that is the case for Aaron. He's probably done it many times in his car. I'm not as experienced as he is.

"Do you want another one, Elle?" He puts pressure with his thumb on my clit, watching me rolling my hips to meet his pace.

"Yes," I pant when he strokes another finger inside me, and I abandon myself to his control and the pleasureful torture he creates. My fingers digging into his hair, he strokes me deeper. Faster. Leaving me breathless. "Aaron. I can't—" I drop, out of air, while he shuts me off with a delicious kiss, sucking my lower lip.

"You'll take it until you can't anymore, *ma belle*." His voice enthralls me, and soon enough, I feel my first orgasm nearing.

I want him to end my agony, and I find myself begging him to be allowed to come. I should be ashamed, but the truth is... I'm not. He pumps his fingers, harder, faster, until he takes all my control. His thumb massaging my clit, he's hitting different pleasures in my body. I can't hold on. Heat. Flashes. I'm spinning. I'm about to—

"Lose it," Wolf orders as my orgasm crashes around me. My stomach vibrates, a blistering ecstasy sends me to the edge. I cry out his name, closing my eyes to meet my pleasure. "Now you are ready for me," he adds.

He caresses my cheek before brushing his lips on mine. "You are mine, Elle."

I want to show him he is mine, too. I want to leave a mark on him, the same way he marked me last night. *Significant*. He pulls me on his lap in the driver seat while I throw off his shirt. He brushes my hair with his fingers before unlocking my bra and sliding it on the seat next to us. He lifts my skirt over my head and squeezes my waist possessively. The light of the moon is warming his face in a blue tone, giving a spiritual connection to this moment.

"I've never had sex in a car," I admit coyly when I notice his gaze take in the sights of each part of my vulnerable, naked body. Stephan never bothered to undress me fully, but with Aaron, he wants to memorize each part of my naked self, every time, and it feels... nice.

"Me neither." I snort at his statement. "But I always wanted to," he adds.

He never did. It is a first for both of us. Meaningful.

When he unzips his pants, I peer at his growing hardness, and I feel the need to try. He's god-like, and I don't want to feel like a random mortal to him. I know men are expecting *that*. I put my hand around his length to start stroking him.

"Fuck, yes," he groans, pulling his head back on the seat.

He spaces the seat from the steering wheel, and I know how things are gonna escalate. He's giving me room to… a shiver runs through my body, my heart aching, old memories rushing back. I angle closer to him, approaching his erection, but when his fingers brush over my hair, I jerk away. *Stephan*. I can't do this.

"I'm sorry, I can't." I swallow as I stop stroking him and wait for his judgment. He stares at me, his expression unreadable.

"It's not an obligation, Elle."

"But, that's what men want, isn't it?"

"I wouldn't lie, saying I wasn't imagining your sweet lips on me." I feel a knot in my stomach, but before I can overthink, his lips close on mine. "But I honestly prefer being buried deep in you and watching you come undone for me." I can help but blush in front of his without filter honesty.

"So, you don't think I'm a prude?" Stephan's voice resonates throughout my head.

"Certainly not. I think you need to trust the person enough to do this… and probably the right man, I guess."

I kiss him, making my lips collide with his, feeling lifted out of a weight I was holding on to. He rips the condom packet with his teeth before pulling it onto his hard shaft. He lowers his mouth to my nipple, kissing it, sucking it, his tongue working across me. His other hand squeezes my breast, his fingers tugging my nipple gently, as a moan of pleasure escapes me.

He enters me with a flex of his hips, and I grip the head of the seat in front of me, burying my face near Aaron's neck while I adjust to his cock inside of me. Our paces synchronize. He cups my cheeks to draw me in and give me another heated kiss while I ride him, rocking my hips to meet his measured drives. When I pull back, I feel sexy and desired in his eyes. That's the thing with Aaron, he creates in me an assurance I never had before.

He thrusts deeper into me, owning each part of my body with his kisses, sending me to a forbidden place in each of his drives. I moan his name as he curses, the world our only witness of the passion exploding between us. Aaron LeBeau isn't the kind to make sweet, gentle love, he's too possessive and passionate for that. But he isn't the type of man to fuck you like a doll and disrespect you. He is not the type of man who makes you feel dirty, like a lower woman after possessing you. No. He brings you to the edge and brings to life something wild in you. You submit him your control willingly—without shame, without regretting your actions.

He pushes the seat down and switches positions, putting himself on top as I lie down on the seat. He opens the roof of the convertible, the warm wind making his hair dance as the full moon lightens my face. I look at him, standing on his knees, his herculean body facing me—he is beautiful but somehow broken. God's blood is running in his veins, while he is inhabited by his demons corrupting his soul.

"Like to be on top, Mr. LeBeau?" I giggle when he brings my knees closer to his chest in one fast movement.

"I'll take you in every fucking position, Miss Monteiro." He lowers himself before trailing addictive kisses along the length of my inner thigh down to my ankle, an insatiable predatory look on his face. Still on his knees, his back straightens up as he puts my ankles on his shoulder.

He pulses in and out as I push my palms to the seat behind me to hold on to his passionate drives. He clutches my waist to push deeper into me before caressing my legs with an erotic touch that makes my whole body shiver. His eyes firmly set on me, watching me fall apart. Watching my breasts bouncing every time he hits the end of me. Watching my belly contracting, feeling my orgasm nearing. I'm wild for him. Slowly. Deeply. Intensely. I'm driven.

"Fuck. You feel amazing. I. Want. All. Of. You." My stomach vibrates with butterflies. Every touch of his is fiery, passionate, rough, but yet—he makes me feel like every woman would want to feel. Secure and desired. With him, a simple word is magnifying, because it means so much more. 'All of you' could mean more than my carnal body, but my whole soul.

He spreads my legs before burying his head into my neck, sucking my earlobe. One of his hand cups my butt cheek while his tempo increases, and my body tingles with pleasure. I wrap my legs around his torso, yanking him toward me to feel him deeper inside me.

His palm cups my nape as his lips fiercely meet mine. "You belong to me, *ma belle.*"

I arch my back with pleasure, feeling my orgasm nearing, incapable of answering him. I scrape my nails down his back. My primal lust taking control. My world is igniting.

"Elle. What do you want?" he moans between kisses.

I feel vulnerable, obligated to reveal things I've never said out loud. I've never given any man the power to read my mind. I have my pride. But him, he could make me break the walls I've built for years in just a flash, and that scares me.

"Only you. I want you to make me come, Aaron. Don't stop. I want to be yours," I yell out, almost crying with pleasure, lost in the heat of heavenly ecstasy. I'll probably regret admitting I want to be his tomorrow, but as for now, I'm blinded by lust.

He slams into me, cursing, his predator's eyes locked on mine. His fingers pressing on my clit with the right amount of pressure. We come together in a last intense thrust, grabbing each other, calling out each other's names at the same time. He remains on top of me as we catch our breath. At this pace, Aaron will own my soul without the certitude that one day I'll own his. He asked me to be his, but he never said he was mine.

He starts pulling away from me, but this time he gives me a soft kiss on my lips. It's just a kiss, and yet, it's the kiss he never gave me after we had sex the first time. I know tonight we will get back to our routine. Me, sleeping in the bed. Him on the sofa. I've promised myself I won't be one of those girls who hope they'd be the special one. The naive ones, the ones hoping they could change a man like Wolf. But I find myself hoping that exact thing tonight. Except that I don't want to change him. I just want to be one day, significant.

"I can't resist you, Elle. Because of you, tomorrow I'll be unable to focus, remembering how good my cock felt buried inside your smoking hot body." He flashes a seductive grin, witnessing my eyes open wildly, due to his bluntness.

I have one certainty.

I've definitely sold my soul to Hell—and I'll do it all over again for him.

CHAPTER 20

Checkered flag

"I could be your personal Grid Girl." I cock my eyebrow at Aaron, knowing that Grid Girls have been removed from Formula 1 since 2018.

We are on our way to the track, approaching his paddock. I'm excited to see Wolf racing, and to be by his side. He seems incredibly relaxed, probably because it's just the drivers' parade, the race starts in two hours. I decided to wear white jeans, my brown wedge heels, and a cute turquoise blouse. I'm starting to feel good in my body, regain my confidence. Wolf fucked Stephan's touched out of me—forever. Now, I'm free to collect the missing pieces of myself.

"Please, don't. I couldn't handle it." He snorts while waving politely at the reporters taking pictures of us. He tugs me toward him, placing his hand behind my back, while I play with my VIP badge around my neck, trying to not quiver under his touch. "All the men will have their eyes on you, wishing you were theirs, and I couldn't protect you from them."

I laugh at him. "How chivalrous of you, Mr. LeBeau."

"Plus, you'll make me lose my focus, which could get very ugly for me," he adds in a playful tone that instantly makes my stomach turn. He is in danger every time he races. He is the epitome of reckless. He is indomitable. A man without the fear of dying. *What if something happens?*

We enter his garage and greet his pit crew, engineers, who are all focused on making the last adjustments to his car. After the parade, Thomas is giving Aaron his last bit of advice on the race, ordering him to take the win today. Wolf closes his racing suit before jumping into his cockpit to take the pole position on the grid formation.

Thomas hands me a headset to follow the race from the monitors, and to be able to listen to Aaron's team radio. I am jerked from my anxiety when Monica pulls me into a hug. I immediately smile at her, glad she is here.

"You know he's never invited a woman to watch a race from his garage, right?" She gives me a dazzling smile.

I pull my headset on, my eyes bewitched on Aaron. "It's weird, Monica. I've known him for like what, a month? But it feels like I've known him for much longer."

"It was the same with Henry and me. Time doesn't matter in the end. Only the connection between two souls does."

Everyone stays silent inside the garage watching the screen as the race is about to start. The crowd is yelling the drivers' names, flags are flying, motors are revving up. Seventy laps to go. I hear the commentator speaking than seven of the drivers chose to start on medium tires, just like Aaron did. *That's a good thing, right?* God, I'm anxious.

Red.

Red.

Red.

Red.

Red.

Go.

The race starts, and the sweltering pace of the cars makes my heart skip a beat. The sounds of the motors spread goose bumps on my skin, igniting my soul. This race is nothing like the qualification race. The drivers are driving angrily, without fear, without holding back. They are like gladiators fighting for their lives in an arena.

"LeBeau is taking the first place during the opening lap, following by Harmil," the commentator yells, as I play nervously with my fingers.

Thomas starts giving instructions to Aaron. "Watch out, Wolf. Louis is going to be in a hurry to get past you."

Just a second later the commentator screams that Harmil is coming straight for LeBeau's car on turn three, and my heart has never raced this fast. Aaron maintains his lead, not letting Louis get past him. *Come on.*

"One-second margin. Push in the last corner. Secure."

Thirty-five laps later, and I'm still feeling anxious. Aaron is taking risks on the track under the instruction of Thomas. The whole team is tense, their eyes stuck on the monitors. When Aaron stayed too long on the pit stop while switching his tires, Louis Harmil takes the lead, following by his teammate, Marvin. Fuck. He is now third.

Aaron asks for a visual of the track, racing faster to get back to Louis, but our screens are blurry. An accident probably happened on the track, as smoke is spreading during the turn. My throat is dry—I have a bad feeling—and Aaron's team starts to feel the panic, as well.

"Marvin is spinning on his own on the circuit. Oh, no! Wolf is arriving just behind him and—" the commentator is interrupted as I hear Thomas yelling with panic in the headset.

"Aaron watch out, Marvin is spinning middle track!"

I can't witness this. He is gonna crash. He is too close. It's too late for him to break during the turn. I cover my mouth with my hand as I see Aaron's car drifting in a 360-degree turn to avoid crashing into Marvin's car. He goes off the track violently, almost hitting the wall in front of him, as I grab Monica's hand, tightening my grip on her.

Wolf goes back on the track in one maneuver, losing some precious seconds, but he's safe. I allow myself to finally exhale, my heart almost breaking, my palms sweating, fearing what could have happened if he hadn't remained in control of his car.

"That freaking idiot! If I had crashed, it could have ended badly! So stupid, man! Get your fucking car out of here," Aaron curses in the headset.

He puts himself back in the race, driving even more angrily and recklessly than before, coming for Louis Harmil. He's feral. The closer Aaron gets to death, the more he is hell-bent on provoking it—which doesn't help me calm my nerves. Thomas congratulates Aaron before asking him to remain calm.

"That was insane! Marvin did something very dangerous! But what an incredible maneuver from LeBeau! He is going for Harmil," the commentator says as I meet Monica's gaze. She gives me a reassuring smile, noticing the mask of fear on my face.

"You need to push, we are tight. Frederich is backing you up." Thomas plays nervously with his hair before putting both of his hands on his forehead. At least someone is as anxious as I am here. Frederich is Aaron's teammate, racing at P4. He follows the orders and race precociously, the total opposite of Wolf.

"I'll overtake him in the chicane," Aaron adds, preparing himself to pass Louis on the turn.

Thomas orders him to stick to the plan, telling him to not act now, or else he risks crashing his car. But Aaron is magnetically attracted to danger. Overcoming small odds is his forte. He doesn't listen to Thomas and breaks his car in the under turn to pass in front of Harmil. Louis hits Aaron's back wheels, almost making him lose control. And it's a penalty for Louis. *Take that, Golden Boy!*

"Amazing! Aaron LeBeau is taking the lead! Ten laps to go," the commentator screams with excitement. My heart is beating, my breath quickens, I've never been so emotionally involved in anything.

I hear Aaron chuckle on the headset, provoking Thomas. "You were saying?"

Thomas rolls his eyes. "You're impossible. Now take the freaking checkered flag home, mate."

"Copy."

The crowds cheer harder when the commentator praises Wolf's racing. I start feeling hopeful, feeling the excitement rushing into my veins. The checkered flag is waved, and Aaron's team jumps, hugging each other. He won. I pull Monica into a hug, feeling happy for him. He deserves it.

"Yeah! Fucking flag! That's a win. Good job, guys." I hear Aaron laughing from my headset. Thomas gives me a thumbs up before I smile back at him. He is proud, I can sense in his eyes his happiness for today's victory and Aaron.

"And that's a win for LeBeau. After his disqualification in Monaco, he dazzled us with an incredible victory. He still has a chance to win the world championship."

That's the last thing I hear before Aaron does the victory lap. He comes back to his garage, throws off his helmet down, before raising his fist in the air. His team congratulate him, pulling Wolf into hugs and giving him a friendly tap on his shoulders. I stay distant. I want him to enjoy this moment with his team.

When his eyes meet mine, I smile genuinely. Wolf starts ambling toward me, like a knight going to kiss the princess, and butterflies start dancing in my stomach. I want to kiss him. I need the passion within me to explode. I need our bodies to speak in a mercurial, flaming, uncontrollable way. With us, there is no in-between. It's all or nothing. Hell or Heaven. But our soon to be kiss is interrupted by his team pushing him to claim his first place on the podium.

He holds the trophy and sprays champagne all around the podium. I can't help but chuckle, appreciating the rare moments of Wolf's happiness. Racing is what makes him whole (alongside his addiction to winning and being in control).

I pass the next hour by Wolf's side. After talking with journalists and his team sponsors, we're back in his garage. I give privacy to Aaron, to let him discuss with his house team CEO, Longfoard. I spot Thomas in the corner, watching the track, his hands in his pockets. He doesn't seem to like the crowd and the reporters either.

"Can I join you?" He gives me a warm smile as acceptance. "It feels good to be alone, hm?"

"You got me." He laughs. "I love racing, but the public events, the cameras, fame, all these kind of things, it exhausts me. I'm probably not setting the best example for Aaron."

"I think it's good to be with someone who can understand you." I clear my throat, a mental note to myself, that I'm not talking about Aaron and me in this discussion. Wolf is about to have what he wants. Which also means he is about to not need me anymore. I've accomplished my part of the agreement. I've broken my rules, but an agreement has an expiration date. *We have an expiration date.*

"You're right." Thomas inspects me as if he senses my confusion. "You know, the after-race is always emotional. You got an adrenaline rush and then you need to get back to reality. It's pretty messed up." He raises an eyebrow. "That's also why racers do it all again."

"I understand what you mean." More than he knows. I just lived it. Aaron being my adrenaline rush. "Well, I should head back."

"It was very nice to meet you, Elle. I hope you'll come more often." When he gives me a kind smile, my stomach turns into a knot knowing this will never happen.

"It was great to meet you."

Back at our hotel, Aaron and I barely speak to each other. This is the end. The end of an unforgettable week. I finish closing my luggage and curse my boss who needs me in New York ASAP. I have to be at the airport in an hour. Aaron offers to accompany me, but he has to hold a press conference at that time before heading to France for the next Grand Prix. This is over. I have to get back to reality, and it goddamn hurts.

We stand awkwardly in the hotel hallway facing each other. I hate goodbyes. I hate that goodbyes with Aaron feel like forever.

"I guess this is it. Our agreement is done," I say uncertainly.

"I guess it is," he adds in a perfectly calm tone. He doesn't care that I'm leaving.

I shrug, somehow feeling hurt. "Right."

He doesn't answer, but his eyes roam my face. My nerves are shaking. I don't like being in a blurry situation. He owes me an answer on what we are. "Are we even friends?" My voice is perched. Totally fake. Totally emotional. Mother used to tell me to never push a man to commit, or you'll scare him away. I did break all the rules with Wolf this few days. I showed him my jealousy and now my emotions.

"We will never be friends, Elle." I swallow, pinching my eyebrows. I was not expecting his dry answer. He smirks when he notices my reaction. "I don't want to fuck my friends."

He is about to take my luggage for me, but I reach it before he does. I don't need a savior. I don't need him to act all knightly with me. I give him a proud smile. "Right. We are an obsession. Good thing you won't be obsessed with me when you are a continent away."

I want to believe we have some sort of bound, whether we want it or not. But I know the story too well. The next bimbo will come, and I'll be a vague memory to Wolf. Insignificant again. He could have my body, but not my pride.

I kiss him on the cheek as a goodbye note. He frowns in surprise, while I limit our eye contact. The only thing I can control is to leave with class. I head toward the exit, my heart aching and ripping. My breath cut, I push my emotions out of my mind. He offered me the illusion of a world full of possibilities, but now I need to wake up.

"*Ma belle.*" Two words from him. Two words, and I'm melting.

I look back at him. "Yes?"

"You are stuck with me, don't forget that," he says in his usual confidence, darting his tongue out of his mouth to lick his upper lip seductively.

"A continent away or not. You won't get rid of me," Wolf promises.

CHAPTER 21

Three words

This thing about feelings, they explode when you expect it the least. I have my blank canvas on my easel, paintings on the side, and I feel the urge to express myself. I tighten my hair in a bow, before taking black paint on my flat brush.

A hateful spurts of iron black on the canvas. Splattering shades of onyx. The blank space is my enemy, my brush for sword, my color shades as witness of the chaos I'm inflecting. The words of Nina are resonating through my mind. *"It's not what I asked you to do. This is crap,"* she commented when I delivered her the interview about Wolf. *I need more black. "There is no dirt. I don't pay you to have a good time."* How come she could never be satisfied? The paint on my fingers is now on my cheek as I pass my hand through my face. I feel like screaming, ripping and damaging everything on my way. Since then, Nina analyzed each of my actions like a stark smelling blood, causing a shiver down my back. I've been back writing about meaningless gossips and I hate it. *"Sleeping with your source should have its benefits. I need more. Give me more."* I guess she did watch the headlines of Wolf and I at the Canadian Grand Prix. I'm tired of this. I want only one thing.

Freedom.

I switch to a sword brush, writing in silver-gray the word *freedom* from the left to the right, lines after lines, like a kid doing her punishment. My column has gained more fans around the world—that's probably the only reason why I'm not fired yet. Readers loved to plunge in the world of Formula 1 and to see the human side of Wolf. I've posted online the recording of the interview as Tania advise me, which changed Wolf's image; from angry god to god-like. Some gossips articles came out about us. The nature of our relationship intrigued the fans—and so do I, where are we standing?

A key.

I paint the shadow of a key, blending the silver and onyx brushstrokes together. I smooth the edges with water. Wolf, the racer who has been occupying my mind is sending me mixed signals. After the French Grand Prix, we went on a few casual dates during his free time, even though they all ended up the same way. Our beach sunset dates ended up in making out sessions, until people began to stare and Wolf went all territorial, narrowing his eyes at them. As for dinner, we never made it on time—and most of the time I was without panties. We've developed a habit of talking by phone. Well, I talk. He listens. Sometimes he makes naughty comments with his usual confidence.

We are almost normal. Who am I kidding? We don't do normal. He's claiming me as his, possessively and ardently, but doesn't let me in his intimacy. Wolf is secretive, there is a strong link uniting us, a whirlwind passion, but his heart is like the Excalibur sword, protected by an unbreakable stone. He's unreachable, letting me see only a glimpse of his soul. We're an obsession neither of us wanted, and right now I'm left with many unanswered questions.

A bird.

With my rigger, I paint a bird in the center of the canvas with sparkling colors of pink, blue, yellow, contrasting with the darkness surrounding it. He's highlighting the whole piece. The bird is about to fly free, spurts of grenade dropping out of his wing. He's his own light, winning over whatever chaos he escaped. *Talk about subconscious.*

I glance at my apron covered in paint, and I can proudly say I've completed my first art piece in months. I take a few steps back to observe it carefully, the brush between my teeth. I feel proud. It's not perfect, but it's real. It has a story.

And, for the first time, I want to share it with one person. I hold my phone to take a picture of it to send it to Aaron. After all, he's been the one encouraging me to take a leap. He just won the Belgium Grand Prix today, I doubt he'll answer me right away, but on my surprise he does—and my heart jumps each fucking time.

Aaron: I'm speechless. Have you thought about showing it to the world yet?

Me: No, I'm not ready.

Aaron: But you share it with me, hm?

Crap.

It doesn't mean anything. We're nothing more than an obsession, right?

Me: Don't get too cocky. I show it to you because I know you're 'hard to please' and brutally honest.

Even I don't believe in my own lie. I showed it to him because an unconscious part of me wants him to feel proud of me. It's bad. Very bad.

I check the time. I'm late. I'm supposed to go for a coffee with Tania and our new intern Joshua. He moved to New York last month and doesn't have any friends in the city. He is very handsome—perfect shiny hair, hazel eyes, a bit younger than us, great sense of fashion, and totally playing for the other team.

Aaron: That's not the only thing hard about me right now, you know.

I'm never gonna leave if I don't end this discussion. But my stomach turns. What if he is with another woman right now? No. Stop. Don't go there. Too late.

Me: Good thing you just won a Grand Prix, it's gonna be easier to find one of those groupies to help you with your problem.

Classy, Elle. First, I admit I just stalked him on TV—buying the F1 TV chain just for him. And then, that I'm jealous of whatever women at his feet.

Aaron: Well, maybe I want *you* to help me with my problem. My hand will do, though.

You. He said you. Don't smile.

Me: Use your imagination, Wolf! Got to go! Xx

I pull off apron, turn off my phone, washed my hands, still smiling before rushing to the coffee bar around the corner, paint probably still on my face.

"We should go to a club to celebrate!" Joshua's excitement makes me laugh.

My birthday is in two weeks, therefore it's a call to celebration for my friends. Clubbing, a thing I haven't done since… Aaron. Stop blushing. *Maybe I should invite him?*

"That's so unfair, I'm single to death while you have a hot male model as a boyfriend," she addresses to Joshua before turning to face me, rolling her eyes. "And you, a fucking Formula 1 driver."

"He's not my boyfriend, Tania. I don't even know where we stand." They both stare at me, eyes wide open, eager for some details. "It's just, we talk, often. And when we're together, I feel alive, you know?"

"It sounds like a relationship to me, you're just too blind to see it." Joshua smiles.

"That said, friends with benefits is the best kind of relationship," Tania comments in a sarcastic tone.

"I don't know, it's not like we have a future anyway." I take a deep breath. "One day, it'll be all over."

Joshua's eyes bore into mine, full of concern. "Opening your heart isn't easy, but maybe you should tell him how you feel?"

I shake my head as a no. "You're too romantic for this world. People are tempted to crush your feelings if you show an ounce of vulnerability."

Not that I feel anything for Wolf.

Not that I'm terrified of feeling something for him.

Not that I do.

Tania encourages me to get physical with Aaron as Joshua encourages me to connect with him emotionally. But there is this thing with three words. They are always so hard to say: I miss you. I love you. I need you. They can be magnificent to hear, but yet self-destructive if the person doesn't say it back to you. Three words can break you. I'll never say those words. My past ruins them for me. Plus, with Aaron, I need only two words: *my significant.*

"I'm sorry I gotta go. I have a deadline." Tania hugs the both of us before leaving. "Don't overthinking this, Elle. Just enjoy the present time, okay?"

It's what I did. And now my heart is involved into a point of no return.

A couple minutes later, Joshua finishes his excess of cookies, and we exit the coffee bar. We talk a bit more in front of it, before ambling on the neighboring street. "Love is a beautiful thing, you know? Since I've met Fabiano, I feel more alive than ever."

"I don't believe in love, neither does Aaron." A part of me does, despite everything. But love is a willing submission that can only bring pain. It's a weakness. No, I *can't* believe in love.

"You know what you need?" He opens his arms, giving me a warm smile. "A hug. Come here."

Joshua pours me into a sweet hug, as we stand awkwardly in that position in the middle of the street. "I still believe you should talk to him, you may be surprised." Not today. By showing Aaron my artwork, I almost let go that I cared for him more than I should. Today, I won't speak more to him.

Joshua brushes a strand of my hair, before staring at my cheek. "Did you know you have paint on your cheek?"

I push him away playfully, both of us laughing. "Thank you for telling me this only now! You're a great friend."

He throws his arm around my shoulder. "You're welcome. You need to show me what you do."

"No. Nobody can see it."

Nobody except Aaron.

The next day, my smile vanishes at the view of the newest gossip article.

Damn it.

Apparently, Joshua and I are involved romantically. The picture portrays us hugging, and from the angle the picture has been taken, it looks like we are kissing. This is bad. I immediately call Aaron's number in case he has seen the article. I feel anxious. Knowing his possessiveness, I fear he'd be enraged right now.

My heart jumps when he answers after the first ring. "Hi, Aaron. Have you seen the—"

"Look, Elle. I'm busy right now. I don't care who you fuck, but please have the decency to at least be discreet. It's embarrassing." I conclude he has seen the article.

"Nothing happ—"

"You fuck who you want, and I fuck who I want. Don't worry, Elle. I have to go." He hangs up without waiting to hear my explanation.

Well, now, I guess I know what we are. *Nothing.*

What just happened? I stare at my phone, my mouth hanging open. Jealousy hits me at full speed. Fuck who I want? A fresh swell of rage rise in me. He didn't hear me out and jumped to conclusions. I know he has trust issues, and so do I, but in just a flash, he erases me from his memory. One mistake. One mistake, and Aaron kicks me out of his life without thinking twice. Without remorse. Without caring. He assumes the worst in me, taking the easy road. I won't run after him. He hurt me more than I thought he would.

You have your pride, Aaron, but so do I.

I'm zipping up my tight black dress in the mirror. Red lipstick. Red heels. Hair free. Tonight, I'm turning twenty-four, and I won't let Aaron haunt my mind. I throw my phone on the bed, ignoring what I've been reading all week. Aaron's latest conquest. *Aaron LeBeau has been seen with beautiful Heiress Francesca Vermont looking close. Is LeBeau already back on the market?* as a headline. He is back in his element, and I'm just yesterday's news.

My phone vibrates, Monica is calling me. I pick up and put her on speaker mode, while finishing to get ready for tonight. "Happy Birthday, Elle! I'm sorry, I couldn't be there."

I ignore the need to ask about Aaron. "Thank you, Monica. And don't worry about it. I didn't expect you to travel from Monaco just for the night."

"I was calling for another motive, I admit." I swallow, waiting for her to speak. "The both of you are so screwed up, you know that, right?" I believe she's referring to Aaron and me.

I try to control my anger, explaining what happened between us, but by the expressive gestures of my hands, I'm not making such a great job out of it. "Why should I tell him the truth? He clearly moved on. If he cared for me, he'd have heard me out."

"Yeah, I understand your point but…" She takes a deep breath. "Look, he started to open up to you, and then he sees that picture. It's hard to trust someone for him. I mean, you know Aaron, how did you expect him to react?"

"Not like that. I expected him to be angry or anything, not this cold guy who doesn't care."

"You should know by now that Aaron has two sides of himself."

Silence.

She's right. Wolf's duality. To the world, he's the heartless racer, a cold man who doesn't care about anyone. And then there is the Aaron I know. The passionate and damaged one. A loner who wears his mask to distance himself from the others. I sit on my bed, hugging my pillow to my chest. *He pushed me away.* Truth is, I can't blame Aaron for not wanting to hear the truth. If I were in his situation, I would have acted the same way. That's what happens when you've been broken, you can't separate the lies from the truth, your past from the present.

But I don't want to run after a man. I don't want to be rejected. If I swallow my pride, he could own me. Relationships are a game for power. There is always someone who cares more than the other. There is always a winner, a dominant, and a loser, a submissive. Aaron might be a dominant, but I'll never be in the loser camp. We can equally heal each other or destroy each other. And right now, we are damaging ourselves, slamming our insecurities in our faces. I'm a mess. He revived me, yes. But he also revived the darkness in me. Jealousy. Hatred. Revenge.

"I know, but maybe it was for the best. He moved on now." I take my phone into my hand before staring at the picture of Aaron and Miss Perfect, his latest conquest. Some *agreements* are meant to be broken. Ripped apart. Forgotten.

"I don't believe he fucked her. The heiress is the daughter of one of his sponsors. He's just trying to make you jealous." She pauses a moment. "I know it's not my place but I hope you'll talk and put both of your egos aside." For that, we would need a chance to talk. "Anyway, gotta go, happy birthday again! I hope to see you soon!"

"Me too, thank you." I hang up and head toward my party, my heart clearly not in it.

A taxi ride later, I arrive at the trendiest nightclub in the city. I meet Joshua's boyfriend, Fabiano, the handsome Italian model, and force myself to pretend to have fun. The club is crowded with people dancing to the rhythms of the EDM. Bartenders are pouring drinks while jumping to the beats. Smoke. Spotlights. Dancers. It's an invitation to celebrate. To forget. I drink one shot. My eyes are locked on Tania jumping in the air with Fabiano. *Two shots.* Joshua asks me if I'm okay, but I'm not. My life went from almost perfect to too complicated. Strong emotions are devastating. Screw it. *Three shots.* I walk toward Tania, deciding to dance to erase Aaron's touch.

I pull my head up—looking at the ceiling, which I believe is spinning—putting my hands in the air, trying to catch the multi-color lights. I move my hips slowly and shake my head to the side, feeling all the emotions inside of me as everyone is jumping with one hand in the air. The DJ lets go of the smoke during the drop. I pass my fingers through my hair, playing with it sensually. A man stops behind me, grabbing my waist, rolling his hips next to mine. I feel nothing under the touch of the stranger. He's not even a good dancer. He's a distraction. And just for a moment, I allow myself to pretend he is… him. I don't look back to see the man's face, I don't care. I close my eyes and dance, abandoning myself freely. The man caresses the exterior of my thighs before putting his hands on my hips. My short dress lifts until it's just under my butt. I caress my collarbone. I'm hot. My head is spinning. I hope the sweat of my body will wash away my sins.

I pass my hand into my hair, opening my mouth to catch my breath. The hand of the stranger reaches my butt, squeezing it as if I'm his possession. I push his hand away, realizing all this is wrong. But he insists, and he kisses my naked shoulder, forcing me to stay close to him. I take a step away before he spins me, blocking my torso against his as his hand slides to my butt cheek again, slapping it like I'm a toy he wants to play with.

I push the man away violently, shaking my head. I feel so weak. He is not Aaron. He doesn't treat me like he does. The man doesn't care for my approval. He yanks me back to him, a vicious smile on his face, reaching for my lips with his disgusting breath. I pull my head away, my eyes searching for my friends. *Let me go.* I feel someone grabbing my hand and jerking me away from the stranger.

"What the fuck are you doing?" a man with a husky voice yells at me. *Am I hallucinating?* When I dare to look up, it's him.

My obsession.

My downfall.

My heartbreak.

Wolf is standing in front of me, his eyes gunning me. They are red from anger, dark as hell. He is wearing an elegant black dress shirt with dress pants the same color. He's even more magnetic than in my memory. I'm confused between hating him or drowning in him. I'm halfway between hell and heaven, incapable to choose which path to take.

"You want to get fucked by an asshole in a dirty club? Is it what you want, seriously, Elle? Fuck!" he screams, clutching my wrist.

And I'm mad.

The stranger tried to steal me—more than a kiss—and yet I'm the one at fault? I push Aaron away while shaking my head in affront. Wolf made me forgot how some men can be disgusting, and how I could feel worthless, a sexual object to them. But he isn't better. Once again, he doesn't trust me.

"Worthless whore," the stranger I danced with insults me.

I close my eyes, swallowing the insult while lowering my dress. Women are whores if their dresses are too short, too tight. Women ask to get fucked if they dress up in such a way. What a great society. Men can make us feel ashamed of our freedom.

When I open my eyes, Aaron is not in front of me anymore. He has grabbed the man by the collar, his jaw clenching, his veins popping from his muscles tensing. His eyes narrow at the stranger like he's about to break him. And when the stranger laughs, Wolf punches him brutally, sending him to the ground. The stranger lands with a loud bang, bleeding from his nose, his eyes bugging out at Aaron with fear. Everyone around us is too busy dancing to pay attention to us.

"You don't call a woman a whore. Especially not my woman." *His woman?* Aaron grabs the man's shirt and lifts him up with his fist. "Apologize. Now."

"I'm sorry man, I didn't mean this," the stranger gurgles.

"Now, get the fuck out." Wolf pushes him violently toward the exit, letting him run like a coward.

Aaron turns back to me, his expression Tartarean. He rolls up his sleeve to hide the blood on his cuff. I take a step away from him, fighting the magnetism that draws us together. But Wolf doesn't let me—he grabs my arm and joins our bodies together. He is dominating me with his height, his superior gaze trying to intimidate me, but he doesn't get to me anymore.

The moment I stopped being enough for him, he lost me. He thinks he can fuck her and get back to whatever we had? I'm not his toy. My veins are boiling with anger. Fury twist inside of me. I'm about to explode. I'm not the second option. I push him away again, my hand hitting his hard chest, but he doesn't move. Everyone is dancing, jumping, while our eyes are stuck in warfare. We aren't moving, only our invisible demons are dancing around us, celebrating our downfall.

"Let me go, Aaron." I was wrong. There are three words I could say to him.

I hate you.

I despise you.

You broke me.

"Why?" His eyes are defying mine. "I told you, I don't like to share. And I won't share you," he threatens me.

I feel worthless to him at this moment. First, I have no idea what he's doing here. Second, he believes he can claim ownership on me. Like I'm just a business deal gone wrong. Third, he made it clear on the phone he couldn't care less about me.

"You're not my boyfriend. 'I fuck who I want, and you fuck who you want.' Your words." I want to hurt him the way he hurt me. I push him once more, rage searing through me.

"I'm not the one who initiated this," he replies in his domineering, superior tone. "You're the one who betrayed me, Elle."

He lets go of my wrist before crossing his arms on his chest. His expression is unreadable. All I see his darkness. No light. "You're the one who went behind my back," he adds.

He clenches his jaw before frowning his eyebrows, and I understand. I hurt him. Seeing me with another man broke him. All along, I thought he'd be the one to break me, while I did it to him. My insecurities, my fears caused our chaos. I don't feel the effect of the alcohol anymore. I want to leave. I can't stand the way he stares at me. I can't stand to be seen as a traitor through his eyes.

Aaron's gaze leaves mine to look at Joshua dancing with Tania and Fabiano. His fists clench. God, I need to clear the air now. This is not too late. I take his hand, wanting to explain to him before he does something reckless. My heart is bouncing across my chest. I feel my world collapsing. If only I had said those three words: He is nothing. I want you.

"Trust me," I whisper before he pushes my hand away and walks by himself toward my friends, Joshua not leaving his sight.

I run after him, trying to push the dancing people away, but I'm not as strong or tall as he is. When I finally reach my friends, they're all looking at Aaron, their eyes sparkling. They have no idea he is probably about to have a non-friendly conversation with Joshua. Sweet, harmless Joshua against reckless and possessive Aaron. I grab Aaron's arm and move my body in front of him before managing a smile to my friends.

"Guys. Aaron, this is Tania." She offers her hand to Aaron, a huge smile on her face. I stare at Wolf. "Aaron, this is Joshua. The man you saw in the picture." Joshua gives him his hand to shake, but Aaron glance at him like he wants to destroys him, playing with his tongue inside his mouth. "And next to him, this is Fabiano… his boyfriend."

Aaron's gaze jumps between Joshua and me as his eyebrows pinch together. He notices Fabiano's hand in the back pocket of Joshua's pants and finally understands. The two men get back to their dancing and exchange a heated kiss. Aaron's expression softens, probably feeling ashamed of his behavior. Our eyes meet again, speaking for ourselves what we couldn't—I am sorry.

All of us walk closer to the bar area in order to be able to talk. My friends end up loving Aaron. They drink his words like children captivated by a magical story. I know Aaron is making a good impression for me. His eyes don't leave mine when he talks with them. He is searching for a sign of my forgiveness. But I'm closed off. I avoid all contact; I could never sleep with another man. But him… he did it. And I can't blame him. His obsession stopped before mine.

"Elle. Can I talk to you?" he asks, leaning toward me, his hand on my lower back.

I nod, and he gives a charming smile to my friends. We move closer to the entrance, to a less crowded space.

"I thought he was—"

"No. And if you'd have heard me out, you'd know that already," I add, crossing my arms on my chest.

"I'm sorry. I'm used to people betraying me. It's hard for me to trust someone." His eyes are concerned. "I should have listened. But words are—" *Words can be lies.*

"It doesn't matter. Why are you even here?" I reply harshly while my heart wishes we could undo the past.

"It's your birthday." I've never mentioned my birthday to him. How could he know? "Monica told me, so I flew to New York to be here." Of course, she did. I'm gonna kill her.

"I have a place I'd like to show you." He searches for my gaze as he takes a step closer to me. My whole body wants to say yes, but my heart can't, but the thought of him with another woman breaks me. *Unless, nothing happened?* I shouldn't be naive, it's Aaron I'm talking about. I wish I could be strong, but I can't handle it. I cannot share him.

"Aaron… I can't." I look down, taking a step back, closing my arms on my chest nervously.

"Nothing happened with Francesca—or any other women, for what matter." I meet his eyes, my heart beating fast, heat reaching my stomach, as I regain my hope for us. He tucks a strand of my hair behind my ear softly, analyzing me with soft eyes. "I wanted you to be jealous. Just like I was. I'm sorry."

"How can I trust you?" My eyes dare him.

"You can't," he admits. "You could call Thomas, he'll tell you the truth. I could tell you you're the only fucking woman on my mind, but that won't make you trust me." His hands caress the length of my arm, his touch soft and addictive. "You can only believe, I'm afraid."

Believe in actions, not in words. It's easy to lie with words, but you can't pretend a touch.

Just like Monica said, we are screwed up. Destruction or passion. Possessing, consuming each other, making the other an addiction. With him, everything is extreme and yet magnifying. We are novices at listening to our feelings. We don't know how to open our hearts. We are learning to heal. To evolve. Maybe one day, we'll destroy each other's walls, but there is a long road left. And yet, I know. I know I belong with him.

"You hurt me." Three words.

He cups my cheeks with his palms, his eyes wounded by my words. And the only thing I want is to feel our proximity. Being under his touch. I need him more than I ever needed anyone. I need him to show me I'm different. Significant.

His lips claim mine in a sweet, tender kiss. The kind of kisses that assures me there is only me. The kind of kisses that makes you believe him. It's his way to say he is sorry for being the way he is. And it's fine. As long as he belongs with me.

"Let's get out of here." I smile shyly. Believing in him. *In us.*

Sometimes a girl needs three words. Sometimes, she just needs a kiss.

CHAPTER 22

Wish upon a lantern

It's uncanny how many things can change in a year.

A year ago, I was with Stephan, not recognizing myself. I was taking the insults. The screaming. The criticism. It had to stop. The more I cried, the happier he seemed to be. Raising himself above my misery. I was never enough. The day of my birthday, I was lying in my bed, feeling miserable. Ugly. Used. Ashamed. I wanted to get out, but I could never break up with him—I feared I wouldn't find anyone else, I kept hoping he'd change.

I remember his words, *"You'll never find someone better than me. Someone who will put up with your personality. To love you for who you are."*

A bouquet of roses—*yellow* roses—a lying post on social media showing how happy we were, that was my birthday gifts. Along with him flirting with a few women. Out of his league. Even though, he kept denying, I wondered what if he was cheating on me? A part of me felt glad. That would give me the green light to break up with him. To have a reason. The other part of me felt I was being paranoid. My mind was too fucked up to think—or even to care at this point.

He brought me an overpriced bag. The one the socialites have. Fancy. Extravagant. Rich. Not my style. But his gesture—that had become rarer—showed that he cares. That's why I was staying. I wanted to believe my misery was all in my head, that I was a paranoiac. That it was all my fault. Sometimes, he showed great acts of kindness, and I was hoping they will be more frequent. I kept remembering how Stephan was when we first met. Gentle. Caring. Loving. I kept thinking he will switch back to how he was before and love me like he did. But I was holding on to a memory—a memory that wasn't even true. I've never been happy. I just got the illusion of happiness. I was holding on to a hope that never existed.

"You're so insecure." That's what he answered when I asked if he loved me. *"Of course I do. It's just some part of yourself that I don't,"* he added.

Pants off. On all fours. Pride swallowing. I remembered staring emotionless at the wall when Stephan entered me.

For my birthday a year ago, I got fucked. Hard. Passionless. Without eye contact. Without a caring touch. Just fucked with one purpose. To satisfy Stephan's own pleasure. To give without receiving. Used and miserable.

I cried without a word. I accepted his humiliation without complaint.

Until a point, I wondered what have I become?

I needed to get out.

I needed someone to help me.

And today, I'm finally free.

"What's this place, Aaron?"

I keep staring at the dazzling penthouse. Everything is spacious. Palatial. The space is occupied only by the strict minimum of furniture. Cold and modern. The colossal windows unveiling a breathtaking view of the city. I wonder if this could be his place? I know his main house is in Monaco.

"Come." He smirks and grabs my hand to lead me toward his balcony.

Balcony is an understatement. I could fit my whole living room in it. He has a giant outdoor infinity pool where the water flows over the largest edge, like it has no boundary. The pool is illuminated with pink and blue lights, opposing the dusky night. I shake my head in disbelief. All this luxury. He is out of my league. He is the dream, the man who is on top of the world, and I'm the harsh reality, one of those thousands of lights from the buildings facing us.

"You didn't have to rent a place to impress me, Aaron." I wrap my arms around my chest, still astonished by the scenery.

He begins to unbutton his shirt slowly, while his eyes sparkle with appetency. "It's my place."

I open my eyes widely. I never knew Aaron had an apartment—or a fucking penthouse—in New York. He seems amused by my confusion. "My main house is in Monaco, but I often have to travel to America. Therefore, I bought this apartment last year." His tongue darts out of his mouth seductively. "We are almost neighbors, *ma belle.*"

A thrill of hope runs through me; I'm making assumptions I probably shouldn't. Aaron doesn't do anything without a reason, and I sense showing me his apartment couldn't be random. It is his privacy. Privacy he shared with me.

"It's very… you." Arrogant. Gorgeous. *Perfect.*

He throws his shirt on the table next to him, his bared muscular torso facing me. "It's a great night for a swim."

He unbuckles his belt before sliding his pants and underwear to the ground, his piercing gaze locked on me. Within a second, his Adonis body stands naked in front of me. His Greek god traits instantly make my body yearn for him. His predator's eyes pierce my soul. Wolf's charisma creates a fire exploding within me, consuming my little remaining self-control.

"Naked only, of course." A ghost of a smile stretches on his lips as his gaze travels the length of my fully dressed body.

He plunges in elegantly and swims underwater until reaching the end of the infinity pool. He passes his hands through his obsidian hair, pulling it away from his forehead. He throws his arms around the border of the pool, cocking his eyebrow, challenging me to take a leap.

He is the epitome of alpha and omega. Leader, dominant and controlling like an alpha. But he doesn't need anyone, he's making his own rules, his own things like an omega. He is my beginning, or my end. My savior, or my hell. Opposite and contradictory, but whole.

I bite my lower lip, feeling the rush of contradictory feelings colliding. My past, digging through the rest of my insecurities, leaving me standing here. My future, wanting to seize the opportunity to be at fifty floors up, to swim with my fallen god.

I take a deep breath and unzip my dress under his demanding stare, contemplating every inch of me. I can never hide with Aaron. I expose my whole self in a way I never did before. My belly is burning, and I lick my lip before feeling a fierce pain inside my heart at how gorgeous he looks. My hands start to shake, I feel my body agonizing in front of the hard truth I've tried to deny. Seeing him between darkness and light has made me realize…

I'm falling hard and fast without control for Aaron.

No warning.

No security.

No come back.

I slide my dress to the floor, confused by my feelings. I take a step closer toward the pool, standing in my red lace underwear. He swims toward me, his pupils darkening with desire. Without knowing it, slowly he is inking my soul until he possesses my entire human being. I let go of my heels before pulling my hair to my back. My eyes connect with his, giving me the strength to overcome my demons. I unclip my bra before swallowing my insecurities. I never thought I'd have the confidence to strip in front of a man. But seeing myself through his eyes, it's overpowering. I slide my bra to the floor as my breasts pop free. My nipples harden because of the cold air around us, and I let go of my panties, before sitting on the border of the pool next to him, putting only my toes in the water.

"Is something wrong?" He furrows his brow, trying to interpret my silence.

Yes. Everything is wrong. I'm aching for him so badly. I feel butterflies. I'm falling too hard. Too soon. And one sign from him will be enough to make me fall fully. Deeply. This is unreal. I shake my head, promising myself I will never let him *own* me. I can't possibly say the L world. Stephan damaged it for me. Everyone did. This is my secret.

He stands in front of me, water reaching his abs. His hands caress my thighs sensually before grabbing my waist and lifting me slowly to pull me closer to his chest. I wrap my legs around his hips and throw my arms around his neck, my breasts connecting with his chest, as I feel the water warming my body. He encircles his arms around my back, and I smile when I feel his hardness pressing against me, but this moment isn't about sex. It's more than that. We are taking our time until we can't take it.

I kiss his wet lips while his fingers tangle in my hair with a tender touch. Slow. Sensual. As if the world stopped spinning, as if everything is disappearing around us, except him. He brings us closer to the edge of the pool to admire the view, and I sit on his lap. He is making it so hard for me. He is torturing my soul without even knowing it.

"This is wonderful, Aaron." *You are wonderful.*

"I also have a gift for you, but that is for later." He grins, but I notice he is uncomfortable. He isn't used to the emotional connection. To proximity. But he is trying. For me.

He clears his throat before showing me the yellowish sky lanterns on the table next to us. "You know what those are for?"

"Not really." I know it is a cultural thing, but I have no idea what they're truly about.

"They're used for cleansing, letting go of everything that troubles you. They symbolize the beginning. A new you, sort of." He stops, struggling to find his words. "Since you're turning twenty-four today, I thought these could erase… some bad memories." I immediately think of Stephan's abusive touch. His devastating words that inked into my heart. The shameful insecurities he created in me.

I stare at Aaron, not finding the right words. He understands me. He knew what I need before I could possibly know it myself. He shows me he cares in his own way. The man who doesn't do romance, gives me today the promise of a future. The promise for us to let go of our demons. The ones who block our futures. The ones who don't allow us to heal.

"Thank you, Aaron." I smile smugly, trying to not sounds so emotional. "How I'm supposed to do it?"

"I'm not really sure. Just make a wish, your deepest desire, and then light up the lantern before sending it to the sky."

"Do it with me," I implore him my doe eyes.

Aaron clears his throat and analyzes me as if he is trying to find out if he can trust me. I take his hand and pull my body closer to his, my voice weak, attempting one more time to get him to open himself to me. "I know your past is off-limits but I…I want to know you. Everything about you."

A deep feeling of sadness washes over him as he takes a deep breath. "Do you remember the first night we arrived at the Canadian Grand Prix?" I nod. It was the day Monica called, and he was exhausting himself at the gym.

"Well, it was my brother's day of death. And I was with you, having such a good time that I—" He stares at the water, his eyes haunted. "That I forgot about it, until Monica made me remember." His mouth twists into a repulsive smile as if he is blaming himself for moving on.

"He died two years ago, and it was my fault." His voice is trembling, his emotions trying to take control. "I killed my brother, Elle." His piercing stare meets mine, and all I see is his pain.

I part my lips, holding my breath. "I'm sure it wasn't your fault," I whisper, caressing his arm to ease his soul. "I'm here, Aaron."

"You won't see me the same way."

"I doubt that." I bring my head to his chest, encircling his body with my arms, before looking up for him. "You can trust me."

He stares at me mournfully, as if he is ready to say goodbye. I take his hand into mine. "You can't keep everything to yourself." I give him an encouraging head nod, feeling he is about to tell me the truth.

After a long silence, he finally speaks. "That day, I had a fight with a bunch of nobodies. I was enraged." He furrows his brow like he is trying to erase a painful memory, his fists tighten, and his eyes redden. "I wasn't myself." He pulls away from me before staring, emotionless, at the view in front of us.

"I was supposed to bring my brother to a work meeting, but our car was at the mechanic to repair a fog light, so I borrowed Thomas' sports car instead." He clenches the border of the pool with his fists. "When I race, I forget. My brother was talking, but I was barely hearing him."

Wolf's expression turns into a disgustful look. "There was a traffic light, I know it was green. I saw it." His throat is trembling, his mouth is shaking, all his muscles are tensing. He turns to face me, a profound pain in his eyes. "I saw it green, Elle, I swear."

I take his hand while he peers away from me again. I try to blink away the tears that are already forming under my eyes, seeing him suffering like this. "So, I continued to race but I don't know what happened. A truck arrived from the other corner of the road at full speed. And slams into us. He was heading straight toward us without slowing down, I tried to turn the car away but it was too late. I'm a fucking Formula 1 driver and I couldn't—"

He thunders a scream of rage, and my heart drops. I struggle to stay standing up, feeling his whole pain as he continues to tell his personal nightmare. "I survived, but my brother... he died from the injuries of the accident. I couldn't save him. I fucking killed him." He walks away from me, his back facing me as if he doesn't want me to notice his agony.

I struggle to speak, erasing the tears that have wet my cheek. "Aaron, accidents happen. I can't imagine—"

"Why did death take him and not me?" he roars. "Every fucking day, I take risks on the track. I don't care if I die, but death keeps saving me. I should have died, not him!" There is only pain left in Wolf's soul. Just like his tattoo. The skull represents his brother's death, and the wolf... it's him. He is the lone wolf. An alpha wolf without a pack.

"We can't control death, Aaron." I can't imagine what he experienced. Seeing the person you love the most die in front of you is the most horrible thing. That's why Wolf never went to his brother's funeral. The shame. The guilt you must carry for destroying what was so precious to you.

"He was the good one. The one who should have survived. I'm just a—" He stops, furrowing his face in repulsion. "—A fucking mistake! His love for me was a mistake."

"Don't say that." I can't endure his pain. I can't let him destroy himself. For an inexplicable reason, everything he's inflicting on himself, he's inflicting on me, too. "The light was green, Aaron, you did nothing wrong!"

"I was the one driving, Elle. Recklessly. I could have avoided it," he erupts with rage. "What if I was wrong? What if the light was red and I—"

"Blaming yourself won't give you your brother back. It will just destroy you." My words are harsh, but I owe him honesty. There is no place for lies between us. "Henry would never have wanted this for you."

"I. Killed. Him." He stares at the pool as if it were his brother's blood.

I don't leave him another choice—I pull myself into his arms. "You are a good person. No matter what happened, you don't deserve this." I take his face into my palms. "You're not a mistake." I lean to find his lips, hoping to comfort him with a tender kiss.

"How can you not be repulsed by me? By what I did?"

"Because you're human. We make mistakes." I kiss him again, his eyes filled with darkness boring into me. "That the light was green or red, that you were mad that day or not, it doesn't change who you are. And you are the opposite of a bad person."

He strokes my cheeks. "You don't know everything about me."

"It won't change what I think of you." I manage a smile, knowing Aaron's brother's death isn't the only darkness in his life. He has other demons, but I'm not scared of ghosts. *Only of mine.* "Let's do this. A new beginning." I glance at the lanterns.

"New beginning." He swims toward the table to grab them and hands me one.

We stand in front of our lanterns. Even Aaron, who acts like he isn't a believer, takes this seriously and stares at his lantern, feeling torn. We are lost in the heartbreaking moment, that feels like a cleansing ritual to save our broken selves. I close my eyes, inhaling the fresh air, thinking about my biggest dream...

And I have one. The biggest and deepest of all.

I wish for Aaron to be free of his demons.

I wish we could heal together.

I wish for love and everything with him. I wish for the fairy tale I, once upon a time, dreamed about.

We light up our lanterns and throw them together in the sky. Aaron positions himself behind my back, his arms encircling my waist, making this moment even more magical. The lanterns fly deeper and higher in the sky, their light warming my soul. They dance together in circles, always finding their way back to each other—like they're magnetically attracted. I smile like a naive child amazed by the spectacle in front of her. I feel all of my emotions taking me at full speed, roaming into my whole body, making me feel alive. Living a romance I've never experienced before. This spellbinding moment will be engraved in my heart. This is a fairy tale scene symbolizing a new beginning. A tear slides down my cheek. How come releasing a simple light creates in me such deep emotions? I feel like I'm letting go of something in me. I know Aaron is watching me, but I couldn't look away or hide my emotions. I don't care if I'm being weak.

In the darkness, there are only two floating lanterns going higher and higher in the sky. Us in the middle of our darkness. Together.

"Thank you, Aaron. This means a lot." I turn to face him, tears of happiness on my cheek.

He erases with his thumb my tears, a protective look on his face. "What did you wish for?"

"I can't tell you or it won't come true," I say in a playful tone, even though—*I wished for you.*

"I wished for something I probably shouldn't." He shakes his head in disbelief, looking at our lights.

His lips captured mine, enhancing the exquisite torture as he switches sides and his back hits the border of the pool. I sit on his lap, needy of the proximity. I grab the edge as I let his hands caress each part of my aching body. I'm not afraid to be close to the edge. To fall down. Because I know. I know he'll be there. Not all men are the same. Not all the stories end up the same way. Ours is yet to be written.

Our kisses grow intense and my need for him becomes vital. He tastes like heaven while sending me into oblivion. He is my Elysian Fields rescuing me from the limbo. I'm trembling beneath his touch, our kisses growing more powerful, more celestial, until he breaks our contact and we catch our breath, regain our spirits. This is a moment for fondness, and when I look into Aaron's dismayed eyes, I know he reached his limit for tonight. Aaron isn't ready to make love to me. I throw my head up to watch the sky and our lanterns beautifully floating together as Aaron pulls me into a caring hug.

The light of our lantern fades slowly and eventually fall, while our bodies lighten up together on top of the world.

CHAPTER 23

Beautifully damaged

"Are you kidding me? It's just the entr'acte?"

I burst into laughter when Aaron sighs while passing both of his hands across his face and throwing his head backward. He attacks me with my pillow, and I giggle harder, lying on his lap trying to get back at him by throwing another cushion at him. He smirks, despite himself.

We've made a bet. We headed back to my place to watch a movie with my old-fashion projector. He said he could keep his focus for an entire movie, and I beg to differ. What he didn't know was that the movie in question was: *Gone with the Wind*, aka four hours. I obviously knew he wouldn't be a fan, but I appreciate his efforts for lasting two hours.

"Are you a sore loser, Mr. LeBeau?" I provoke, a naughty smile on my face.

"You're playing with fire, *ma belle*," he defies, cocking his eyebrow while leaning on top of me dangerously.

"I don't know what you're talking a—"

Too late. Aaron stands up from the couch and swoops me on top of his shoulders. I'm definitely weak under his manly body.

"Aaron! Put me down," I order in a non-convincing way, still laughing.

He walks toward my bathroom, carrying me over his shoulder like I'm weightless, and when he opens my shower faucet, I instantly know what he has in mind. He lets the water warm for a few seconds.

"Aaron! Don't even think about it!"

Too late. He puts me down in my shower, and it's just a matter of seconds before I'm fully wet while fully dressed. My white pajama is now transparent, and I know he is enjoying the show.

"I love to see you wet for me." He darts his tongue out of his mouth, his sinister smile spreading on his face.

"If I'm going down, you're coming down with me." I grab him by his shirt, pulling him toward me under the shower.

He follows, not even trying to resist me. We are now standing like two idiots fully dressed in my big shower. We laugh, wondering how we ended up here in the first place. Every moment with him ends up in something unexpected, he makes everything unique.

But then a series of events change the course of the night. I bite my lower lip. His eyes darken with desire. My breath quickens. He pins me against my shower wall. I'm burning. He's cursing.

Our lips collide in a rough explosion, without warning, without holding back. Our playful mood from earlier is now replaced by the need of the other. A burning passion irradiates from my whole soul, and it's uncontrollable. He cups my cheeks with his palms, claiming control over me, as I savor him fully.

In a matter of seconds, we've undressed each other, feeling impatient and needy. I encircle my leg around his hip as he squeezes it possessively, and he dots my neck with his addictive kisses. I run my nails down his back, not hiding the powerful effect he has on me. The transparent door of my shower becomes blurry from the fog all around us.

His predatory gaze is fixed on me, making me his prey—a not so innocent prey.

"I want to fuck you endlessly, deeply, fully, until you're entirely mine," he whispers in my ear, his longing for me in his husky voice. His fingers caress my naked flesh. "Until your body melts just at the thought of my cock buried inside you."

I'm aroused by his words. I'm bewitched by the contact of our skin. I'm consumed by the man who is my obsession. It's not healthy, it's brutal and addictive.

I want you to fuck me endlessly, deeply, fully, until you're irrevocably, unconditionally, mine.

And just like he has read my mind, his lips crush mine with intense fervor, creating a sweltering symphony, exposing our true need. The need to belong significantly. Together, we're creating a blistering explosion revealing our carnal need. I'm melting. Collapsing. Demanding more of the man who shakes my world upside down. Insatiable, he sets me on fire, driving me to a place I've never explored before.

He slams into me and ignites my world in an instant. My whole body responds to him at twice the intensity it has received. Moaning stronger. Squeezing harder. Falling deeper. He owns a piece of my soul, and I'm dominated by the lecherous ecstasy. I can't stop. I can't think. I'm caught between pain and pleasure, darkness and light, destructive feelings and healing ones, opposite and yet one can't exist without the other. Just like Aaron and me.

He thrusts deeper, harder, into me, his hands squeezing my waist more passionately. My eyes start to roll under his forceful pushes. I wrap my legs around his strong torso, incapable of standing anymore. He lifts me up and I submit my control to him. Multiple emotions explode within me. Passion. Eagerness. Possession. Our chemistry exploding in flaming animal sex. Our kisses violent, torrid, erotic.

He is a tornado of emotions, creating a devastating yet pleasurable spiral of sin. My emotions are colliding. I need him, fuck—*I need him so much*. I'm afraid he might leave me, I feel the pain of the day when I'll be insignificant. Can two broken people really overcome their fears and the damage their pasts have caused them? Or are we damned from the start and we're just hiding, lying to ourselves? He pushes into me, and I feel him inside my belly and yell out his name in my trembling voice.

"*Ma belle.*" He slows down, his predator gaze is now replaced by a genuine concern look. It feels like he was possessed, and hearing me brings him back. "Did I hurt you?" In just a flash, he switches from the possessive alpha male to a lost and broken man, as if he could sense the pain aching in my chest.

The pain to lose someone who was never mine in the first place.

Someone who never wanted to belong to anyone.

Our eyes connect, the only noise is the water still running. He knits his eyebrows and caresses my cheek with his thumb. *Don't be sweet, Aaron. Don't look at me like I'm precious to you. Don't torture my soul.* I feel emotions reaching through my eyes. *Not now. Remember Elle, don't be vulnerable.*

"Lose control." *I need you.*

"Elle. I don't want to hurt you." *Stop looking at me this way.*

"I want you to show me how much you want me." *I want your body to speak for the words we can't admit. I want you to make me forget I'm falling too hard.*

Our bodies connect more intensely than before. We're possessing each other until fully belonging to the other. Until our souls are endlessly marked. Until I believe I'm significant. His palms grab my wrists, pulling both of them against the wall, our kisses growing. I intertwine my fingers with his, digging my nails into his hands, as a heat invades my belly each time I met with his passionate thrusts. He is groaning. I'm moaning. He is slamming into me at different paces and intensity. I'm rolling my hips, abandoning myself to him. His gaze locks on me. I close my eyelids.

I feel hot sparks flash and let my orgasm explode inside me, rippling through every nerve in my body. He comes right after me, and we stay there breathless, his body capturing mine, our heads on each other's shoulders, my arms wrapped around him. My legs are shaking, trembling upon the intensity of our exchanges. He holds my waist, not letting me go. The hot water is warming us, washing away our sins, our heartbeats synchronizing.

A while later, he clears his throat and we pull away from each other. We exit the shower and get dressed. I dry out my hair quickly with the towel before I change into my silk rose-gold shorts and my crop top, while he stands with my towel surrounding his hips.

"Do you want to stay?" I ask, unsure of myself.

"I have an early flight tomorrow." His tone is dry, indifferent, just like nothing happened between us.

"Oh. Yes, sure." I manage a smile. "Well, I'll let you… finish. I—" I point toward my bedroom before passing my fingers through my hair as countenance to hide my emotions.

I exit the bathroom, running away from him to take a deep breath. I hop into my bed, my back facing the bathroom door, as I hug my bed pillow across my chest. He opens the door and doesn't say a word to me. I hear his footsteps leaving my bedroom as he walks toward the living room area.

I don't turn back. My heart is breaking again. He opened up to me in a way he never did, and yet I'm alone. I hear him sigh and grab his car keys as I close my eyes and a tear slides down. The front door closes brutally. Gone. I turn off my lights, wishing I could switch off my heart the same way. I was ready to fight for him, to give him the time he needs to open up. But Aaron takes what you offer to him willingly, he isn't afraid to go for what he wants. And he isn't afraid to leave once he obtains it. Nothing more. Nothing less.

I'm lost in my thoughts. The nightmares of my past begin to reach back to me. The tears of my mother after having her heart broken, warning me to never fall in love. The way my dad left me when I was crying on the floor after falling from the tree. The way Stephan used me. *They abandoned me.* I'm falling deeper into my broken past, until I feel someone pulling me away from my ghosts.

Aaron is behind me. He pulls himself under my sheets and spoons me into a hug, pulling me closer to his chest as he wraps me under his protective arms. He didn't leave. He battled his demons to stay, to be there when I needed him. For the first time in my life, I feel secure, as if someone is here to catch me. *He didn't leave me.* Not like the others.

"What are you doing?" I whisper.

"I have no idea." He squeezes me closer to his strong physique, and my whole body is warmed under his contact. "Is it okay?"

"It's more than okay." It's the proof I'm not insignificant. He lets me in, into his intimacy.

We intertwine our fingers together, our hands near my collarbone, his other arm under my head. I feel his breath near my neck before he kisses my nape softly. Just a simple hug warms my heart, this delicious moment eternally engraved. He squeezes me tighter, connecting our bodies like he is afraid to let me go. No matter how long it takes, I'll wait for him. We'll heal. His thumb caresses my fingers and the top of my breast before goose bumps travel the length of my whole body.

My heart is his. He can tear it apart, break it, it belongs to him in a way it never belonged to anyone before.

"It feels good," he whispers, falling asleep. "Having you in my arms, it feels good," he adds slowly.

"I'm yours." I smile, my eyes close, savoring *our* moment.

"I won't let you go."

He slides his hand under my top to caress my breast and cups it fully, while his other hand is still intertwined with mine. It's a first time for both of us. A proximity we feared for so long and yet is what we needed all along. Our thumbs caress each other's skin, and I fall asleep under his arms, knowing there is no coming back from this moment.

He shows me he is mine, too.

I wake up in the middle of the night suddenly.

Aaron is squeezing my body painfully, pulling it harder against him, hurting me under his strong grip. I gasp for air, incapable of pulling away. I ask him to not hold me so tight, but he doesn't answer. I try to move away, but he keeps throwing me back against him. Something is wrong. His palms are sweaty. His body is shaking. He is breathing heavily and moaning incomprehensible things. I try to calm down when I notice he is having a violent nightmare.

I finally succeed in pulling myself away from him and turn on the light in a rush. I notice the red mark of his grip on my wrist, and I feel my heart pounding in my throat. He is having a nightmare, a terrible one. His eyebrows are frowning, and a mask of terror is on his face. He is soaked in sweat and he is thrashing around in the bed. I've never seen him this way.

"Don't leave me with him. Don't abandon me," he yells, his breath quickens and shortens, he shakes his head hard.

He grabs the sheets around him, and I stand here, not knowing how to react. I panic and try to call out to him, but the more I'm speaking the more he seems to be hurting, fighting against something as his fists clench. I'm scared, seeing him facing such threatening and scary terrors. I want to help him, but I can't reach him—like he is stuck in limbo.

"Stop, Dad… no…" He keeps repeating it, his voice imploring something to stop. His dad? What's happening?

I shake him, imploring him to wake up. "Aaron, please wake up!" I cry out, terrified, probably doing all the wrong things.

"Yes, Dad. Yes, I am. Now, please, stop I—" He frowns his eyebrows, his eyelids and mouth shaking. All I see is a frightened kid stuck in his own hell.

I can't take it. I pull myself closer to his chest trying to hug him, to kiss him, anything to trigger him to wake up. I have no experience; I've never seen someone having such violent flashbacks. I've had a few nightmares about Stephan, but nothing as horrifying as his. *Aaron, come back to me.* The closer I get to him, the more I see his terror transform into violent hatred.

"Aaron, please."

"Don't touch me! I don't want to—" He grabs my wrists violently and continues to debate with his demons.

I keep repeating that it's me, that he has nothing to fear, but he doesn't hear me nor believe me and squeezes me harder. I understand at this moment that Aaron's past contains more than his brother's death. It's a succession of tragic events, leaving him haunted. Broken. I feel his pain. I feel his fear. It's nothing like I could have imagined it, nothing a normal human should be able to support. His need for control, his need to forget, his need to not get close to anyone—I understand.

I release my wrist by turning it into the exterior, before cupping his face with my palms, imploring him to wake up, I want to end his torment, but at the approach of my contact, he pushes me violently out of the bed. I fall down on the carpet. I'm lost. Confused. Heartbroken.

He gasps for air and jerks up out of the bed. He looks around him, his eyes full of fear. He is breathing heavily, as if he doesn't know where he is. His face is flushed, and his pupils are dilated. He panics, throwing his hands around his hair, searching for something. Probably for me. I hear him cursing fuck, his body still shaking, as he blinks forcefully looking at the floor to try to calm himself. *Oh, Aaron, what happened to you…*

I'm out of breath, unable to speak. I try to stand up, but I'm shaking after what I've witnessed and immediately fall back on my buttocks. His gaze finds mine, and his expression changes radically. He notices my tears, looks at the bed, and back at me in a petrified way. He takes a few steps back, hitting the wall behind him. He swallows harshly, his mouth shaking. His eyes are wet, and he curves his lips into an expression of disgust. I hide the marks he left by squeezing my wrist too hard with my other hand. But it's too late. He has seen it. He shakes his head saying no, walking backward along the length of the wall, keeping his distance from me. He thinks he hurt me. It's destroying him.

"Elle."

Ashamed. Lost. Vulnerable.

He isn't my downfall. I'm his.

CHAPTER 24

Hell-Bound

"I—I'm sorry, I—"

He can't find his words. He mumbles, repeating the word *sorry* like a mantra. He stares at me, lost and confused. The Aaron I know—so confident, cocky, powerful—is gone and replaced by a side of him I've never uncovered before. Regrets. Pain. Blame. His broken part emerged for the first time in the most violent way.

He passes his hands through his hair. It's as if I can hear from here the palpitations of his heart. He has sweat drowning the length of his Apollo body. His remorse is taming him, enslaving him to his pain. I know he is sorry, it's not his fault if he is haunted by something stronger than him. I've felt ashamed for so long from the way Stephan treated me, but Aaron made me see the light.

I want to be his light in the darkness of our pasts colliding.

I stand up from the floor, my legs still shaking. I swallow, feeling that each second of my silence is a second closer to losing the man who changed my whole self. The man who helped me gain confidence and overcome my fears is now the one in need. I need to remain strong. I take a step closer to him, whispering his name, but he takes a step backward, shaking his head. I'm losing him. I remain still, hoping I'll be enough.

"I'm fine, Aaron." I'm not afraid of him, nor of his past. We knew we were broken, and it was just a matter of time before our demons manifested. My soul is in pain. I'm crashing with him. I take a step toward him again. I won't let him go.

"Don't come near me, Elle." He swallows harshly, his nostrils flare, his pupils darkening of hatred. The inside of his eyes is the color of Hell, his lips still curved in repugnance.

"Aaron. You didn't hurt me." Abhorrence, horror, atrocity, are consuming the broken soul of the man who was my savior. He doesn't belong here. He is worth so much more than what he inflicts on himself.

"I did this. Don't you see it, Elle? I fucking hurt you! I'm a freaking monster! I'm just like—" he roars, his eyes spreading flames of rage, as he turns his back on me, banging his elbows violently on the wall, his head down.

He curses and searches for his clothes, dressing quickly. He wants to escape me. Escape us. I won't let his demons win. I rush toward the door, blocking his way. I don't want him to leave like this. I probably should give him the time he needs, the space he requires, but I know Aaron. All or nothing. I need to tell him before he blames himself, before he creates a devastating tornado transforming the both of us into ashes.

"I want to be there for you. You don't have to talk to me, but let me be here," I implore him.

"You heard." He turns to face me, staring at me like I'm a ghost, his tone is dry, menacing, authoritative. He is terrified about me knowing something about him. Something that happened to him.

"No, Aaron. I couldn't understand and—"

"Elle. Get. Out. Of my way." He stands in front of me, looking down, his powerful demons trying to dominate me.

I take a step toward him, my hands caressing his chest. But it's not the same. He doesn't react. My touch doesn't awaken him anymore. It's... hurting him? Tearing him apart? I reach for his cheek, for our eyes to connect to feel the proximity, to give myself to him, to let him use me. I want to make him forget, but he grabs my wrist and pushes my hand away.

I yell at the contact, the pain and mark his nightmare caused still tender. He takes my hand softly on his, and his expression becomes paralyzed when he peers over the mark he created. His fingers caress my skin around the mark as I see him falling apart slowly and fully. I call out to him, but he doesn't answer nor react.

A mark will heal, but I know he'll never forgive himself. He squeezed me under the fear of his nightmare. He squeezed me because he needed someone. And, in the end, he inked his nightmare into my skin. He shared his pain with me, and that, he can't handle. He always tries to protect me, and tonight he was the one destroying me. The step he took tonight for me is the reinsurance that he doesn't belong with me. He closes his eyelids, and I notice a subtle tear sliding down his face. He swallows hard, his eyebrows and eyelids trembling.

"Aaron…" Tears are spreading, bleeding across my face.

"I don't need you, Elle. Stop trying to save me. You're desperate!" he shouts, taking me by surprise with his violent tone.

"You don't mean that."

"I fucked you. Now, I just want to go home. You were a mistake." Pupils dilated, he stares wide-eyed at me. He is gone, drowning with his nightmares, selling his soul to the darkness. His cruel words sink into my heart and blacken my soul. They are meant to push me away, to make me give up on him.

"I'm not going anywhere."

He looks at the ceiling, at every angle of my room except me. When his expression is back on me, a dry smirk appears on his face, making my stomach turn.

"I will. Never. Love. You. I played with you for my own amusement. Remember, just an agreement?" he says harshly. Brutally.

"I'm not going anywhere," I repeat slowly.

"I'm bored with you. I was in it just for fucking. And I did fuck you good, right? You were just a challenge. Now you're old news." When I don't react, he continues his cruelty. "I told you about my brother, hoping to be finally done with you. I came here to fuck you out of my life, nothing more."

"Aaron, you're hurting me, don't say that," I howl, my heart bouncing across my chest. I'm hurting. Breaking. I want to fight for him, but his words are devastating me. I don't want to believe him—but it could be true. My demons begin to crash into me, I don't know what to think, how to fight them.

"You're insignificant to me, Elle." He articulates every word, taking a step closer as I take a step backward. It feels like he has put a dagger into my heart. Making it bleed. Tearing it apart. Ripping it bloodily.

"It's not true! Aaron, look at me!" I cry out, tears sliding down my cheeks when I find his gaze empty. Blank. Without any emotions. "You're making me feel worthless, you're humiliating me." *Don't do this to me, Aaron. Don't do like he did. Don't push the one button in me that will make me fall apart and break me again.*

"Because it's what you are to me. And to everyone else."

To everyone else... he hits me with the hard truth. The truth that opens the hole of my insecurities. The truth that can devastate me. I collapse on my bed, not feeling strong enough to stand. I feel humiliated in a way I've never felt. Some words are destructive, cataclysmic, detrimental.

"I hate you," I yell out, my face on my pillow, as my pain is crippling me, ravaging my whole self.

"Good. And you'll keep hating me for your own good."

I hear him leaving without a word. He closes the door, exiting my life. This is over. The silence consumes me. Alone. Broken. He is my downfall, and he broke me in unexpected ways. I've reached the abyss of my soul, I'm bruising and I can't heal.

I hate him the same way I've fallen for him. Deeply, fully, without warning until I crashed. Until he left me, taking my soul with him.

I don't know for how long I sit next to my bed, looking blankly at the wall in front of me, surrounded by my darkness. Daytime begins to rise, and I feel like death, replaying the events of a few hours ago. I feel empty. My hatred is gone, I feel nothing. Chaos. He is like a poison running through my veins. He took my dignity, and everything with him when he left.

We were so close, but the closer we have become, the deeper we have fallen.

I look over my wrist. His mark is gone. Just like him. But the pain he caused inside my heart can't be erased, it won't heal. He is a part of me, we connected through our darkness, we hid behind our passion, and we caused destruction. We can't love. We aren't capable of such a pure feeling.

My doorbell rings, bringing me back to reality. I pray for the person to leave, I'm not in the mood for anything. I just want to hide and cease to exist. But it keeps ringing and ringing, creating a deafening noise, hurting my ears. I get up, pissed, and open the door violently.

"Good morning, Miss Monteiro. I have a delivery for you." An old man dressed in a fancy suit stands with a commercial smile as he hands me a huge wooden box, probably one by one meter, with a *fragile* sign on it.

I take the package, looking at it with confusion. There is no address on it. No shipment date. No expeditor. "I haven't ordered anything. This must be a mistake."

The man looks over his document, playing with his glasses, before smiling at me again. "Mr. LeBeau requested a week ago for our company to deliver this to you today. Can you sign here?"

Aaron? I don't understand. This must be a joke. Probably more of his games. A new way to makes me feel insignificant. A thank-you note for fucking me. I sign the paper in dubiety, and the man leaves, calling someone. I close the door and set the box on my living room table. I take a cutter and decide to open it, in spite of myself. Inside the box, I distinguish something well-cushioned under the tons of bubble-wrap and rigid Styrofoam. I cut all of it, to see what's inside.

I believe it's a painting. At least, the back of a painting. My heart starts to bounce. My cells come to life again. I feel suddenly afraid to turn over the painting, to face what it could be. My breath quickens. I stand in front of it, incapable of turning it around. I finally find the courage and face the hard truth. I exhale violently, my breath cut, as I take a step back, noticing what it is. This can't be. It's not possible. I stay shocked, unable to speak or to think.

It's a Romeo Di Angelo. And not just a Di Angelo painting but the one, *Everlasting*. The painting that saved my childhood, that comforted me, the one that accompanied me my whole life. The one I have as a print in the middle of my living room. The significant one. My dream. My hope. My idea of romance. How could he remember? How could he know? I must be dreaming. It's unbelievable.

The mark is engraved, it's the original dating from 1856. I shake my head, this can't be true. I try to remember, searching on my phone for the proofs to collide. I find a few articles. The painting was in an auction a week ago in Italy. It had been sold to an anonymous buyer for ten million. There is a picture of the woman who bet for her client in question. I recognize her. It's Francesca Vermont, the heiress. The one I was jealous of. The one who was photographed with Aaron on the same date.

He did it for me. I find the contract attached to the painting. The contract stipulates the painting belongs to me. It's signed by the auction house—and Aaron, who paid in full for the painting. He bought a Di Angelo for me. I stand breathless, my emotions cannoning together. I knew Aaron was incredibly rich, but this is something else. Something significant. I don't know what to think, what to believe.

The man who just left, breaking my heart, telling me I'm worth nothing to him, just bought me the greatest gift I could ever wish for. He went to Italy. He remembered something I told him months ago. He gave me my dream, my escape. He did something incredibly romantic and galvanizing.

You can only believe, I'm afraid. Those were the words he told me at the club. Words can be lies. Actions are proof. I stare over the painting, crying the rest of my heart out.

I was significant.

Until he broke me to free myself from him.

He is capable of the greatest and of the worst. My savior or my downfall.

Devastating or healing.

Hell-bound or Heaven-sent.

He is the man I love.

PART II
HEAVEN-SENT

Significant *adjective*
/sɪgˈnɪfəkənt/
Synonyms: Unique. Heaven-sent. Unforgettable.
1. Something you can't ignore. Something that shakes your world.
2. The thing that matters the most.
3. The one who understands you.
4. Elle Monteiro.

CHAPTER 25
The sea, the waves, the sand

Eight years old.

Dishes breaking.
    Screaming.
    Darkness consuming.
    I sit upon the stairs, my face between the railing. Men don't cry. Men don't hide. Father was right, I'm a little boy. Maman yelps one more time before I hear a cracking loud sound. Henry told me to stay in bed, but I cannot. I dream of monsters, again. The stairs creak when I step closer to the kitchen. The wailing. The bouncing. I want Maman to hug me. Other boys' parents hug them—but not my parents.
    I open the door of the kitchen to stare at Papa, his arm clutching Maman whose tears have swallowed her face. He looks enraged, like the monster of my nightmare. Papa is a scary man, especially when his vein pops up on his forehead. Everyone is scared of him, no one says no to him, and when I grow up, I wanna be like him. A man and not a boy anymore.
    Maman is howling that she loves Daddy so much that she wishes that

he dies. And now, Maman is laughing with blood on her teeth. *What's wrong with Maman?* She's usually beautiful. Grown-up people said I look just like Maman, but now she is looking… dirty?

"Aaron!" Papa stares, furious at me, before grasping my arm violently, and I howl under his painful touch.

Why is Papa hurting me? He throws me against the wall, making me stumble and fall on the tiling. Blood. Oh no. The blood of my knee is spreading over my pajamas. It hurts, but I won't cry. I glance at Maman, but she stares at me emotionless. Papa grabs my collar, forcing me to stand up. I don't like his breath. It smells like the bottles he hides in his cabinet. It smells rotten.

"You're gonna stay here, Aaron, and watch. If I see you move or cry, I'll get very angry. *Compris?*" I nod. I never say no to Papa. But my body is trembling. I should have listened to Henry. I'm doing all the wrong things.

"Leave the kid alone, André," Maman spits before rolling her eyes.

Papa laughs wickedly before bending Maman over the kitchen counter. "You never wanted him, Monique."

Papa grabs Mother's hair, fitting it into a fist like girls who wear ponytails. I see Maman closing her eyelids, while her throat is exposed in front of me; it seems to hurt Maman. "She never loved you, Aaron. Your mother is a whore. A cheating whore." He pushes her head back on the table, her legs opening wider. *Don't close your eyes, Aaron, or Papa will be mad again.* "I've given her a choice. Leaving with you, or accepting money and leaving us alone. And you know what she chose? Tell him, Monique." My hands are sweating, my throat is dry, my belly turns into a knot. *What Papa is talking about?*

"Money. I'm sorry, Aaron. I just can't. Forgive me—" Maman starts to howl, tears in her eyes, as Father covers her mouth with his fingers. *Leaving me? But Maman loves me!*

Papa unzips his pants as he takes Mom's hair into his fist again. I'm scared. I take a step forward toward Maman, I don't like what Papa is doing. He has an evil look on his face, it terrorizes me. But Papa points his finger at me, ordering me to not step forward.

"She chose money instead of you. She's a whore, and tonight she'll be treated like one in exchange for money." My mouth starts to shake, and tears are in my eyes. *Father is cruel and Maman doesn't love me.*

I close my eyelids, thinking this is all a nightmare. Breath Aaron. Think about your happy place. And it works. I don't hear the sob, the screaming, I just see the ocean. The sea. The waves. The sand. Until I hear Father's voice. "I told you to watch, Aaron!" I open my eyes wildly, a knot in my throat—I feel like I'm unable to breathe. "I'll show you how to treat a woman."

And then Papa hurts Maman. I hear a slamming sound, making Maman bounce all over the counter. Her legs spread, her skirt up. *Are they making a baby?* Papa is brutal, slapping Mama like Grandfather does to punish Henry and me when we behave badly. But Maman becomes red and—*I can't*—I can't watch that.

"Stop! Papa, stop!" I cry, collapsing against the wall. This is just a nightmare. Think about your happy place. *The sea. The waves. The sand.*

But Papa turns me around and slaps my cheek brutally. I looked away. I went against his orders. He pushes me on the floor, and even more blood comes. No. Not again. I look up, begging for Dad to stop, but my papa is gone. Only hatred. A monster. Papa's *thing* is pointed up at me, it's big. He stands me up and leads me by squeezing my hair to take a seat on the chair, to watch Maman from her profile. I cry out for her, but Maman stares blankly into nothing, telling me to stop crying. *Why isn't Maman dressing herself? Or moving?* Maman doesn't want that.

Papa continues to brutalize Maman, doing what beasts do in nature. Making babies. This is disgusting. I look away, but Dad's voice frightens me. So I watch, but blood reaches my head, my body is trembling, and— Oh, no. I vomit on the floor. I'm in trouble. Papa makes a deep groan before pushing Maman away and telling her to take her bags and leave immediately. I call out for Maman, opening my arms for her to hold me and take me to bed. I don't want to be alone with Papa, he scares me.

When she stares at me, I know Maman is gone, too. She mouths to me, "One day you'll forget." And she leaves. Abandoning me. Maman will never come back. She was wrong. I can't forget what Papa did to her. I'm cold. Dirty. Ashamed. I did nothing to protect Maman. *It's my fault.* If Maman never had me, would Papa never have hurt her? Papa walks toward me before he pushes me against the refrigerator. *Is he gonna hurt me, too?*

"Now, you belong to me, Aaron. Only me. I'm the only one who could ever love you, you know that, right?" Papa shakes my shoulders, forcing me to nod yes. I can't stop my tears. Maman said she loves Papa, and now she's gone. Papa says he loves me, but I'm terrified. Is this what love is? *I wish to never love.* "I love you, Aaron. That's why I need to tame you. I'm gonna shape you until you're just like me. And don't forget women are whores, just like your mother. You love me, right? Tell me."

A dry smile curves on his lips, and I feel disgusted. I want to vomit again. I nod at my father as he shakes my shoulders once more. He asks me to speak louder, yelling at me. I close my eyelids and cry out, "Yes, Papa. Yes, I love you. I'll never leave you."

"So if you love me, you'll do as I say. You'll obey me. You'll watch until you don't turn your eyes, like a man, okay? You'll be like me, son." *But I'm scared, Dad. I don't want to be like you.* My head is heavy, I feel my heart inside of it, and I'm spinning. Again? He'll do this again? No. No. No.

The sea. The waves. The sand.
The sea. The waves. The sand.
The sea. The waves. The sand.

Submitting because I love*d* Dad.

I learn and promise myself three things.

1) Loving someone is hurting them. Love = pain. *So, if I'm like Papa, I'll hurt people? So, I'll love no one.*

2) I promise myself I will never love. *And no one will love me.*

3) I'm ashamed. No one could love me, apart from Papa—*André.* If humans have a soul, mine is broken. *The sea. The waves. The sand.*

No more feelings. I don't want to feel pain anymore.

Love transformed me into a slave.

CHAPTER 26

Bound by blood

Present time

I can't forget the expression of disgust on her face. Her doe eyes wild as she collapsed on her bed. I broke her. I did it to protect her from me. The thought of hurting her is eating me alive, I had no choice. I couldn't let her see *me*. *Fuck*. Hopefully, she'll forget my existence. She deserves better. Fucking nightmare. The first time I let myself get close to someone and this happened. I saw my grip on her wrist, it was red. I bruised her. I became just like André. That's the price I had to pay for breaking my rules. How could she ever look at me the same way? She fucked me. I can't think straight.

I swore to never let feelings consume me. I don't feel. I don't have a heart. I'm used to pain. But her eyes terrified, the pain I've caused—it goddamn hurts. Usually, I would have used a distraction to forget. But racing isn't enough. I could still go for a quick fuck, but I can't. Other women aren't Elle. They're insignificant.

Elle.

Only Elle.

Fucking obsession.

"You should let go, Aaron." I awaken from my thoughts as my eyes dart to André sitting in his renaissance couch in our family manor. He's like a shadow, hiding in the darkness of the curtains, stopping the light from entering. A cold smile spreads on his face. The bastard is enjoying this.

He made me who I am. And he's proud of his creation.

"Why did you ask me here, André?" I swore to myself when I turned eighteen to never see him again. And I didn't, until Henry's death. Since that day, he's trapped me with him. I'm his only son left. His legacy. Which means, he's trying to ruin my life, to shape me as his own project.

As he said, we are bound by a chain only death can break. I wish death didn't take her sweet time.

"I want you to take over LeBeau's hotel." I snort. Wrong son, André. "You owe me for what happened to Henry." The features of my face close, hearing the name of my dead brother. André never had a heart, but for an unknown reason, he was less cruel to Henry. I'd prefer to die than to work for him.

He stands from his chair before walking slowly toward the ray of light in front of his desk, our eyes connecting like blades. "I haven't told you, but I'm sick, Aaron. I have a terminal illness." He swallows, his jaw trembling. Of course, he's afraid of death. He'll not go to heaven or shit like that. "I have multiple system atrophy. I doubt I have a long time now."

My jaw clenches as I scan over André, searching for the truth. But when I see fear and cowardice in his eyes, a smirk eradicates my lips. He's afraid to die. He knows he'll die alone. Good. I hate my father for everything he has done to me, for breaking me, turning me into his personal project.

"I'd never work for you. You can give your money to someone else, I don't want to be in your fucking will," I reply deadly, but André laughs wickedly.

"You don't even have a heart for your dying father? I taught you well." He coughs before standing in front of me with his imposing figure. But I'm not a little kid anymore. I'm a man he cannot abuse. "You are mine, Aaron. You don't want to turn your back on the only person that loves you." *I don't want your freaking love.*

"You don't have a choice, Aaron. If you go against my will, I'll destroy you." Even in his dying hours, this man is up to tame me until the end. But I won't give him that satisfaction. I'll get to watch him die unsatisfied, and that's my gift.

"So, do so. Destroy me, *Father*." I articulate each of my words, leaning toward him. "You already broke me, you can't do anything else."

I walk away, his dry laugh resonating through my mind.

Elle

The past weeks seem like years. I see him, my downfall, everywhere, and my heart rips with the same intensity each time. I've tried to paint, but the truth is, my creativity was linked to Aaron. I broke so many canvases. I tore down everything I did. He was my inspiration and my damnation. Without him, I'm just a ghost. People are talking, laughing, living and I—am stuck in limbo. He has been impregnated in me, I can't deny that we have been. I've spent most of my time losing myself, staring at the painting he bought me. Crying. Begging for him to come back. I realize he pushed me away on purpose, but the fact he let go so easily of me, scares me. I know he could come back, only on his terms.

Tania and Joshua have tried everything to cheer me up. But as extreme as Aaron and I have been, we've bruised each other until we cannot forget. By being each other's escape, by using each other, we've trapped ourselves into an endless nightmare. I've looked over my phone so many times. I should have fought more for us. But I can't. We need time to heal, and maybe one day, destiny will bring us back together.

Flashes spark. The crowd of reporters push me in front of the barrier, and I suddenly emerge back to reality. My heart starts to shake, my gut haunting me. Goose bumps run coldly down my spine at the approach of the French multibillionaire, owner of several luxury resorts. He steps onto the stage to take place in front of the microphone followed by his security guards. The businessman waves at the crowd, exposing his charismatic figure with a dry smile. He makes my stomach turn, as I swallow hard. I can't believe Celebrity Magazine chose him for the upcoming article about men married to their careers. Men of power. And of course, I was the one assigned the mission for one reason.

He is André LeBeau. Aaron's father.

Everything about him is imposing. From his six-foot height to the square, sharp edges of his face showing his authoritative personality. His deep black eyes are contrasting with his silver-gray hair pulled back perfectly from his forehead with gel. André LeBeau is approximately fifty years old, and yet judging by the cut of his tuxedo, he is in shape for a man of his age. He has the typical Mediterranean tan; his white teeth are the only thing illuminating his face. He seems like the type of boss who doesn't take no for an answer, that he has the power to break you if you make one false move.

Aaron's father adjusts his tie, and when his gaze meets mine, a wicked, dry smile stretches on his face. I instantly gasp for air, Aaron's nightmare resurfacing in my mind. I remember him staring at me wide-eyed, petrified, his face flushed, his pupils dilated. If he had the power to break Aaron, the man who is known to be indomitable—it could only mean one thing. I take a step back from the front row feeling a dominant and enigmatic vibe from his father that scares me. The Lebeaus exude power in a different way. With Aaron, I felt safe. With his father, I feel trapped.

The national TV journalists, all the media fall silent the moment André LeBeau starts to speak. He announces his prestigious hotels' chain expansion to Abu Dhabi, a business choice that places him at the top of the list of Forbes richest men. "I'll take your questions now." He projects his voice, rogue and authoritative.

In a matter of seconds, journalists transform themselves into sharks, pushing to get closer, speaking louder to be heard. André LeBeau answers only the questions of men, ignoring the few of us women standing here. It's clear that for a man like him, women are good at only two things: the kitchen and the bedroom.

Suddenly, the questions take another direction. "What about your son, Aaron LeBeau? Will he join the family business after his racing career is over?"

"Hopefully. However, he has more of a reckless temperament, it's hard to predict." The crowd laughs at Aaron's father's comment.

Another reporter follows up. "Do you support your son's racing career?"

The questions continue to aim toward Aaron, and I realize something is off. This is a setup. All the reporters were meant to ask the questions in advance. It was in André LeBeau's plans to talk about his son at the launch of his overseas business from the beginning. But, why? What motive could he possibly have?

He remains silent, shaking his head, as he inhales for a few seconds. "The truth is, I've hidden something from you." The crowd falls silent, and I'm fearing the worst. "As you know, two years ago, my son and I had suffered a great loss." He swallows, knitting his eyebrows together almost like he is giving a *fake* performance. "My older son, Henry, died in a car crash, the seventh of June."

I almost fall down as the crowd passes in front of me, yelling their questions at the businessman. The reason of the accident has been hidden for two years, and now he reveals it? It doesn't make sense. My thoughts go instantly toward Aaron and how this announcement will hurt him.

"That's the time your son's career started to change drastically," a reporter comments as another question follows.

"Is his reckless driving related to his brother's death? Can you tell us why he never went to his brother's funeral?"

"My son, Aaron, is emotionally unstable," André says in a condolent tone, with fake display of emotion. *Jerk.* "I'm hoping one day, he'll heal completely."

This is career suicide to put Aaron in the spotlight like that. He is waiting to sign his contract; revealing this now is the worse timing. It shows how dangerous Aaron could be.

"I don't want to lie to you anymore. I'm not perfect, I've made mistakes, but today it's about moving forward. So, I want to say to my son…" He pauses for a long moment, the crowd gasping for air, waiting for the juicy news to come out, cameras braking on him, my stomach turning into a knot.

"Son. I forgive you." His gaze is stuck on the camera.

No.

André waves at the crowd with rigidity, before looking at me for the second time, his eyes defying me. I swallow, struggling to keep eye contact with him, his cold look making my skin shiver. He leaves, escorted by his bodyguards as the questions of the reporters rise.

"Does that mean Aaron LeBeau had any implication in his brother's accident?"

"Sir! What did you mean by that?"

The questions don't stop, even after André LeBeau leaves. The journalists want more of this scandal, and they won't stop. I advance in the opposite direction, trying to exit this media manifestation. André implied the worst for Aaron with his comment. He already feels responsible for his brother's death, doing this now is like stabbing him in the back right when he's finishing his season. I can't imagine how Aaron or even Monica will feel after this announcement. The media will harass him in to giving answers. Henry's memory will be tarnished by a media-worthy story. My heart is bleeding, I need to know how he feels. But first, I need to leave.

"Aaron LeBeau's past is finally revealed, right before signing his next season contract," the reporter announces, the cameras of national television braking on her.

I hide my face, fearing they'd recognized me, and run toward my car to have some privacy. I open my phone and notice a few missed calls from Nina telling me to come back ASAP. Tania is informing me the calls at the office are blowing up. Great. I need to stay calm. I take a deep breath and dial Aaron's phone number. It goes straight to voicemail.

I leave the message, struggling to speak. "Aaron, it's Elle… I heard your father's speech. I'm… I'm sorry I—I'm here if you need me. I hope you are okay. Please call me back."

When I'm back at the office, Joshua fills me in quickly. Nina Braham has been on the phone with the director of the business magazine OC and the national sports channel a few moments ago. They want some information relating to Aaron's brother's death. Wolf, usually so secretive, whose past and secrets have never been uncovered, are now the source of worldwide attraction. This is too juicy for the media, it's the best thing that has happened to them since a royal wedding. They'll go to any length to have info and to be the first ones.

Which means I would be their number one candidate as a columnist, and one of the closest people to Wolf. I hope I'm wrong. I hope I won't have to deliver the article that could ruin Aaron.

I enter Nina's office as she stands up from her desk, looking shaken. "I need to have an inside scoop of the whole Aaron situation." She walks toward me, putting her hands on my shoulders and giving me a fake smile, while she guides me to take a seat.

"You know what this means? You get to write an international article outside your column. This can be the beginning of everything! And I'm talking about international exposure here. Multiple translations. Invitations to talk shows." She smiles wickedly, taking a seat behind her desk. "Of course, I'll increase your paycheck. Welcome to the big leagues. I'm so proud of you." She grins as she throws her pencil on her desk, leaning back in her seat.

"You can't ask me to write an article about my *boyfriend's* past." I shake my head as her dragon's eyes crash flames at me.

"A good columnist knows how to have the right information. Plus, his secrets won't stay hidden for long. We need to be the first ones to uncover the truth about what happened to LeBeau's brother." She analyzes my reaction, her eyes sparkling at the vision of all the money and fame the magazine could win with my upcoming article. "You know what happened, don't you?"

"That's not the point. You know, I can't write this article," I assure her. "It will destroy him…" I can't betray Aaron; no matter what happened between us, I care for him deeply. I can't be bought. I will not serve her Aaron's past on a silver platter. I'm not that type of person.

"You need to be a shark if you want to succeed."

"I'm sorry. I can't," I murmur, my voice trembling, fearing what's next.

"If you refuse, Elle, I'll make sure no one will ever employ you. I can destroy you." She leans toward me, her eyebrow arching. "You can kiss your career goodbye, and your reputation." She shakes her head, a repulsive smile on her face. "I knew this was a bad idea! How could you let your career go to ashes just for a man?"

I swallow my feelings, as I know she won't hesitate to use her power to ruin me—and Nina could easily. If the media are sharks, she is the megalodon. At my silence, her face softens and a wicked smile stretches on her lips.

"Plus, he is Aaron LeBeau. Is a man really worth sacrificing your whole life? You might be the flag he claimed this season, but he won't commit to you. Don't be naive."

I remain silent for a moment, knowing it already happened. That he claimed me and left. *But Aaron has been good to me.* "You're wrong, Nina. Not all men are like—"

She pushes her fists on her table before lifting herself up from her chair, anger in her eyes. "Stop being naive, Elle! You're being weak! He's manipulating you!"

"He's not. Aaron is genuine, kind, generous and loving. He's—" A smile curves on my face, thinking about him. Maybe she'll understand? I start regaining hope, thinking Nina wouldn't mind, but then I meet her icy eyes. The last time I saw this paralyzed expression on Nina's face was when... *he left.*

She points her finger at me, her hand and mouth shaking. Oh, no. My hands are sweaty, I feel my pulse on my neck. *I shouldn't have said that.* Her eyes are wild, like she's trying to keep them open so her tears won't fall on her cheeks. She advances toward me like she's possessed, scanning me as if I've committed an unholy crime.

"I didn't think it was serious between you." She stares at the floor blankly, like her soul left her body. She thought I was just using Aaron for information, that's why she was proud. "But you actually fell for that freaking bastard?" She articulates each word with disgust as she glares at me, making me feel little and ashamed of my feelings.

"Did you fall for him, Elle?" She clutches my arm, and I can't contain my tears anymore. I cry and betray my feelings. I shake my head—no, I cannot admit that to her. I cannot tell her I went against everything she taught me. She'll resent me.

She shakes her head as my tears speak for themselves. She lets go of my arm, taking a step away like I'm infected with sickness. "After everything I did for you, everything I taught you! Stupid child, you didn't listen to me."

"Aaron isn't my father," I howl, my voice begging her to hear me out.

Her eyes meet mine once more, her mouth closes, her lips shaking and curving toward her chin. "Men are the same. They use our weakness against us. He doesn't love you, he uses you. I read it all about him. This will get you nowhere."

"Because Stephan did?" Tears fall on my cheeks. Aaron might not be perfect on paper, judging by his background and reputation, but he taught me how to live again. I was a dead rose without petals, just thorns. And thanks to him, I grew back. I regained my petals.

"You messed up things with him last year, and I forgave you. Don't disappoint me, twice." I feel my world collapsing. She never wanted to listen to what Stephan did to me. She never knew. She just cared about his superficial, perfect facade of him.

"Stephan broke me, *Mother!* Because of you! I went with him and suffered because of you!" I cry out and collapse on the floor, my knees at her feet, ready to admit to her the horrible mental torture I suffered. "You don't know how he treated me and—"

Nina stares in front of her, her chin up, disdaining me. She ignores the tears forming under her eyes and remains like a general at war. No pity. No heart. No love. "I told you to not fall for a man. You can't put that on me." *But you won't listen.*

"It's not my love for him that destroys me, Mother. It's my love for you."

She's too proud. Rigid and cold as ice. Her mouth starts to shake again, and one of her tears hits my cheek—but she is still turning a blind eye to the truth. The truth that, by trying to protect me, she broke me and inflict chaos into my life. She took my love. She stole my job by becoming my boss. She made me forget my dreams by trying to accomplish hers.

She created my pretty cage, chaining me into a life I never wanted, breaking my wings. During all this time, I was the bird.

"The article, Elle. It's your last chance. If you don't, I'll never forgive you. You'll lose me for a man that will play you."

So this is what's going to be, losing the hope to find again my mother behind Nina's mask or losing the man I love who never wanted to be mine in the first place.

I nod, stand up, and leave.

Either way, I'll lose.

CHAPTER 27

Everlasting

Elle

I've been calling and texting Aaron. Of course, he is unreachable. He shut down his social media. He couldn't escape his father's words. I just watched his last race of the season, in which he placed P5. A pretty bad position for Wolf, but yet he still claimed the world champion title. I'm proud of him, he deserves it. But seeing him, on screen, it hurts. I increase the sound, watching Wolf doing a press conference because of his title—a title tarnished by the questions of the reporters.

"Your mindset wasn't on the race. Does it have anything to do with your brother's death?" a reporter asks.

Another question follows. "You claimed the world champion title and yet your contract isn't secure for next year. How do you feel?"

"Are you close to your brother's fiancée, Monica? Is it the reason why you never came to his funeral?"

My heart broke when I see Aaron staring at the floor blankly, completely mute. When his eyes meet the cameras, I know he is breaking inside. That's the thing between him and I. We never needed words. Even if we are apart, even if we had broken something that hadn't even begun yet,

I can still feel his presence, like our souls are one. He has left a part of him within me, and I believe I did the same. And right now, Aaron needs me.

Wolf stands up from his chair and leaves without a word.

I shut off the TV, the same way I wish I could just shut us off.

After three days without an answer from him, I'm left with a decision to make. The article. Our story began with one and ironically will end with one. I push my computer away from my bed, facing a blank page. He stole all my inspiration away.

I walk with my huge blanket toward my living room to drown my misery with food. On my way, I stare at *Everlasting*. I'm a martyr for my beliefs. Love. *Bullshit*. A shiver runs through my naked legs, as a reminder that I should be freezing. The radiator of my living room is broken, but I'm too emotionless to care.

My phone awakens in my bedroom and I rush to it. I don't need to look at the screen to know who's calling me.

I know it's him.

I don't think twice. I pick up.

"Hi, Elle. I…" I hear Aaron sigh on the phone, struggling to find his words, my heart shattering at the sound of his husky voice. I feel again. All the emotions I've tried to deny get back to the surface.

"Are you okay, Aaron?" My voice is weak and trembling.

"I don't know. Elle, I'm… I'm sorry. For everything." He waits for me to speak, despair in his voice, but I'm incapable of replying. He sounds so miserable, and so am I. Sometimes words can't express our deepest emotions unless—

"I need you," he affirms.

Words can't express our deepest emotions unless it's the words you have never been able to say before. *I need you. I miss you. I love you.* I was for so long waiting for him to need me, to allow me in his heart, for his acceptance that we belong together.

I need you. Words of hope. Despair. Fate.

"I'm here." Unconditionally. Irrevocably. Truthfully. No matter the heartbreak. As his silence follows, I know it's the same for him. I don't want to be here, he doesn't want to need me—but it's not our choice to make, it's a part of us.

"I took a flight to New York. Impulsively. I'm parked in front of your building. I wanted to see you." He curses, I can sense his agitation. My reckless Wolf is back. He is here. "Gosh, I sound desperate, I understand if you—"

"I'm coming down." I throw my phone on my bed, not taking the time to grab a jacket, before running toward the front door to meet him.

I can't wait. I need to see him. I can't think straight, I'm not conscious of what I'm doing, something took control of me, something I can't fight. I run toward the stairs until reaching the last door separating us.

Outside, it's snowing. My flesh freezes. My breath cuts. In the white carpet of snow on the street, there is my lonely Wolf, warming the storm. He stands outside of his car, looking just as I remember him. Handsome and troubled. A dark knight. I notice the dark circles under his eyes, his gaze red like he is holding Hell inside of him. A contrast between darkness with his black ripped jeans, black coat, and his obsidian hair with the light of his blue, celestine eyes. *Oh, Aaron.*

I take a leap. Running toward him in the cold, my bare feet struggling in the snow, him walking toward me. I'm only wearing my long shirt, no bra and panties, probably exposed to the view of the few pedestrians, but I don't care. All I see is him. We are lost in a slow-motion moment, stuck in a romance movie scene, and yet our story has nothing to do with a fairy tale. That's the thing—when you're drawn to someone, a second is too painful to wait. I jump into his arms, hugging him tightly, my arms around his neck. He squeezes me harder against him, his arms protectively wrapped around my waist like they always belonged here. Harder. Closer. Melting together. We are one again, standing like the world is ours, the snow the only witness of our reunion.

"Fuck, *ma belle*, it's freezing, don't stay like that." He pulls off his coat, standing only in his black shirt. He wraps his jacket around me, tugging me in, his cologne still on it, arousing my desire of him. He frowns his eyebrows, conveying his worry for me.

He swoops me under his arms, carrying me to my apartment and I don't complain. There are so many unsaid things between us, but I'm not ready to break this moment. After carrying me for the last two floors, he deposits me in my living room before closing the door behind him.

"Why is it so cold in here?" His voice isn't judgmental, he is concerned. *Gosh, Aaron, you're sending me mixed signals.* I can't play anymore.

"The radiator of my living room is broken. But the heat is fine on my other rooms." Goose bumps spreading on my skin, my teeth shaking, I cross my arms on my chest, tightening his jacket around me.

"Where are your tools?"

"Kitchen, last drawer."

His gaze stops at the painting he bought on the wall, his lips curving into a ghost of a smile.

"I've never said thank you for the painting. It was very generous of you. Too much, even. You can have it back if you want?"

He doesn't answer.

For reasons I don't want to tell him, I've cried for a week because of his gesture, thinking about how happy he made me. But I remain stoic, just like him. Aaron hasn't shown me any emotions since he arrived. He reduced his eye contact with me to the minimum. And yet, he is standing a few inches from me. I feel our chemistry, but he does nothing.

"Your shirt is wet. You're gonna catch a cold, you need to stay warm." His eyes travel in direction of the bathroom and I'm… mad.

How can he stay so casual in front of me? Acting as though nothing has happened? I want to explode and tell him I *love* him as much as I hate him. I don't want his normal tone and false civility. I take off his jacket and throw it on the ground. *Not my best move*. I'm freezing to death with my excuses of clothing, trying to make a point. We have never been average or medium. We are extreme. My eyes dare him, challenging him to be the Aaron I know.

"*Ma belle*, please." His voice is like a whisper, but I'm hell-bent.

I don't move.

He swallows before carrying me, the same way he did the night before my world fell apart to my heated bedroom. He puts me down gently, before we face each other, without a word. His hands slide gently on my thighs to grab the end of my top. His eyes meet mine, asking for… permission? Forgiveness? I can't picture what it is. I want to see the real Aaron. The man who stares at me with an intense craving, the man who is straightforward with me. I don't want this polite Aaron. I want all of him.

I put my hands in the air, waiting for his action. I want to know why he broke me. Eyes don't lie. His fingers pull my top up to my belly, revealing my pastel blue panties, until he has pulled it off completely over of my head. Until I stand almost naked in front of him. Until I know if *we* are real.

His eyes drag over my body, and I can remember every touch of his, his scent, his mark he left on me. Memories. He stops his gaze at my breasts, my nipples pointing at him, and I'm remembering the way he used to suck them. His pupils darken. His eyes shift to my belly, to the places he used to caress me, to my hips that he grabbed passionately during our ardent exchanges. His gaze now stuck on my mouth which he claimed and used abundantly, and I know.

He craves me.

I've marked him.

But his memory of us is tainted by deep pain. His nightmare. He left me out of fear. Fear of hurting me. His fingers caress my belly, climbing higher to the edge of my breasts, our eyes stuck on each other. He approaches me, our lips begging to connect, my need of him growing, and just when I think he's gonna kiss me—and that I'll let him—he puts the blanket of my bed on my shoulders and wraps me in it. He takes a step backward, before leaving my bedroom. I'm left confused. *What happened?*

I change quickly putting on my ugly comfy sweats, before storming in the living room. I was at his disposal and he didn't kiss me? Aaron never backs away from a challenge. From a prey who submits herself willingly. My anger vanishes when I see him sitting on the floor fixing my broken radiator.

I should yell at him. Kiss him. Slap him. Anything. But what do I do? I watch him fixing it, as he hides the shame and regret piercing through his eyes. Silence flies over us. Minutes passed, and finally he stands up, turning the heat of the radiator.

He fixed it. But could he fix us?

He cleans up the area, while I take a seat on my couch confused by this whole situation. "Thank you."

Once he is done, he sits on the chair in front of me. He's maintaining a distance between us. When the conflict in his eyes strikes me, my heart bounces in my chest, my emotions colliding into me. "I'm sorry, Elle. I've pushed you away, I was afraid. I would never hurt you. I wanted to protect you from me."

"I know." And I understand, I'd have done the same thing for him. *But I can't forget his words.*

"I tried to stay away from you, but fuck, Elle, you haunt my mind. I'd like if you could give me a second chance." He furrows his brow like he wants to say more, but something is stopping him. "I'm not ready to share my past yet, but I… I want to try." His eyes are now stuck on mine, reading into me, unveiling himself without filters.

Trying. Trying to heal. Trying to love.

"You can't push me away again. You humiliated me, what you said to me… I won't be able to handle that a second time. Never again," I say firmly, my eyes wet, expressing the pain he caused me.

"I won't."

My tears slide down as I turn my head away, because if I don't, I'll cry and crawl back to him so easily—too easily. We stay silent. I don't understand why we always need to play the game of cat and mouse. Chasing each other. Escaping each other. Saving the other or tearing ourselves. Probably because our pasts have been stronger than us. Our need for power, our need to not be weak, our need to own. But he is the only one knowing me.

He hands me the envelope he took from his jacket. "I know I can't offer you what a nice and sweet guy could offer you. I'm screwed up with a deadly job. You've seen a part of me, I'm—" He stops, and I know he isn't ready to talk.

Soul mates. I'm convinced Aaron is mine. Probabilities will be against us, and yet here we are defying all the odds once again. Out of billions of people. A continent away. Out of the improbable factors we met.

"I need you. I want to try with you." He sets the envelope on the table in front of me. "This is a ticket to Paris and a hotel reservation. I'd like you to come as my date to the FIA Prize ceremony award. I'll be waiting at your hotel until eight, after I'll leave. It's your choice, Elle." He leans toward me and kisses my forehead softly. "Whatever you choose, thank you for seeing in me what nobody ever saw."

I'm in shock. A rush of feelings is invading me and I'm unable to speak. My answer is yes. *I can't live without you,* but I can't say it to him. I was miserable without him, but my ego is getting in my way. He walks closer to the door. I don't have time. *Think, Elle. Speak. Fight. Do something.* I turn my face in his direction.

When I do, it's too late. He is gone.

I take the tickets in my hands. Paris. The gala is in two days. It's officially the end of the racing season. People say you're always one decision away from changing your life. But I don't think you can choose who you love. I didn't choose to fall hard, deep, fast, for Aaron. He is a part of me. He completed me. He is more powerful than my free will.

We belong like magnets.

A positive and a negative. We aren't perfect. We're equal to our chaos, but light can't exist without darkness.

And together we found our balance.

I run toward my window, open it, and look at the street. His car is still here. I haven't missed him. I spot Aaron walking under the white snow. I want to talk about the painting, I want to talk about everything he has done for me, but the only word I manage to say is—

"Everlasting!"

"Everlasting." He mouths, his lips curving into a smile.

CHAPTER 28

The Villain

Elle

Paris, the city of love.

A Prize Giving Ceremony.

The perfect mixture between money, power and… love.

I take Aaron's hand, leading me out of the limo. My body is rebelling. Legs shaking. Heart bouncing. He gives me a comforting smile, and we walk side by side toward the entrance. Do you know that surreal moment when everything feels so pure and perfect? When it couldn't be possibly true? I went to Paris, ready to fight for the man I cannot live without. The man who waited for me alongside his limo, after eight p.m., even if he said he wouldn't. I have put my hair into a tight ponytail. I'm dressed in a long raven black satin dress with a split on the side. I wear an elegant cleavage; the tight fabric of the dress is showing each of my curves, revealing my body shape underneath. A red lipstick, with an eyeliner touch, I feel like Grace Kelly. After all, fairy tale princesses have a ball to meet a prince.

But I've never been a princess. I'm just a woman.

I look over at Aaron playing the prince, wearing his tuxedo, his arm wrapped around my waist looking handsome with an empyrean superiority. I'm dazzled when his eyes explore my whole body, savoring me fully, not tiring of the view of me. But it isn't just lust, it is something else. Something powerful. I can see myself, mirroring through his cerulean eyes. I feel beautiful—just the way I am.

But Aaron isn't a prince, either. He is a fallen god.

The mortal and the god. It sounds like Greek mythology—*and we know how those end up.* Together, we're equally powerful and destructive.

We passed the whole ride to the gala with a desire to kiss, caress, stroke each other. But I don't want to rush it. I want to crave him—all night. I want our attraction to sparkle all around the room for everyone to witness it. I want them to know: Aaron LeBeau's soul belongs to me. It's mental torture, and the more we suffer, the more our pleasure is going to explode into fireworks. Tonight, I want him to crave me until he reaches his torment. I need to know where we stand. If we belong in a fairy tale or a Greek tragedy.

Once we enter, it feels like a red-carpet event. The huge chandeliers and the seventeen-century French architecture are owning the room. This event is like a monarchy. The elite are sipping expensive champagne, women wear their most distinguished dresses, hors d'oeuvres are served with a French service. It's a first-class happening with the most valuable guests, a mix of celebrities, businessmen, and investors. I've been to this kind of event before—*with the wrong man by my side.* It's a universe where money is the center of every discussion, when people smile at you depending on your net worth, your accomplishments, or who you're accompanying. Politeness is required to hide how this world is fake. It's a competition off the track.

A competition in which Aaron excels. He claimed first place and exudes charisma. Charisma that people in this room are breathing and envying.

"Everyone is staring," I whisper, a part of me enjoying this.

He connects my body to his chest, a possessive arm encircled around my waist, claiming my lips in front of the crowd with raw hunger. That's a thing I love about him. Wolf isn't afraid to go for what he wants. He isn't afraid to allege me as his in front of all the crowd by stealing a kiss. He doesn't care what people think of him, and that's incredibly sexy.

"Well, that's probably because I'm the lucky bastard who won the world championship, and have by far the most beautiful woman in the room by my side."

"Maybe I'm the lucky one." I play with my lower lip, biting it, drawing his attention to it.

"Is it a competition?" He raises his eyebrow.

"No, I had my fair share of bets and games." I chuckle, but behind my playful tone is the truth. I don't want games to come against us. I don't want an agreement. I want something real.

"You're right. Same team? No games. Just the truth," he adds, as if he has read my thoughts.

He furrows his eyebrows, taking a step closer to me, magnetic electricity invading us. "Elle, I—" He contemplates my gaze, a rush of emotions battling in his eyes, and I'm in a haze. His confidence vanishes, replaced by vulnerability—the one he has when he is about to show his feelings.

I gasp for air, and when he's about to speak, his gaze drifts to something else entirely. And what's left of him is obscurity. His eyes become onyx and stygian. His veins throb in his neck, his full lips become narrow, conveying his revulsion.

I turn around to find what is causing him such enmity. In the middle of the crowd, there is one man standing like a rock alone, hands in his pocket, his strong stature showing his supremacy. André LeBeau. His black raven eyes are stuck on his son, a dry smirk spreading on his face, his square jaw up in pride. The two men are caught in a staring warfare. A war of ice and fire. Aaron struggles to contain his annihilating feelings, while André is calm, not showing an ounce of emotion.

"Aaron?" I call out to him, but he doesn't move. It feels like a wall stands between us.

His father greets a few businessmen and starts roaming toward us with a rare elegance and a charisma that leaves you frozen in place. He is the type of man that makes you feel small next to him. Aaron's grip tightens around my waist as he yanks me closer to him. A sign of… possession?

"Son. Congratulations, on your prize." André chortles, amused by his son's reaction.

André's gaze encounters mine, and it pains me to maintain eye contact, my gut telling me to escape. "You must be, Elle? My son has great taste in women." He switches his gaze back to Aaron, who tenses immediately.

Aaron steps in front of me, facing his father, like fighters provoking each other before a duel. The tension is unbearable. "André. You weren't invited."

"I'm your father, Aaron." He challenges Wolf's display of power with a half-smile twisting his lips. It's a war for dominance between them. Both are of an impressive height, emanating of alpha hormones. "Plus, Formula 1 can be a great business investment."

André quits his staring warfare with his son, taking his silence as a statement. "Well, Elle, are you here on business or as my son's date?"

I don't have time to reply, because Aaron has turned his back on his father and is facing me. "Elle. Can you wait for me by the bar?" He takes my hand, his eyes begging for me to listen to him.

I nod, and he squeezes my hand as a sign that everything is okay. I give him his privacy and amble toward the bar area, looking back a few times, wondering which man André really is behind his all-too-perfect appearance.

I order a glass of water when I notice Louis Harmil—probably not on his first glass of champagne—occupying the bar area by himself. Most of the people are busy eating hors d'oeuvres on the golden plates, talking in groups; even the young bartender is checking his phone, not paying attention to us.

"Look who's here. The outsider." Louis smirks arrogantly, pouring himself another drink. God, the ceremony hasn't even begun, and he is already hammered.

"You really enjoy everyone hating you, do you?" I roll my eyes, despising him. Especially since I discovered the truth about what he did to Monica.

"You'll never belong to his world, you know that, right?" He squints his eyes, his anger eating him alive. I know Louis is a sore loser, but still, he wouldn't drink that recklessly for finishing second. He is the Golden Boy, after all. He swallows his drink in one go, laughing way too loudly for an event of this luxury. He's destroying himself willingly. But why?

"Nobody can understand what it is to be a Formula 1 driver," he spits with repulsion.

"Are you okay?" *Not that I care.*

A red-haired woman, approximately fifty, approaches us. Pearl necklaces on her neck, designer dress, nude makeup, her hair designed into a chignon—she's definitely from old money. Her emerald gaze sparkles with her peerless and condescending attitude. She forces a smile on me before focusing her attention on Louis.

"Louis. What are you doing?" she mutters.

"Celebrating, Mother." He smirks, raising his glass in provocation in front of his mother's face. She closes her thin lips harshly, her eyes doubling in size, daring him to stop this affront.

"Celebrating?" she sputters. She glances over at me, and I turn in the opposite direction, pretending to be focused on… well, nothing. She lowers her voice. "You know how much money your father and I invested in you? For you to be second? I thought you said you were the best, Louis."

"It's sports, Mom. You can't always win." Louis shrugs like he couldn't care less. She sighs and storms away.

I peek over at Louis, who's snorting and waving at a few people in the back. *Nobody can understand what it is to be a Formula 1 driver.* Maybe he is right. The race isn't only on the track, it's also off the track. It's about money. Investors. Branding. And Louis is certainly losing that race, as well.

"Hey," he calls out to me, leaning toward me, his elbow on the counter of the bar. "I'm not a jerk."

"You kinda are, Louis."

"Well, maybe." He laughs. "But if you are a jerk, you can't disappoint people, right? And sometimes, Outsider, it's better to be hated. It makes life so much simpler." He cracks a smile and leaves when the Prize Giving Ceremony is about to begin. *What was that about?*

I search for Aaron around the room, but he and his father are nowhere to be found. I decide to head toward the stage as everyone is gathering to take a seat. I sit in the second row, behind the reporters, near the drivers and their families. The speaker opens the ceremony, and I'm still without Aaron. I keep texting him, my gut telling me that something is wrong.

The lights of the room switch off to illuminate only the stage in a bluish tone. Behind it, there is a big screen opening this year's ceremony. My anxiety stops when I notice Aaron storming from behind the curtain and takes the seat I reserved next to me. He seems tense; his face is glazed as he readjusts his suit nervously.

"Aaron, are you okay?" I pose my hand on his knee, but he pushes it away.

A cold shoulder. I swallow, my insecurities hitting me. The scare of him pushing me away again leaves me stoic. The crowd applauds and cheers as the speaker calls out Aaron on stage to receive his world champion prize.

"We'll talk later, Elle." Wolf doesn't look at me, his dry tone cutting me off as he jumps on stage.

That's when I spot André LeBeau. He appears from the same curtain Aaron walked out from a few minutes before. He smiles wickedly at me, freezing me in my seat.

Something is wrong.

CHAPTER 29
Rules are meant to be broken

"Why do you believe she's really here, Aaron?" André spits his venom.

"She's here for me. Now, you back off from Elle." I don't need to threaten André twice. Everything he touched, he destroyed.

"She uses you. She's here for an article. Her boss asked her to deliver information on you... Since the start."

I shake my head, not believing a word he's saying. "Stop your bullshit, André."

"I got the information from Mr. Black himself. She never loved you, Aaron. Do you really think someone could care for you apart from your money and fame? She betrayed you."

"No, you're fucking lying. I trust her." She would have told me. She promised me she wouldn't. She couldn't. I can't believe I'm even considering this.

"See for yourself. She's writing an article about you and Henry, that's why she's here. You know how the media are? They wait for the perfect opportunity to strike. An opportunity I gave her as a test of her loyalty at my press conference. I did that because I love you, and I wanted you to see her real color."

"Bullshit. You're desperate, André." My irritation starts to grow, knowing he's up to no good. "I'm going and you stay the fuck away from my woman."

"Think about it. She had an opportunity, and she seized it even at the risk of crashing your life. She stays with you for information or maybe, who knows, money or fame? All of that is fake, she never cared, and you're stupid to believe she ever did." He puts his hand on my shoulder. "Now you know what I've been feeling. You really believe she could have loved someone like you? With everything that you did? With what you are? You're a joke to her. You're weak. Far from a man."

I awaken from my thoughts when the speaker shakes my hand, handing me the microphone on stage. I need to stop replaying in my mind the talk with André. Why can't I forget his fucking words?

Damn it—all of this shit. I'll give these vultures what they are here for. I don't have a choice. Betrayal is the only color of the night. I stare over at the only person I trusted, Elle. She smiles coyly at me, encouraging me to speak up.

But she used me, too.

"I would like to thank my team, my sponsors, and my coach for their support this season. We won this together." I show the crowd the trophy before they start to applaud. Truth is, I'm not a man of words, but sometimes you have to put on a show. But all I want is to explode. I need to remain in control. If I don't, I'll lose the only thing I've left.

"I've dedicated my life to racing and let me tell you… it's one hell of a ride. That's the thing with racing, you can hate it, and yet you can't live without it. It's in your blood." I smirk. "Judging by the front row of reporters, I suppose they're all here to know about my brother's death." I narrow my eyes at each of them, speaking to them directly, while they swallow under the intensity of my gaze. People say you can see the soul of a man in his eyes, well mine is definitely dark. "You'll be pleased to know that today, I'm gonna give you exactly what you're here for. A story."

I don't have a choice. If I don't speak the truth, the media will continue to look for dirt—*I couldn't let her betray me.*

So I tell them.

I tell them about the accident we had. Without blinking. Ignoring how my heart is breaking at each of my words. I've never felt so naked. Exposing myself publicly is a nightmare. The mental images of my brother's blood on the passenger seat are flashing in my mind. My throat is dry. This is worse than therapy.

I'm no freaking hero. I race because I'm a fucking coward. I'm the villain. And today I'm exposing my skin. A coward who couldn't save his brother. A coward who never had the courage to verify if the traffic light was green or red. I got left free of charges for killing my brother. Supposedly, it wasn't my fault—or André paid the judges and police. I glare at their faces with disgust. I don't want their fucking pity.

"Henry was the greatest brother, friend, boyfriend a person could have." Each time I call out Henry's name, I feel like a blade is cutting my twisted, rotten heart out. *The sea. The waves. The sand.* I should have died and not him. I keep pushing my feelings away. I cannot be weak. "He gave me the strength I needed. I raced with him. Some people say I'm reckless, I would say I'm driven…"

Driven by fear. Sorrow. Hatred.

I know what these vultures are thinking.

Wolf has a heart.

I wanted to become a better man for Henry—and for *her*. Truth is, I want to honor his death and be the man that he was. I want to be good. To give back. To ask for redemption. And I want to make her *lo*—Bullshit.

"As for today, I'm creating a foundation under his name. We will give a future to kids who don't have the necessary funding to pursue their dreams." White flashes haunt my mind, the same I feel when I race. "When I was fourteen, I stole a kart and raced it when I wasn't allowed to. Thomas discovered me and took me under his wing, but Henry had to pay for my mistake. All of his savings were put into it. Henry was working two jobs. He invested in me. He believed in me. Without him, I'd be a nobody." *And I thank him by killing him.*

"I had a dream. To be a racing driver. And thanks to my brother, I became one. And in this world, there are plenty of kids like me. Thanks to Henry, they'll have a chance to touch their dreams. Thank you for your time."

I'm a fraud. People stand up from their seats and applaud. Pity. Caring. Sensibility. Everyone is feeling something, even André has a dry smirk across his face. I stare over at Elle, and she has tears in her eyes, her expression showing how proud she is. She bites her lower lip, a naive smile on her face, a gesture that usually makes me weak toward her. *She's gorgeous.* But I don't return her elation. *Could she have betrayed me?* I trust Elle.

But I also trusted my mother, who abandoned me for money.
I trusted my father, who broke me.
I trusted my best friend, who fucked and humiliated my sister-in-law.
Every person I care about used me. *Why would she be different?*
Only one way to find out.

As soon as the ceremony ends, I rush to find her. People are congratulating me, waving at me, asking me about next season. I don't listen. I manage a few smiles, but I just want to be out. I clutch Elle's arm from behind, recognizing her beautiful raven dress that fits her curves perfectly, her scent of rose. She's heaven-sent. A beauty.

"We need to talk, Elle." She gives me a head nod and trots behind me to keep up with my fast pace.

We walk toward the darkness, the only light being the ones of the bridge of Alexandre III, the statues of angels, Pegasus and the gods, the only witnesses of our presence. I broke my first two promises I've made to my younger self, and tonight I want to know if she would break my promise number three. *No one could ever love me.*

"Why are you with me, Elle? Tell me the truth." My eyes dare her, a threat in my low voice.

"Aaron, what's wrong?" She shakes her head, her eyes wild. She's hiding something.

"Were you planning on writing an article about my brother's death?" I scream at her as she takes a step back. I don't want to scare her, but she's unleashing my demons. "Were you planning on writing some private information I told you confidentially? I fucking trusted you, Elle," I roar as she breathes faster feeling the flames of betrayal I have inside my heart.

I peer over the bridge, my hands grabbing the border as I try to remain in control. *Fuck, Aaron, you're terrorizing your woman. Calm down.* But I can't control myself, she exercises such a powerful thing on me. I can only be intense. I could hurt her so easily. *I could be like him.* I curse as I see the face of a little girl, afraid, and not of the feisty woman I know. She looks so freaking innocent, and yet she stares at me like she's guilty and afraid.

"It's not what you think," she whispers—not denying. Too late. She's a weakness.

"I bet it doesn't please you that I confessed what happened to Henry on stage earlier. You'll not get to write the exclusivity anymore. My secret is out," I snort, and what's left of me is just bitterness. She usually awakens the best in me, the remaining light in my corrupted soul, but tonight, she awakens the worst in me. Each of my darkest emotions. My fears and needs are multiplied. I can't find peace. And yet, all I want is my lips on hers, my cock inside her, I want her to be mine. But it feels like an ocean is standing between us.

"Tell me you would have never used me for another article? Without even speaking about it with me, first." I drift my dark gaze to her, only anger inside me. The real me. "Was it all a lie? Tell me it's not true!"

She feels it and rushes toward me, taking my hand into hers, her eyes imploring for forgiveness. "I wanted to talk to you tonight about it. My boss forced me, I fought and refused, but you can't refuse Nina for long," her sweet voice murmurs, but it's not enough. We always used each other from the start, how can we trust the other?

I scan her, searching for the truth, as her eyes shift to the ground under my forceful staring. "I haven't written anything, but I'll lose everything if I don't. She threatened me saying, she'd destroy me." She bites her lower lip, frowning her eyebrows as if she's trying to contain her crying. "I haven't told you this, but my boss… she's my mother."

I look up to the sky. Elle never mentioned her mother to me. Just once, and it was a story she didn't want to discuss further. Fuck. We're so screwed up. I feel like the statues of the gods are laughing at us. "If you had been honest with me, I'd have fought for you. I wouldn't have let you lose your job." I'm trying to remain placid, because if I let my emotions out, I'll explode.

"You can trust me," she pleads, reaching to put her hands on my chest.

I take a step back. "People used me, Elle. All of them." *Even you.*

"Really? That's what you think? I tried to call you, Aaron! You never answered me for days! I called you, but you pushed me away, again! When was I supposed to talk about the article?" she explodes, unleashing her hellions, howling like she's in pain. "I had other things on my mind, Aaron! I was freaking broken." She slumps to the ground, like a child hiding from a nightmare, head on her knees. It takes me all the willing in the world to not take her into my arms. "And when you showed up at my door, I was afraid. Afraid that you'd leave me… again. I don't want to be weak."

"You see, you don't trust me either." I know my passionless tone hits her deep, and a part of me wanted to. I don't want her to know how weak she makes me. I don't want her to possess me.

I help her stand, my fingers tangling with hers, our souls merging as I caress her cheek. *Mine*. Her eyes are wet, her cheeks red from anger, her sweet lips begging to be kissed. "I need the ultimate proof, Elle," I whisper. She looks stern, confused, but she *knows* what I'm talking about. I need what she couldn't give to any other men. I need her soul. I need her to be mine. "There is only one proof. The one to show me that I'm special to you, to show me it was more than pretending."

I need her to belong to me fully.

I need her to say the words I for so long, feared.

She stares at me, emotionless. I'm losing her, and my eight-year-old self is coming back to the surface. Her mouth is open, she doesn't know what to say. By lack of words, she captures my face in her palms, crashing her lips into mine. It's as if she's losing herself in me, trying to give me her whole soul. But it's not enough. We cannot hide anymore. I don't want to be her escape. I want to be more. I pull away, my hands meshing with hers, acting like a wall against our bodies.

"Say it, Elle."

Show me, my father was wrong. Show me you could love me. Show me this was the truth.

Don't destroy me now.

"Say it, Elle," I plead, and I see her trembling as she takes a step back, shaking her head.

She doesn't love me.

She breaks the last of humanity within me.

CHAPTER 30
Eros & Psyché

Elle

Panic reaches my veins, I gasp for air, my body shaking. He wants me to say the L-word. *I love him.* I love him so much, but I can't say it. Love is a destructive word. Mental images come back to my mind. My mother on her knees, pleading my father to not leave us. Crying at him, imploring, begging. She threw her pride at his feet, but he ripped it apart. He owned her, enslaved her, with the three words—I love you. She said it and he left us. Since that day, I was forbidden to use these words. Saying I love you, is a way to submit fully to the other. It has been banned from my language, a secret I shall keep for myself.

What if I say those words and he doesn't say it back? What if history repeats itself? Like my mother said, a man is incapable of love. You can't trust them.

That's why I chose Stephan. He was a man I was sure I would have never fallen in love with. He was nice, polite, boring, the perfect husband to be. The good man, the one your family loves, the one who will never break you, on paper. And yet, he exercised a mental torture in me. *I know you love me, my sweet.* He knew he was owning me. Once I finally opened myself up to him, believing I'd found a contemporary prince, he showed his true face. My castle became my prison. Stephan became my nightmare. And my princess beauty vanished, became bruised, my soul consumed with pain and shame. And I never loved him. I love Aaron. The damages he could cost me are bigger. I'm not ready to live this nightmare again.

"I can't," I gasp. I can give him everything—*everything but the word love.* "Aaron, I—"

"It's, fine, Elle. I don't want your pity." He draws a long breath, and I know I just put a dagger into his heart. His face, half-scintillant from the moonlight, half aphotic. The bioluminescence of our chemistry is silently fading. "You were looking for a prince all along, and I'm not that type of man, right?" Tears slide down as I watch Aaron breaking for the first time. He is mortal, after all. "He was right," he speaks to himself, a loathsome expression on his face.

He is just like me. Unconfident about love. I see only an empyrean, seraphic beauty in him. And yet someone in his past damaged him, to the point he sees only his own darkness. We're the same. That's why I can't give him what he wants.

"Don't say that. You're incredible, you're—"

"—Do you know why I proposed you the agreement?" He cuts me off, his agitation growing.

"No."

"I always wanted you. From the moment I saw you, Elle."

My heart drops. Crashing into the ground, dividing itself, as pieces of broken glass. The sharpened edges of my remaining heart like daggers cutting my soul. His piercing eyes don't leave mine and assist in my decomposition.

"It was physical at first. But that night, you weren't like any of the women I've met. I wanted to get to know you." He takes a step toward me, domineering me with his height. "But the only way I could have made you fall for me, or have you, was to have an agreement with you."

"Why?" My voice is trembling, weeping, howling.

"Because, if I'd have asked you on a date without playing a game, you would have never accepted it. I needed an opportunity to see you again." He looks at the ground for an instant. "So, if I had an agreement with you, we would have to see each other, and with time… I could conquer you."

Just as I feel stuck in limbo, completely belonging to the darkness, the rain falls, the storm grounding around us. The few people on the street are running away, escaping the brutality of the downpour, but we don't move. Accepting it fully. The elements a reflection of what's inside our hearts.

"But the first night we slept together, you ran away? And what about your sponsors and your house team?" Hundreds of questions are spiraling in my mind.

I always thought I was a game for him. But he made the game for me.

"I was afraid to hurt you. I lost control, and it never happened to me. I finally felt, and it scared the shit out of me." He clears his throat before his eyes provoke mine. "I'm Aaron LeBeau, do you really think I needed to do all that to have a racing contract? Sure, the media were on my back, but a part of me wanted the world to know you're mine." I remember Monica's words. *Aaron doesn't do something he doesn't want to do.* The agreement was a lie. Aaron did all that because he wanted me. All along.

He trapped himself by wanting to possess me, but I ended up possessing him.

"Like I told you. I always wanted you. Even when I didn't know it myself." He caresses my cheek, bringing his forehead closer to mine, the deluge of the rain washing away our sins, our pasts.

We're both a Masquerade. We wear masks hiding our true selves from everyone, except for us. I always knew something stronger was uniting us. He is the missing half of my soul. We're from the same essence, and yet, we're the opposite parts, completing each other.

"Aaron... I..." I lean in to kiss him, but he pulls away.

"I know how painful it is for you to say it. I know it'll rip you apart. I know what it'll mean for you. That you lose your control to me. That you belong to me." His eyes darken, and all I see is pain. He demands for me to hurt myself on purpose, to give him what his demons need. Destroying myself to save us. A sacrifice. "That's why it's the ultimate proof." His eyes lock on mine, trying to make me sink into his side. "I'm fighting for you. But now it's your time to fight for me."

Against all odds, Aaron did fight his demons for me. He was always here. Rescuing me. Giving me what I yearn for. And now, he needs me to rescue him. I wish I could say it. I want to. But I can't. The destruction he can cause me is equal to the love I have for him. It's as strong as the anger of the gods. He pushed me away once, leaving me like a soulless ghost. Admitting my love for him will mean I'm enslaving myself. My tears are bleeding through my eyes, I'm hurting, but I'm incapable to say those words. I'm damaged, I know that. But my fears are owning me, paralyzing me.

"Can we take it slow?" I beg, knowing we've never been able to take it slow. With us, it has always been all or nothing.

"No, it's not enough, Elle."

And just like that, I created our apocalypse. The beginning of our end. As he turns his back to walk away from me, I feel like I'm drowning deeper in the water, until I reach the end of the aphotic zone. I remain stoic, owned by chaos.

"I can't leave you here alone. I'll accompany you to your hotel." He turns away, and I nod, incapable of speaking.

We walk in silence until reaching the door that symbolizes the end. The storm becomes quiet, I feel the nothingness. The nil. We stand here awkwardly, knowing that each second of silence is tearing us miles away from each other. Our story, all the months I knew him, scrolling through my mind, the passion and the heartbreaks, from the end to the beginning.

"I don't want to lose you," I whisper, looking nowhere, my fingers trying to interlace with his.

"Goodbye, Elle." He lets go of my hand and disappears like a dream, as I'm left with my own hell.

When I close the door, I cry. I cry my heart out, but all the tears of the words aren't enough to erase the memory of him. I'm collapsing, my pain crashing, erasing me. *What did I do?* I freaking love him, why can't I say it? He was the right one for me. The only one.

I thought Aaron was the one who was Hell-bound. But it was me.

I was the one who destroyed us.

He fought his darkness for me, but I let mine consumed me.

It's him.

The look in his eyes, fearless and haunted. Strong and vulnerable. Beautiful and damaged.

A lone Wolf. Half human, half animal.

Between obscurity and light, his eyebrows frown like he is in an eternal war. The black oil paint in the background representing his hellions, while he has splattered red paint of passion.

A light of orange behind him, like the speed of a race car or burning flames. The left edge of his face is decomposing into white little birds flying away from the darkness.

Wolf's duality.

A three foot by three foot canvas, and my best creation. I couldn't stop my tears while painting, my heart bleeding from the heartbreak. The painting has dried now, and I covered it with a sheet before hiding it behind my couch. The man who stole my heart eternally immortalized. Us, we're over. But he will continue to live.

Days passed, and nothing changed. The white snow has covered everything. I stare over my Angelo Di Romeo, a tear in my eye, convinced I'm not meant for love. I did learn about it through a painting, and my experience at true love ended up more painful than I could ever imagine. But when I look closely, my vision perceives new details, and for the first time, I understand the irony of it.

Everlasting was us. We weren't a fairy tale, we were mythology.

Aaron has the beauty of a god, to the point where he could be Aphrodite's son. His hell-bent desire to win, the power exuding from him such as he could be the son of Arès. He wasn't sent to fall in love with me, I wasn't supposed to strike him at his own game and burn him with his own arrow. I was supposed to be left with a monster that night, Stephan, but instead, destiny gave me my Eros.

We could have been a myth. The myth of Eros and Psyché, how a god fell for the mortal he was supposed to use.

I wasn't supposed to see Aaron's vulnerability, to see his whole self, until that night. The night of his—and our—nightmare. The night he ran from me, just as Eros ran from Psyché after she burned him with a candle, discovering he wasn't a monster but a celestial being. And then, we were both left alone and broken. Love consumed me until the point where I wasn't feeling alive. My insecurities became my own Pandora's box.

But in this mythology, Eros came back for Psyché, and together they flew toward heaven. My Eros has left.

But maybe it's not the end?

Maybe, after all, I need to open my own Pandora's box. To unleash my insecurities, my past, without filters. I rush toward my computer and start typing. Typing until twilight rises and the sun fades.

It began with an article, and today, it'll end with one.

Ask. E. Monteiro: The truth about Aaron LeBeau.

Aaron means: bearer of martyrs or mountain of strength. The etymology couldn't have been more accurate. He is reckless. Indomitable. Tenebrous. He is the man you defined as a lone Wolf. A man who carries darkness. The traumatic loss of a brother, his hell-bent desire to excel. He is a man who always fought harder than anyone. He is the man who drives without fear, provoking death without shame.

But today, I'm gonna expose Aaron's secret. The one he has been hiding from you. The one unknown.

Bearer of martyrs. I was a martyr. I had faith in love, even if it broke me, made me bleed and suffer. I had faith in love to the point where my soul belonged to the nothingness. I was trapped in my own hell... Until him. He was the light, rescuing me from my nightmare. He was the one who showed me that the cause I was fighting for, the cause that made me bleed, was worth it.

Love.

Aaron's secret is his undeniable love for others. Aaron LeBeau has been driven by love all of his life. His love for his brother kept him alive. Made him the fastest racing driver. Driven and invincible. His love for others made him protect them. He offered them a life full of possibilities. A chance for redemption. He saved me. He saved my soul. My life. I was reborn like a phoenix from her ashes. He brings out the light in others.

Love is the opposite of indifference. It's an intense feeling, as strong and destructive as death. You can't love halfway; you love fully, deeply, until it consumes your whole being, your cells. It is just like passion. Passion means suffering. Passion is devastating or healing. It's intense.

Love isn't all beautiful and divine. Love is a path, a fight. Along the road, you'll hate, you'll be a martyr of your own beliefs, and yet in the end—you'll find your significant one. The one worth fighting for. The missing part of your soul.

Aaron LeBeau hid himself, pretending to be only capable of Ludus love while he is the four types of love. Eros, passionate and full. Philia and Pragma, capable of everlasting love and friendship. Agapé, for his love of others.

As for me, he is my two words.

Some people say I love you.

I'll say, he is my significant.

And... posted.

I decide it's time to take a leap. Aaron made me realize I was living a life that wasn't mine. I had a dream I ignored. I took on a job I wasn't happy about, to please my mother. I pretended to be someone else to be loved my whole life. It never worked.

It has to end.

All of it.

He taught me that sometimes the most broken people encounter the most successful paths. Because we're survivors. Fighters. Every pain, every shattered part of myself makes me whole and can be turned into positivity. Aaron races. I will paint. I'm not alone. I will matter. Just like he mattered to me.

Sometimes, all you need is one person to make you see the light.

I need to change my life, and that's just what I'm going to do.

Elle: Mother, I'm sending you my resignation. I'm done working for you. I'm taking my own path. I know that you don't believe me, but if you wish one day to act like my mother, I'll be ready to tell you the truth, and be your daughter.

Nina: Goodbye, Elle.

Alone.

Again.

CHAPTER 31

My significant

I have no idea what I'm doing here. It's already night, and God knows how I'm doing the hundreds of steps to her door. I've read her article. *Of course, Elle, you couldn't tell me in front of me I was your significant; you had to write it for the world to know.* I snort, only she could do that. Elle isn't perfect. She is broken, too. She has too much pride. She has her way to push my boundaries. Playing me at my own game, fighting me for power. And yet, she's perfection to me. An equal version of myself. My light.

I knock.

When she opens the door of her apartment, we stare. No words are needed. *Ma belle* has circles under her eyes. Her blond honey hair is the only light on her face. She's gorgeous, even while wearing sweatpants and no makeup. But she's ripping me apart. She looks miserable, so am I. Why has she inflicted this on herself? I signed my contract for the next three upcoming seasons. Got sixty million out of it per year. Pretty good. I got what I wanted all along. I even bought out a few shares of Amorino racing. This way I could do whatever the fuck I want. *See, André, I, too, can do business.* And yet, without her, it doesn't fucking matter. I take a step toward her, and her hazel eyes lighten. She looks so freaking weak and vulnerable, I hate this.

I hand her the article I've printed. "Is that true?"

She beholds my tormented gaze and nods. I'm fighting for her, and she's staring at me like she's afraid of me. Afraid I'd break her. Own her. She might be stubborn, but I'm feral. I won't give up until she lets her heart speak. I'm not Stephan. I'm not her father. I'm screwed up, but I would protect her, not damage her. She needs to trust me. She's mine—whatever she wants it or not—and I'll cherish what's mine. Her lips curve into a shy smile as she poses her hands on my chest.

"You're my significant, Aaron," she whispers.

Finally. I don't think twice. I take her into my arms, pinning her against her wall, and close the door behind us. She hasn't said the L-word, but I know admitting it was a painful step for her and that's all that matters. She offers me a part of her soul, and soon I'll claim the rest. I kiss her without restraint, letting her know I'll be the only one to possess her. Sending her into oblivion. My tongue is claiming her. She's melting under the intensity of my kiss, accepting my control, accepting the hunger I have for her. She's a part of me. The lighter part, but *ma belle* is mine.

I carry her to her bedroom with only one thought in mind. Making her mine. But tonight, it will be different. I always made love to her, even if she never knew that. But it was hard. Passionate. Possessive. I wanted to erase the mark of all the men she had been with, for her to belong to me. But tonight, I'll take my sweet time with her, I'll bring her to the edge. I honestly don't know if I'm capable of sweetness. I've never fucked sweet, never even witnessed sweetness in my life. Plus, I haven't had sex since the night I've pushed her away—and pleasing myself with my hand was definitely giving me blue balls. What about her? Did she wait for me? The thought of another man touching her makes me cringe. However, the thought of her touching herself makes me hard.

I pull her on her bed, hovering on top of her. She pulls my shirt over my head—she seems as eager as I am for physical contact. I do the same with her shirt that is way too large for her perfect body. I slide her pants on the floor as she rests on her bed in underwear in front of me. God, I've missed that view. She flushes when I scan my eyes over her whole body. I've memorized her by heart, and yet she reacts like I just discovered her for the first time. And honestly, it feels like that. Still fucking amazing. I slide her panties to the floor, and she starts to bite her lower lip. I smirk, noticing her wetness she tries to hide. I unlock her bra to push it away and stand in front of her to admire her sultry, naked body. Gorgeous. And mine.

"Everything about you is beautiful." I groan as she stares at me like an angel. An angel with a body that tortures me.

"I love how strong you look." She wanders her hand on my chest, to my biceps, observing my muscles contracting.

"You're mine, Elle. You are my woman." It's an affirmation, and yet, it's my way to ask her to be my girlfriend—or better, to inform her of it.

"I am." She bites her lower lip. "And you're mine, too."

Now that we officially established our exclusivity, I lean toward her, positioning myself between her legs. I claim her mouth before biting and sucking her lower lip slowly. I kiss the soft spot on her neck as she starts to moan. She moves her hips to feel the friction of our bodies before I descend, kissing her collarbone while her fingers pass through my hair. I cup both of her small, perfect breasts into my palms, my forefingers playing with her pink nipples, tugging them. Then I claim them with my tongue. Elle arches her back and her eyelids start to close, her breath quickening. I'm leading her where I want her to be. Hot and ready. I stop for a fraction of a second, and she opens her eyes, begging me to continue. Again, that's what I wanted. I continue to suck and kiss her nipples as she watches me pleasuring her. God, I could come just by watching her.

I continue claiming her breasts as mine, my hand sliding between her inner thigh. She starts to roll her hips, embracing the friction fully, my fingers tracing pleasureful circles on her center gently, pulling her wetness around her clit. *Ma belle* moans louder, and I see the muscles in her belly contracting. I descend a trail of kisses down around her stomach before focusing my attention on her inner thighs.

"Open your legs," I order, and she looks over me shyly like she's ashamed of something.

She finally opens her legs, probably noticing it wouldn't be negotiable, and allows me full access. Burying my head between her legs, my mouth starts to explore her, preparing her for what's to come, even if she is already wet and ready for my touch. She gasps for air and seizes the sheets next to her as I drift my attention to her clit. Kissing it. Licking it. Sucking it. She grips my hair with her hands, like she wants to push my head deeper into her. Not that I would mind.

"You taste divine," I groan, and her moans increase. She's getting me hard just by watching her lose control.

If I'm being honest, I never liked going down on a woman. I was an asshole, I took my blowjob and never gave anything back. It was hard sex with women who knew what they were doing and whose faces I've never really seen. It was never about emotions. But her, she's different. I want to watch her come, tingling with pleasure under my touch, I want to treat her right.

I continue to kiss her, my tongue and lips claiming her clit, as I feel her climax nearing. I stroke one finger inside her before she starts to call out my name from her sweet mouth, which almost makes me jerk off. I increase my pace, sucking her clit harder, pushing more pressure into her core, and squeeze one of her breasts while she arches her back even more. I stroke another finger inside, tug her nipple around my forefinger, while my tongue pushes into her clit and she explodes. I maintain the pace, letting her enjoy her orgasm as long as she can. She starts to relax once her orgasm crashes all around her, and I pull over, watching her out of breath with a satisfied smile on her face. She looks flushed. Good. I lick my lips, swallowing the last taste of her. I usher over her fully as she clutches our bodies together, her breasts connecting with my chest.

"That was very good," she whispers while my lips collide with hers. "No man ever did that." I tense when she speaks of the other bastards unworthy of her. But that is the past. I stroke her cheek softly, knowing I'll give her many orgasms to come.

Her hand starts to cup my manhood as her lips curve into a smile. Damn. She was always so shy to touch me here, I never wanted to impose on her, or ask her to do anything she didn't want. She starts to stroke me, and I fall on my back next to her, allowing her to be on top. I'm already hard from going down on her, and if she continues to tease me, I could come right here. I caress her back while she kisses my chest, stroking me faster. The feel of her touching my cock feels so good that my muscles start to tense of pleasure. But when I cup her nape to lean her over to kiss me, her eyes are drawn with fear. Something is terrifying her. She lowers herself over my cock to suck me, but something feels wrong. I fucking want her mouth on me, and it takes all the strength in the world to pull her body on my lap, preventing her of doing something she was obviously doing because I went down on her. I want her willing.

"*Ma belle*, what happened?"

When she notices my concern, she glances away, afraid to look into my eyes. "You know, before you, I slept with one man only." That Stephan asshole, what did he do to her? He didn't deserve her. "And Stephan, he forced me to…" She looks over my manhood as she starts to feel embarrassed. I give her a kiss, encouraging her to go on. "Suck him. Hard. He didn't care if I would vomit, or if I felt like a whore. He said it was my job to do this. That men want this." My jaw clenches, and I promise myself if I ever meet this bastard, I'll give him a lesson. I'll shove his dick in his head. "That he would cheat if I never gave him this. And I don't want to lose you." Her voice is weak and shuddering.

I don't want to lose you. God, Elle. Like she thought I'd cheat on her if I didn't have a blowjob? I would never treat her like that. I'm not a bastard. At least, not with her. Sure, her sweet mouth on me would make me come in record time, but I'm not an animal. I can wait. I stroke her cheeks, forcing her to catch my gaze. "That man was an asshole. You'll not lose me, and if one day you want to try—I'd not force you." I switch positions, pulling myself on top of her, before scanning her lovely face. "I'll make love to your mouth, the same way I'm doing with your body. It's not fucking between us." On that note, I kiss her. "And if you don't want to, as I told you before, it's fine."

She relaxes, and I start regaining my hardness as her hands caress my back. "Will you make love to me tonight?"

She didn't need to repeat this twice. "Yes."

She assures me she's on the pill. Good. I don't want a piece of latex to come between us. She wraps her legs around my back as she bites her lower lip playfully. The thought of Stephan touching and hurting her has made me so angry and possessive. Not having her for so long has escalated my need to claim her body. But what if… what if I'm incapable of being sweet?

"I'm afraid to hurt—" I stop, cursing myself for saying my thought out loud. I kiss her neck, praying she didn't hear me.

She cups my cheeks with her hands, staring into my soul. "I won't hurt you."

I snort; I wasn't talking about her. "No, I'm afraid to hurt you. That I'll become like my father if I lose control."

The image of my mother haunts my mind. All the pain I witnessed in my childhood. Maybe our past doesn't define us, but it clearly shapes us. I want to treat her right, but what if my desire for her ends up hurting her? I've been raised to treat women badly, and with what she suffered from her ex, someone like me would only destroy her. I have to always be careful. What if I inflict on her what my bloody father did to the women? Fucking like an animal, breaking her.

She smiles before kissing me again. "You'll not. Now, make love to me, Wolf."

And so I oblige. I enter her slowly, letting her adjust to my length. She's tight, which hardens my cock even more. Our tongues dance together, my heartbeat slamming across my chest. My hips flex gently against her, pushing deeper each time. I kiss her neck as she tightens the grip of her legs around me. I thrust into her, changing the angles to hit her with pleasure, finding the right spot. She moans, her fingers raking my back, before I take her hands into mine and pull them to each side of her head. She digs her nails on my skin, toughening the grip of our clutching hands. I push deeper into her, kissing her collarbone as she arches her back, serving her hard nipples next to my face as temptation. I lick, suck, kiss, before I bury my full cock into her.

I remain at a controlled pace, probably the first tier of what I could do to her. Pushing deep but slow, and it feels… insanely good. This is lovemaking. The opposite of who I am. Pure and sweet. Emotional. In each of my thrusts, her body responds to mine. She rolls her hips. Kisses my neck. Her soul pierces me through her eyes. It's mutual ownership.

I let go of her hands, rub the rough pads of my fingers along her cheekbones before kissing her fully. When her eyelids close, her breath quickens, and I know she is close. I push deeper, accentuating my pace, as her eyebrows frown with pleasure and her lips part. I pull my head into her neck, grabbing her butt cheek, making her come for the second time, reaching my release at the same time. Slowly but strongly.

We stay in that position for a couple of minutes before I roll to the other side of the bed, staring at the ceiling. She tries to reach for something to wear and get away from the bed, but I take her hand and bring her back to me. She stares at me in confusion, clearly not used to my display of affection. I open my arm, leading her to lie on my chest, and she obliges happily. I caress her hair, my arm wrapped protectively around her. She hugs me, her fingers caressing my torso, and I kiss her forehead.

Mine.

I've never been hugged or hugged anyone before her. I thought it would weaken me, and honestly, I've never felt the need to get close to someone. But having her in my arms feels good and right. I can't let her go. She's mine to protect. Mine, to lie naked with. Mine, to take care of. She starts to relax on my chest, and I wait for her to fall asleep.

When I know she's fully sleeping a few hours later, I continue stroking her hair, watching her angelic, peaceful face sleep like a creep. I move away without awakening her and put her under her covers. I cannot sleep with her, not that I don't want to. I couldn't. As I said, she's mine and I couldn't forgive myself if I hurt her again. If I had a nightmare and she discovered what happened to me, she wouldn't forgive me. Losing her would break me.

So I walk toward her living room and sleep on the couch, knowing she will be safe from me.

And I'm planning on doing that every fucking night.

CHAPTER 32

Crushing my demons

Elle

Aaron and I make progress during his winter break. I've been sleeping at his place, or he at mine. He hugs me every night, and it feels good. But I know after I fall asleep, he goes to sleep on the couch. His nightmare and what he did to me is still haunting him and bruising him. He'll need time to heal.

Last week he went to his pre-season testing and being apart from him was harder than I thought it would be. The first race of the season will start in two weeks, and I'm hoping by then to be able to reach his heart.

I'm finishing clipping my diamond earring, which matches my ballerina pink dress perfectly. I simper when Aaron's arms embrace me from behind. He disposes a soft kiss on my nape before telling me how beautiful I look tonight, his hardness pressing on my back.

"I wish I could keep you for myself."

He groans at my comment. I clutch my hands around his arms, biting my lower lip to admire him in his marine-blue suit.

We both hate the elite socialite kind of events, and attending this charity gala isn't something we are looking forward to. But everyone whose names are known attends. Everyone, including my mother, to whom I haven't spoken since I sent her my resignation.

I've finally taken a leap to share my artworks to the world. I created a website and a social media account. So far, I've finished two contemporary pieces of birds in oil painting—and, the painting of Wolf. But this one is personal. I'm awaiting the right moment to show it to him. Financially, I've been running low on money and I was on the verge to become a starving artist if it wasn't for Aaron who insisted on helping me. I obviously refused, and he obviously argued it was not negotiable, buying me all the art supplies I needed. He has a blind faith in me, feeling proud of my little accomplishments. Supporting my art, even if it isn't a passion of him. That's why I *love* him. He never wants to change me.

"Don't tempt me, or I might want to fuck you in some private room."

I raise my eyebrow, considering his idea. He definitely has corrupted my soul.

"But I prefer to enjoy what's mine alone. The idea of someone else seeing your naked body is driving me insane." He winks, placing his hand behind my lower back.

I don't mind Aaron's possessiveness. On the contrary, it arouses me most of the time. Stephan's possessiveness was to tame me, putting a leash around my neck. Aaron's possessiveness is freeing, making me feel significant.

I'm not even dazzled by the luxury of the gala we're at. Here or in France, it's always the same thing. Money. Power. Extravagance. Everywhere Wolf goes, the crowd is always following him, scanning him. He inspires either great admiration or profound hatred. Aaron shakes the hands of a few older men, discussing the next season with them as I talk to their wives about my... boyfriend. Because in this type of society, a woman doesn't exist without her man. It's incredibly sexist, and I'm glad Aaron doesn't treat me like one of these green plants. Some younger models throw themselves at his feet, flirting with him, even though I'm standing next to him. My heart immediately races with jealousy. Luckily for Wolf, he ignores them by claiming my mouth, his arms around me, showing me I'm the one on his mind and showing them he belongs fully to me.

We greet Thomas, who seems to be as jaded by this event as I am. Aaron scans him from head to toe before laughing at Thomas' annoyed face. "You didn't even bother to dress up. I don't believe you even own a suit."

"You're right, I don't. I just hate this world and those clowns." I chuckle at Thomas' comment, loving his personality even more. He has a lot of money and yet remains simple. I think that aside from me, he is the only person Aaron really wants to speak with tonight. "Glad to see you, Elle. You look stunning. Aaron is gonna have a hard time keeping the men away from you." Thomas stares at Aaron playfully, like he knew something I didn't. No doubt, Thomas knows Aaron well.

A bunch of old men ask him to join them. Aaron's gaze meets mine, asking my permission. Of course, I oblige, even though standing here alone by myself isn't very pleasant. He gives me a kiss and assures me he'll be right back. I find my mother talking with her husband, playing the perfect wife, even though she's wearing a black dress like she attended a funeral right before. She stares coldly at me before searching for my boyfriend. *No, Mother, my heart hasn't been broken yet.* She doesn't bother to greet me. I decide to not stand by the wall like a kid being punished and head toward the champagne area when a hand grabs me.

"Elle." My stomach turns into a knot when I recognize the voice behind me. A voice that shouldn't be here. A voice I forgot about.

I turn around to meet Stephan with his perfect beige suit, the perfect haircut, and the perfect smile. All those doses of perfection to cover such an imperfect man. Before, I would have been afraid to confront him, but now only my anger remains. I've always wondered why he treated me that way, and tonight I won't let him go away until I have my answers.

"Where is your lapdog?" He gives me his polite—manipulative—lawyer smile.

"My boyfriend, Aaron, isn't far away, and if he sees you, I believe he'll not act kindly toward you." Especially now that I've told Aaron what happened between him and me, knowing his temper, he'll probably beat him to death.

"I understand. I wanted to talk to you, privately, about what happened between us." His expression is unreadable, and for a moment I believe he's gonna repent. "Please, Elle. Just for five minutes." He is extraordinarily calm, almost pleading, which doesn't look like the Stephan I remember.

I nod, accepting to follow him. My gut is screaming to get out, but I need to be brave. I need to face him, to find my closure and move on. And it's not a discussion we could have had among the curious ears of the old money people. On our way to the hallway, I find Louis. He stares at me weirdly, probably wondering why I'm going with another man instead of my boyfriend into a library. I swallow, hoping he won't tell him. I don't want any damage tonight. Stephan closes the door behind him. No lock. I remind myself that I'm stronger now, and that he wouldn't dare do anything to me with his parents right behind the door. Stephan likes to keep up appearances, he would never hurt me—in public.

"What do you want, Stephan?" My eyes narrow as he walks in a circle around me, inspecting me from head to toe, his vicious gaze disgusting me. "Are you here to apologize?"

"You're the one who left me, Elle. Why should I apologize?"

I snort. Of course, it's again one of his manipulative games. "Because you're everything I despise. You treated me horribly. You were a huge asshole." He starts to smirk, proud of himself to still get under my nerves. I breathe heavily, keeping my cool. I'll find my closure whatever way he wants to give it to me, or not. "But now I've found someone who treats me with love and the respect I deserve. I pity you, Stephan. You can't get to me anymore."

"You were lucky to be with me. Other women would have—"

"No, you were lucky. You're an egocentric and manipulative—"

He pushes me violently against the shelf of books, hovering over me with both of his hands caging me. My jaw tightens, my eyes sending blades at him. I hate him. I hate what he has done to me. I'm repulsed by his entire being. I know Stephan is too weak and afraid to punch me or to hurt me. He'd never do that. He is smart. A bruise on my body will mean proof. And as a lawyer, he never left any proof behind.

"Let me go, Stephan, or I swear I'm gonna tell the truth to everyone here tonight. Your mother. Your company. Everyone."

He laughs wickedly. And he's right—Aaron is the only one to know; I'm too ashamed to admit what he did to me. Nobody will ever believe me. Not even my own mother did. As an avid manipulator, he knows my flaws. But maybe I could play him at his own game.

"You won't, we both know that." He clutches my arm, tightening his grip to search for my pain. I wish he could hurt me. Leave a mark on my skin. That way, I would have proof. A proof to cause his downfall. "Nice dress. But I know what's underneath."

"Only my boyfriend knows, and you're not a quarter of what he is." My eyes narrow, I'll provoke him until he commits one mistake that will free me of him. I don't care if he'll hurt me, I want revenge. I want the proof it wasn't in my head. "I give him everything I was reluctant to do with you." I lick my lips. *Bastard.*

His jaw tenses as he pushes me again against the shelf and a few books fall on the floor, hitting us on their descent. "So, you can suck LeBeau's cock and not mine?" I remain silent and proud, waiting for his reaction. But when he doesn't notice the mask of fear on my face, he smiles. "Oh, my sweet. So predictable." He reduces his grip enough to not leave a bruise and starts to spread his mental manipulation on me. "I'm still haunting your nights. You will never forget. When you fuck him, you think of my cock." He speaks his devastating words to shame me, thinking he has control over me, but I don't even hear him anymore.

He can't reach me. This is my closure. It was never me. It was never my fault. Stephan can't bear to see me happy while he is miserable and lonely. He has put me down—not because of me, but because he never believed in himself, so he exercised his control to tame me. To make him look bigger. Stronger. Happier. But alone, he can't stand himself. He suffers from an inferiority complex. I was too good for him, all along.

"You can't live with yourself," I mumble under my breath, before shoving him away. "You'll never have me, Stephan."

He frowns his eyebrows, clearly unsatisfied with my freedom. I start walking away from him and from the past when he shoves me against the shelf. This time, brutally—and not caring if he hurts me. "I'll have what you gave him, whore." I feel his breath of alcohol next to my cheek as his eyes squint with deep hatred.

I try to kick him in his little manhood, but he turns my wrist violently, making me howl in pain as he shuts me off with his hand on my mouth. I hear only my heartbeat when Stephan forces my hand to stroke him on top of his pants. I'd never have believed he would do that publicly, and now I'm scared. I push him, try to kick him, to move away, but he tightens his grip on me, hurting me to bend to his desire. Flashbacks come back to my mind, and my blood runs of fear. I feel my head spinning. I feel so stupid. His strong hold on my wrist stops the circulation of my blood. I keep moving, but yet he stills controls me. Please. No. He tightens his other grip on my throat, making me gasp for air. Taking pleasure in choking me. I would never forgive myself. And Aaron? I would lose him, he'll hate me. I can't lose Aaron.

I see a blurry shadow grabbing Stephan's shoulder and throwing him on the floor. I catch my breath, my vision is getting better, and I notice Louis standing over Stephan on the ground. He must have followed us here.

"Are you okay, Elle?" he asks concerned, his fist ready to hits Stephan. I nod a yes, I can't let Aaron know what almost happened. Louis' gaze shifts to Stephan before grabbing him by his collar. "If I see you near us again, me and my men will kick the shit out of you until you have no teeth. Understood, asshole?" He pushes him toward the door, and Stephan runs like a coward into the hallway. Hurting a woman—that he could do, but having the balls to hurt a man was out of question.

I sit on the desk behind me, trying to regain my spirit, my heartbeat slowing, my nerves still wrecking. I was stupid facing Stephan alone. And now, I'm terrified. I'm terrified to see him again and to never be able to speak the truth about him. I feel ashamed. Vulnerable. What would have happened if Louis didn't arrive? Today, Stephan took a step he never did, and now I'm not feeling safe anymore. My body is trembling when I feel Louis' hand on my knee as he sits next to me.

"Elle? What happened?" His eyes glance over me with worry.

"Nothing. Don't tell Aaron, please," I plead, trying to ignore the tears of my weakness devouring me inside. If Aaron knew, he would cause damages that I'm not ready to face. A truth I'm not ready to reveal after what happened.

Louis nods. "I won't. But if he learns what this jerk was about to do, you know that he won't forgive you for keeping this secret from him?"

"I know, but I don't want him to get into trouble. Stephan isn't worth Aaron's future." I don't know if I can trust Louis, but I have no other choice. "Why did you help me? You hate me." I readjust my dress and pull my hair free.

"I don't hate you." I arch my eyebrow, as he sighs. "I told you, I'm not a jerk."

"Not a jerk to help me out with a dickhead, but a jerk to publish compromising pictures of Monica," I murmur, not daring to meet his eyes.

"Would you believe me if I told you I never published those pictures?"

I stare at him, my eyes wildly open. His emerald gaze is dark, his face serious. "Why should I trust you?"

"You shouldn't, but I'm telling the truth," he adds dolefully. "Since I'm holding one of your secrets, you'll hold one of mine. You can never tell Monica, promise?"

I nod, the seriousness of his tone almost frightening me. He takes a long breath before speaking like a patient does with a therapist. "I was hammered on the track. Monica had lost her fiancé, and we already fucked. I saw her and Aaron, who was my best friend at that time, looking quite close, hugging each other."

He snorts before staring at the wall in front of him, as if he were reliving an event. "I got freaking jealous. And then, Monica said she loved Aaron. I lost it and broke up with her. I now know they love each other as brother and sister, but back then, I was already tense because of my rivalry with him. That was too much for me."

For some reason, I believe Louis' words. I understand how destructive jealousy can be.

"Anyway, I was at a bar that night, and I got drunk watching her pictures. I passed out and lost my phone." He swallows. "When I woke up, I was back at my parent's place, and my mother had found my phone." He gives me a repulsive smile, glancing at me for a few seconds—just long enough for me to notice the broken expression on his face and his wet eyes. He drifts away immediately, and my heart starts to feel for him, replacing the pieces together.

"Did your mother share the pictures?"

"Yeah, she did. My parents didn't appreciate I was losing my time over a girl while I should focus on racing. They hated Aaron, and the fact he stole my spot." He smolders with resentment as his fingers clutch the edge of the desk.

"But she's your mother. She knew you'd be in trouble for that?" A dazed look on my face, I wonder how we could all have fucked up parents.

"If it'd mean that I finished first, she didn't care." He struggles to continue. "Anyway, when I knew what she had done, I erased the pictures from the group, but it was too late. All the drivers had seen it, saved it, and Monica's reputation was already destroyed. The same day, Aaron's fist hit my face." He shakes his head. "The worst in that, is that in our world, fucking and recording the women we've fucked, or even sharing them, are a recurring thing," he says, staring at the floor as an expression of disgust appears on my face.

"Why didn't you say the truth then? It doesn't make sense."

His stare meets mine, his mouth shaking, hesitating to tell me something. "For the same reason you don't want to tell Aaron about that jerk."

Shame. Guilt. Afraid to hurt the person you—

"I fell in love with Monica. I still am." He tries to hold a smile, his lips close, before playing nervously with the end of his suit. "I knew she would hate me at some point. I never deserved her, so it was easier for her to hate me than breaking her heart later on."

My mouth hangs open, witnessing cocky Louis Harmil tearing himself apart, capable of loving another human being more than himself. His story is the truth. I remember his jealousy when I first met Monica in the lobby with Aaron. The way he stared at her like a ghost later that day. At the Prize Giving Ceremony, the fight he had with his mother.

"Why did you tell me the truth?"

"Because, Outsider, you don't know me enough to have your mind already made up about me. And for once it's nice to have someone who looks at you differently than being a playboy jerk." He tries to smile and joke, but he is hiding behind a mask. Like all of us. Louis is lonely. "Keeping up my reputation isn't as easy as it appears. I owe my parents everything. They invested in me. You know, when people love you, they expect a lot of you, and most of the time I end up deceiving them."

"You deserve better, Louis. And where you are today isn't thanks to them. You are the one racing in that car, not your parents. You deserve to be happy too."

I lean in to hug him and show my support, but he is hesitant to hug me back. "Your boyfriend is gonna kill me if he sees you're hugging me."

"Not if you tell him and Monica the truth."

He starts to relax and hugs me back—without overstepping. Tonight, we both shared a secret to protect the one we love from us. In our loneliness, maybe we created a new friendship. An improbable one.

"Monica deserves better, and Aaron isn't the forgiving type." He clears his throat. "Even if I hate to admit it, he's a good guy. At least, a better one, thanks to you."

"He is. And you shouldn't give up on Monica. Be worthy of her."

"Elle. What the fuck?!"

We both jump when we hear an enraged voice screaming, slamming the door behind him.

Aaron.

Fuck.

CHAPTER 33

My light in the darkness

Aaron

"Elle. What the fuck?!"

I roar, watching my girlfriend in a compromising position with this fucker, Louis. I've been looking for her for God knows how long, and I catch her in a fucking old library with the man I despise above everything else? They both stare at me with wide eyes, and I don't think twice. Anger contracts my face, my fists close, my blood runs hot throughout my body.

"Aaron. It's not what you—" Too late. I grab Louis by his collar and shove him against the wall. Elle keeps begging for me to put him down, but I can't. This bastard made a move on her, and I'll punch him with twice the intensity I did when he hurt my sister-in-law.

"Aaron! Stop! He has done nothing wrong!" Elle clutches my arm, trying to get some sense into me, but I tighten my grip around Louis' throat. He doesn't even dare say a word, and for that, he knows me well. One word could set me on fire, and my patience is rather limited.

"What were you doing with my girlfriend?" This bastard stares over at Elle, like he's waiting for her to speak. She shakes her head, a no. What the fuck? Her lips are shaking as her gaze drifts between Louis and me. "If you don't tell me what's going now, I swear my fist is gonna hit your freaking face," I erupt at Louis.

"Stop! Let him go." Elle's eyes soften my rage, looking at me like a traumatized doe. I let go of Louis, and my eyes narrow at her for an explanation. She nods at Golden Boy, who stares at the both of us before leaving. "Louis kinda saved me."

"Saved you? What the fuck were you even doing here?" I raise my voice, but when she rushes to hug me tight, her head on my chest, I know something is wrong. I relax and stroke her back gently.

"You have to promise me you won't act impulsively, okay?" I nod, even though we both know 'not acting impulsively' isn't my forte, especially with her. I'm a protective asshole.

And so, I listen to the whole story.

That freaking trash Stephan tried to abuse my girlfriend. Why did I ever leave her alone tonight? One thing is sure, Stephan is a dead man.

I storm toward the exit of the library to find him, ignoring Elle yelling after me to not do a thing. You bet I will. She's mine, and he bruises a beauty like her because he's a sadist. I search around the gala to find him, but I'm interrupted by people trying to have conversations with me. Luckily, when they notice the killer look in my eyes, they don't bother. Finally, I find Stephan in a pleasant discussion with some old billionaires. Just the sight of him makes me want to destroy that microbe.

"Stephan." He turns to face me, recognizing who I am. He swallows, his eyes filled with fear when he meets the rage in mine. I can't help but smirk as I approach him, grabbing his jacket. "I've been meaning to talk to you. Follow me."

Not that he has a choice. I tighten my grip and shove him outside. Nobody is in the back garden at this time of the night. I give a head sign to Thomas; I don't want anyone to interrupt us. I bet he won't approve, but he knows me enough to know that the only orders he can give me are the ones on track. *And not always.*

"You'll stay away from Elle. I know everything you did to her, and I can promise you that you'll pay for that." I remain in control, but my low voice is terrifying him enough. I'm twice his height, twice his muscles, twice the man that he is.

"You can't hit me. This event is full of important people. You can't do anything."

I burst into laughter. He might be a lawyer, but he's not a smart one. And I'm definitely not the type to obey the rules, but to make them.

I shove my fist in his face, blood jerks off, a cracking sound resounds. A broken nose. He drops violently to the ground. His eyes bug out, stuck between confusion and terror—I believe he finally understands what man he has in front of him. I'll do everything for Elle. Including killing that piece of garbage. He disrespected *ma belle*, he tried to destroy her, and that I will not permit. At this moment, I'm happy to be a monster just like my father. I pull him up with my fist, making him stand on his tiptoes. I hear Elle running in our direction and stopping behind me breathlessly before noticing two witnesses walking around the garden. I couldn't care less.

"You won't touch her anymore. I promise I'll send you to jail, freaking bastard," I roar as he curves his mouth into repulsion, incapable to move around my grip.

"Aaron, let him go please," Elle's sweet voice calls me out. "Aaron, he's not worth it."

"Listen to your whore," Stephan mumbles, his gaze drifting to the floor cowardly. The thought of him touching her, tarnishing her, makes me go nuts. I punch him again in his face, his blood spraying onto my fist. Fuck. My suit is ruined.

I don't notice Elle's voice howling, I'm only focused on Stephan. He tries to punch me back, but I intercept his fist, scratching his hand like the microbe that he is. He screams in pain and falls onto his knees.

"What's all this?" An older woman dressed in black narrows her eyes at me. "I'm calling security, you bloody asshole," she screams before grabbing Elle's arm fiercely. I immediately tense. "Elle, keep your boyfriend on a leash! See what he's doing to a gentleman like Stephan? I don't recognize my own daughter." *Her mother.*

Why isn't Elle saying anything? She keeps staring at the floor, like a bullied person accepting her fate. Screw it. I don't think twice. I twist Stephan's hand before making him stand up, and my eyes gun at Elle's mother. "Tell her what you did to my girlfriend! Tell her what a bastard you are." I tighten my grip on Stephan as he keeps howling in pain. *What a pussy, I'm sure he's faking it.*

"This man ruined your daughter. He treated her like a slave, forcing her and abused her." Elle shakes her head telling me to stop, a mask of fear on her face, but I can't. I'm breaking my promise, but I can't let people keep disrespecting her. "Stephan is an abuser. He was in the library trying to force himself on her." I push him on the ground. Stephan swallows, searching all around him fearfully. His mask is finally revealed.

Elle's mother scrutinizes me for the truth. I take a step closer to her to let her see me in the light. I know my eyes have reddened of anger, my gaze black, every muscle in my body is tensing.

She takes a step away from me before staring at Stephan on the floor, who is trying to defend himself with another lie. "It's not true. I was helping her and wishing her all the best when she kissed me and wanted to—"

"Shut up," Elle's mother drops before turning to face her daughter, her mouth hanging open, her lips shaking. "Elle. Is what Aaron is saying the truth?"

Elle's tears are falling on her cheeks as she nods a yes. *What did I do?* I didn't think about the pain I would cause her, enraged by my own anger. I've never seen Elle so broken. She's crying, her whole body shaking. I've never witnessed my Elle so afraid and vulnerable.

"Yes, Mother. You never believed me." Elle's tears don't stop, and my whole heart is breaking, knowing I caused her deep pain.

"Elle, I'm—" I reach to hug her, but she pushes me away. Fuck.

"You humiliated me." *No, I saved you.*

She storms away from us, escaping her own nightmare. It wasn't my truth to tell. I forced her and betrayed her trust. I fucked up badly, but I'd do it all over again. I won't allow her past to destroy her. I failed my brother, but I won't fail her, even if she hates me. That's why I don't run after her. I know she needs to be alone right now. For that, we're the same.

I look over Stephan's blood on my hand. I could have beat him to death. I didn't care about the consequences. I'm just like André. And I don't even regret it. Elle's mother's face is like a ghost, staring nowhere. She's going into shock from the truth. After all, she pushed her daughter into the arms of *another* monster.

"Don't worry about security. I'll take care of this," she says mechanically before returning to the gala. She keeps murmuring the same sentence, "I never believed her."

I glance at the bastard on the floor one more time, my eyes promising him he'll go to jail, and that on my life he'll never touch her ever again.

Thomas walks over to me, he had witnessed the whole scene. "That was quite a show." I remain silent. I know he won't judge me for it, nor ask further questions. The security guards arrive, eying me. They take Stephan under their shoulders and tell me I can stay if I clean up myself.

"The press will not know about your fight," Thomas assures me.

"Do you think I care about the press?" I give a sign to the security guards informing them I'm leaving, I have no desire to stay. Thomas follows me, probably happy to escape the gala. "I fucked up. Elle will not forgive me."

"That won't be easy, but I would have done the same. Sometimes the truth needs to get out, no matter how hard it is to hear it." Thomas, a freaking Yoda like usual.

"Don't get me wrong, I don't regret what I did." I shake my head as we walk toward the exit. "But I shouldn't have stolen the truth from her. She wasn't ready. I broke her trust."

"You're a good man, Aaron. Don't punish yourself. Elle will forgive you."

"You don't know her like I do."

"No, but I know you. I've seen how you are with her, how both of you look at each other. You're alike." I feel sometimes that Thomas can read in me as well as he can read a race.

"She's a better person than me."

"Probably." He laughs. *Bastard.* "Now, go do right by her the same way you take the checkered flag."

I can't help but smile. He gets me. "Your words are like music to my ears."

"No, really. I'm proud of you, Aaron." I look fixedly at Thomas muddled by his wording. We are used to joking around, communication and shitloads of emotions aren't our forte. "Not just as a racer, but as a person."

"Glad you think so, because I'm afraid you're stuck with me for a good twenty years. I'm not planning on retiring anytime soon." I smirk before my stomach turns into a knot. Racing will always be in my life. But what about Elle? "Anyway, I need to go. Thank you, Thomas."

We nod at each other and eventually, we drift apart. I feel miserable as I'm heading toward the garage to pick up my car. Louis runs after me, but I don't have the time to hear him out. What on earth could he possibly want? Can't he see I have more important matters than him? I ignore him, but he stops me by grabbing my shoulder from behind. I instantly shove him against the wall for the second time tonight.

"I just want to know if Elle is okay," he defends himself, and I loosen my grip on his expensive dress shirt.

"What do you think?" I shout before swallowing my pride and stepping away from him. "Thank you, for what you did for her earlier." Louis gives me a smile, and I hate myself for thanking him. I have only repugnance for him. He got to play the hero, while I remain the fucking villain.

"I'm sorry, Aaron." He stares at the ground, zoning out. "When you have a moment, I'd like to talk to you on the track."

"We have nothing to talk about, Louis."

"I owe you an apology."

Is he drunk? He has a defeated expression on his face I've never seen before, even on his worst days. The bastard is serious.

"I don't have time for this." I storm away, ready to get home to what really matters.

All I care about is her.

Elle

I can't believe Aaron slammed the truth in my mother's face. His expression was so dark and enraged. And now, I'm certain every one of the elite socialites will know what Stephan did to me. There is no point for him to lie anymore, everyone discovered his true colors. I should feel relieved, but on the contrary, I feel ashamed and weak. Sharing my darkest secret with Aaron was heartbreaking, but hearing the truth out loud from his voice made me realize I hadn't healed completely of Stephan's abuse. I wasn't strong enough. I'm still ashamed and humiliated.

I hear Aaron's voice calling out to me from the living room. But I don't answer. Instead, I try to erase my tears, but I know my eyes have reddened since I've spent the past hour crying. When he enters my bedroom and sees what a mess I am, his dark expression softens as he kneels in front of me, his hands stroking my cheeks.

"I'm sorry, Elle." He kisses my forehead, his eyes plunging into my soul. His touch is sweet and caring, contrasting with his feral and forceful expression of earlier. They all know Wolf as a cold, indomitable, all-alpha man. But I know him just as he truly is. Capable of the greatest and the worst. An extreme, only I could ease.

He gave me my closure, I shouldn't be mad. But he stole it from me. I wasn't ready to face how weak I am, to face the judgment on my mother's face. Maybe I wasn't ready to move on? Maybe I'm still punishing myself for having fallen into Stephan's trap. To have been his victim. His toy. People will probably ask, *Why didn't you get out sooner?* but no one apart from someone who had lived it can understand how manipulation is almost impossible to get away from. Tonight, I realize how blind I was, and it makes me want to punish myself. And so, I hide my emotions the best way I can, by pushing him away.

"You had no right, Aaron! You humiliated me in front of my mother! You showed her how weak I am." I storm around the room, shame inking into my blood.

"If I hadn't told her the truth, he would have stayed engraved in you. You can't keep everything to yourself, Elle." I stare over at him looking god-like, while I'm just a broken mess. He takes a careful step toward me. "I'm sorry, but it would have eaten you alive if you never spoke up. I know you weren't ready. I know I acted like an asshole." His fingers caress mine before he kisses my knuckles. "But sometimes you need someone to help you face your fears. You aren't alone in this. I'm with you, and you don't have to feel ashamed. You are wonderful." He pulls me into his chest, his thumb brushing my back. "I wish I could tell you I regret what I did, but I don't. Any of it. You're mine, and I don't want a part of your soul to belong to him and the atrocity of your past."

I want to ease into his touch, I want him to make love to me. I need him physically, but I, too, need his whole soul to belong to me. Just like he wants all of mine. Aaron might be right, some truths are too hard to face alone, you need someone to pull you out from your nightmare, just like *Everlasting*. But that applies to him, as well. I don't own his whole soul; it still belongs to his dark past. He's still hiding many things from me.

"What about you, Aaron?" I press my hands on his hard chest, my eyes looking up at him. "You said, sometimes you need someone to help you face your fears. Why don't you sleep with me? Why do you leave after I fall asleep?"

"I don't want to hurt you," he whispers, reaching for my lips to kiss.

I shake my head, refusing his kiss. I know he'll try to distract me, but I'm hell-bent. "Why? What are you afraid of? What are your nightmares about?"

"Elle. Don't." His jaw tenses as he takes my hands away from his chest.

"I won't. You know the darkest part of me. You know what Stephan did. I trusted you with something I'm ashamed of. I've been worried you'd look at me differently. I lowered myself, sharing the most broken part of me. Tonight, you owe me the same truth." I raise my voice, imploring him to let me in.

He walks across the room, ignoring me as his back faces me. Both of his hands are on the wall, his head down. My voice is sharp, I won't let him escape me. "What happened to you, Aaron?"

"You'll never look at me the same way. I can't lose you," he articulates painfully.

I walk toward him and clutch our hands together. He faces me, and I press my body against his. "You'll never lose me. Nothing can push me away from you. What happened to you? What are you afraid of?"

"Elle, please don't ask me that." His eyes beg.

"Sometimes you need someone to face the truth with you. I'm that someone, Aaron. I need you to tell me. For me. For us."

He tries to get away from me, but my weak body pulls him back on the wall, and he contemplates me with confusion. We both know he's stronger than I am and can pull away at any moment, yet he doesn't try to escape me. "I need you to explain to me, Aaron. Don't run away from me again. I want all of you."

"You'll leave. You'll be disgusted by me." His voice hard, he stares at me shamefaced.

"I won't. Let me prove it to you." I take his face into my palms before kissing him passionately, tenderly, obsessively, letting him know he belongs with me. "I'm yours, Aaron, nothing will change that," I whisper while our mouths collide. "I need you. If I'm significant, let me help, let me show you."

Every muscles in his body tense as he breaks our kiss. His eyes meet mine, conflicted between darkness, pain, and fear. I nod, encouraging him, pulling myself in his embrace. When his calloused fingers caress my cheek, my lips, my neck, just as he's looking at me for the last time, convinced he'll lose me, I know he's about to tell me the whole truth.

Tonight, I'll meet his darkness. And tonight, I'll be his light.

CHAPTER 34

Remedy

Aaron

For the first time in my entire life, I expose my cruel past to the only person that ever mattered. I'm convinced she'll leave me and will confirm my rules as I hit her with the somber truth. My father forcing me to watch while he fucked my mother, punishing her for cheating. My mother, who couldn't love me more than she loved money. The years that came after that. My father beat me to lower myself under his ruling. Owning me by my love for him. Forcing me to watch when he handled women like objects.

I tell her what happened on the day of my brother's death. André came back into my life that same day, and had threatened to destroy my career, shaming me publicly on the track. I was weak and angry, and those fuckers heard us. I fought them. Six against one. I kicked the shit out of them. But that wasn't enough. I needed revenge. I was consumed by my anger. Ashamed of what they witnessed. That led me to speed racing and killing my brother in the car crash. Elle keeps listening to the darkness of my past, without blinking, without reaching for me, without any emotions.

So, I continue. My nightmares. I didn't do anything to help my mother. A coward. I fear that he has twisted my mind and I'm afraid to hurt Elle. Bruise her. To treat her the same way my father treated women. It was worse than hard sex, it was ownership. I'm afraid to lose control. To be like him. To have the impulses André created in me. With the other women I never lost control—it was fucking, and I was emotionless. But her, she awakens my heart and also my demons. I can't hide anything about me. If I'm meant to lose her, she'll destroy me and I'll probably transform myself into a soulless monster.

When I finish telling her about my gloomy past, my voice is trembling and I've never felt so weak and vulnerable. I'm fucking ashamed. How could she love me? Love someone like me? A coward. A villain. A heartless man. I stare at her as she shakes her head no, her pure eyes aghast and appalled. I was right. I scared her away. I need to leave. I can't bear the look on her face. I'm disgusting her. She proved that she couldn't love me fully, just the lighter part. With her gaze switching between me and the floor, I rise up from the bed and head toward the door.

"I'm sorry, you deserve better."

But then out of surprise, she explodes in tears and rushes toward me, capturing me into a hug. "I'm the one who is sorry." *Sorry?* She shouldn't be sorry for not being able to love me. I want the best for her, and if I'm not it, so be it.

She erases her tears with her long feminine fingers, opening her sultry mouth as if she's about to say something. But instead, she exits her bedroom, leaving me alone. I'm terrorizing her. She can't stand the sight of me. I ignore my ripping bloody heart, the fact I've lost the most precious—

"I've made this weeks ago." She came back. She's here. With a one by one meter canvas.

My eyebrows knit together, not understanding where she's going with this. She holds the painting close to her chest, her hands trembling as if she's hesitant to reveal it to me. Her eyes are begging, tarnished by the darkness I shared with her. She finally uncovers the strength to show the art she's holding and…

Shit. She painted me. Fucking me.

She painted me as if she knew me all along.

The real me. No mask. No game. Just me.

My eyes, between conflict, pain, and determination. Birds, her trademark. I look haunted and yet there is light. A promise of the possibility of happiness. Her. She's my light. Everything she touches, she's healing it, illuminated it. I have no words. Where was she all this time? I can't let her go. I need her. I can't give up on the best part of me.

She poses the painting on the ground, positioning her hands on my chest, my jaw still open. "That's the man I—"

Her eyes rise to mine, full of tenderness, before she caresses my face. "I love you."

I stare at her in shock as a wave of emotions reaches me. I feel a pain in my chest, my heart waking up after all this time. She loves me. She said it. The word that means everything to her, the word she couldn't say. The word meaning her soul belongs to me. The word allowing her to be mine. And tonight, she said it twice. With her painting, and with her words. Two declarations. She's the best thing that has ever happened to me, and…

She loves me.

She loves me, knowing the darkest part of my soul.

And I love her, too. But I can't tell her yet.

Elle

"I love you."

I admitted it to him. There is no return. Aaron needs me, and I can't live without him. His father broke him, he witnessed so much darkness, more than a human being could handle, and yet he turned out to be a sweet and caring man with me. I know what this word means to us. That I give him my soul, that he could rip me apart, that I'm his. But I trust him. Not all men are the same. I've given him the key to my heart, and the secret of my inspiration. Him. It's always been him. The one I was waiting for during all those years. He's damaged but beautiful. Painful but healing. Together, we're Yin and Yang, opposite but whole.

He stares at me in shock, and Aaron—who's known to hide his

emotions—pains to do so. His face softens, his eyes wild and filled with tenderness.

"How could you love me?" He shakes his head, his tongue wetting his mouth, scanning me.

"For everything that you are. I love you, Aaron." I pull him closer, my hands cupping his cheeks, while I'm standing on my tiptoes to reach his face. "I love you for your darkness and your light. For everything, Aaron. I'm yours." He clutches my hips, separating the remaining space between our bodies, before pulling me in for a heated kiss. "And you're not your father, Aaron. You're everything he isn't."

"You're the only one seeing the best in me." I know this isn't true. Thomas seems to care for Aaron like his son. Monica loves him like a brother. But I'm the only person he opened entirely to. The one person he gave his soul almost fully.

The look in his eyes betrays the fact he wants to say something but can't. Instead, he pulls me back for an intoxicating kiss, my heart hammering in my chest. "I need you," he drops, hot and desperate.

"My heart is yours, but don't break it please." I manage a simper, trying to joke while I'm scared to death. I love him, and yet now I'm fearing to lose him. My insecurities are still crushing me. "I can't bear to see you getting bored with me. You know my body by heart, maybe you'll need another woman," I add.

"There is only you, Elle." His thumb pulls up my face for my gaze to meet his. "Only you." His lips seal mine, silencing my insecurities, promising there is only us. "You're the most gorgeous woman I know. You're driving me crazy like no one else has." I make a small laugh when I notice his hardness pressing on my stomach. "I adore your laugh. Everything about you is perfection to me. And that painting you did, you have so much talent."

My heart flushes, knowing Aaron isn't a man of words. Our kiss deepens until we're molding into each other's souls. He's mine. His grip tightens, my body panting to feel him under me. My hand starts to reach Aaron's pants, stroking him on top of them while he furrows his brow, contemplating me. With my other hand on his neck, I pull him into another kiss as I start unzipping his pants. We undress each other as fast as we can, our lips always connecting, his fingers starting their descent down to tease my entire V zone.

With my heart slamming across my chest, I'm ready to leave the past behind us. I bite my lower lip, admiring the man that I just confessed my love to, before my hand touches his hardness. I fall onto my knees, deciding to erase a bad memory with a new one. But before I can act, Aaron pulls me up for another kiss, caressing my hair. "You don't have to do this, ma belle."

"I want to," I assure him.

He puts a strand of my hair behind my ear. "Are you sure?" I nod, a smile on my face, as he analyzes me. "If you feel uncomfortable, you tell me. I don't want you to force yourself."

I kiss him again before kneeling in front of him. His stare doesn't leave mine, and I know he isn't relaxed. I've never seen someone as protective as Aaron, but he doesn't have to protect me from him. I know I can trust him. My hand stroking his length, I tease his tip, drawing circles with my tongue, his muscles immediately tensing. He starts to groan when my mouth focuses her attention on it, our eye contact not breaking. Aaron's fingers brush my hair, his other hand gripping the desk behind him. Seeing him tensing, moaning with pleasure, his eyes darkening with lust, creates in me a new form of power. I take him fully into my mouth, slowly at first, my tongue offering him more friction. He groans and curses, and a simper eradicates my face. It is the opposite of Stephan. I felt so little and ashamed with him, but with Aaron it's different. Good, even. Thrilling.

"Fuck, Elle. I could come right here." My tongue darts of my mouth to caress his tip, before tasting his precum. "You're torturing me."

I increase my pace, taking him deeper, spurred on by the gasps of pleasure my mouth is eliciting. His hand fists my hair, his hips following my movement. I know he's close to his release when his groans grow in intensity and he resists the urge to be in control. "Elle, I can't hold on. Move if you—"

I don't listen; I suck, lick and slide my mouth over him faster—a thing that isn't easy to do, due to his length. Our paces are passionate. We collide in a lustful explosion, his orgasm crashing around him, taking him a full force.

I lick my lips, surprised to like the taste of him, and even more surprised to be wet from what just happened. Weirdly, bringing him to the edge empowered me. He pulls me up before kissing me deeply. As a thank you? An act of love? I can't tell. "How did you feel?"

"It was actually good." Was it for him, though? Was I even good? "Did you like it?"

"Loved it. The best head I've ever received. I could come just by watching you." I smile, noticing he's already regaining his strength. "You're mine, Elle. Now, let me please you."

His fingers try to reach for my entrance, but I can't wait. I want him. "I need you inside me, now." My voice is weak by the need for him.

"I want you so badly right now, I don't know if I can be in control." His eyes meet mine, stuck between darkness and desire.

"I don't care, I want you." I crush my lips into his, our tongues tangle, our teeth clash.

The next thing I know I'm pinned against the wall, my legs wrapped around his hips, firmly locked onto him. My fingers run through his hair while his hand roams the curve of my butt cheek. He grasps my waist, holding me with his manly muscles, trapping me with him. Skin against skin. Soul against soul.

His mouth marks my throat and my aching breasts with delicious and addictive kisses. I can't hold on to this torture. He's hard against my belly, a heat flaring between my legs, the need to belong with him has never been so deep. A tropical storm in his ocean eyes, my pulse spikes when he sucks on my nipple.

When he enters me fully, I cry out his name. His pace hard and passionate, my body tenses at first between pain and pleasure under his forceful thrusts. I scrape my nails down his back as he squeezes my butt cheek harder than he ever has before. Our ardent exchanges make me bounce on the wall. Giving and taking, it's a battlefield where passion meets possession. My body is burning of an unstoppable fire. A fire he creates, feeds, entertains, eases, satisfies.

He carries me to the bathroom, positioning himself behind my back in front of the mirror, offering me a view of my whole naked body. Old Elle would have drifted her gaze away instantly. But new Elle is empowered by the way Aaron is staring at her. I don't shame my body, nor my desires anymore. I'm *free*. Aaron kisses my neck, his arms encircled around my waist.

"You're beautiful. I want you to watch yourself come. I want you to watch how I look at you."

I understand this isn't a request when he slams into me, sending an electric shock along my skin. My mouth hangs open as one of his hands holds my back to his sculpted body, and his other cups my breast. I never thought I'd be aroused watching us.

Watching his animality, when he fists my hair, tilting my head back for our lips to connect roughly in a possessive and hungry kiss. The way his muscles contract, the lust in his eyes when he's caressing my clit, making me fall apart. Watching me, flushing, feeling I'm at the mercy of a man who worships my body. A body that could easily bring him to his knees.

He pounds into me with wild abandon, contemplating my whole body responding to each of his thrusts and touches. My eyes rolling, Aaron LeBeau has the gift to awaken me, to bend me to his desire willingly. In our intimacy, he grants me the control I need. Giving me what I need to ease my insecurities. And yet, I know there is no war for control during sex with Aaron. I already lose. My body is happy to submit and oblige, accepting the pleasure.

He releases my body, bending me over the counter, offering him total control over me. His fingers caress my back before capturing my waist, as he thrusts with no mercy, hitting a new spot I never knew existed. My back arching, my legs shaking, I'm tingling with pleasure. Hot flashes spark, facing an intensity he has never reached with me before. Our moans melt together. When I find the strength to meet his gaze in the mirror in front, I recognize his expression. The haunted Aaron. Wolf. I know him too well to know he needs the proximity of the flesh to ease and forget his darkness. What he had admitted to me earlier left a mark of insecurity in his soul and claiming my body with passion is his way to reassure himself. To feel manly, to know that I belong to him. Liberating his past through me. Sharing his darkness with me in each of his thrusts. Possessing me by allowing me to be his remedy. His significant.

Seizing and pounding. Pain and pleasure. He slaps my butt cheek while I feel my whole orgasm crashing roughly around me, howling his name. He cups both of my breasts, leaning toward me, and with a flex of his hips hits the end of me in one last intense thrust before finding his release. We come together, completely washed out, incapable to speak. He kisses my shoulder and nape softly, staying in that position for maybe minutes, regaining our spirits. I can't even turn around to face him. I'm panting breathlessly by our animal exchange, my body sore and weak.

Aaron's hands find my waist, spinning me so my front collides with his. He pushes my wet hair from my forehead before caressing my cheeks, worry in his eyes. His haunted expression is gone, he has recovered his tenderness. He stares at the mirror, swallowing and clenching his jaw when he notices the passionate grip marks he left on my butt cheek. I know it'll shift back to normal in a few minutes, but the fear in his eyes is killing me.

"I'm okay, Aaron," I reassure him by brushing my lips on his, but he's still laying eyes on me like I'm a porcelain doll capable of breaking.

"I shouldn't have gone that hard, I don't know what happened." He caresses my whole body, probably verifying if I had lied to him.

My fingertips brush on his strong chest, tracing the shape of his tattoo, before I put myself on my tiptoes to kiss his throat. "You aren't your father. You didn't hurt me."

"I fucked you, Elle. I've put all my freaking darkness on you." He wraps his arms protectively around my waist to keep me steady. "I should take care of you, not damage you."

"You didn't, and I liked it. If I didn't, I would have told you." He frowns, scanning me for the truth. "Obviously, I'll be sore tomorrow, but from time to time it's good." My cheeks flush red, thinking of what we just did.

Aaron has his darkness, and I have mine. I doubt we could completely change, but with love, we could give what the other needs and evolve. We are probably far from a standard couple, but we are us. With him, nothing is boring. With him, I can be myself. No matter his darkness, no matter the path we're taking, I'll follow him because I know he's mine. I love equally his darkness and his light.

"When you allow me, I'll make sweet, gentle love to you for weeks." He takes me under his arms, carrying us to the shower. "I'll go down on you until you're ready."

"That sounds perfect."

Plus, there is always light in the dark. A hope. His blackness created his overprotective side; without it he wouldn't be my Wolf. Our pasts don't own our futures. Our blood doesn't shape us.

We are the masters of our fate after all.

I feel at peace. The night had promised to be a nightmare, and yet I feel closer to him than I have ever have. My eyes are slowly closing to sleep, my head on Aaron's chest, my hand on his torso. I've gotten so used to him. I hear his heartbeat slowing while he's caressing my hair, his thumb brushing my arm. I chuckle when I feel his erection on my stomach. He insisted he wanted to feel my bare skin on him, not allowing me to dress up—well, now he'll have to deal with his bulge.

When I wake up early in the morning, I find Aaron spooning me into a hug. He hasn't let go of me all night. A simper reaches my face, savoring the moment. *He slept with me the whole night without a nightmare.* He accepted the intimacy that had triggered his demons before. He beat them. I spin to face him. He looks so peaceful and angelic. His eyes are still closed, and yet he pulls me onto his chest, like he knew I was watching him. And I know it's the best night's sleep either of us has had in a while.

I lean in to kiss him. His eyes open, full of hunger when he stares at my naked body sitting on his lap. He smirks, and I giggle when he steals me a galvanizing kiss that makes my heart shiver, hammering so hard each time. We both know what will happen next.

Our demons can't reach us anymore.

We are each other's remedy.

CHAPTER 35

Wolf

Life has been good. Too good. The worst enemy of a Formula 1 driver is happiness. It dulls your killer instinct. You should have your head on the track, give everything to it, even your life, if you have to. But lately, I've been driven by my cock and the organ that serves as my heart. I've been training harder to take the win this season, but I've changed my habits. If it wasn't for her, I would have been at my main residence in Monaco, but instead, I've passed my winter holidays at my penthouse in New York. I've spent every night with Elle and haven't had another nightmare. Slowly she's inking my soul and erasing André's print. Speaking of whom, I haven't returned any of his calls.

Ma belle is at the Australian Grand Prix with me. First race of the season. I couldn't be happier that she finally decided to do what she loves. What she doesn't know is that I may have submitted her paintings to art galleries. I know it's her dream, even if she's still uncertain, but I have no doubts in her. They'll be idiots to not take her. Plus, her, being an artist would mean she could come with me all around the globe. We'll take her art supplies, and then I'll have her with me. All. The. Fucking. Time.

It's freaking bullshit. I live in Monaco. She lives in New York. I travel all year. We're doomed to fail. What if she lives with me? Would she leave New York? I've never lived with anyone. Would she agree to travel with me? *Focus on the race, Aaron, damn it.* She's messing with my mind.

She offers me a sweet smile, her headset on, ready to follow the race from my paddock. I love how anxious she looks. Then again, I'm known to be indomitable, not the easiest boyfriend to deal with. I saw all the men ogling over her when we arrived. But, Elle is mine. She's also glanced at me a few times when a woman gave me the bedroom eyes, or when a woman she defined as attractive spoke to us. She doesn't have to fear anything. None of them could compare to a quarter of her. She's more gorgeous than all of them, and even if I hate to admit it, she completely ruins me for other women. *Damn it, the race Aaron.*

Monica makes fun of me when she sees my gaze stuck on Elle, like a softy fucker. You bet she couldn't resist the urge to come, she doesn't miss an opportunity to travel in the sun. Plus, she loves Elle. But who couldn't love her? Louis keeps staring at Mon, and I can't help but grin, the bastard has his mind as fucked as mine because of a woman. Since he told me the whole truth, I still hate him but I believe his hatred for himself is enough to make him suffer. Plus, by the way he's yearning Monica from afar, I guess she hasn't forgiven him. Knowing her, she's just gonna make him work hard for it. Good girl. I just hope Elle won't soften her. She's too good for this world sometimes.

It's time.

I jump into my cockpit and wrap my mind around the race. Gloves on. Helmet on. When I race, Aaron disappears to let Wolf in. Reckless. Dangerous. A sinner. I'm all of the above. We are all dealing with our traumas differently. Me, I race. Racing is what keeps me sane. I need the blistering pace, I race against my own demons. *Hopefully, happiness won't wreck my race.*

I align my car on the grid, and excitement rushes through my veins. I miss this. When the red light disappears, I press the accelerator. 200. 210. 220 mph. I race my car without fear taking the lead. But a race isn't a sprint.

Faster.

A mistake causes me to withdraw from two places. Currently P3,

Louis is taking the lead, followed by another contender. *Freaking happiness.* I focus only on the grinding sound of the motor, shutting my mind off. I don't even pay attention to Thomas' voice in the headset. I race my car faster, gaining microseconds during the turns, taking risks. And I'm at that point again. The point where the same images appear through my mind. Henry. The accident. I let the adrenaline rush consume me. Inside the cockpit, I'm the one in control. I'm powerful. Invincible. When I race I'm a step closer to death. I can feel it racing against me. I've never felt more alive while being closer to death. 225 mph…

Haunted.

I need to get a step closer.

I'm here. I'm at that point, I'm not feeling anything. I'm at that point, I'm feeling at peace. The point when everything can change. When a bad maneuver can make me crash. Just one movement, just one breath away. But I can't help it, I need to see the demons of my past one more time. I need to see Henry.

227 mph…

Henry's spirit is with me. Watching me racing. I feel close again to my brother. Time seems to slow. I feel stuck between life and death. *Henry, I'm so sorry. Forgive me.*

"Aaron. You have an opening to overtake Louis, but it's risky," Thomas speaks in the headset.

I increase the pace, struggling to keep a hold on my steering wheel. One mistake and I'll crash. One mistake, and I'll be with Henry. But this time, something changes. I've always have that fury and that anger inside of me. I'm feral by blood. But I find my peace.

I'm ready to let Henry go.

I love you, brother. I hit the pedal as Thomas screams in the headset, but I smile. I shift it into the turn and overtake Louis.

And at that moment, I know—I will win the race.

Because I don't race against my heart anymore. I race with it. Before, when the races were over, I was alone. Alone with my thoughts, alone with my dark soul. There was only one formula. A game. A haunt. Flirting. Fucking. Controlling. And repeat. But now there is her. I have something to go home to, to fight for. I will not live in the past, but in the future.

I'll race toward the woman I *love.*

Elle

I hug Monica tight when I witness Aaron's victory for the first race of the season. I feel like everything is finally falling into place for us. I'm fearing only one thing. The distance between us. Aaron will be busy with racing, and I'll be on the other side of the globe. He asked me to come to Australia with him, but it would just be a one-time thing, right? Is that so bad I want to travel the world with him? The other drivers don't have their women cheering for them at each race. And Wolf is the alpha type. The type who needs his freedom. Can I really trust him? Can I stay apart from him for so long? The thought of an empty bed at night is something that turns my stomach. I got addicted to him so fast.

"Well, love looks good on Aaron's face." Monica smiles as she sees Aaron jumping into his teams' arms.

"What about you?" I arch my eyebrow into the direction of Louis who trots toward his pit before shaking hands with Aaron, congratulating him on his victory.

"He's gonna work hard for it." By watching Monica's expression, I can sense she will make him wait for months. "I'm pretty sure he won't give up, though. Seeing Aaron happy in a relationship has made him want to be a better man." She chuckles. "I surely won't be a better woman."

"You're an amazing person, Monica." I roll my eyes. "Sometimes you're just like Aaron." Both of them are teasing, seductive, and don't allow themselves to love.

"Just like me, hmm?" I feel Aaron's arms grabbing my waist from behind.

"And that's my cue to go." Monica waves at us.

I turn around, pulling my arms to his shoulders, biting my lower lip. "Great race, Wolf. Tonight is worth celebrating…"

His eyes grow with lust, sparkling as he starts to groan. He moves his gaze to the deep plunging neckline of my flower print summer dress. "You're not wearing any bra?" I shake a no with my head, cocking my eyebrow playfully. "You'll be the death of me, Elle."

"Don't you like that I'm a step closer to get naked soon?"

"God, Elle, I love you," he says instantly, and I open my eyes in shock. He loves me?

As I notice Aaron's eyes wilder, I realize he didn't mean to let it slide. Or maybe to say it at all? He probably meant he loves that I'm a step closer to get naked, right? Not love me? My heart is hammering.

But our moment has to wait as Thomas calls Aaron out on the podium to celebrate his victory.

I can't stop thinking about Aaron's words. Should I confront him? Being in the incertitude is making me anxious. I should forget it. It's nothing, right? Aaron comes back to me once he finished handling a press conference. Tonight, he says he wants to invite me to one of his favorite restaurants. Maybe he'll tell me there?

He kisses me softly when his phone interrupts us. "Damn it, this is the fourth time. I'm sorry, Elle."

He picks up and his whole expression changes. For a couple minutes, he remains silent, his face completely closed off. "Okay." A beat. "I don't know." A beat. "I'll keep you informed." He hangs up.

"What is it?" I start to worry, my fingers caressing his arm.

"The hospital. André is dying." He pauses. "He won't make it through the week."

CHAPTER 36

Like father like son

My bastard of a father is dying. I shouldn't care. Hell, I shouldn't even be here. He is cruel, and he deserves to die alone. But Elle convinced me to fly to France to meet him. She said it would give me the closure I need. To know why he hated his own blood. To know why he couldn't be my father. One thing is sure, if he's hoping for forgiveness, he can still hope. I will never give him this satisfaction. But Elle is right. I should watch him agonize. I should see him going into ashes and laugh at his death. I should be the last person he sees when he quits this world. He'll know how much I despise him, and how much I'll never forgive him. Redemption is not something I will offer him.

It's my revenge.

"Are you gonna be okay?" Elle asks, intertwining her fingers with mine as we stand in the middle of the hospital hallway. *I have been wanting him dead all my life, of course, I'm okay.* "I'm here if you need me."

I stare at her; she's pure kindness. I had planned the perfect romantic night for us. I promised her an exotic vacation, and instead, I dragged her into a freaking hospital, made her fly for twenty hours. "I'll be fine. I won't be long." I kiss her forehead before walking through the white corridor to his room.

Revenge. It's all I have in my mind. Hospitals give me goose bumps. I hate these places. People die. People are sick. They are dependent, and being caged in your own body is the worst human curse. I've never been afraid to die, but being here sends a chill in my spin. I'm facing his room number and hesitate to enter for a fraction of a second. Finally, I open the door, ready to glare at his face.

But when I witness André's mouth hanging open, his eyes stuck on the wall, his face white as a ghost, I don't smile. André, usually so powerful and scary, is now lying in his bed, incapable of getting out of it, with a feeding tube in his stomach. Peeing in his own clothes. Needing someone to wipe his ass.

Dependent.

Vulnerable.

Weak.

The man who terrorized me is now reduced to less than nothing. I should glare, but I don't wish this ending on anyone. I stand in front of him, my face cold and emotionless. He takes a complete minute to shift his eyes on me.

"You came." He struggles to articulate, his hand wanting to reach mine but falling back on his bed.

"Only to watch you die," I say harshly when his lips try to curve into a slow lethal smile, but miserably fail.

"Don't be too happy, you'll die alone, too."

"No, André." I lean toward him, gunning my eyes. "I have someone. Elle knows everything, and she loves me. You failed, *Father*."

"The company is yours," he whispers, the timbre of his voice slurred at low volume.

I smirk, happy to destroy his dear business. His hotel chains were his life. I know he gave them to me because he had simply no one. He thinks I'm stupid enough to save his legacy. "I don't give a damn about your will. Tell me something, André." I take the chair near his bed, and bring it next to him to sit. "Why did you do this? Why did you hate your own son so much?"

He stares at me, this bastard probably thinking about dying without giving me an answer. He would enjoy that too much. But I won't beg for the truth. His face muscles try to tense, but he remains with a mask-like appearance. "Your mother cheated."

"And? What does it have to do with me?" I raise my voice, unable to hide all the hatred I have for this man.

"You look just like her." He swallows, his lungs gasping for air. *Don't die yet.* "Love is a weakness." A pause. "I wanted to break you."

"Why?" I yell. "Why did you hurt me? For your own pleasure? Or because you hated my mother?"

"I wanted your loyalty." He almost manages a sick, twisted smile. "My possession." He struggles to breathe, and I know his dying hour is approaching. "The day of Henry's death…" He pauses.

I tighten my fists. That same day, he hit me on the track and pressured me to give up racing. That day, my whole career almost burst into flames. "What happened? Speak, now!" I scream.

"The truth." What truth? Can't this man even manage to speak one sentence? I'm tired of his mind games.

"What truth?"

"She cheated with your fucking coach." Thomas? My mother cheated with Thomas? How could that even be possible? "Twenty-seven years ago," he adds, emotionless.

"Thomas? That's not possible, I wasn't even born." Even in his dying hour, he finds the time to lie.

"You were born ten months after." A pause. "He's your biological father."

My blood runs cold, my heart hammering. He's trying to mess with my mind. "I don't believe you."

"Both paternity tests are on the counter. Do one yourself if you don't believe me." He struggles to speak as I stare in the void. "You were my revenge. My blood type is AB. Yours is O. Check yourself."

I don't want to believe this. I shake my head, my eyes darkening as I walk like a tiger in a cage across the room. I finally grab both paternity tests, and the truth makes my world collide. Maybe he could have trafficked them? But why would André go to all this trouble for a lie? A lie that wouldn't serve him. All my life he wanted to own me, the unique thing linking us was blood. The only purpose of hitting me with this news would be his hope for redemption, or his sadistic way to watch me fall apart.

"She hid it from me for years. That whore didn't want to tell me who it was when I banished her. I found a letter almost three years ago. She left it on purpose. To punish me. There were only two words written: screw you, with a picture of that bastard. That day, I got a second paternity test."

The first paternity test is dated from the day he pushed my mother to leave, eighteen years ago, when I was only eight. Zero percent. André isn't my father. The second report is dated from the day before Henry's accident, almost three years ago, the date he found the letter. Thomas shows compatibility of ninety-nine percent.

Fuck.

I throw the papers on the ground violently, trying to contain my anger. My freaking life is a lie. I know by losing my control, I'm giving André what he was wishing to see. Me, tearing myself apart. Me, discovering the reason why he could never treat me like a son. Because he has never been my father. For him, I was the bastard of the infidelity of the woman he used to love. A woman he hated with all his soul, due to her betrayal. He wanted to use me to ease his pain. I was meant to serve his revenge. By owning me, he was owning her. Giving me away would have drawn media attention on himself as he's a figure of power. He didn't have another choice other than keeping me for his image. I was innocent. And most importantly, André's blood isn't running in my veins. I won't become like him. I'm not a monster.

But, Thomas? Life is twisted. Something isn't adding up. If André knew all these years why would he hide it? He's a believer in pain and punishment, he'd have never kept his calm this long. No. It doesn't make sense. "Why didn't you hurt Thomas, then? If you knew all along, why did you let me race?"

"He was meant to die," he says coldly. "The truck was supposed to hit Thomas."

The truck.

The traffic light.

The accident.

I remain silent. Shocked. Broken. Empty.

The truck was supposed to hit Thomas.

That same day, I took Henry's car to the mechanic to repair the fog lights. We were supposed to pick it up the day after. That night, Thomas offered me to take his car as his girlfriend was driving him back to his place.

My father had orchestrated the truck that hit us.

It wasn't my fault.

He is the one that killed my brother.

I burst out of my chair, hitting the wall vehemently with my fist. Blood all around my knuckles, I fall into the wall, not even feeling the pain. At that moment, I want to kill André, to hurt him for taking my brother from me because of his hatred for my mother. But it would mean I would be offering him a quick death, and he needs to agonize his soul out. I spent the past three years blaming and hating myself and all the while it was because of him. And fate. The cheating of my mother, my birth, the broken light on Henry's car, the succession of small events had created a devastating outcome. André destroyed the only thing he ever loved, Henry.

"The light was green," I rumble.

"Yes. When he died, I couldn't lose you, too. I wanted you by my side." He breathes heavily. "Because you felt guilty, I let you believe it was your fault, so you wouldn't leave me. That's why I allowed Thomas to live, for now. You grew close to him, and if I had taken him away, you'd have lost it. It was better to turn everyone against you, so you'll come work with me." He pauses. "I can't lose that too."

Everyone.

Was it his fault too about my contract being in danger? And about the sponsors stopping their investment on the team? It was his plan all along—to take Formula 1 away from me, to be stuck with him. André is selfish and wanted to ease his own pain, by blaming and tearing down others like puppets to his misery. He replaced his child with his Empire, probably thinking that having his name on a building will make him better.

"You sick bastard! You killed Henry! You killed your own son!" I roar. My fury spring to life. I'm nearly suffocating on my own rage. Chaos stabs me. I'm on the verge of letting my pain consume me, but I won't give André the pleasure.

And for the first time, I see a tear sliding into André's ghostly expression. A freaking tear. Like that could forgive it all?

"I bet you're happy now," he says as if he is about to say his goodbye. Happy? Happy to realize how twisted and blinded by revenge he was? "I could have died without telling you the truth." It wasn't out of love he did this, it was because he is scared to go to hell—and he will. "I loved Henry."

Another fucking tear.

"I pity you, André." He broke his own heart, he destroyed my innocent brother. "You'll never meet Henry again. Never."

"I know. But I'll meet you." He stares at the ceiling, the monitor hammering, the doctors rushing toward his bed to try to save him. "See you in hell, *son*."

André takes his last breath.

I walk into the hall like a soulless ghost, struggling to even stand. The blood on my fist has dried, and yet nothing can make me forget the truth. I didn't kill my brother, none of it has been my fault. My whole life is falling at my feet. André is cruel. A liar. A man who had a heart once and ended up using it to create chaos. He isn't my blood, my genes. But his darkness tarnished me.

Elle runs toward me, calling me, probably seeing how defeated I look. She's like an angel encircled by light, while I feel like a mess. A bastard. She hugs me tight, speaking to me, but I don't hear her. Everything is blurry. I fall to the ground, sitting against the wall, staring and thinking about Henry. He was the only good thing in all of this mess, and he died. I see my life in front of me, my head spinning as if I'm high. Elle kneeks before me, kissing me, trying to bring me back, and for the first time in my life, I let myself get consumed. I allow my feelings to rush back into me. I allow myself to feel and be vulnerable.

I cry.

I cry my bleeding fucking heart out.

CHAPTER 37

Goddess-like

The funeral of André LeBeau. Multibillionaire. A tyrannical boss. A public figure. You'd expect a lot of people to have come, and yet, no one is here—apart from his business associates. But they aren't here to mourn the man. They are here to fight for the pieces of his company and the money he left behind. (Truth is, I wanted to destroy it and watch it burn to the ground, but someone named Elle brought me back to my senses.) So, imagine their surprise when I told them I gave my share of LeBeau's hotels to Monica. LeBeau's hotels should have been Henry's heritage. He was the smart one, the one interested in business. He and Monica were planning on opening their own business together—in fact, she had founded a successful start up, but her financiers bailed when Louis leaked her pictures, and she left the business world. She deserves to have it, and I know she'll be a better boss than all of these ancient pricks. As for André's billions, most of it went to the foundation I created in Henry's memory. Helping kids to have a future, that would have been Henry's wish.

    I've also gathered my courage to visit for the first time my brother's grave. He'll always be with me. But, I'm ready to let him go. For the first time, I finally feel at peace. I stand in front of André's grave. I did accomplish the last wish of his will. He is isolated from the other graves in Monaco's cemetery, next to his favorite and only blossoming tree. There is no point in hating the dead, you'll let them haunt you. I did learn a lot from him after all. He ran after wealth and power all his life and look at him now. Insignificant to everyone. Miserable during his living life. I won't make the same mistakes as he did. I won't die alone.

I spot Thomas standing awkwardly in the middle of the cemetery. As usual, he is wearing his lumberjack outfit. We haven't talked since I asked him to take a paternity test and the results were positive. André had at least the decency to speak the truth. Thomas, the man who always acted like a father in my racing career is indeed my blood. It was shocking news for both of us. Thomas married but never had children. We never talked about this, I just assumed that racing was taking all of his time. And now that he's in his late fifties, it's probably too late for him.

We walk toward each other, and I'm determined to let him know things between us don't have to change. I don't expect him to be my father. "Hi, Thomas." He salutes me with restraint. "You don't have to feel cornered, it's a shock for me, too." He stays silent, not even daring to look into my eyes.

Thomas and I both suck at expressing our feelings with words. During all these years working together, we never had any sweet words toward the other. And yet, I know even if I'm making him go through hell with my reckless driving and my temper, he cares for me. He always had my back.

"I never knew Monique was married, and even less to André. We'd met at the beach, she was taking pictures there, and one thing led to another." He clears his throat. "It was just a short affair. She hid everything from me, I never knew. I never saw her again." He looks away, taking a deep breath, excusing himself for something that isn't his fault. I never mentioned my mother's name since the day she abandoned me. "André came to see me a long time ago, telling me to stop managing you. I obviously told him to fuck off, since you were at an age to do what you wanted and had a great season in Formula 1. I was smoking at that time, he probably used that for a sample, or maybe a piece of my gum. I have no idea."

"Yeah. André had a lot of contacts." I decide to not tell him about the truck. Thomas is an important person in my life, and he looks already defeated and freaked out by knowing he's a father of a twenty-six-year-old man. "Look, Thomas, you don't owe me anything. I'm grateful to have you in my life, as you've always been."

"I should have known. You have her eyes. I'm sorry, Aaron. Life hasn't been easy on you." He gives me a tap on the shoulder, which is a pretty demonstrative gesture for a man like Thomas. He is the opposite of André. Thomas has a warm soul, he sees the best in everyone. A good man. *The ideal father.*

"It's fine, Thomas. Thank you for coming. We have a Grand Prix to win soon, right?" I grin, trying to cool the atmosphere between us.

"Right. See you on the track, Wolf." He nods and starts walking away, hands in his pocket. Then he stops and massages his scalp nervously, before turning back. "Would it be okay if we talk? Outside the track, I mean. We could get a drink or something?" He takes a step toward me, a timid expression on his face. "If that's okay, of course? I know you're already, well, old and don't need me."

I can't help but smirk. I don't know if it's because it means Thomas acknowledges me, wants to know me as his son, or because of how clumsy he is with his wording.

"That would be nice."

He smiles, and the worry leaves his face. "Great. I—Hmm… well…"

I laugh when I see how awkward he is. Damn, Thomas. I pull him into a *manly* hug. Both of us are tense at first, but we relax after a few seconds.

"This is getting too emotional for me. We have a reputation to hold on to." He snorts.

I grin. "You're right. But the rest of the team doesn't have to know."

"I'm sure you'll find a way to keep them entertained by worrying us all on the track."

"Thank you for always looking out for me." As I see tears start forming in Thomas' eyes, I quickly switch the subject to racing. That is a subject the both of us are comfortable with.

Elle

It warms my heart noticing how close Aaron and Thomas are. Looking at their faces, I'm pretty sure they are surprised by this display of affection themselves. Like father, like son. I decided to give them the privacy they need and walk a bit outside the cemetery to admire the nature. Seeing Aaron burying his father has torn my heart. Not for the repugnant man that he was, but because of my mother. I don't know if I could stay soulless if I were to lose her. Her expression when she discovered the truth about Stephan and me showed that she does love me. She wasn't as bad as André, she just meant to protect me from what she experienced. That's why I can't bear the thought of her dying alone.

"Elle." *And now I hear her voice calling me—how paranoid am I?* I start walking away, ignoring the voice. "I flew from Paris to see you, you can at least hear me out!"

What? I turn around and watch Nina, standing in her usual black businesswomen outfit. I stare at her in shock, but then I remember that André is a public figure. She's probably just here to find dirt about him for an article. Aaron closed the access to the media for the funeral, before promising them a public announcement the next day if they respect his privacy. I was surprised they agreed and kept their promises.

"Fine, I'll talk." She sighs before rolling her eyes. "I'm sorry," she says in a harsh tone like it has ripped her heart out.

"Sorry?" I take a step closer to her. I've never heard that word come out of her mouth.

"For Stephan. I should have listened and I…" She puts her big sunglasses on, trying to mask her expression. "I pushed you toward him, and he did to you what…" I notice her throat and mouth trembling while she manages a forced smile.

I pull her into a hug, and for the second time in twenty-four hours, another person burst into tears on my shoulder. I witnessed Aaron crying for the first time and my heart was bleeding, knowing it probably had cost him everything within him to finally let go. And now Nina. The last time I saw her crying was when my father left her and she begged at his feet. *Maybe I'll regain my mother back?*

"I wanted to protect you, Elle. From love and men. And he did what your father did to me..." She tries to regain her control, but she's still sobbing despite herself. "I failed. I didn't want you to suffer. I thought it was what's best for you." My mother was unhappy in her relationships. She married for money and prestige, and now she realizes it's not what happiness is.

If life taught me something, it's that we can't prevent certain events from happening. But we can rise up. Not give up on our hopes and dreams, no matter how hard life hits us. I choose to see the light instead of feeding my pain.

"I forgive you, Mother." I blink away the tears, looking at the blue sky. "But you are wrong. Not all men are the same." I pull away from her to force her to stare into my soul. "We can heal. One bad relationship doesn't mean the end of us. It's time to move on, Mom." She nods her head before wiping her tears with a tissue.

"Does he treat you well?" She regains her cold tone.

"Yes. I love him."

An expression of resentment appears on her face at the mention of love, but she manages a fake smile instead. "Well, let's hope you're right."

"*Ma belle.*" Aaron caresses my arm gently, his gaze switching between my mother and me. I give him a head nod to let him know we are good. "Nice to see you again, Madame Monteiro." Aaron offers his hand to shake, and she stares at it with confusion, as if she would betray her beliefs if she accepts his hand.

"Braham, I remarried." She finally goes for his hand, and I know how much it costs her. It's a sign of truce. An armistice. "I hope you're serious about my daughter." Her eyes run over him like a general leading his troupe to war. Her hatred for men will not disappear, but I know that if Aaron could heal me, maybe one day he could show her I'm right.

"All I want is Elle's happiness."

"We'll see." She arches her eyebrow, clearly not believing him. "I better head back. I'll text you, okay?" She grabs my hand, and I nod with a smile on my face. "Great. Goodbye, Elle." She starts to walk away, completely ignoring Aaron, when she stops and—in spite of herself—glances at him one more time before leaving. "I hope to see more of you, Aaron." I chuckle, she's trying.

Aaron kisses my forehead. "I think I'm growing on your mother."

"It's hard for her to trust a man, but I'm sure you'll prove her wrong, like you did with me." I smile coyly at him.

"Let's go." He takes my hand and leads me toward his car.

"Where?"

"Remember when I told you that's for me to know and for you to find out?" I laugh. Of course, I do.

We arrive at the fateful summit in the cliffs of Monaco. The place that marked the beginning of us somehow. The place he shared only with me and his brother. And now we're back at the top of the world, where it's only us. We walk toward the edge of the rock. The highest point on the cliff. This time, I stand up, even if just a few steps farther I would be stepping into the void. When I focus on the horizon, I'm still afraid—most of my body is trembling, but now, I'm not alone anymore.

Aaron is behind me, his arms encircling my waist. I pull both of my hands in the air, my hair wild with the breeze. I feel free. Like a bird who just found her freedom after being caged for so long.

Like I could finally fly.

With him.

I chuckle. I'm not weak anymore. I've found my way back to myself. Aaron squeezes me closer to him before kissing my neck. "You're not afraid anymore?"

"I am. But you're here, I know you won't let me down."

And that's how, on top of the world, we share an everlasting kiss. He possesses me like the first time, sending shivers in my whole body.

Inflaming me.

Enthralling me.

Enrapturing me.

An eternal addiction. A need.

He catches me into his arms, carrying me to the white myrtle tree. The tree of Aphrodite. A symbol of love.

"Remember the other day when I told you I love you?" His eyes are locked to mine while we take a seat on the grass.

My lips part, my heart leaping, as my eyes grow wild and impatient. "Yes. I remember."

"Well, I do, Elle. I love you." *I love you.* Those words hit my soul so deep, it feels like a dream. I'm in heaven.

I jump into his arms, kissing him fully while his back hits the wild grass, and I fall on top of him. I giggle, biting my lower lip and looking over my fallen god. He pulls my hair away from my face, scanning my whole soul with a light smile. Seeing myself through his eyes, I feel gorgeous. Significant. Eternal.

"I love you, Elle. I love all of you, for everything that makes you, you. I love you deeply and fully, and fuck, it feels so good telling you this." My eyes sparkle as he cups my jaw to seal his declaration with a kiss. "You always have been significant. And I'm so fucking lucky to have your love." *Gosh, don't cry, Elle.* "You're mine eternally, and I'm yours."

"I love you too, Aaron." Two broken people. Two souls for whom love was something impossible. A god-like man and a mortal who succeeded in finding happiness. An Eros and Psyché type of love.

Passionate.

World-shaking.

Boundless.

"Live with me, *ma belle*. I want to wake up next to you. I want to have you close. I don't care if it's in New York or Monaco. I want you to travel around the world with me, while we both do what we love." His face serious, the lone Wolf who couldn't let anyone in his intimacy offers me everything I could possibly ever dream of. I nuzzle into his neck, knowing there is only one answer to his question.

Yes.

And just like him, I'd go everywhere he goes, because he's my home.

My significant.

The other part of my soul.

Our beginning might have been a Greek tragedy, but our ending promises to be a fairy tale one.

EPILOGUE

A couple of months later

Victory tasted sweet today in Monaco.

Ma belle has been traveling the world with me, being there in each of my races. I wouldn't exchange my life for anything. I love the way she kisses me after each victory as I take her into my arms—showing to the world my biggest victory. I've asked her if she wishes to stay in Monaco in our mansion to focus on her paintings, she told me her inspiration was linked with me—thank fuck for that, I need her with me. She didn't have to repeat this twice, I was glad to carry her art supplies into my jet, and I'll continue to do it for every race to come. Collectors and galleries around the world have shown interest in her. Yes, my girlfriend is talented as fuck.

We made a new agreement.

In each Grand Prix, I shall take the checkered flag and she shall create an art piece. No expiration date. No fucking rules.

"I found a name for my collection. '*Finding the beauty in the most broken things. Significant by Elle Monteiro.*' What do you think?" Her eyes sparkle of enthusiasm.

What do I think? That she looks gorgeous wearing that black tight dress who reveals every inch of her body—she's probably not even wearing underwear. *Focus, Aaron, you're a man on a mission tonight.* Even the fact that her fingers are colored with paint turns me on. Sexy and natural. An angelic beauty and a stunning temptress. My goddess.

Today, I took the win, and tonight I'll take the girl. My girl. *And I'm not giving her back. Ever.*

"I think it's incredible." I intertwine my fingers with hers, leading her toward the racetrack. I asked Thomas for a favor earlier. To let open the Monaco Grand Prix just for us tonight. A year ago, I was a lonely asshole who wrecked his race. Best day of my life. For one obvious reason.

"You remember that storefront by the beach?" It's not really a question. I know she does. I recognized the way she glanced at it as I drove in front of it voluntarily a couple of times. It's an empty storefront for sale, near the beach of Monte Carlo.

"Yes, why?"

"I bought it. That's your future gallery." Her eyes open wildly while I can't help but smile, seeing her happy makes me feel like a goddamn god. I saw the plans she left regarding *Everlasting*—her dream art gallery. "Happy, one-year anniversary." It's technically the day we met. But hell, the moment I'd met her I knew she was mine and no one else, may as well call that anniversary—because she wasn't going anywhere without me.

"You're kidding me? I can't believe this, it's too much, I—"

She tries to argue, but I shut her off with a heated, possessive kiss. I love her for being so stubborn, but she knows that everything related to her happiness is not negotiable. She finally jumps into my arms, letting her joy invading her. "I can't believe you did that. You're wonderful to me. I love you."

I'm not getting tired of hearing it. Not one bit.

"Can you say it again?" I swoop her into my arms, as she keeps repeating that she loves me. *Definitely not tired of hearing it.* Nor saying it for what matters.

We arrive in front of the two-seater Formula 1, who's at the departure of the track. I know each track by heart, but Elle probably only sees the darkness surrounding us. Almost all the lights are switched off except from the one of our Formula 1. I've planned everything.

"Ready for a ride, *ma belle?*"

She bites her lower lip as I set her down. "You keep on surprising me tonight."

We enter the cockpit, Elle behind me. I race as she throws her arms in the air, welcoming the speed, her laugh making me smirk. We do a couple of laps before I stop the Formula 1 at the turn in front of the yachts. I send a text to Thomas. *It's time.*

"What are you doing?" she asks.

I get out of the cockpit to position myself in front of her.

In one minute, everything will be operational.

In one minute, I'll ask her to be my wife.

In one minute, she'll be mine forever.

"Remember when I told you, you'll be stuck with me?"

"Aaron…" Her voice starts to quiver. I take her hand and get down on one knee in front of her.

3…2…1…

Fireworks rise up in the sky.

The lights switch on to reveal the petals of roses surrounding us.

I open the jewelry box with inside a twenty-four carat pink diamond ring, a happy fucker smile on my face.

"Spend your eternity with me? Because one life is certainly not enough."

And she seals eternity with a kiss.

Mine.

ACKNOWLEDGMENTS

Warning, I'm gonna be overemotional.

To my readers, I could never thank you enough for taking a chance on my debut novel, it matters more than you could ever imagine. Sometimes, all you need is a small action, a person, or even a word to change your life. In my case, it's every one of your reads, words, trust, that impacted me.

You matter.

You're significant.

I hope you'll never cease to believe in your dreams, and more importantly in yourself. There is always light in darkness, possibility in what seems rather impossible.

You can heal.

You can find true love.

You can fly free in the direction of your dreams.

After all, we're the heroes of our own book, right? Our story is written every second, and today is a blank page with infinite possibilities.

www.ingramcontent.com/pod-product-compliance
Lightning Source LLC
LaVergne TN
LVHW041658060526
838201LV00043B/480